About the Author

Joseph Croall was born, raised and educated in Glasgow, Scotland, where he began his career as an engineer. His passion for travel began in 1984 when he left his native Scotland to apply his professional skills globally.

The attraction he found towards worldly cultures and writing increased whilst working and travelling overseas. He became inspired to commit to the publication of this novel.

Dedication

I would like to dedicate this book to all of my friends, to those who I have adventured and run with. This story would never have been written without you.

Thanks to you all

Joseph Croall

AFRICA AND BEYOND

AUSTIN MACAULEY PUBLISHERS™

LONDON · CAMBRIDGE · NEW YORK · SHARJAH

A CIP catalogue record for this title is available from the British Library.

ISBN 9781398408708 (Paperback)
ISBN 9781398408715 (ePub e-book)

www.austinmacauley.com

First Published (2021)
Austin Macauley Publishers Ltd
25 Canada Square
Canary Wharf
London
E14 5LQ

PROLOGUE

The New Year celebrations began with music, cheering and embracing, with salvos of large Chinese rockets releasing their thunderous booms and uniform radiance high in the evening sky above the town.

The noises from the celebrations were loud and slightly more than irritating for some. This would soon settle down to leave a healthy shared ambience through this warm and humid evening. The three Farang, two men and a woman, were seated at a well-presented table at one of the floating restaurants in Pattaya.

They took a break from their drinks and colourful Thai cuisine to text their New Year greetings to friends and relatives. This was going to be a very happy year for them.

The Savanna House

The day was transforming from a sun-baked afternoon into a breezeless July evening in the Msasani Bay neighbourhood. The groundkeepers were finishing up for the day and security guards were beginning to appear from the shaded gateposts that they occupied 24/7. An occasional dog barked, a contented bark that avoided any attention from the black cat making her way effortlessly along the top of a perimeter wall. Her evening was looking perfect as she blended into her territory, programmed as always to hunt, kill.

Vince was relaxing on his fourth floor balcony, thankful to be part of this African evening beneath the rapidly changing deep-orange, crimson and blue sky. He was enjoying his first mouthful of a perfectly chilled local beer. Beer always tasted better to Vince straight from the bottle. No point in pouring it twice, he thought.

He had given up cigarettes more than a decade ago and never had the craving for one since. He could even savour the taste and smell of a fine cigar occasionally but only over a cold beer or three in the correct ambiance. The bay was looking tremendous and time was hung for a moment, that moment in the now, he thought, the moment that he frequently wished was an option to exist in for as long as he pleased. The thought was a welcome distraction away from the more profound thoughts he had deep seated in his mind.

The sun was almost completely down with the shaded light blanketed over the bay; he enjoyed another chilled bottle and collected his thoughts for the day. *Shit*, he thought to himself; he felt the creeping itch of a couple of irritating mosquito bumps on his ankle, developing. Looking towards the bay, the stillness of the evening was confirmed by the appearance of the green Saudi Arabian flag hanging lifelessly in the embassy grounds; it was time to head indoors.

Miriam and Lisa were busy preparing the drinks selection in the K Bar. They had worked together since March this year. The K Bar was a part-time job for them, as fulltime jobs in the area just now were few and far between. Miriam came from the seaport town of Tanga, not too far from the Kenyan border. She grew up there with her two sisters and three brothers. She felt the port town had nothing much to offer her as she reached her late teens and travelled to Dar es Salaam the year before in the hope of employment opportunities. Many young adults were drawn to the former capital with the same intent. She would return to Tanga when she could afford to or when work was slack; the financial commitment to her parents was continuously demanding.

Miriam's parents were long-term residents of the Tanga region, her mother was a strong healthy woman and well-respected in the area. None of her parents were ever involved in alcohol consumption or used tobacco. Her brothers were known to indulge moderately. Her mother took each day as it came and was always capable of adjusting to the requirements in the town to earn some money.

Miriam had spent her last week in Tanga, helping to nurse her father back to full health following a head injury. Rashidi had been involved in a road accident while riding his scooter. An oncoming truck had shed some of its load onto the main road after a securing strap had snapped, sacks of charcoal littered the road and the impact between Rashidi, Piagio and the charcoal was unavoidable. She did worry about her father.

Her father had since invested in an open-faced crash helmet, the helmet carried the usual fake manufacturer's label so often seen in Africa, but it was at least some form of protection.

"Hey, Miriam, check out who is here."

Miriam glanced around from the far end of the bar and she curiously studied Lisa smirking with raised eyebrows, tilting her head backwards towards the other end of the bar. She noticed the attraction and prompted Lisa to serve the guy sitting on a barstool, lighting a cigarette. A man in his late 40s of medium height, stalky and unshaven was seated. He was casually dressed in light-coloured shorts and T-shirt with sandals and wearing a beige ball cap over close-cut hair. The small, round tinted spectacles he was wearing attracted a second glance at the man. Miriam heard the familiar loud voice from the previous evening.

"Hey, babe, a double JD and a cold Safari, *s'il vous plait*."

The *mzungu* had an Australian accent and had occupied the same barstool on the previous evening. The Swahili word *mzungu* 'white foreigner' was a common term in Tanzania. Lisa placed the cold Safari beer on the bar surface and opened the bottle for him. She greeted him and dispatched a large Jack Daniels from the bottle into the smaller empty glass in front of him.

Miriam strolled across with a bucket of ice and sat the ice down next to the man along with a clean ashtray. The Jack Daniels disappeared rapidly and he ordered another.

"Hey, you two are looking fucking tasty tonight, yeh? Do me a favour, babe, and fire up the sports channel."

It was probably the closest thing to a compliment that the girls were going to get from the Aussie. As far as they were concerned though, it was a compliment.

The time was early, only 7 p.m., and the band was setting up; Wednesdays and Fridays were usually live music nights. The two girls were starting to serve the arriving customers and were chatting in Swahili and keen to see the coming of the weekend.

They both knew that the Aussie had been pretty drunk during the previous evening and they also knew that he had rented a room upstairs and spent the night with two of their friends; they had seen the two girls leaving around 7 a.m. The bar girls had settled on a reasonable payment from him for their services and the room rental. Considering that the room rented at half the total cost, the guy was probably happy with the deal, or what he could remember of it, thought Lisa.

Neil McPherson, an Australian from Queensland, born to Scottish parents, had moved to Tanzania in 2005. He and his partner, Ron Pringle, a white Zimbabwean, had come to Tanzania together from Zimbabwe. They managed a hunting safari business there and left, following the Robert Mugabe land-reform structure which was embedded in the country since 2003. They had invested in a fair-sized lodge in the Regency estate area in Dar es Salaam. With minimal upgrades, they began operating as a halfway house hunting lodge to accommodate overseas guests arriving and departing Tanzania as part of their safari or hunting trips. 12 large bedrooms with three communal areas as well as the huge downstairs kitchen ensured adequate room for its intended purpose. A traditional African thatched roof had quite a fast pitch and matted perfectly with the bright, white exterior walls. The interior was beautiful; a selection of rich African mahogany and teak were used extensively throughout, and the teak flooring seemed to go on forever. Ground and top-floor porches were open-sided. Inside, the bedrooms were spacious, neutral and had a warm rural feel to them. Mahogany interior wall panelling rose up from the teak floor for a metre or so; from there, stacked stone panels covered the walls blending greys, browns and shell shades ascending up to the pitched cane ceilings. With the choice of air conditioning or ceiling fan, residents could relax in comfort.

Over the years, Tanzanians had their fair share of power outages and the national power provider frequently found itself the subject of news headlines in the country. There was always the mention of various temporary or permanent outside power companies contracted in to supplement the national grid. Tanzanian nationals were asking the same questions every two or three years and, at the same time, stocking their homes with candles.

The Savanna House, as the hunting lodge had been named, rarely needed candles, although each room had supplies. At the rear of the lodge, a backup generator had been installed in the past and sat on a concrete base.

The machine kicked in frequently during the day for short periods and the grid was fairly stable through the night. It was an aggressively noisy machine, smoky and the rich smell of half-cooked diesel exhaust fumes suggested that major engine and fuel system attention was probably overdue. There were plus points to the noisy, smoky generator set, as well as supplying backup power to the lodge. Once it was switched off, the day would return to the relative neighbourhood silence. Indoors, all that could be heard were the refrigerator compressors and satellite television. Outdoors, the sharp cawing sound of Pied Crows along with the relaxing hiss of the sprinkler systems feeding the rich green blades of grass that complimented the lawns.

Hunting season in Tanzania runs from the beginning of July to the end of December depending on the desired game or trophies being stalked; an extended period had been approved and put in place this year till March 2012.

The vacationers were made up of mixed nationalities. American, British, German, Belgian and Australian were probably the most frequent visitors to The Savanna House. Ron, together with Neil, would tailor the complete package for the visitor if this service was required.

One of the rooms on the ground floor was converted into a strong room using engineering brick and concrete; housed within those walls was a large multi-gun, walk-in, steel, gun cabinet. This certainly provided assurance for the armed guests; the unarmed guests never seemed to notice. Although The Savanna House was a well-equipped hunting lodge complete with adequate security, the lodge accommodated random guests and a few foreign resident contractors. There was always a good mix of company to socialise with.

Regency estate is a residential area not too far from Ursino Street shopper's plaza. Access roads were covered with huge potholes that never complimented this area; the problem worsened during the rainy seasons. The president had a property nearby and the American Embassy was not too far away. Potholed, unsurfaced, service roads were part of life and accepted.

The main practice that was frowned upon at The Savanna House, and regarded as unacceptable, was any of the residents returning in the evening with subcontractors in the form of bar girls; most guests and residents were unaccompanied men. Ron had always made a point of informing people that although he understood the attraction and fun involved, the bar girls were a terrible thing, as he put it.

This house policy had been broken from time to time. A few weeks previous, four new long-term residents checked in. They were engineers involved in commissioning a new power generation plant in Dar es Salaam. They had probably been there a couple of weeks and were just getting used to the long hours onsite.

On this occasion during a Friday evening, some of them decided to head out and enjoy themselves. It was around ten and they had a recommended choice of bars and clubs from some local colleagues to choose from, and they decided on the K Bar. Following a 20-minute taxi ride through the bumps and potholes, they arrived at the busy bar.

They soon became acquainted with Safari beer, a much-stronger Tanzanian option to Tusker, a popular Kenyan beer. A fun-packed night was enjoyed and they found each of themselves leaving with attractive African girls. One of the guys whistled himself a taxi and climbed in along with his new friend and left ten minutes before the other two. On arrival at The Savanna House, the advance party found that they were in luck; there was a power outage and the generator set's two-and-a-half cylinder Deutz air-cooled diesel engine was refusing to start.

The happy couple noticed that the security guard was occupied with Deutz and two or three spare batteries.

The contractor called the guard over to the gate. Wanzagi, the guard, approached and opened the latch, then quickly returned to the generator with a handful of wire and a hammer. The girl had been out of sight; she was slipped in and went unnoticed by the security and they had forgotten to close the latch as they made their way quickly to the lodge-entrance door. The engineer knew his assistance may be requested.

Shoes and heels got slipped off and they quietly made their way to the upstairs floor; home run was complete and the room door was locked; a candle was soon lit in the darkness.

The other four were not so nimble; during the cranking of the generator set engine, they had all managed to stay under the guard's radar, come through the open gate and made it to the lodge-entrance door.

The journey to the upstairs floor was organised a bit more carefree; alcohol-charged guys and girls decided that they were all home and dry, and after all, it was only just beyond three in the morning. More than one of the guests had been wakened by the disturbance and they were now hearing the contact of stiletto heels against the hardwood staircase and floors.

"Don't make so much fucking noise," in an English accent from one of the contractors was heard over the clattering heels, this prompted more loud giggling and laughter from the girls.

At this point, if the noise had been just about enough for the disturbed guests, some more disturbances lay just ahead. The residents who were now awake were greeted by a huge bang from Deutz down in the rear garden. The engine popped, growled and spluttered before letting out a loud backfire up through the air induction manifold and out through the empty filter housing; there was no air-filter element fitted. The carnage was completed by a bright fireball exiting out of the open engine-area canopy door and into the night before the engine ramped up to the rated noisy 1500 rpm. Wanzagi was less than amused; the black stubbled hair on his head together with his eyebrows and moustache and eyelashes were now partly singed brown.

Saturday morning came around too quickly for three of the contractors. Saturday was a normal working day for them, especially today; there was a large transformer being released from the port today and expected onsite. *These things always seem to mobilise at the fucking weekends*, Matt thought. He had a good idea that the cause of this lay somewhere between the roads being quiet to accommodate transport with wide loads and the Tanzanian port authority carefully planning overtime. Plenty of organisation was needed to be done and a day off was not an option.

The four of them were seated downstairs in the large breakfast area, waiting for breakfast to be served; the time was 06:15 and they were all enjoying coffee. American and English breakfasts were available.

Andy and Gary came from the Glasgow area in Scotland, Matt from Manchester in England and Les from Johannesburg in South Africa; all were in their mid-30s to mid-40s.

Les was feeling the best among them all. He even slept through the lodge and garden fracas. Gary and Matt were wishing they had also stayed in the previous evening; they had no sleep, spent more money than planned and just to round it off, the girls had left just one hour after arriving. Matt had been having a laugh, giving Gary a hard time as Gary's girl had decided to leave and phoned her friend who was with Matt; the two of them demanded payment, gave the guys their mobile contact numbers and left. Wanzagi seemed a little happier in the morning, as he had received a generous tip from the girls to simply let them out of the grounds without any fuss; their taxi was already waiting for them.

"What time did your chick leave, Andy?"

"What chick?" Andy replied to Matt. "What are you on about, mate?"

"That chick from the bar last night," Matt continued.

Andy had managed to convince Matt and Gary that he had got into the cab with the girl but dropped her off at the Bogamoyo Road and carried on to the lodge on his own. Andy was very casual in his reply, and Gary and Matt seemed to have accepted his story but still seemed to appear baffled and short-changed. This was Andy setting himself up for the day at their expense. The girl had left about an hour before breakfast time during darkness, and he had also tipped Wanzagi at the entrance door when she left.

Breakfast arrived from the kitchen. One of the maids placed down toast and butter, fried eggs and the bacon, and beef links sausage were coming shortly with some more coffee. As the guys started serving themselves and eating, two other guests arrived for breakfast and sat down across from the contractors.

"Hey good morning, how ya'awl doing today?" one of the two fairly heavy Americans greeted them.

"Aye, not too bad thanks," Andy replied. "Yourselves?"

"Yeh, we're good, buddy. Were you guys having a turn with the local bush meat during the night?"

Andy quickly offered a reply.

"These two here, mate."

Andy had his arms raised in the air and pointed his both index fingers downwards towards Matt and Gary. Les was laughing and joined forces with Andy. Les mentioned to the Americans that Matt and Gary were trying to lose their virginity. The two Americans let out some loud laughter.

"Hey, do you two come from fucking Idaho?" one American said.

Both the tables were joined in loud laughter; they had all shared a laugh regarding the previous evening and chatted about their presence in Tanzania. The Americans, Brad and Jim, were hunters from Montana.

The contractors were starting to make a move to work as the company driver had arrived quite sharp at 06:45; they all shook hands and arranged to meet up later. Matt and Gary apologised for the noise in the early hours.

"Hey no worries, man, ya'awl take it easy, you hear."

Jim added that there was another guest upstairs who was really pissed; big guy from Idaho. He just got engaged to one of those girls a couple of nights previous.

"Ya'awl watch out now, and could one of you boys take a look at that fucking generator out in the backyard?"

The team were laughing hysterically as they headed out to the vehicle.

Later in the day, when the team had returned from the site, Neil was relaxing outside; he invited them to have a beer in the front patio area. He had a chat with the guys and touched on the activity of the early hours; they all gave their apologies and assured Neil that there would be no repetition. That was the end of it, they promised.

Ron had not been there that evening. He would also know about it, but he would not mention it again after Neil had already dealt with it. Better Neil than Ron. Ron was much more serious regarding these matters. He was tea total and almost intimidating sometimes, and his size seemed to dominate most conversations or discussions regarding problem-solving. He was a big guy and many people viewed him as a racist. There was word on the street that Ron had survived a struggle with a lion in Zimbabwe and had the scars to prove it; nobody ever pressed him on the authenticity of this story or more details and the big cat remained unidentified as a lion or lioness.

Lisa was beginning to clear up for the evening. She had some holidays due to her and was planning to finish up early this evening. Her trip to Mwanza in the morning would involve a couple of days' travel by road.

"Miriam, is it cool with you if I head off shortly, honey? I got to make a move real early tomorrow morning."

"Yes, babe, do it; I can finish up here. There's plenty of security on tonight and I can get some help from any of the boys. I also got Neil to keep me company at the bar," she joked. "No seriously, Lisa, go for it, babe."

Lisa moved back into the kitchen to prepare coffee and a sandwich and have a chat with Ben, the chef. She sat down and felt glad to be free of the bar with her thoughts on tomorrow, the Ubungo Bus Terminal, Morogoro, Dodoma then Mwanza.

All her family lived there as well as her daughter who was still a young child, just three-and-a-half years old. She named the girl Diana; this was in memory of Princess Diana of England who had always been a legend to Lisa and she had thought along with many others that the late princess had done more than her share of good in this world. She collected as much memorabilia related to Princess Diana as she could find. Even if she was having any traditional African dress made for any occasion, she would choose the colours and style as she thought the princess would choose.

Her daughter lived with her mother, but this was a temporary arrangement that was necessary for Lisa until she could find some stability in her life. Her child had no real father and she had lost her own father two years previous to malaria. She had two brothers and two sisters as well as a number of relatives in Mwanza, so her daughter had no shortage of company and loved ones. Her pregnancy was unplanned; her boyfriend, at the time, denied all possibility of him being the father and had left the area before the birth of Diana. Lisa went through with the birth, she had wanted to.

She planned to return to Mwanza and live permanently as she had before. She knew the city was steadily becoming more prosperous. One of her brothers worked in one of the large fish-processing plants and he had mentioned to her that more and more of these plants were being built in the area and people could enjoy overtime hours. These plants had been introduced to supply an increasing global demand that was developing for Nile Perch; maybe this time she would not return to Dar es Salaam.

Friday night was early, especially by K Bar standards; 12:30 and the place was just beginning to see the main volume of customers arriving. The atmosphere was always vibrant on Wednesdays and Fridays, the band was tuned in and the pool tables were busy. No chalkboard queuing here, just small piles of coins in a line along the table edge. The local Tanzanian guys and girls were dominating both tables, some of them high on the local weed and most folk steadily becoming louder as the effects of Safari lager and vodka and Red Bull steadily intoxicated them. The bar had a reputation of attracting a fair amount of fun-loving girls with flexible morals, price negotiable; this, in turn, attracted more single guys than couples. Along with the smell of flame-grilled fish, steaks and mishkaki mingling with the smell of cigar and pipe-tobacco smoke reminded visitors from the western world that Africa enjoyed freedom of choice in everything when socialising.

No matter how busy things became in the K Bar, the service was excellent. You never seemed to wait longer than five or ten minutes for your drinks to arrive at your table or almost immediately if you chose to occupy the bar area. Albert, one of the security supervisors, manned the entrance door tonight. Entry usually involved three different processes, a fee could be paid that authorised entry and a voucher for two drinks, tipping the doorman authorised your entry and regulars and local girls entered free of charge.

Neil was having a 'cool as bananas' night as he would often describe things; he was overindulging a bit on the late evening, socialising these past few days, but what the hell, he thought, who wasn't on the start of the weekend again?

Neil and three of his friends were together at the end of the top bar. Paul was Scottish; Osaiya, Tanzanian and Darren claimed British and South African nationality, sometimes!

Apparently, Darren was from Newcastle in England, had dual nationality and his home was in Johannesburg. After sampling his accent and attitude for a short period of time, most folks labelled him as South African.

"Hey, Osaiya, are you in Dar for a while or what, mate? Last time I saw you was in October time I think. You were in the market for a Land Cruiser. Did you ever see anything?" Paul shouted.

Osaiya gleamed a huge smile, the kind of smile that only an African could present. He tuned into Paul.

"Yes, I got myself a nice one, 2005 model and the spec I was after."

This was now his pride and joy. Osaiya explained that he had found a silver Land Cruiser Prado with the 3.0 D4D turbo-diesel motor, a peach of an engine, he boasted. The model was an LC4 with all the toys, electric everything, sat nav, sunroof, leather and alloys.

"It was worth the shopping around, Paul; you know the deal with Cruisers in Tanzania. The place is full of them, all are in good order and you will never find a cheap one. Just single out the colour and spec you like and have plenty money ready. I got a buddy in Libreville. His reckoning is if you get knocked over by a vehicle while crossing the road there, 90% chance it will be a Cruiser. I paid $18,000 US for this one. Shit, the sound system is worth that, man."

Paul ordered a round of drinks.

"Osaiya, whatever you do, don't lend your new wheels to this fucking rampant Aussie here. His female conquests are a no-go back at The Savanna House at the moment."

"Piss off, don't tell me you don't have any heel marks on your roof lining yet, mate," Neil replied.

"If you were at the controls on a Friday night, mate, the heel marks would be on the driver's foot well," Paul replied to him.

Their end of the bar was cranking up fine. Miriam and some of the other customers were settling into the chat from the middle of the bar. Darren's attention was diverted and he was occupied with a very dark slim girl seated on the barstool next to him.

Miriam saw her chance to have a friendly go at Paul. She shouted across to tell him she had seen his daughter today. The word on the street was that Paul had a child to a local girl. The child was just a small baby, a claim he profusely denied but had been noticed a few times meeting with the girl, and he seemed to be supporting her. He was trying to avoid the issue and this just made Miriam laugh more.

"Paul, the baby looks like you," she yelled.

"Miriam, all babies look like me, fat and ugly. Would you like a drink, babe?"

Miriam opted for a beer as she tried to contain her laughter.

Darren was keeping busy, chatting to his new friend, and the bar girls were all pretty much independent operators, not too pushy or in your face; for a single guy looking for some female company, the choice was wide. The girls knew exactly when a guy was easily approachable. Guys would normally be confident in their understanding that they were the ones who were in control of choosing a girl that led to a transactional sex agreement; depending on the timing, things could work the other way around; the outcome was the same however.

Most guys never noticed the move. Either that, or they simply accepted it. The band was thumping out a welcome variety of American and British rock, Reggae and Congolese style music; the place was busy but not crowded.

The dance floor now had more attention than the wall-mounted sports screens that decorated some of the walls. A few middle-aged mzungu, who were probably too drunk even to walk to the toilets, now insisted in displaying their talents on the dance floor. Osaiya had already left. Cruising around in his Toyota in downtown Dar S was much more appealing to him than a late, late K Bar Friday. The other three would be there a while yet. Some more drinks and platters of mishkaki had been ordered and just the savoury smell of the flame-cooked beef had many people unable to resist ordering some.

Bar girls were starting to mingle more with the male customers now, and the girls usually well-outnumbered the guys. Occasional female as well as adventurous couple's desires and pleasures extended their customer base. Jim and Neil had bought two girls a beer each, and this gesture was more or less accepted as personal invitations for the evening if one desired. Darren returned from the toilet and joined his slim, dark, Kenyan friend at the bar. She must have been as bored as a kid in church, listening to his personal documentary on Johannesburg. Tonight he was wearing his South African head. Neil was content with his Tanzanian hook-up for the evening and he had already decided to make a room reservation. Jim was looking uninterested with his girl's company and appeared quite tired. Neil had considered the thought that he may end up double-booked again tonight. The K Bar was seedy, definitely seedy, he thought to himself with a contented grin on his face.

River Tiger

On the floor of the front porch, a battalion of ants was going about their routine activities. Across the sunlit and shaded floor areas, the formations were dismantling an upturned cockroach carcase. The legs, antennae and some other extremities were being systematically severed and transported through a crack in the tiling joint a metre or so away as if riding a conveyor. Jim was amused watching the tiny creatures. The disciplined determination, communication, strength and speed of these insects never failed to interest him. The events had an added attraction. A tiny lizard was darting out and in from the edge of the flowerbeds and picking off some of the ants. Jim and Brad had another few weeks to spend on a game safari in the Selous in Tanzania; they had moved from The Crystal Lodge two days ago. The Mambo Lodge was more remote and the area less frequently stalked by hunters, and the area also permitted bow hunting for small game. Jim poured himself another coffee from the pot and lit up a Marlboro. He was studying a map of the area while enjoying the view from the lodge. The view was pleasant, mainly savanna scrub land. The Rufiji River was more or less on their doorstep, and some of the faster moving parts of the river in the distance hinted good fishing spots. He had made a mental note of trying to fish there and looked forward to wetting a line maybe in the early evening or morning.

The time was approaching 08:00 and the temperature was around 25 Celsius and dry. Until now, they seemed to be the only guests at the lodge.

Brad arrived with the Toyota. He had gone out for a drive at 06:15 and he pulled up, got out of the vehicle and grabbed his bag, rifle and cigars.

"Hey, trooper, howz it going?" Brad said.

"Cool, buddy. I got some hot coffee here. You see much out there?"

"Not a God dammed thing, buddy, apart from vultures and some wild dogs fighting over a carcass; plenty of tracks though, but I had to cut it short. The gas gauge is approaching E for fucking excellent."

Jim pushed the plate of doughnuts towards the other chair at the table.

"What do you recon swims in that river, Brad? I fancy wetting a line later."

Jim unconsciously swatted a fly and flicked it into the ant's path.

"Gaitors, why ya'awl wanna mess with that river today, Jim?"

Jim convinced Brad that he might not get a chance later, as tomorrow would probably see the whole area limited to hunters, so they decided to try to find time to check out the river later in the day. Brad had mentioned that he only ventured out around 15 kilometres northeast, and a few times he was forced to change direction due to the changing course of one of the river's endless tributaries. He had seen some baboons and hyenas in the distance through his riflescope. The vultures had made themselves airborne and the wild dogs scattered to distance themselves as he approached the carcass; the remains looked like a wild pig, probably a plundered leopard kill.

They decided to give the vehicle a check over and gas it up. Brad suggested an inventory and check of all equipment, ammunition and firearms. The hunting bow had not been unpacked yet; that was something that Brad was keen to have a go with. The last time he and the bow had seen any action was in Montana. He claimed that a good bowman with a good bow was good for anything from salmon to bear. 70 pounds draw weight or whatever, Jim was never convinced of that claim.

The bow-hunting permit cost double the rifle fee in Tanzania. In reality, anyone involved in bow-hunting was required to carry a suitable rifle as backup; large or dangerous game were also out of bounds for bow hunters.

Africa was a completely different style of hunting for the Americans compared with their home state, Montana. A hunter there could find himself completely out on his own if he pleased; a bit more challenging they thought. The rules on the game reserves in Africa generally demanded the presence of a professional hunter to advise, guide and protect the client in the event of any danger arising.

They started to arrange the kit and remove the unnecessary items from the truck; the truck was pretty tight and a quick check of the tyres, pressures, lights and levels proved satisfactory. Jim walked over to the porch to answer his cell phone. Brad moved the rifles aside and unpacked his bow to reveal a fairly expensive compound bow in desert-camouflage colours. In reality, he knew that he may not get the chance to use it. The terrain, in general, was too open and not ideal for a surprise short-distance bowshot. Positioning yourself in a tree hide was out of the question.

The style of hunting done here would be vehicle dependent to get to a key point before stalking on foot, and no rifle shots would be permitted from the vehicle.

Jim walked back across and mentioned that Ron had called. The professional hunter and guide would arrive in the morning to arrange their requirements. Ron had mentioned that he would most likely take a trip over next week to meet up. Neil was interested to make it over also. This just depended on him arranging a couple of hunting firearms permits from the Tanzanian Game Division for a couple of clients arriving.

Jim mentioned that the guide in the morning would be Osaiya.

"Excellent," Brad replied. "That guy knows his shit; I like the guy. I was with him for a week last year at Mondulijuu. Crazy about SUVs and bikes, he is. Whatever you do, don't talk about either or you will be getting your brain fried for most of the day."

Jim smiled and slid the Marlboro from his mouth.

"Tell you what, buddy, you don't mention bow-hunting and I won't mention Toyotas, Harleys or whatever the fuck. I am gonna give that river a bash before dark, Brad."

Brad agreed to head to the river later with Jim. Although he was an experienced angler, he preferred to give the fishing a miss this evening. Jim mentioned that they would not be taking too much gear, just the usual mosquito repellent, torch, rod reel and landing net and a couple of rifles.

"Take along your bow, Brad. What do you recon?"

"My bow indeed; well, I would recon if I did that along with a big net and two rifles. What the hell would you need a fishing rod for?"

At this moment, they noticed a vehicle approaching from the main access track; the white crew cab pick-up pulled up and parked behind the Toyota. The two Americans observed two game-reserve representatives and a tall buxom policewoman getting out the vehicle. It appeared to be a routine visit and permit check, and the two of them approached the vehicle as the occupants were getting out and introduced themselves. The two casually uniformed men wearing shorts introduced themselves; one was Tanzanian and the other appeared to be either South African or maybe Zimbabwean; the woman was an officer in the country's national police force. After they completed their introductions, Brad offered them some coffee and cold drinks.

They sat down in the porch area and things quickly became apparent that the reason for the visit was not a permit or firearms issue. The police officer did most of the talking and explained in very clear English that the authorities were concerned of the whereabouts of three French nationals. Two men and a woman had been missing for three days, the woman possibly the girlfriend of one of the men.

Jim explained that they themselves had just arrived here in this area the day before and were expecting their PH (Professional Hunter) in the morning, and this official visit was the first folk they had seen with exception of the management and staff. This area was 15 kilometres or so east of the Blane River camp area. The police officer informed them that the police and game-reserve authorities were putting out awareness to as much people as they could in regards to the missing three. The French had been based about 175 kilometres away in Mahenge and were last seen heading out on some bush trails in a white Toyota crew cab; they were en route to this area and were expected to arrive here yesterday afternoon. Brad found himself continuously admiring this lady from every angle possible, nice uniform, not pretty and not unattractive, definitely not unattractive and definitely something about her. *Mid-40s, five-feet ten and in perfect shape*, he thought to himself. Yes, Brad could have happily just sat there for hours just watching her movements and facial expressions. Brad had asked the obvious question regarding cell phone communication. The information which the authorities believed to be accurate was that the French all had cell phones in their possession. The police officer passed over the three contact numbers to Brad and informed them that no connection was available at present. The guys assured the visitors that they would frequently try those numbers in whatever locations they were at. As the visitors were leaving, the officer informed them that an aerial search was due to begin in the afternoon, and she answered Jim's earlier question in regards to the equipment and supplies they may be carrying.

As far as they had been informed, there were a couple of cool boxes containing food and drinks, a lot of camera equipment, a high-powered rifle and a rifle that was leaning towards minimum hunting calibre. Just after they left to talk to the lodge management, Brad tried the three numbers but got the response confirming that connection was not possible. They completed the arrangements with the equipment for the morning and Jim was complete in arranging his fishing gear for the evening. The sky had clouded quite a bit, and the wind was very light; the V8 diesel engine cranked over and settled into a healthy idle. The time was just before four in the afternoon as they set off on a track directly towards the river's faster-moving flows. Brad decided to leave the bow behind; the time was not enough to familiarise with this new location and riverbank before nightfall. There was not much to see on the way down in the heat of the late afternoon apart from an abundance of birds as they approached the river. The area that they were approaching had started to become inaccessible for the vehicle; large rocks and changing ground levels halted them. They got out to have a look around and were surprised at how wide the river was at this point. The river was taking a turn in direction to the right as they looked downstream; it looked about 300 metres to the opposite bank.

"Hey, Jim, check that out." Jim looked downstream and saw a tributary mouth about 500 metres away on their side of the river.

"That's where we want to be, buddy. Let's head down there," Jim said.

"Here ain't manageable even if we got down to the river's edge, there ain't no level bank there, Brad."

After a short drive and a bit of manoeuvring, they managed to reverse park away from the river just about 50 metres from the tributary mouth; they were on the upstream bank as it joined the main river.

Brad mentioned that there seemed to be a fair bit of depth as the tributary joined the river, and both banks were steep and were about 15 metres apart. A huge rock was breaking the surface just upstream of the tributary mouth five or six metres from the bank with ten or 12-foot width either direction. It was creating an eddy as the flow passed both sides of the rock. "Looks not too bad, Jim; you got a break in the trees as well and there's not much sign of prowlers around us here. Still, keep your eyes and ears peeled."

Back over at the vehicle, Jim slid the rod out of its cover; he had brought his ten-and-a-half-foot sea-trout rod in carbon fibre, expensive, strong and very light. This rod was a two-piece and had a reversible handle that allowed the angler to use as a fly fishing rod or the option of a spinning rod if the handle was reversed. The immediate terrain was open with grass that was not too long in most places, and the clear break in the trees prompted him to try some fly-fishing.

Realising the time, Jim quickly set up the rod and coupled the fly reel onto the screw clamps. He clipped in a spool loaded with a slow sink line and linked on the herringbone braiding loop to the line before tying on an eight-feet monofilament tapered leader. The lure flies that he had were mainly rainbow trout and steelhead lures. *What the hell?* he thought. *A fly is a fly.* The fly he had chosen was black, yellow and red, about three inches long with a size three, single hook together with a wired treble.

Brad picked up the landing net and he lifted out one of the rifles from the hard case.

Jim had worked out 15 metres or so of line from the reel; the lure was causing quite a bit of drag, especially on the back cast, so he decided to trim down some of the feathers.

He replaced his line with a fast sink tip and shortened his leader to six feet.

He was casting traditionally downstream wide and allowing the line to swing into the bank with the current; the river was deep, dark and clear. No surface activity was present, but they were confident that the approaching evening would encourage some feeding activity. Brad seemed content viewing the surroundings through his 8x40 binoculars and giving Jim the rundown on some things he was seeing. There was activity about a kilometre upstream on the opposite bank; wild dogs barking and generally playing around, at the same time cautiously approaching the river's edge to drink. Some sub-surface activity had started now and again around the large rock. Jim was working 20 metres of line in the air and a couple of his casts had been placed between the rock and the riverbank. He decided to cast out from the rock and let the lure swing in just upstream of it. Brad was focused between surveying the surroundings for unwelcome visitors and the dogs when he was startled by a loud, heavy splash and a sudden movement from Jim. Jim was recovering his balance and his footing on the sloping riverbank; something had hit the lure hard just upstream of the rock and the line was being hauled deeper and in an upstream direction with the rod tip thumping downwards and the rod taking on a deep curve. He had no choice but to release some line to the fish and start to move upstream with it.

"Hey, buddy, this fish sure is fit; ain't no catfish that's for sure."

Brad was laughing and coughing at the same time.

"Come again, big guy, when did you ever use a rod and line to bag catfish, man?"

Brad stood leaning on the net with the rifle strapped over his shoulder. He knew the net would not be required just yet. The fish still had plenty of power and had not even surfaced yet. Jim knew that he had 30 metres of line left on the reel as the line backing started to roll out.

So far things were going well. The fish was moving upstream and Jim had a steady tension on the line; after ten minutes, he managed to gain back some line and now putting 20 metres of line between himself and the fish. Some trees were lining the riverbank 50 metres upstream. He decided to move upstream a bit and place himself more or less in line with the fish. Jim started to apply some more tension by clamping the line against the cork handle with his fingers, and raising the rod while moving backwards, he was trying to encourage the fish to the surface. This tactic worked. The fish reacted quite suddenly by swimming outwards and upwards, a fast gold-and-silvery shape appeared through the clear, deep, black water. The fish broke the surface with enough power to clear the water by a metre, shaking its head and body violently; this was repeated a few times, prompting Jim to lend the fish some slack while skilfully keeping firm tension on the line and tackle. Ten minutes later, the fish had spent much of its energy and was showing signs of submission. Brad had positioned himself low on the bank with the net placed under the surface so as to prevent spooking the fish as Jim was leading it towards the bank. The fish was quickly scooped up in the net without fuss and they headed up the riverbank. The fish lay gasping on the grass; the teeth-filled jaw moving up and down in time with its gill movement, with its defiant predatory eye fixed on the Americans. The fish was beautiful, a female tiger fish, weighing about 15 pounds. After a very quick photo shoot, they released the fish back to the river and watched as the fish swam slowly downwards, fading away into the dark depth.

Saturday Night Fever

He awakened before the alarm as he did most mornings. Miriam was still asleep as he leaned over her and kissed her on the side of the lips and she smiled while raising her arm to hold his head without opening her eyes. Vince got out of bed and put on some shorts and made his way out to the balcony. It was just after 6:30; he planned to check his emails over a coffee.

Miriam decided to get up also as the constant noise on the bedroom window had denied her a late rise. A small colourful bird was outside, flying at the window and pecking the glass with its beak. Vince was surprised to see her up as early as she sat down at the table, wrapped in a white bath towel and holding a cup of coffee. The bird story had him laughing and he stood up and had a quick look across the bedroom. He watched the blue, black and red bird continuing this activity. He explained to Miriam that this was no doubt a male bird attempting to see off his own reflection from his territory; she acknowledged the explanation but seemed uninterested.

"Vince, you do remember that you promised to drop me at work tonight. You would have to collect me at five. Is it OK to stay here till then?"

Vince was engrossed in his inbox.

"Vince!" Miriam continued.

"Yeh, yeh, Miriam, sorry. I heard you the first time, no problem, hang out here, yeh."

There was no real relationship between them apart from randomly meeting up and spending a night or two together; there were never any complications. Vince was unattached and preferred to get involved with women whenever he felt like it and with whoever he chose to be with. He was 45 and had been in Tanzania for about 15 months. He had spent 12 years in the United States Military, Sergeant Vince Joseph Kelly, with most of that time spent in Saudi Arabia and Iraq.

The Saudi period gained him experience as a mechanical expert and weapons systems specialist with the patriot missile air-defence battalions in Riyadh. Once the Iraq invasion began in March 2003, he accepted a posting in Iraq as a light weapons specialist, covering covert assignments until he left the military in 2006.

After a failed period trying to get his own truck-repair business off the ground in Texas, he was successful in securing a 24-month overseas assignment in Dar es Salaam, supervising a heavy plant workshop for a large plant-rental company.

Vince had an arrangement to meet up with Ron and Neil later at The Savanna House; the day was pretty much free for him.

"I am heading out for a bit, Miriam. No doubt you will be spending some time under the blankets with Doctor Z for a while."

"Doctor who?"

"Never mind, babe. I am sure going to fix that noisy bird problem for you right now."

He rolled down the external roller shutter to cover the bedroom window.

"There you go, no more tapping here today."

She thanked him and strolled over and put her arms around his neck and demanded a hug and a kiss. She made no effort to stop the towel sliding off her dark, slim body. She released him and slipped away just as he was beginning to feel the urge to change his mind and join her back in bed.

"Do me a favour, honey, and be careful out on that moto and remember I have to work the next three Saturdays."

He slipped on a pair of motorcycle boots over his Levis.

Vince left as Miriam was doing a wash up in the kitchen and headed to the elevator with his gloves, full-face helmet and a lightweight, summer, leather jacket.

Once in the basement-parking area, he disarmed the Honda alarm and immobiliser, pushed the key into the switch barrel and turned on the ignition circuit. A quick system check followed together with the buzz of the fuel-injection pump energising and charging up the fuel system. The finely tuned motor snarled into life instantly as the starter button was pressed. The black 2009 model Fireblade settled into a deep throaty high idle and the sound invaded every corner of the underground parking area. Vince had taken his time securing his helmet, jacket and gloves and he sometimes admired the bike from different angles after parking or before riding away. He repeatedly told himself that the Blade appeared like it was travelling at 100 mph even when parked. Had he leased a ground-floor apartment, the Blade would be sitting room furniture when not in use.

Ron was enjoying breakfast outdoors on the lower patio area of The Savanna House. He had quite an appetite this morning and asked his wife to prepare some more sausage and eggs.

Deborah was working the kitchen with one of the maids as she normally did on weekends. The resident guests were probably half a dozen or so at present, and the vacant rooms were being prepared for new arrivals after the weekend.

"There you go, Captain, sunny side up and bangers sizzling." Deborah laid down the second helpings in front of Ron as he was finishing off his coffee.

"Hey cheers, Debs, I'm bloody starving this morning. You gonna sit down?"

"Yeh sure, if I get a minute. Our guests all seem to be arriving for breakie at the same time." She headed back to the kitchen with Ron's plate and mug.

Deborah was South African who had done a fair bit of travelling. It would be fair to say she was pretty, much the opposite of Ron in a few ways. The both of them in some ways were free spirits and this was mutually accepted by each other. They both had done their fair share of travelling. They had two grown-up children, a son and daughter, who both settled in South Africa, and a big part of Ron and Deborah was now set in their ways, but they were definitely a team.

Not long had passed when Ron had finished his breakfast. He tidied up the table and strolled around the villa to check up on the generator set. All looked well and a new, modified, monitoring and protection panel and fuel-system repairs promptly inspired confidence in the machines operation and performance. The resident power-generation engineers had repaired and modified the set in their own time for a very modest price. *Now diesel in one end and electrical energy out the other hassle-free*, Ron thought to himself. The engineers had moved away not so long ago to permanent accommodation in apartments not so far away. Their duration of stay in Dar es Salaam had been extended considerably.

The distinct sound of a large multi-cylinder motorcycle could be heard approaching The Savanna House. The rider was revving up and down with skilled clutch control while dodging and negotiating large potholes. Wanzagi opened the main gate to allow Vince to ride inside.

"Good morning, Mr Vince, I am happy to see you. You like me to clean your moto?"

Vince pushed down the side stand, cut the engine and stepped off parking the bike in a nicely shaded area next to Wanzagi's guardhouse.

"Good morning, Wanzagi, yeh good idea, buddy, but better let her cool down a bit first. Oh, and don't clean the engine area."

Wanzagi was always happy to earn a few extra dollars.

Ron and Vince had just got together and sat down when Neil appeared. Neil appeared quite fresh today, considering his recent late-night socialising. The time was just around 8:15 when Ron suggested coffees all around and two 'yeps' from the guys confirmed agreement.

"You guys have a think about what you want to eat, I'm done for now," Ron mentioned.

"Hey, guys, good morning to you," came a loud jovial voice from Deborah as she just seemed to appear from nowhere.

"Coffees coming up and I am going to prepare you two guys' bangers and eggs, bacon too if you like. I hear you are all going on a sea-fishing trip this morning," she said in a strong South-African accent.

Vince and Neil looked at each other and then towards Ron who just smiled and shook his head while looking at Deborah.

"She's just screwing with you."

"Thank Christ for that, Debs," Neil said. "I feel not too bad this morning, not quite 100%, but sea, boat and the smell of fish is way off for me, madam."

Deborah laughed while giving Neil a mischievous grin. She headed back to the kitchen area, still smiling while asking Neil who the lucky lady was the night before. Neil was a sitting duck for Deborah when he did not stay overnight at his room at The Savanna House.

"C'mon, Debs, you know me better than that. I did not ask her name and she sure ain't no lady."

Deborah was forced to smile and shake her head a little as she left to prepare breakfast.

Ron immediately informed them of the mishap that Osaiya had the previous evening. Osaiya was apparently downtown Dar S and had spent some time at the Chinese casino followed by a visit to one of the nightclubs. The female he was dancing and hugging most of the evening turned out to be the girlfriend of some local big shot. Cutting the story short, Ron mentioned that Osaiya had got into a brawl with two guys and he now had two broken fingers, carpals, knuckles or whatever on his right hand. That put Osaiya out the game for a while. The hospital had released him with his hand set in plaster.

Vince put his hands behind his head, leaned back on his chair and expressed his feeling by just exhaling the words 'awe shit'. Neil rocked back on his chair, looking kind of blank and then just cracked up laughing.

"What a silly fucker, of all the available malaya, hookers, bar babes, whatever you want to call them, he ends up with a live wire."

Vince could not hold back with his laughing either. He reminded Neil that Osaiya was also married. This even had Ron letting out a snigger.

"Yeh, well, we got to find a solution to cover for him to take care of the American boys down in the Selous," Ron explained. "How do you fancy some bush time down there, Neil? I can follow up with the licencing applications for you. It's up to you, mate."

Neil finished off his coffee, lit a cigarette and agreed to cover for Osaiya. He mentioned to Ron that the Americans planned two or three weeks there and suggested that Monday would be good to go. Ron agreed, thanked Neil and said he would phone Brad and Jim shortly. Ron explained that they should have their meeting as planned regarding some other issues that had been developing.

"Yup, that works for me, guys," Vince said. "Let's meet up at the Sea View Hotel in an hour or so."

It was around midday and Ron was on his way to the Sea View. He was dropping off one of the maids on his way. He had already touched base with Brad in the Selous.

He was beginning to feel like he was settling into Tanzania but still had his mind on assets and issues in Zimbabwe. He had done a power of moving around and ducking and diving. It seemed a constant issue in Africa that required adapting to. Ron was a big clean-shaven man around six-foot five and tried to keep himself around 115 kilograms. He followed his own exercise plan that involved walking and swimming. He was in pretty good shape for his 63 years. He had spent some time serving in the Rhodesian security forces back in the day. This was the period in his life when he met Deborah who had also served in the forces.

Neil and Ron had met up in Zimbabwe and had decided to become partners in the accommodation and hunting business. At the time, Neil had been there on a game-hunting holiday break. Zimbabwe during this period did not require foreign prospectors to involve any Zimbabwean business partners. It seemed promising for investors within the correct sectors; there was enough potential there to convince Neil to set up in business with Ron.

Vince and Neil were seated at a table overlooking the Indian Ocean shoreline when Ron arrived. The hotel complex was quite upmarket, and the bar restaurant was famed for the menu and hospitality. Ron had phoned the Americans to explain the short delay and that arrangements had been made for Neil to fly down on Monday morning. A couple of cold beers arrived and Ron ordered himself some freshly squeezed orange juice.

Ron asked Neil to get an inventory together of what he intended to carry with him. They would touch base tomorrow evening on that. "Yeh no probs, Ron. I'm gonna call them tomorrow to see what they have in mind to chase, anything on their tickets with a tail no doubt, and thank Christ we don't do elephants."

Vince ordered up two more beers and an orange juice for Ron. Ron was sitting, smiling and chuckling at Neil's statement regarding creatures with tails.

"What are you laughing at, Ron?" Neil said with a grin. "I'm serious about some of those guys. Who the fuck is gonna help you when one of those guys gets pissed off and decides to destroy you, vehicle and all? They don't usually leave the job half-finished either. Buffalo and lion are challenging enough, mate, without those beautiful eight-ton lumps."

Neil had a thing about elephants and he did not agree with hunting those creatures. When Neil had piped down a little, Ron laughed; a glance at Vince, then back at Neil.

"Neil, mate, I could not agree with you more. When you were sharing your knowledge of animals with and without tails, my mind kept straying towards yourself and your weekend conquests."

Ron went on to tell Vince of Neil's guidelines in regards to the available obliging opposite sex in downtown Dar S, and once the beer goggles were on, anything without a tail was fair game.

Neil was not rising to it, instead just sitting, smiling and enjoying his beer.

"Hey, Ron," Vince commented. "I ain't so sure about all that. My money would be on odds with Neil regarding anything with or without a tail as fair game on weekends."

"Absolutely," Neil offered, "something to hold onto, mate." He then strolled off to the men's room.

"OK, guys, I'm not gonna stay much longer. Neil, you should be up to speed tomorrow. Vince, are you still up for getting your guys to give the two vehicles a real good going over? I prefer to talk to you now about that. I heard in the pipeline that you are thinking on quitting the workshop game and moving on."

"Ha, I was wondering when you guys would get wind of that," Vince replied. "The answers to that are yes can do and yes on the cards, buddy."

Ron was checking his messages while Neil and Vince were chatting. He was wondering whether or not to contact Jim and Brad again but decided to leave it just now.

"Right, guys, sorry to interrupt, but I need to leave fairly shortly, got an appointment with the game authority," Ron said.

"A Saturday appointment," Neil said. "You better not miss that."

"Yeh, I know. Anyway, a kind of weird, well, maybe concerning, situation got brought up when I was talking to Brad earlier. Vince, do you recall a while back maybe four months or so there was an issue in Dar regarding diamonds, tanzanite and shit, French and Americans involved?"

Vince was leaning with elbows on the table, clasped hands and chin on the thumbs, looking at Ron.

"Yeh, I sure do, but I can't recall the story to it all."

"I know you remember, Neil. You had some conversation with one of the French guys in one of the bars, yeh? Do you feel that this guy was involved in that incident?"

"I recon he was for sure. He never mentioned any of his business to me, but I overheard some stuff in the piss house when he was talking to his American buddy. I was in the shitter at the time. They did not talk much at all because other folk entered and they left. I'm a good listener even if I have had a few.

"I learned years ago in the mines in South Africa, never to even mention the fucking word diamond outside work; if it got reported, you got instant dismissal from the job; fuck those mines," Neil continued.

"So what's the deal with this?" Vince asked.

Ron went on to tell them of the phone conversation with Brad and the police and game warden's visit they had and the mention of the missing French folk between Mahenge and Lake Tagalala area.

"Maybe I am putting two and two together and making five. I don't know. What do you recon? I was going to mention to Brad, but I didn't."

"No need to," Neil offered. "If you like, I will mention to them on Monday; if you don't, I won't."

"What do you recon, Vince?" Ron asked.

Vince seemed to be staring out to the sea in the direction of the small ferryboats crossing to and from Zanzibar.

Vince added that he thought whatever they decide, better not to get thinking too much with these folks that are missing.

Vince dropped Miriam off for her shift at the K bar and thought that he may as well hang around. Neil had talked him into a night out, as it was Neil's last weekend in Dar for a couple of weeks and he would probably arrive in a couple of hours.

The bar was fairly quiet and a couple of hours had passed without any power outages. The grid seemed pretty stable, no doubt due to many industrial consumers presently not operating, he thought.

He could relax this evening. He was not driving and had decided to just go with the flow. He sat at the top end of the bar that displayed the large TV screens and this was also the main bar that Miriam worked. The lower bar next to the entrance was the smaller bar that provided and prepared cocktails as well as everything else.

Miriam had Lisa's replacement working with her. Husna was one of the girls who normally worked between the kitchen and both bars as a waitress.

Miriam opened another beer for Vince and he asked her for a small plate of mishkaki. She took the offer of a drink from Vince and pegged it for later. She made no conversation with him regarding the night before; it never worked like that with the two of them.

He was watching some football on the large screen, some African league that could have been anywhere on the sub-Saharan side of the continent. A large man had entered and took up a barstool a few metres from him and ordered a short and a cold beer. The man was dressed in the normal K bar dress code: shorts, soft casual shoes, loose shirt and he was wearing a ball cap. The man was quite overweight, and the light-khaki green shirt he was wearing allowed the fresh, expanding, underarm sweat marks to be easily noticed.

Vince was never really fond of shorts on an evening out. He usually preferred his Levis, t-shirt and soft shoes with socks. He still kept well within the realm of casual dress of course. He was a good-looking guy around five ten, slim and muscular and kept his dark, straight, shoulder-length hair pushed behind his ears and normally clean shaven. His dark brown eyes were gifted from his mother's side and his strong jawline from his father. One of the local bar girls strolled over from the pool tables and sat down next to him on his right in between him and the big guy. She leaned towards Vince, said hello and asked if he could buy her a drink; he agreed, providing she had either a beer or soft drink. Miriam came over and gave the girl a beer and they exchanged a few words in Swahili.

The girl was quite pleasant and appeared to have tuned herself into early evening mode. He had already given her the split second look over when she arrived and sat down. She was within Vince's taste, mid-20s, average height with a slim firm body, wearing heels, short skirt and top and a nice choice of longish bob-style hairpiece. He was thinking how attractive she was and she was on the dark side of perfect; he found himself mentally entering her onto his to-do list.

After a chat with her, he bought her another beer and mentioned that he would be occupied with his friend shortly. He ordered himself another beer, excused himself and went to the men's room. The toilet was fairly clean, quiet and dry. *Just wait till later on*, he thought. He returned back to his beer where the large guy was talking to the girl. Vince noticed from the drawl of his accent that he was from the States, probably Kentucky or Tennessee. The big guy asked the girl if she was waiting for someone.

"Yes, you, babe," came the reply to him.

The time had moved onto 7:30 p.m. and customers were arriving at a steady pace. The big American was joined by another man and their conversation was becoming more raised. Vince was chatting to another girl and reckoned that Neil should be along fairly soon. The girl was quite young, very late teens maybe and very chatty. He was receiving the pre-assessment enquiries from her, "What you do here, how long you stay, where you stay and are you married?" You could be anyone you wanted to be in Dar without any comebacks. Vince just basically answered her quickly with the facts as they were; it was much easier.

He caught a glimpse of Neil entering through the main door at the opposite end of the bar. He nodded to Miriam and she brought over two Safari beers and a large Jack Daniels and some ice.

Neil arrived wide-eyed, bushy-tailed and sober.

"Howz it going, mate, been here long?"

Vince thumbed in the direction of the bar space to his left side.

"Just about that long, buddy," he said and quickly realised that his four or five empties were already cleaned up.

"Couple of hours; I dropped Miriam off for her shift."

Neil swallowed the whiskey, sat the glass on the bar and gestured with his forefinger to order another. He said cheers to Vince as he lifted the beer from the bar and sat down on the vacant barstool. Vince was in his preferred position, standing with his elbow on the bar. Neil went on to say how good he was feeling tonight with his free day tomorrow, then the Selous on Monday. He had prepared most of his packing and informed Vince that he had already spoken to both Brad and Jim.

"No problem," Neil said. "Those boys really don't give a fuck for the delay, and they are keeping themselves busy fishing, target practice and reloading shell casings and stuff. They will arrange my pick up on Monday and fluff up my pillows. You will have to come out on one of these bashes sometime, mate, really; see if you can make some time next week. Ron will be heading down I reckon. You ever shot a rifle, Vince?"

Vince just smiled at Neil and gave him a raised closed hand all except an extended middle finger. Neil ordered some more drinks through some controlled laughing.

Neil picked up a full bottle of beer next to him on the bar.

"Hey, did I miss this one?"

"Na, buddy, hers."

He nodded his head in a direction behind and beyond Neil.

At that moment, the girl turned around to pick up her beer and noticed Neil.

"Hi, babes, how are you? I miss you. Where have you been?"

She gave Neil a kiss on the cheek.

"I've been looking for you, gorgeous. Where's your buddy tonight then?" Neil replied.

Just then, another girl arrived. She was a mirror image of the girl already standing at the bar with them. Neil looked at Vince and, casually thinking out loud, muttered, "What the fuck?"

The girls mentioned that they were twin sisters, or 'sistas' as they put it.

"No shit," Vince said, laughing.

The twins began moving to see some people at the other end of the bar. The first girl was laughing.

"You like two again tonight?" she asked Neil.

Neil drew on his hand-rolled cigarette.

"Yeh, you bet. Later, babe."

"Hey, Vince, if I ever pay for two, I certainly don't want two that look the fucking same. That would be a head fuck, that would."

Vince was hanging over the bar, laughing loudly. He was also having a good laugh at the 'Rouge Rubis' smooch mark on Neil's right cheek.

"Yeh, you got it, buddy, but you could maybe try the 'buy one get one free' deal."

Neil got talking to the big American guy and Vince ordered some more drinks. Vince had a quick chat with Miriam, then headed out front to make a phone call. When he returned, Neil was just finishing off a game of pool with one of the bar girls. He thought, *Shit, that must have been a quick game.* He heard Neil giving the girl a false promise of a date as he was leaving the table. Vince took a long drink of his beer and asked Neil if he got his ass whipped.

"Yep, why be different tonight, mate?"

"You know, any girls on those tables look like amateurs; the way they hold and use those pool cues looks like shit. Tell you what though, they are bloody good," Neil continued to say.

Vince mentioned to Neil that he had a terrific view of the table and it was worth watching, especially when she leaned over with those heels and that short skirt.

"Neil, buddy, my thoughts and heart was on you winning that game, but my wager had 'cute sexy chick' written all over it."

"Yeh, fuck you too, Vince; c'mon, let's get some drinks."

Vince laughed, shaking his head. Neil still had the red lips on his cheek.

Neil was chatting to a couple of the power contractors that had just arrived, looking for a game of pool. Vince was chilling at the bar, enjoying his beer and thankful to a break from the passing bar girls. The big American was in deep conversation with his buddy, and the twins were on the hustle. His cell phone chimed a message announcement and he checked it. It was from Miriam. She and Husna were up to their ears in clearing up empties as well as setting up full ones. It was just approaching 11, the start of the busy period. The content of her message was asking him if he required her company tonight. He thought, *What the hell, why not?* He was in a chilled-out relaxed mood tonight and could not be bothered hooking up and exploring any of the available new territory that was moving around. *The same cannot be said for Neil,* he thought with a smile on his face. He returned her text and asked her what she had in mind. 15

minutes had passed when his cell phone chimed again, Vince was chatting to another girl who had moved in beside him at the bar. He picked up his phone. The message read '*how about no complications and we just fuck each other all night.*' A smiley was entered at the end.

Vince liked her directness. He excused himself for a minute with the girl at the bar, and, while smiling, he replied, '*my thoughts entirely, guess where you are going tonight, babe?*' He could see her checking her phone. She smiled over at him and carried on with her work. His phone chimed again, the message read, '*Whaoh, that will be two nights in a row, is this an upgrade, Mr Kelly?*' Vince smiled, slid the phone into his jeans pocket and continued chatting with the girl.

Vince's realm of sustained harmony was suddenly shattered by a loud disturbance at the other end of the bar. Tables, bottles, glasses and at least one person was on the floor. Vince quickly assessed the incident and noticed that Neil was away from it and he remained where he was. He noticed the big American's buddy lunging at the individual who was picking himself up off the floor. The two of them collided and the American's buddy had the other guy in a neck hold and hitting him with his free hand.

To Vince's surprise, all within a second or two, Neil had dumped his beer on a table and raced towards them. Neil pounced on the American guy's friend's back like a hungry alley cat and locked his right arm around the guy's neck. Vince muttered, "Shit," to himself and instinctively ran over, grabbed the friend's both forearms while dodging a couple of kicks and the three of them stumbled and fell onto a table and a bench seating area.

At least four Tanzanian doormen and the big American were now on the scene and dealt with it without any more violence developing. The four Tanzanians were pretty big and solid guys. Just their presence deterred any fracas re-igniting. Vince then noticed that the guy who had been on the floor was one of the power contractors.

Two of the doormen left and the other two had a chat with the three of them; the other two contractors were asked to go to the bottom bar. Nobody ended up being asked to leave the premises, just some cash was required for breakages along with some drinks and tips for the doormen. The doormen were quite confident of no repetitions arising and would keep a keen eye on things. The available girls around were normally quite good at smoothing out any animosity among those involved following these incidents. Vince headed back to the bar and his beer with Neil and just laughed.

"Fuck me!" he said to Neil. "The bar staff paid no attention at all to all that."

The two of them went into serious laughter.

"Hey, Neil, what was the deal over there anyway?"

"Haven't got a clue, mate. I will ask Matt later or tomorrow. I reckon he is fine, looks like a busted lip and no doubt a few head lumps. I see that other guy is South African, mate; got one of those funny accents."

Vince sniggered and ordered a couple of beers and a Jack Daniels as if nothing had happened.

Vince had just come out of the shower and got himself a cold beer from the cooler. He was happy to have arrived home. The taxi that took him home managed the 20-minute journey without incident and that was a bonus. There seemed to be not even a millimetre of the old Toyota Corolla pointing in the correct direction. The safety belt in the rear had been tied around the interior handle of the right-hand door to keep it closed.

He drank his beer and had a chuckle to himself about the taxi. He checked the time and his mobile lit up 1:20 in the morning.

Miriam had mentioned she would be finished around two maximum; he had given her a spare key to let herself in.

She was in the elevator and on her way to the fourth floor to Vince's apartment at around 2:30. She had tried calling Vince, but he was ringing out. The security guard assured her he was in. *Probably fell asleep,* she thought. She entered the apartment and heard the snoring and the lighting was low from the one uplighter that was on in the sitting room. She removed her heels and moved towards the main bedroom door which was opened. Vince was lying on his back, wearing just black boxers and sound asleep. She smirked to herself and moved to the kitchen. She cleared the two empty beer bottles from the table and headed to the bathroom. Miriam stood in the shower and lathered herself for the second time and let the cool water from the showerhead comfort her head and face.

After drying off, she wrapped a light sarong around herself and poured herself a large glass of chilled white wine. She felt the welcoming warmth in her stomach and the effect of the wine hitting her almost instantly. Her mind was on getting into bed beside Vince; she was smiling to herself, wondering what direction Neil was heading. She had left the premises before him and he was still there with one of the twins and another girl. Miriam decided to wear a fresh hairpiece from her bag; it was an expensive one made from human Chinese black hair that lay straight to the level of her breasts with blue tints either side at the front.

She emptied her glass and applied some perfume to her neck and cleavage. Vince was still snoring. She decided that Vince would smell of beer and she poured herself another white wine.

The apartment temperature was maintaining a nice 25 degrees Celsius through the air-condition system. She finished her wine and was feeling really relaxed now, almost high as she got into bed. Vince had moved onto his left side and the snoring had ceased for now. She was naked and came in close to him with her arm over his waist and her hand moving over his lower tummy. She rested her cheek and nose on his neck and ear area and started to kiss him behind the ear and down his neck at the same time running her nails lightly up and down his side and his tummy.

Vince realised she was there and gave a contented moan of satisfaction and quietly asked her who she was. She laughed through her nose and pushed her nails into his stomach. He could feel her breasts against his back and the scent of her perfume was overwhelming as if taking over his very thoughts and controlling every move he would make tonight.

He took her hand and kissed and tonged her palm and wrist. He then moved her hand down his stomach and against his boxers. Miriam moved her hand around the front of his neat-fitting shorts and she could feel how erect he was becoming. He had moved his right arm behind him against her buttocks to push her vaginal area into his buttocks.

Her hand was now inside his shorts, feeling how hard he had become. She steadily pulled down the shorts and removed them.

Her hand went back to his erect penis that was now free from obstruction. Vince turned around to face her and he could see the black hair with the blue highlights; he thought how attractive she was and started to kiss her passionately.

He leaned back a little and let her lie down on her back. His hand moved over her breasts and erected nipples. She had put some personal lubricant from the bedside table onto her palm and was slowly masturbating him; he felt like he was as hard as he could ever become. He started to kiss her intensely with his hand exploring her vaginal area with the intoxicating scent of her fragrance influencing him even more.

Both of them were tense; their tongues firming up and equally exploring with the more than wet taste of lust.

They made love and pleasured each other with intense, adventurous, sexual intercourse until almost first light. Sleep came to them like a couple of dead-beat toddlers.

Peckish Pooch

Sunday morning greeted Ron with a bright ray of sunshine that brightened the bedroom through the open patio shutters and warmed up his pillow. He smiled and stretched his arms and legs as if attempting to increase his body length by a few inches. The area was quiet outside apart from a number of disturbed pigeons flapping their wings while ascending from the lawn to the roof thatch. Ron leaned over and clasped his hand on Deborah's shoulder and kissed her on the cheek. She smiled and dug herself further into the pillow, appreciating the fact that she still had some time left in bed. Ron slid open the two mosquito-net doors that were access to the balcony.

The time was 07:20 and he watched Wanzagi at the end of the grounds with the two dogs, giving them some exercise after feeding them. The dogs were black Labradors that Ron and Debs had acquired in Tanzania a few years ago; both were males from the same litter.

The family had their experiences with a few breeds in the past in Zimbabwe, mainly Rhodesian ridgebacks and Dobermans. These animals were kept with the primary purpose being security. In Tanzania, although more secure, it was wise to have dogs for this purpose, especially in the more privileged areas. Labradors were always favourable to Ron and he thought well of the pedigree in these animals. The labs, being of good nature, obedient and predictable, fitted in well within this guesthouse environment.

These two dogs were very rarely indoors of the building; this was out of bounds for them. A purpose-built kennel outbuilding housed the dogs within the grounds.

They were probably the only labs in the Ursino area, as many of the dogs in the neighbouring properties were German shepherds or Dobermans. There was a fair amount of these dogs that were clearly undisciplined to the point that some temporary, subcontracted, security guards dreaded some of their placement posts. Having a stroll in some of the avenues could prove more than irritating when dogs would sometimes bark and display their teeth against the fences when an individual walked past.

Ron was of the opinion that this entire big, mean, guard-dog image was unnecessary. Labradors were quiet, strong and pretty much fearless and pound-for-pound would see off most breeds.

Let's face it, he thought, *how many times did anyone ever see an angry Lab growling deeply in a pre-charging position with hackles pointing upwards between the shoulder blades and baring its teeth like a determined wolf? It is not a comforting sight or easily induced, but when seriously provoked or commanded, this breed can take care of business.*

Two years ago, just a few days before Christmas, Debs had prepared a Christmas cake. The preparation had consumed many hours of her time. She placed the cake on top of the large kitchen table resting on a stainless steel tray to cool down overnight.

The following morning, Ron was awakened by loud screaming and crying from downstairs. He rushed down and was faced with Debs and Alison, the maid, in the kitchen. Alison was attempting to comfort and calm down Debs who was crying from both sorrow and rage. Ron noticed the cake and the tray on the floor but with half of the cake missing.

The floor and under the table were a mess of cake pieces and scattered cloths that once covered the cake during the cooling process. He had a fair assumption in his mind in regards to what had happened, and before he could say anything, Debs screamed.

"Those bastard dogs, Ron."

Just as Ron was trying to prevent Debs from going into a frenzy, Wanzagi entered the kitchen and began to explain what he had observed at around 03:20 hours. Half a minute into Wanzagi's report, Debs ran out the kitchen and towards the kennel, with Alison running right after her. Ron instructed Wanzagi to wait in the kitchen together with him.

The carnage that followed was nothing less than what Ron expected. One dog ran past the kitchen on the lawn and out of sight in the foliage behind the generator area. Debs, just 50 metres away, could be heard screaming at the other dog. Alison was shouting at Debs, and the dog was yelping in fright and from pain. All then fell silent and both ladies made their way back to the kitchen. Ron asked Wanzagi to go and attend to the dogs. Debs cuddled up to Ron, still crying with her head against his chest. He understood her feelings, as he knew she had spent days preparing and baking this cake. *Merry Christmas,* he thought.

Debs said quietly and sternly to Ron that if either of the two handguns that they kept hidden upstairs for protection had been within reach, she would have shot the dog. He believed her.

Wanzagi had explained that in the early hours whilst doing his rounds, he had noticed the kitchen door was ajar.

He had moved quickly towards the door, grasping his baton and torch. The torch beam exposed one of the dogs named Sam eating the cake on the floor, and on sight of Wanzagi entering, the dog quickly ran out. He had observed the key inserted on the inside of the door but unlocked. He closed the door, locked it and gave the key to Alison when she arrived. Debs had mistakenly forgotten to lock the door the previous evening. Sam had probably got an irresistible scent of the cake, made his way to the source and leaned on the handle, opening the door. The animal must then have grasped the tray in his jaws and lowered it to the floor before feasting on it. Wanzagi had asked Ron if this theory was plausible. Ron went on to tell Wanzagi that Labradors have very powerful neck and jaw muscles and they are greedy opportunist bastards when unattended food is around. Yes, more than plausible. Jazz, the other dog, had not been involved in the raid.

The unfortunate animal, Sam, had not escaped Deborah unpunished. As she ran towards the kennel, she picked up a long piece of two-by-two-inch white-pine framing wood. Sam was inside the kennel building and his stomach was swollen so large with cake that he could not move normally. He probably found it difficult to move at all, considering he had eaten half of a 14lb Christmas cake that was moderately laced with Brandy.

He ran to try to evade Debs, but as he passed, she dealt a hard blow driven by anger across the dog's back. The dog yelped in pain and was vomiting the cake as he escaped. The blow was hard enough to cause the pinewood to snap into two pieces.

Just as Ron was about to head back indoors from the balcony, Neil's voice boomed from the external ground area.

"Good morning, Ron, you coming down for breaky?"

Ron was more than surprised as he expected Neil to be slumming it somewhere with some good time girl during his last Saturday evening in Dar for a few weeks.

"Hey, Neil, good morning. What's happening, don't tell me you crashed in your own pad last night?"

A monotone half sleepy voice came from the bedroom.

"Ask the dirty stop out if he has just arrived back, Ron."

"Ha, you will never know, Debs; na, I took it easy last night. See you guys when you come down, I'm starving here," Neil loudly replied.

Neil headed into the kitchen and set up the coffeemaker.

He had a sneaky look in the wall mirror in the lounge to double check that no sign of any lipstick was visible on his cheeks. The last thing he needed this morning was handing Debs an easy target to focus her comments on. He sat outside and rolled himself a cigarette. The two dogs spotted him and raced over with their tails wagging puppy-style and tongues ready and prepared to remove any trace evidence of lipstick on his cheeks. Ron appeared and started to get the coffee and things together and placed some paperwork on the table. Ron sat the coffee pot on the table.

"Right, Neil, I got the guys a three-by-two ticket, two *simba* and one *chui* between the pair of them." This was Swahili language describing two lions and one leopard.

"The two buffalo are one-on-one and covered by the three-week hunt, and Richard at the game authority says hi and you owe him a few beers when you get back."

"Oh yeh, Neil, forgot to mention, forget the bow-hunting thing, too restricted, no dangerous game hunting and twice the licencing and government area fees of a rifle. Brad and Jim were not interested when I phoned them."

Selous Bound

Ron asked the maid to prepare two full English breakfasts but prioritise any guests that arrive.

"Your flight departure is 08:20 tomorrow with coastal, mate, e-ticket in your email. I am far from tied up with things to do today, so I can give you a hand kitting up. What kind of kit do the guys have down there?"

"Not sure, Ron. I think a couple of RPGs and fully auto 50-cals," Neil jokingly replied.

"Will let you know, mate, got it in my email."

Neil asked Ron how many guests at present were going to be game hunting and found out that none were. Some folks were due in next week, and there were a couple of professional hunters that could stand in for Osaiya. Ron had mentioned that a couple of female guests were going to be staying a while, but they had not fully decided on their plans or timetable until now. He reckoned, judging from their conversation, that they would probably be opting for some photography in one of the closer reserves; they were Canadian.

The rest of the guests were tourists or business folk. Apparently, there was an Irishman and an Englishman who were more than fond of a drink or two. They were independents and something to do with the power contractor site and the Tanzanian client, compliance or audit folk or something.

"Well, Ron, I certainly can't knock them."

The unique smell of sausage and bacon was thick in the air now. Neil headed off to the toilet to scrub up and Ron sent the two dogs packing. Sausage, bacon, fried eggs and black pudding arrived at the table along with toast and more coffee.

As they were enjoying breakfast, Debs appeared briefly.

"Good morning, guys, *bon appetite*."

"*Merci*, madam," Neil answered.

Debs said she had to go, as guests were appearing for breakfast now. She placed a ring of keys on the table.

"Gunroom, gentlemen, catch up later."

Neil printed off his flight ticket and some documents from Ron. He printed out Brad and Jim's asset's list and forwarded the email to Ron along with serial numbers.

Ruger .375 Holland & Holland M77 Magnum Express
Winchester .375 H&H Model 70 Safari Express
Mauser .416 Rigby M96 Magnum

CZ 550 USA .416 Rigby Safari Magnum
Tikka T3 .270 Winchester Magnum Varmint
Tikka T3 30-06 Springfield Hunter
Bowtech BT Mag Smart Bow

Neil already had most of his kit arranged. Ron was inside the gunroom, checking on a few things. The English guest walked past on his return from breakfast. He introduced himself to Ron as Brian and he seemed keen to have a look in the gunroom when Ron invited him inside. The guest was quite impressed by the size of the room and the firearms that were neatly displayed in their racks with a common coated chain and lock linking them together through the trigger guards.

The room had a 20-square-metre floor area and the walls reached to 2.3 metres in height. The guest mentioned that he knew very little of guns except for airgun ownership as a kid and he once had an opportunity to take part in some clay-pigeon shooting.

Ron was quick to advise him that shotguns are a good start but firearms were much more rewarding and an endless subject of study. He offered any advice to the guest if he was planning to stay in Tanzania for a while and developed an interest in shooting. All guests that resided in The Savanna House could be potential future clients in Ron and Neil's thinking. Brian thanked Ron and asked him if he could give any advice regarding good places to socialise on a Sunday that were not too far away.

"Yes, I can advise you of that too," Ron said.

As Brian was making his way out, Ron introduced him to Neil who was on his way in.

"I'm not gonna need too much, Ron; just a hunter and a backup rifle, I think the Steyr and the Heym."

Ron arranged a couple of lightweight tripods and the appropriate ammunition for Neil.

"All reloads, Ron?"

"Yep, there are soft points and solids there."

Neil grabbed two plastic gun cases and a low-powered scope. He would decide down there if he was going to mount the scope or stick with open sights. It was just around 15:20 in the afternoon and Neil was more or less good to go.

The rifles he had arranged to take were quality pieces of engineering and both were equipped with open express sights. The double barrel was a very expensive rifle, a Heym 89B in .450-nitro express calibre, a German-made side-by-side British-style double. In anyone's book, this was a serious rifle of high velocity and energy mainly used as backup or a first-shot rifle in heavy scrub areas, a real stopper in the correct hands.

In a situation that has developed into a close proximity charge from a dangerous game animal, many PHs and hunters alike would probably prefer this equipment in their hands. The assurance of being in control of sending two, rapid, 400-grain, high-velocity projectiles in the direction of the danger was welcome.

The hunting rifle was a Steyr Mannilicher S in .375 H-and-H calibre. An Austrian rifle chambered in the minimum calibre required to hunt African dangerous game in Tanzania.

Neil sat outside, having a cigarette and a beer. Dusk had already settled, and the first sounds that could be heard were the haunting calls of nearby and distant peacocks. He had set up the fan and the vape mosquito coils under the table.

He dialled up Jim's cell phone and got a connection. As things turned out, Jim and Brad were engaged in the same activity outside the lodge as Neil was, less the peacock calls.

They discussed some options and plans for the coming few weeks, and the conversation progressively swung into the bow-hunting plan being dropped.

"Hey, buddy, Brad ain't too much pissed at that at all, not at those fees. He can still use the thing on small shit if the big stuff don't keep us occupied."

Neil cracked open another beer and wished the guys a good evening. They were not wanting or needing for anything taken down there.

Neil picked up a copy of the 'Citizen' newspaper that was on the table, probably left by one of the guests.

The copy was a couple of days old and he was not reading anything in particular, just an addition to his beer and cigarette to keep him occupied. He was reading through the small articles when something jumped right out at him on the fourth page. There was an article and an appeal on behalf of the Tanzanian authorities regarding three missing persons in the Selous area. Neil carefully read through the content a second time and learned that the media described the people as French Canadians. The common knowledge that Neil and the guys had been led to believe was these folk were French nationals, not so apparently. Neil was searching for any useful detailed information, but the article more or less described them as visitors to Tanzania, all in their 30s.

"Hey, Ron, I am just reading an article in the 'Citizen' on those missing Frenchies, only they are not French apparently; unless there are six missing folk; they are Canadian."

Ron came out from the gunroom, sweating and pledging to have the air conditioner checked out and recharged in the morning. He looked over the article and shrugged his shoulders.

"Hmm, maybe you guys will come across them down there."

"Maybe, Ron, but you would not want to get lost in that area with no means of communication, would you? What did the guys down there say? Three cell phones and all unresponsive! What the fuck is all that about, unless you are trying to stay under the radar or you have no means of charging. That is serious shit, mate, something wrong there."

"Yeh, I know what you're saying, Neil, sure don't add up at all."

Neil placed the newspaper into his luggage.

41

The Selous Lodge

The PC12 Eagle touched down on the airstrip at Kiba in Selous and Neil was more than happy for that. The flight from Dar was a short one, way under two hours from boarding, but it seemed like an eternity for him. He had a window seat and his companion on the flight next to him had started a conversation long before departing Dar, and she was still on it as they were approaching the small apron in Selous.

He felt that he now knew everything she had done and everything that she planned to do. The woman was American, in her 50s and fairly overweight, wearing large dark sunglasses. Neil never usually drank much on these short internal flights apart from a couple of small beers. This occasion prompted him to stray from this routine and sink a couple of whiskey chasers for the beers. He wished he could slip on a kid's Halloween false facemask backwards and stare out the window, wearing his tailor-made earplugs. He had probably managed to digest a fraction of what she bombarded him with and she was now informing him that her husband could not make the Selous trip due to his presence being required at an event in Dar. *That's one lucky guy,* Neil thought. *Must be a tree hugger's convention.* They walked across the apron to the small terminal when Neil found himself wondering when he was going to be blessed with her business card. Just at that moment, she produced one from her bag and handed it to him. He returned the gesture by removing one from his shirt pocket and giving it to her. She gave the card a brief glance and put it in her bag, and they both shook hands again and greeted each other by their given names.

Nancy Bell
Consultant and Photographer
African Wildlife Conservation
El Paso County, Colorado, USA.

Judging by her conversation, Neil did not expect much less regarding powdered rhino-horn snorting and the diminishing lion population etc. etc. He was smirking to himself, realising that she had not taken the time to study his card where the first two lines read *Neil McPherson, Firearms Consultant and Professional Hunter.* She would notice later, he thought, thankfully unobserved to his advantage. He was grateful with the cards being exchanged as they departed each other's company and not at the beginning, that would for sure have directed her conversation in another direction. He wondered how many American women were called Nancy and Deloris.

Neil caught sight of Jim and Brad beside the Toyota, and as he walked towards them, a four-by-four vehicle drove past with Nancy Bell leaning out the window, waving and shouting over to Neil.

Neil waved back and returned the verbal gesture.

"See you around, ma'am," Neil shouted.

"Oh ho, who is she, Neil?" Brad asked.

"I'll explain later, mate. Give me a hand with this gear, please, guys."

They manhandled the bags and cases and rested them down at the exit gate to allow the police to carry out their checks. Everything was in order, including the paperwork.

One of the police had a short assault rifle fitted with a scope.

"Hey, guys, that copper must be a right arse of a shot if he needs a scope from this distance," Neil said to the Americans. Loud laughter followed.

"Hey, Neil buddy, you can be a God-dammed motherfucker sometimes. Give the guy a break," Brad replied with a chuckle.

It was only an 11-kilometre drive to the lodge. Jim was driving and mentioned how good it was to have the entire luggage on the back pick-up area without being tied down and covered over.

"In Dar S, they would have the eyes out your head, then ask you where you lost them, buddy," Jim said.

They discussed the accommodation and Neil would fill them in with the permits and allocation later in the afternoon.

Neil was informed that they were the only guests at the camp and some new arrivals were due to arrive midweek. Neil knew the camp manager well, Simon, who was also a PH and had completed his training in Tanzania. His hometown was Mbea, not too far from the Mozambique border. They arrived at camp after a dusty but not too bumpy journey through a couple of small villages on the way. After a chat with Simon, Neil opted for one of the small raised Bandas for his accommodation; the two Americans shared a spacious tent lodge that had adequate room inside as well as two en suite bathrooms. They all had views of the river from the north bank.

"Hey, Simon, is there any chance of a late breakfast or brunch or something? I missed out on breakfast this morning," Neil asked.

"Yes, just give Tatou a shout, Neil."

Simon shouted to ask the cook to come through, and then Neil and Simon caught up with the latest gossip.

Simon had found Osaya's mishap in Dar quite amusing and he let Neil know that he had called him the day before.

"Tell you what, Neil, he will sure save himself a fortune by not being able to answer his cell phone while he is driving in Dar now. You see those big, fat, mama kilo traffic cops there? I recon Osaya is the main source of income for their lunch."

Simon enquired into the police visit on Friday and asked what was going on with those missing French folk.

"That's another story that, mate," Neil said. "When I find out, I will sure let you know; oh, they ain't French as in French France, apparently Canadians as in French Canadians."

Neil strolled over to let Tatou know that the three of them were up for eating.

"Hey, Tatou, ain't Brad shot you anything for the pot with that bow yet?"

Neil ducked as an incoming empty cigar tube that Brad had launched flew over his head while Brad was simulating the release of a bowstring.

The three of them sat outside under the shade of one of the table parasols, enjoying sausages, bread, French fries and coffee. They shared their lunch with a tag team of uninvited sparrows and an ashy starling.

"Don't matter where you find yourself on this planet, guys, there ain't no getting away from those little house sparrows, you know—" Jim commented.

"That's a fact, buddy," Brad cut in. "I spent a bit of time in Lebanon a few years after the civil war was officially over. I got invited to a colleague's house in the mountain area somewhere between Beirut and Tripoli for a barbeque. I'll tell you, buddy, that was some amount of food and quite a few bottles of Johnnie Walker on the table. I got to eat these tiny little birds that were skewered along with some peppers and onions and all that shit. I thought they were maybe chicks from advanced incubated eggs, something like those Filipino boiled eggs with the chick inside.

"They tasted really nice. They sure did, especially with a whisky chaser, and you just eat the lot, head and all, only the feet missing. You know, there was no feeling of sharp or hard bones there at all, just kind of melted in your mouth after a few chews."

"What were they, Brad?" Neil asked.

"Fucking house sparrows. The deal there was the grandfather was more than protective over his olive trees that surrounded the house. He had the tree trunks painted with that white shit about five feet up from the ground. I dare say that kept the goats and lots of critters away.

"Those little birds never kept away though. When enough of them congregated in the trees, the old man would scare them off the trees from the rear balcony and shoot off some buckshot from his old 410 shotgun into the small airborne flock. The girls would collect, pluck, clean and salt them ready for the flame. I still prefer turkey though," Brad said with a smile.

"What took you over there, Brad, the military?" Neil asked.

"No, not at all. I was over there in the position of resident engineer, working for a UK company, overseeing some American compacting equipment being fitted onto British trucks' chassis. These were specialist vehicles, trash trucks, you know. The project was sponsored by the Lebanese government with some generous assistance from the Saudis.

"The Greater Beirut upgrade project I think it was named, and I was there for 12 months. The place was a God-dammed mess and I remember a huge landfill site that ended up reclaiming and occupying part of the sea and that was known as City Clean Mountain. City Clean was the name of the operation side of the business, we were the engineering side."

"There was a huge difference in the city by the time I left with regular garbage collections in place. Anyway, are we having a beer?"

Three cold beers arrived with ice crystals starting to form inside the bottlenecks.

"What's the deal with the fishing then, Jim? Did you get some more time in? I had a look at your tiger on the email photos, beautiful fish."

"Na, Neil, not yet. I caught it over there a couple of miles, west I recon."

Jim was pointing in a direction where the river flowed in quite a curve where it appeared much wider. The grass, scrub, trees and background hills were shimmering in the afternoon heat haze. The time was around 13:30 and just a couple of hours away from the hottest part of the day. Neil reminded the guys of the chat they would have regarding the plan for tomorrow; he felt more tired than he usually did and this was no doubt urged on a little by the couple of large whiskies he had on the flight. He excused himself and headed off to get his head down for a couple of hours.

"Oh yeh, by the way, guys, have a peak at this, page four."

Neil pulled out the copy of the 'Citizen' newspaper from his carry bag and tossed it onto the table and left for his room.

The welcoming warm breeze was flowing through the Banda and Neil switched off the overhead fan. He lay down and gave some thought to the riveting conversation he had with Nancy Bell. He smiled as he thought it could have been more challenging if she had decided to have a couple of drinks also. He thought that he had somehow not seen the end of her. It was not long before he was lying on his back in a deep sleep.

The Americans had read the newspaper article and dismissed the nationality confusion as irrelevant. They were discussing which options might lay ahead for the following day. Excitement and maybe a little apprehension were developing between the two of them.

They had hunted in Tanzania before mainly for plains game and once on an unsuccessful hunt for Cape buffalo that was abandoned due to weather. A visit to Namibia had been previously accomplished chasing plains game mainly antelope and warthog.

A successful hunt involving any of the big five was new to them, and the possibility of lion or leopard was the appeal; this was the main purpose of the trip. A trophy each was an absolute achievement they wished to accomplish. The discussion moved onto the potential dangers of dangerous game hunting in Africa and the creatures that were probably responsible for the most human deaths each year. They both agreed on the mosquito, common knowledge had that down to more than 750,000 deaths each year, and hippos, crocodiles and snakes and things seemed to follow.

Jim had a friend and acquaintance that had died in Africa three years previous. His name was Phil Burns who came from Texas. He worked in the oil industry and had spent some small periods of time on job placement in Africa, usually offshore.

In 2008, his company sent him to Nigeria to spend a couple of months consulting. His first week was spent in hotel accommodation in Lagos. The remainder of his time was also in hotel accommodation in Sapele. Sapele was one of the hotspots within the troubled delta region and well-known for kidnappings, robberies and killings; this was the first time Phil had worked onshore.

He had become ill and was mainly experiencing cold or flu symptoms. He was visiting pharmacies and taking flu-relief medicines. The symptoms came and went. There was a time a few days before he was going home on leave that he did not show up for work; this was unusual for him. He contacted his colleagues to let them know he needed a couple of days off to try to rest as he had felt feverish. An arrangement was made for a driver to drive to Phil's accommodation with some documents that required his signature. This was carried out and the driver advised Phil to visit the doctor to get checked for malaria. He assured the driver that he would be fine. Besides, he was travelling home in a couple of days and would visit his doctor there if he still felt under the weather.

The day Phil was travelling, he stopped by the Sapele office to say goodbye to everyone and collect a couple of things. He appeared to have lost a little weight and looked like he had not shaven for a few days; they were always used to him being clean-shaven. He had mentioned that he had some fever the last couple of days but felt quite good after the medication he had taken. The drive from Sapele to Benin Airport was a fast 90-minute drive with an armed police officer in the front passenger seat. The flight route was Benin to Lagos, then Lagos to Dallas via Amsterdam. He lived alone and was due back in Texas on the Wednesday evening, but Thursday morning had passed and none of his family had heard from him. His ex-wife had called the company who had got back to her to inform her that all seemed normal and there had not been any 'no show' status on Phil's flight connections.

Early Thursday afternoon, his ex-wife and his brother entered his home, and there they immediately noticed the unopened luggage in the entrance hall. There was no answer as they moved through the house, calling his name. His brother, Scott, entered the main bedroom upstairs and found Phil deceased on the bed, fully clothed. The coroner's findings following the autopsy disclosed that the cause of death had been malaria.

It was a tragedy to his family, friends and his company, especially since it was probably so preventable. Phil was only 42 years old.

"Yeh, poor old Phil," Jim commented. "He must have been real messed up on his way home. You know, I recon busy hotels in Africa are probably prime areas to contract malaria if mosquitos are not managed efficiently indoors. The way I see it is most of the guests there are from all over Africa and many African folk have malaria, more than one strain sometimes. The African folk have built up a fair degree of immunity to it and so has other foreign folk that have lived there for a long time. That puts someone new to Africa on a visit in a pretty high risk; you got to be real careful. The best management is not to let the fuckers in your room in the first place, and don't hang around in open bars dressed in shorts and shit in the evenings."

"Yeh right, Jim, no shit, get drunk during the day then. Anyway, we ain't hunting mosquitos. We should go for a drive; I don't think Neil will be around for a couple of hours."

They grabbed a cool box with some water and sodas and sat it on the rear of the pick-up bed. A .375-calibre rifle along with a 12-gauge shotgun and camera occupied the rear seating area.

They set out in a westerly direction. The opposite direction from before which now kept the river behind them. They decided to follow the main roads which were tracks by any standard. In front of them was a vast savanna grass and scrubland terrain and there was some sort of distant settlement in view. As they approached closer, the outline of a small village with fenced off farmland became apparent and villagers could be seen attending to whatever produce was being cultivated and managed within these boundaries. Brad reduced speed as they came through the village. Basic accommodation consisting of breeze block structures supporting corrugated steel and fibreglass roofing dominated the neighbourhood. Familiar worn-out and badly corroded shipping containers lay on stone or wood foundations and seemed to accommodate tools and supplies and some served as local trading posts.

One of the raised 10,000-gallon, black, plastic, water-supply tanks had developed a leak that created a large puddle right up to the roadside. Most of the village kids and dogs were attracted to the deluge and were having as much fun as a free trip to the carnival; even the dogs seemed to be smiling. As their journey made progress, the village faded away to give to a view of the road, beginning to offer a steeper gradient and snaking up to higher ground. The rocks became larger and some rocks resembled areas of a possible ancient volcanic past.

The effortless exhaust note pulsing from the big turbocharged V8 diesel engine as they climbed was pleasing and echoed high horsepower to the listener. Brad frequently monitored the vehicle-fuel content and warning gauges on the display consoles.

The road soon offered the option to carry on straight or verge off on another track to the right. Without giving any thought to decide, Brad carried on the straight option mainly due to being more used in appearance. As the road gradient levelled down quite a bit, he pulled over and let Jim know that he had to relieve himself and, on the way out, asked Jim to take a turn at the wheel. There was no shade in this immediate area and the flies were a serious nuisance if you were not in motion. When Brad had finished and was walking back to the Toyota, he was looking in a few different directions, trying to source a noise that he had heard. Jim had moved into the driving seat and was smoking a cigarette.

"Hey, Jim, did you hear that?"

"Hear what?"

Brad strolled back over to the vehicle passenger's side.

"I did hear something over there, a kind of rustling and light sort of thumping sound."

"Pass," Jim said as the two of them stayed quiet and motionless for a few seconds without any forthcoming sounds. Just as Brad parted his lips to say something, the sound returned quite clearly.

"I heard that, buddy," Jim said.

"Hold on a second, Jim; I'm gonna take a peak over there."

Brad walked slowly and quietly towards the noise. It was close and coming from rocks just beyond some thicket. He decided to stay still and observe the general direction where the noise was coming from. A moment later, a couple of flapping wings appeared from behind the rocks, then disappeared again. Brad turned around to ask Jim to hand him over the camera.

"What's the deal, Brad? Don't be walking in there."

Jim came over with the camera and carrying the shotgun. Brad informed Jim that it would be fine, as he had seen wings flapping.

"Don't worry, buddy. It's some kind of bird. I want to snap a photo as it takes off."

Brad was 20 metres away from the vehicle and Jim was in between the two of them. With the camera in hand, he moved to the left a little in an attempt to improve his view by stepping up onto a rock. The wind picked up and a cloud of dust and birds' feathers became airborne, moving around in all directions. He was about to move to a higher point on the rock when a scurry of movement and flapping wings exposed the source of activity. Two birds appeared on the ground in front of him just a few metres away; one was a large pigeon half plucked and torn open. The other was a large bird of prey with one set of talons firmly grasping the prey and the other claws fixed onto an exposed plant root; the wings were spread out and curving downwards over its prize. The raptor's yellow-and-black fearless eyes focused on Brad. He quickly turned to look at Jim, then straight back at the bird. With the camera raised, he managed a couple of shots just before the bird flapped its wings and dragged the prey a few more metres away under some thicket.

"Jim, did you see that? She was not freaked at all, man."

After a quick look behind the rocks to see only some feathers and some morsels of flesh, Brad headed on back to the vehicle.

The two of them drove on, intent on finding some kind of summit offering a view below.

"You recon that was a female bird. I did not get close enough to notice."

"Yeh, for sure a female, Jim. Big and brown, but not sure what type of hawk she is, but going by the wings, definitely a hawk. Hey, Jim buddy, I know we are in rural Tanzania, but don't you think it would be more polite and courteous to other road users to drive on the left side of the road?"

Jim gave Brad the middle-finger gesture and corrected the vehicle's position.

They reached a point that commanded a view of the landscape below as well as the higher ground. They shared a set of binoculars and took in some of the vast scenery around them. It was the time of day when the sun was high and the view in any direction was almost colourless. The higher ground appeared darker and the distant Rufiji River focused in and out of the heat haze. The immediate terrain in view was a varied mix but mainly scrubland with close-clustered thicket and stubbled trees with mangroves and tall, lush greenery in abundance along most of the riverbanks spreading outwards. The huge baobab trees were in no shortage and had probably been around for thousands of years wherever they grew. A permanent presence in the area that dominated sporadic locations, especially in higher ground, was the large clusters of huge, dark, grey and brown rocks that claimed their positions for more years than the baobab. Unscathed by the merciless sun but sculptured by the wind, rain and sand, the rocks provided either a safe haven or an area best avoided for various wildlife.

"It's quite a view and hot as hell," Jim said. "Dry heat though, I like dry. We ain't gonna see too much wildlife at this time, but I dare say there's plenty hiding in those forests down there and the big cats no doubt having a snooze. Did you get enough photos?"

"Hell yeh, but they won't look like shit worth keeping though; sunrise or sunset would be the deal. Let's head back to base, driver, what do you recon?"

After drinking some bottled water, they began the 45-minute drive back to the lodge.

On the way through the village, the carnival at the puddle was at an end. Someone had promptly repaired the leaking water supply tank, prompting the kids to occupy their time playing football. Jim halted the Toyota and they gave the kids a slab of Mirinda from the cool box.

The time was not long before 5 p.m. when they arrived back at the lodge. Brad ordered a couple of cold beers and they sat down, feeling contented after their drive. The savage heat of the day was beginning to reduce towards the start of a pleasant, calm and perfect evening before dusk approached. This lodge had been well-sited, offering tremendous views of varied landscape and contrasts over far distances. The immediate area being dry savanna grassland owing its abundance to the endless supply of sunlight passing through the widespread forests of stunted trees. The rocky formations increased with altitude and the green, lush, distant jungles stretching over marshland and riverbank created an environment to compete for height while forming tall canopies. Separating all this is the Rufiji River magically snaking along its flow path preformed so long ago.

The three of them met up at dusk for dinner in the open-roofed area of the restaurant, and Neil appeared considerably more alert owing to his afternoon siesta. They planned to retire early this evening after discussing the plan for the following day. Neil had mentioned his knowledge of the area that Jim and Brad had visited earlier during the day. He confirmed to the Americans the breed of bird they had encountered from the photograph taken by Brad. He was in no doubt it was a female black sparrow hawk. Jim commented to Brad facetiously that he had been half correct with the female and hawk part.

A carafe of red wine arrived along with three menus while Neil did the honours and charged up the glasses. As they were consulting the menus, a small hard bug struck the table, rolled to a halt, and after a brief period of playing perfectly still, then extended out half a dozen or so legs and proceeded to crawl along the table on its way.

Neil's eyes strayed from the menu to look at the steep cane ceiling above them, then casually placed a beer mat over the carafe. Nobody wasted much time deciding over the ample choices available. They skipped on the starters and settled for Angus steaks; more-exotic preferences would no doubt be sampled when more time was at their disposal.

The steaks were well-received and washed down with the fine South African Shiraz while Neil was laying out a brief idea of options for the following day. Coffees along with another carafe of wine arrived and Brad used the occasion to ignite one of his fine Cuban cigars.

"Anyway, guys, it looks like we are going to stick to our baseline plan by meeting here an hour before dawn and take some time to have a proper breakfast. Just two other guys are coming, a tracker and a driver. The driver is actually a driver skinner and these guys will have all the necessaries packed into the vehicle, packed lunches and all. I'm not sure how the day will progress, but if we prefer and depending where we are, we could maybe head back here for lunch, maybe even a nap. Sometimes it's good practice to avoid the peak temperatures if the opportunity arises," Neil said.

They were basically going to head out for high ground in order to have a clear view around as much as they could see and determine whether spot and stalk or ambush-type hunting would be appropriate.

Everyone seemed happy with that. Brad poured out the remainder of the wine into the three glasses and drew on his cigar.

"Hey, Neil, what kind of radius or diameter can we cover out there, and is south of the river an option?" Jim asked.

"It's permitted to operate across the river, mate, but, remember, the vehicle must cross. There are some people that can get everything across safely, but then time is against you and you have to set up fly camps over there, as you ain't coming back the same day. We can look into it if you like, mate. Remember, though, it ain't permitted to fire a shot across river, not like USA, and the range we can cover is more or less 30 square miles of unfenced wilderness."

Jim let out a satisfied whistle.

Neil was looking forward to this hunting trip just as much as the Americans. After all, he was covering for Osaya and it came as a welcome relocation from Dar S for a while. He had completed his training in Australia and Zimbabwe for his professional hunter's licence and Tanzania was another obstacle he had to contend with to be legally within the law to guide and manage hunting parties. Ron and Neil operated under the company name

Outback Expeditions and had retained the same name from Zimbabwe. The time was approaching 10 p.m. as they finished off the wine and coffee when Neil reminded himself to make sure that the rifles had been zeroed at 35 metres.

They retired to their rooms and the distant chattering of hyenas and snorting of hippos in the river were the only sounds that disturbed the otherwise silent evening.

Darkness prevailed as Jim leaned on the fencing surrounding the balcony outside the room, smoking a cigarette.

He had wakened to his cell-phone alarm and was surprised that he had an appetite. *Must have been the vino*, he thought. Some coffee first was foremost on his mind. He remembered and had taken some time to apply some sun block to his face and neck area after shaving. Jim seemed to be the first to rise, and he could tell by the dim lighting visible in the kitchen area beyond the darkened restaurant that Tatu was already quietly working away in the kitchen.

Jim was giving some thought to his family in Montana, and he had arranged to get together with his son in El-Paso in Texas next month. His son had moved there to work for a defence contractor and quickly favoured the weather there to Montana. Jim was in his mid-50s and had accepted the offer of a redundancy package from the engineering company that he worked for two years previous. Brad, being a few years older, had worked for the same company and had accepted a similar early retirement package a few years before Jim opted out. The both of them were casualties of failed marriages, and they grew up in the city of Great Falls. Brad had been Jim's manager for a period while they both worked together. He had also fathered a son and daughter who lived in Montana.

Coffee arrived at the table, and Brad and Jim arrived to find Neil already there with Tatu laying down a large pie tray laden with sausage, bacon, scrambled eggs and bread cleverly laid out together.

"Looks like it's help yourselves, guys," Neil said while trying to contain his yawning.

They had just finished up with breakfast as the darkness was giving way to the arrival of a new grey dawn. Thomas and Juma arrived in the Toyota and the two of them helped with the carry bags and arranging the rifles in the rack at the rear of the cab. Neil discussed briefly with Thomas the route they had planned the day before. They would be heading in a north-westerly direction via the main road, leading to various tracks providing access to clearings on the rocky slopes.

Neil sat up on the rear bench seat beside Jim and Brad at the right-hand side behind Thomas, the driver.

"The weather should be fine, guys, fine and bloody hot," Neil said. "How did you guys fair on that last trip you went on?"

"What, in the States or Africa?" Brad said.

"The States, mate. I heard about the Tanza one already that was the buff one that ended up swinging to plains game, yeh?"

"Correct," Brad mentioned. "Well, the last States trip took us to Idaho for a long weekend, that's right, Jim, eh?"

Jim just nodded his head in agreement while mildly laughing a little.

"Yeh, Jim and I had a hoot of a time on that one, boy."

Neil was asking anxiously what sort of time they had.

"Well, we were hunting black bear at the end of April this year, dammed cold it was too. We were on the correct side or maybe the wrong side of the Lochsa River; well, that all depends on which side of the river that you make a kill. Snow was down but manageable and made tracking fairly easy. We were tracking some fresh spoor leading uphill from the river. The next thing there, he was standing up with the front legs hanging by his side. He was watching us over some fallen pines and ferns maybe 50 metres or so away, and boy did he bolt. By the time we got to where he was, the ground was thankfully levelling off and we assumed he ran along the path that carved through the thicket and undergrowth.

"We had assumed correct; after we carefully made our way along a hundred metres or so and navigated across a couple of sizeable fallen trees, here is this big fella walking towards us about 70 metres away. The thing was, he looked more brown, and why the fuck was he heading back in the direction he had been running from?

"We stopped and the big fella kept coming, and at this point, Jim here is down on one knee with the Savage .270 Winchester right on him. Something to the left in among the thicket distracted the bear and took his attention enough for him to stop and turn with the nose sniffing and moving up and down in the air in that direction. *'Bang'*, off went Jim's rifle. That bear jumped more than a few feet in the air and looked like he spun round about 100 times in a couple of seconds before he went straight down on his chin with all four legs pointing way backwards."

"It ain't over there either, Neil," Jim offered.

"As I stood up, I caught a glimpse of something black moving towards us to my right through the ferns about 20 feet away. I yelled to Brad. You know how so many thoughts can get processed through your brain in a fucking millisecond during a fearful situation. Black, moving, bushes, another bear, etc. Shit, I was already reloaded, but before I could think exactly where to point the rifle, Brad's rifle echoed a loud bang followed by the sound of the bolt action delivering another round into the chamber.

"We rapidly stepped into the trees and thicket on the opposite side of the path and realised that the movement had ceased and not a sound was to be heard apart from the shower of dead pine needles dropping around us," Jim said.

Neil was wide-eyed and leaning into Jim's face.

"Well, what the fuck, Jim, you dropped him, yeh?"

"We sure did, buddy, a great big fucking turkey, man, what a day that was."

Neil leaned back, grinning.

"OK, guys, now I know that a 30-06 works for turkey," Neil commented.

Thomas and Juma in the front were looking interested and curious as to what brought on the laughing.

They had driven back home to Montana via the Bitterroot Range and Missoula with the bearskin packed on the pick-up. The poor old turkey was left in the ferns. The soft point .270-calibre bullet had ripped through the bear's heart. He had weighed around 220 pounds.

As the Land Cruiser continued following the direction of the tracks leading off to the right, Neil informed the guys that many of the tighter tracks descended into impenetrable rock-covered ground unsuitable for any type of vehicles.

This chosen route was mainly smooth and firm, but progress was slow due to tree branches becoming lower and thicker. Frequent low-level branches demanded careful attention to avoid any injury from the branches or any unwelcome resident occupying the foliage. Once clear of the cool forest floor, the bright skies dominated once again to reveal the dry, parched and cracked surface of the open savanna. Neil went on to explain some facts regarding the area in general and the local occupants of the area, including wildlife.

The Americans had earlier been enquiring into some facts concerning leopards and the rules of hunting them in this region.

"The villagers and farming community over various locations in the region were just as resident and territorial as anything else is," Neil said. "Probably more. They do understand, tolerate and deal with issues and situations as they arise.

"The most common issue which can occur occasionally or frequently is mainly wildlife breaching boundaries, resulting in damage and loss to assets, impairing quality of life and safety to the residents. It is for example more than welcome within the villagers and farming community for any hunting parties to shoot baboons if desired. Both guys in the front of the vehicle are quite locally connected, and most game meat given to them is always well-received. These guys, in turn, would carry out customary distribution of the meat to various villages. The villagers are always aware of the source, and the meat is always thankfully well-received. On the flip side, the pelts and trophies were the reward of the hunter. Any wildlife that chooses to stray onto domesticated land causing damage to crops or targeting livestock is generally dealt with by the local population. This could range from anything from snakes to elephants. There is one creature that is presently at large, and although incidents have been rare, the threat is more than irritable to the locals. He has been identified as a male leopard. Some small livestock and dogs have vanished, and five miles from this area either, this male or maybe another leopard caused some carnage in a farm and apparently killed all 15 farm ducks in a pen. The leopards have eluded any attempt to trap them for many months. The locals would more than welcome assistance in compromising the cat or cats.

"Lions do not seem to be much of an issue at present, probably down to the abundance of prey species in this area and their nature of hunting. An extended dry season can change all that though."

Neil went on to mention the man eaters of Tsavo during the late 1800s as a typical example. These two male lions in Uganda had been responsible for killing and eating 28 Indian railroad construction workers before they were eventually shot and killed by Col. John Henry Patterson in late 1898. They had terrorised the massive imported workforce and locals alike and were becoming increasingly portrayed as demons and not lions. Neil expressed a reminder that he believed there was an unusual period of drought that year when many species moved away in search of water sources and healthy foliage. The poor old lions being territorial would generally be stuck there. Especially two males, probably brothers banished from a large pride occupying a neighbouring territory. At the end of the day, a thousand or so Indian workers assembling on the lions' territory with nothing more than canvas separating them from the darkness; every night would be considered more than an opportunity by the lions. That was the lions' effortless access to live stockpiles of fresh meat right there.

"Yeh, well Mr Patterson was clearly not in possession of a 375 H&H magnum rifle," Jim said.

"Nope, more than likely a black powder job or a Brit 303 with iron sights if he was lucky, mate," Neil replied.

Jim was keen to know the process involved in leopard-hunting in Tanzania, particularly the mentioned nuisance at large being an option. He was informed of the basic method in Africa of baiting high in a tree within the cat's territory in a frequently visited area and waiting in a purpose-built blind. In Tanzania, protocol dictated your hunt for game to be planned between dawn and dusk, as no hunting is permitted during the night. Neil mentioned that he was in agreement of the process in place, as it was dangerous to hunt during the evening outside and away from a vehicle due to a human being's night-vision ability.

Another reason to avoid this is that anyone shooting and injuring a big cat or any dangerous game in the dark is a real problem and it does happen in places.

"A man with a wooden head would probably refrain from tracking any injured beasts on foot during the night," Neil said.

Probably the main problem developing from an unfortunate occurrence like that would be the cat that is presently an occasional nuisance to livestock would no doubt become a man eater targeting all and children. Not an animal that anyone would consider less than dangerous to be around. Animal casualties running around with painful bullet wounds are not popular and need to be dispatched quickly. Brad asked what size of territory leopards generally occupied.

"Quite a deal, mate. 10, 20, 30 square miles, take your pick. Males obviously roam the largest areas, and female's territory usually crosses over the male's at some points. There are plenty around when you consider Africa, Middle East and Asia, with South America being home to the jaguar of course, amazing creatures."

"Let me tell you the story of my first leopard hunt," Neil offered.

While Neil was resident in Zimbabwe, his first hunt had been arranged with a local professional hunter named Jeremy. Jeremy's pregnant wife was rushed into hospital in labour the day before the hunt, with some complications that were overcome, and had given birth to a baby girl. Jeremy had stayed in the hospital all night and had made his way home early in the morning. He had missed an evening's sleep and Neil had suggested rescheduling the hunt and advised him to go home and rest. Circumstances and bookings with clients led Jeremy to prioritise and follow the present carefully arranged scheduling and he informed Neil that there was no problem for him to stick to their plan this day.

A preferred area had been chosen previously and a competent tracker had confirmed the presence of frequent fresh spoor confirming regular visits from a male leopard. The PH and Neil had already installed a blind system a few days previous complete with an integrated blinded toilet area 30 metres away from the tall shaded bait tree in the forest. They arrived there late morning with an impala that had been shot the day before, and they secured the impala firmly on some outgoing branch forks 25 feet above the ground. The vehicle left and waited about half a mile away and they settled into the blind that was 80 metres away from a river on the edge of the forest where the trees were sparse. The both of them got settled into the blind and adjusted into this small environment that demanded total silence and controlled movement. The shotgun was inside along with the rifle with the safety system engaged and complimented with a chambered cartridge.

The arrangement in place was dependent on a cat arriving. Jeremy would give Neil one silent tap on his leg to indicate that the animal was within legal boundaries and a shot could be taken. Three taps would indicate that the animal did not meet the requirements and could not be targeted. Hours passed without as much of a whisper from either of them, and water was taken silently when required. Any gentle breeze that came along provided such comfortable cooling while flowing over the rivers of sweat that flowed down their bodies. They had seen various types of wildlife passing during the afternoon, including a couple of warthogs and a family of mongooses.

As dusk was approaching, maybe an hour or so away, when the sky was becoming more redder in colour than blue, some noisy guinea fowl flew from the river's edge to the treetops. Some alarm calls followed from birds and monkeys 200 metres away. *Could an approaching cat be the reason for the disturbance?* Neil thought to himself. He made eye contact with Jeremy who nodded to signal to Neil to direct the rifle in the direction of the bait with the safety off and the .375-magnum rifle was carefully manoeuvred into position. More than 15 minutes passed, which seemed like hours to Neil, without a sound or movement from anywhere. Suddenly, without any warning, Neil's attention was drawn to some kind of movement or change in surroundings, he was not sure which. Higher in the bait tree, he raised his eyes without any head movement, and there he was as if he had been there all day, a beautiful golden male leopard covered in perfect dark rosettes among the higher foliage of the tree. Neil realised the illusive stealth of this animal and was afraid to even blink; he was sure the cat had seen him and was just passing time, watching, but the cat had not seen him.

The big cat gave a contented lick to his lips and moved down the opposite side of the tree, out of sight. Seconds later, the cat appeared at the outgoing branch that the bait rested on, his front half in view outside of the trunk of the tree with the bait just two metres away from him.

The full view of the animal's right-hand side was only two steps away from the bait; the plan was folding out as good as it could get. The leopard was cautious and carefully looked around, ensuring himself that everything was as it was during his last visit.

Suddenly, in a couple of quick steps, the cat was on the bait. No tap on Neil's leg was forthcoming as Neil's heart was pounding like a steam train. He slowly turned around to glance at Jeremy and was shocked to see he had fallen asleep. Neil carefully and reluctantly prodded him on the leg, resulting with Jeremy's body giving a slight jerk with a small release of air expelling from his nostrils. The next event was over in a flash as the cat angrily looked in the direction of the blind, spun around out of sight behind the tree trunk and was gone. His paws coming in contact with the ground made no sound.

"I was fucking pissed off," Neil said. "That kind of shit never happens, but it did on this occasion. The thing is, I played by the rules, you have to; he managed to fall asleep, crikey fucking unbelievable! It is fortunate that this all ended in disappointment, but under different circumstances these things can end in tragedy. We recovered the bait, pissed off back to base and decided to put it down to a fuck up and learned from it. He was wrong to ignore my advice, advising him to head back home and sleep."

Thomas slowed down the vehicle and caught Neil's attention to ask which area they were going to stop at. He was advised to carry on a couple of miles and use the clearing as the track started to descend.

The natural clearing where they stopped at appeared to have been constructed in the past by the actions of engineers rather than Mother Nature. This area where a few vehicles could be parked up next to the kopje while keeping the road clear could have been cleverly designed. On the opposite side of the track, an almost-flat platform of rock gave anyone a feeling of standing on top of the African continent itself.

Hunters of past centuries surely profited from the view of the plain's wildlife below. The area was a completely natural feat of engineering less the track that conveniently intruded through. The Americans along with Neil stood on the plateau, enjoying the view and appreciating the vantage point while Juma and Thomas lay on their backs in the shade.

The view below was vast; everything was typical savanna colours and greys on account of masses of stubbled leafless trees and scattering of large rocks. The river was not in view from here, and the kopje behind begged to be explored as most of them do.

Neil explained that the previous excursion that Jim and Brad had taken had led them to a clearing that lay seven miles around this mountain in a south-westerly direction from their present position. The plan was to scan the area in view and choose some game to follow and stalk, depending on what was there. The desired game on this outing was buffalo.

Neil came back from the vehicle with his binoculars, and it was not long before he could make out two buffalo herds through his lenses. He passed on their positions to the Americans who also focused in on them. One herd to the left about 1.5 miles away was fair-sized and made up mainly from cows, probably 200 or so. Another herd more to the right and closer had 60 or 80 animals, and Neil put his money on many of those being old bulls, maybe one or two young ones.

"Gents, we should try to concentrate on that smaller bunch over there. We can have a chat with the boys and let them plan the best route to get us downwind of them," Neil said.

"Do you guys have any qualms or issues that need to be addressed?" Neil asked.

"Not really, buddy," Jim replied. "Myself and Brad read each other pretty good in this game but will be making every move based on your advice. Are we looking at 30 yards?"

"Maybe, it depends on where they lead us to, and remember, it's a thorny, thick, sparse, wet and dry and sometimes open or pleasant fucking wilderness down there. These beasts can travel quite slow or pretty quick, and to be honest, we may or may not get a shot in today, you know the score, and sometimes you can end up tracking a certain animal of interest, especially a trophy animal for a few days. Who knows, maybe we will get lucky. You know the deal though, stay behind Juma and myself and always be aware of your surroundings, front, either side and behind. Keep eyes where they should be and never get distracted looking at tracks. Juma has that well-covered. We can check wind direction down there, if any."

They journeyed down another 800 metres off the track where Thomas negotiated the vehicle slowly through welcome breaks between the rocks that cursed any four-wheel travel. A puncture would be as welcome as a skunk at a lawn party. They eventually arrived at the savanna level and enjoyed a more-civilised drive. Thomas brought the Toyota to a halt and parked up. Jim stood up at the rear and intensely scanned what he could see of the area through his binoculars. The stubbled trees and bush appeared fairly sparse from the view from the platform but now took on a new appearance resembling an impenetrable blind.

They were downwind of the herd with a moderate breeze present and kept their voices to the level of a whisper. Neil exchanged some conversation with the driver regarding their choices of communication with two-way radios and cell phones. Thomas would stay there with the vehicle until needed.

Neil secured his ammo belt and camera and rested his Heym 450 on his shoulder. The Americans kitted up with their 375 and 416.

"OK, guys, let's get cracking. That's 10 a.m., it's gonna heat up. I recon they are probably a kilometre away. This sparse shit will become somewhat thicker and even lighter on occasion, so we will either go around or under it."

They were all wearing light but strong, long, khaki trousers with long-sleeved shirts and hats. Juma led the way with Neil and the Americans following, and the progress was fairly slow but constant. The higher grass demanded higher steps and some stooping was required to avoid thorny branches but no crawling was necessary. Juma was leading them to the smaller heard while keeping a keen watch for any predators that might be sharing the same interests and intentions towards the herd as themselves. Buffalo ranked up there as one of the most dangerous animals in Africa and fearless to any situation which made them feel vulnerable. On a straightforward hunt, Neil and Juma would normally ensure success for clients, for most times this could be time consuming. They were very aware that sometimes a perfect situation could immediately change to ugly and a backup plan is always in place. Foremost though, preventive practices in place and adhered to in an effort to avoid these situations developing prevailed at all times.

Juma had slowed down the pace, then stopped. They all followed suit and waited. He paced back to talk to Neil and the communication was basically passed across in lip motion and hand signalling.

They were close to the herd now at around 100 metres. Neil was surprised as he thought they would be moving much further on, these animals seemed to be happy at this spot.

They decided to go straight to them while the herd was on their feet and easier to read. Juma carried on much slower and moved out to the right, away from the deep thicket and dead foliage. Neil stopped and kneeled down on one knee and encouraged the Americans to do the same.

They let Juma carve out a final approach to secure an advantageous position of cover to observe and shoot from. A stealthy advance was required and these animals were hopefully concentrating on feeding on shrubs and low pickings on the trees. Juma waved them to approach and pointed out a path to follow; he was just 30 metres away from the guys. When they arrived beside him, he nodded in two directions where buffalos could be seen moving and grazing. The wind was on their side and the black mass had not yet appeared intimidated.

As previously arranged, Brad would have the shot at the first buffalo. Communication was limited now and there was not much left up for question. Brad would be ready to position himself and wait for Neil's instruction to fire. All that would be left for Brad to control would be the accuracy of the placement shot and just as important the timing of the shot during the opportunity.

If timing was slow enough for the opportunity to move out of position, the shot would be aborted. On the other hand, if the shot was taken too early due to excitement or taken too hastily under pressing circumstances, this could impair accuracy and the outcome of events could change dramatically for the worse.

They had sufficient cover as good as could be had in this demanding environment. Most of their cover was provided by the uprooted part of a long past fallen tree and the trunk and grass around it. Brad nodded in the direction of a large buffalo that seemed to appear from nowhere only 20 metres away.

Neil shook his head at Brad and described the word 'cow' with the movement of his lips. Brad thought to himself, *Shit, which herd are we in among?* Neil suddenly took Brad's attention to a large bull that had put himself in view. He had changed his position and was now front facing in their direction about 40 metres away. The vegetation between the bull and them was quite sparse; an advantage for the shot had offered opportunity.

Neil was reaching over to take the tripod that Juma was offering, but Brad signalled there was no need. He preferred the stability of the tree-roots cluster that was conveniently in front of him.

He rested the rifle and positioned himself with his left foot placed on top of the fallen tree trunk. They waited for the bull to expose himself a little more, and Neil slowly moved close to Brad's left side. Brad knew there would be a nod from Neil to signal him to take the shot. The bull was still facing them, and Brad concentrated in focusing his eye relief on the low-powered scope's lens and keeping the crosshairs on the animal's vital area.

The bull moved his head up and down, then up again, sniffing the air; this massive black beast was looking in their direction. Neil then nodded an approval to Brad. Brad was in the same ball park as Neil, and within probably less than two seconds, he squeezed the trigger home, sending a 410-grain solid Rigby 416 bullet at the buffalo, and he immediately actioned the bolt to chamber another round.

Due to the recoil of the big rifle, Brad's view of events through the scope were impossible to monitor after the trigger was squeezed; he had been accurate though, very accurate. The bull was down.

The bull attempted to swing around but immediately staggered backward with no control of his legs.

His hind legs collapsed first, then his whole mass crashed to the ground. The free hind leg gave a few violent movements, then stopped as the noise of air expelling from the lungs in powerful gasps could be heard.

Two other bulls came to investigate their comrade while two other animals could be seen trotting off through the bush. The two bulls spent a few moments moving around to the rear of the fallen animal, then decided to leave as the others had done. None of the guys moved from their location and Neil decided they would wait five minutes; he saw no reason for a follow-up shot to be taken, as there was no sign of life there. He clearly saw the spray from the headshot that Brad had taken. He was a slight surprised as he had assumed that Brad would have taken the heart or lungs option at that distance, but hell. *What a shot!* he thought.

They moved to the animal and carried out the proven-dead checks. The big bull was shot between the eyes with a hole off the centre laterally towards the left eye that did not look too large and no exit wound was visible. This presented an indication that the bullet probably carried on through the brain and skull and lodged in the spine or shoulder area, resulting in an instant kill.

Not much blood was around and Neil announced that this was one of the cleanest kills he had witnessed on a large game animal. Everyone else agreed and congratulated Brad who, in turn, thanked Juma and Neil. Juma explained to Brad that the bull had caught their scent just before he took the shot. Brad knew this and he did not announce to everybody of his original intention to take the heart shot. He had seen the bull looking directly at them and decided quickly to stay on the head rather than risk moving his crosshairs and loose both placement opportunities.

Neil called Thomas to inform him of the kill; Thomas did hear the shot. He drove over to the kill area and informed Neil that another more-appropriate vehicle and help was already mobilised from the lodge to help him deal with the trophy and carcass.

Neil was feeling jovial and admitted to the guys that he did not remotely expect to get close to those buffalos today, as he thought they would be tracking and following them for a few days. He reminded everyone of his comment earlier in the day that they may get lucky.

Lucky so quickly was unusual but welcome, he said.

Thomas's help arrived in the form of another man and two, young, thin, muscular boys.

Following a photo shoot and some cool drinks, Neil and the Americans were happy to call it a day and parted to make their way back to the lodge.

Hunter and Hunted

With some encouragement from the Canadian mission in Dar es Salaam, Tanzanian law enforcement directed some resources to prioritise efforts to uncover the whereabouts of the missing individuals in the Selous area. A few days had passed since the buffalo kill and Neil and the Americans were enjoying some late afternoon coffee and snacks on the patio bar area.

They had ventured out on an unsuccessful buffalo hunt the day before and most of today was spent searching some potential leopard territory and checking out some river issues.

A crossing point had been located 12 miles upstream that was capable of ferrying a vehicle across and returning on the same day. This was unexpected but welcome.

The atmosphere at the lodge had recently become a slight more colourful following the arrival of another two guests. An English professor had arrived with his wife and both were apparently obsessive trophy hunters.

South Africa and Zambia was their preferred area of adventure, and the Tanzania visit was a first for them. They had all been together the previous evening and had been acquainted a little with each other. The professor appeared very quiet and methodical with a clever sense of humour. His wife was far from quiet and she seemed to lack any sense of humour at all, or maybe she was rarely even listening to what anyone was saying. Neil had learned this quite early on during the evening while in conversation with her on the subject of Australia and the Commonwealth. The Americans had enjoyed some entertainment that had generated from the discussion and they both decided to listen without offering any opinions.

They had noticed that the professor appeared to routinely adopt the same practice, and he maintained his conversation with Brad and Jim.

The following day was planned for tracking two areas they had noted could be likely to attract a territorial leopard or leopard's visits. Over the next few days, a trip across the river had been discussed and planned.

Today was more of a reconnaissance and photographic pastime. They had come across some plains' antelope, kudu and a couple of cheetahs. The buffalos had moved well away on their travels from their location yesterday, and baboons were in abundance on some rocky mounds and close to parts of the river's edge. The guys were not tempted enough to have a shot. No shots were fired this day.

The distinct thumping of a two-bladed main-rotor helicopter approaching soon became apparent, but it was anyone's guess from which direction it was coming from.

"This would normally be police or game conservation people," Brad said.

Jim was unconcerned while scrolling through the photographs on the digital SLR camera. Neil was just adding the finishing touches to his hand-rolled cigarette.

"Well, I pray it's not Nancy Bell." He had already informed Brad and Jim of his acquaintance with her during his flight over.

The chopper suddenly appeared on a slow decent within the lodge area, confirming the pilot's intention to land there. The Robinson craft was white and unmarked all but for a number on the underside and with the same number displayed either side of the fuselage close to the tail rotor. The birds and tree dwellers parted company with the nearby trees. The skids touched down and the main rotor blades timely came to a halt 200 metres away.

Brad and Jim recognised Inspector Adimo as she stepped out the front passenger's side. Neil offered a comment suggesting that this must be a fairly prioritised search now. Adimo approached with her two officers.

"Good day, gentlemen, I decided to stop by."

She introduced her two officers, and Neil was introduced.

"Has the hunting been successful?"

"Oh yes, ma'am, we're just getting started," Jim said.

Adimo and the officers brought over some chairs and joined them at the table. She asked one of the officers to arrange some water.

"Maybe you gentlemen can do some hunting for me," she said with a smile as she laid down her holstered police-issued revolver on the table.

"Would love to, ma'am, but I think it would be safe to assume that we would possibly fall beyond the legal boundaries of best operating practices," Brad replied.

Neil reminded her that she had the best equipment at her disposal. She agreed and turned towards the chopper where the pilot was carrying out some checks. She instructed one of the officers to take over a bottle of water for him.

"Yes, gentlemen, the pressure is on us now and the powers that be are beginning to take it seriously. This would normally appear to me to present a fairly easy task, but so far we have absolutely nothing to go on. We need some leads from the ground. I am sure things will change direction soon. I assume that you have all heard or seen nothing in relation to this enquiry?"

"Nothing at all," Neil replied. "The only other mzungu we have seen is the professor and his good wife who have just arrived here and an American lady on the flight from Dar. I would be inclined to imagine that they are not in this area at all or they could have met with some unfortunate circumstances.

"The Selous would not be my first choice of area of natural beauty to be touring around, especially during the night, that's just an opinion," Neil continued.

"I would agree with you, and it certainly appears that way at present. We will map out an aerial-search pattern to cover a radius more than could be covered by a vehicle since the time they left Mahenge; there are certainly no Total or Shell filling stations every few hundred metres here. Who knows though, they may have been hauling some containerised fuel with them," Adimo said.

"Did you ever find out what type of rifle they were traveling with, Inspector?" Brad asked. Adimo consulted her notebook for a few moments and answered that although she had no information relating to the firearm type or manufacturer. The ammunition found at the Mahenge apartment was solely Springfield 30-06 and would assume the firearm to be a bolt-action rifle.

"That's a handy tool, but they sure don't appear to be hunting any dangerous game," Neil offered. "At least not legally."

"Dangerous game!" Adimo replied.

"Yes, Inspector, buff, elephant, leopard, rhino and lion, minimum required calibre is Holland & Holland .375, a good all-rounder Brit cartridge," Neil replied.

"Really! Surely you would not require such a large calibre to take down a lion or lioness, the mighty Simba. When we were kids, we took them down with a spear double handed; it's as easy as breaking a chocolate bar, gentlemen."

Neil and the Americans glanced at each other while Adimo and her team were quietly smiling.

"No, I am just teasing you gents, but our Masai regularly practice this. I do have my firearms permit. My first rifle was a Ruger .22 LR calibre bolt-action rifle, second a .223 and third a .308. My father was a keen hunter and target shooter and there was no encouragement needed to lure me towards firearms; I was always interested. I have dropped a fair amount of game since becoming competent."

The three police officers stood up in preparation for departing. She left a few of her cards on the table and Neil handed her his.

"Please keep in touch, gentlemen, and enjoy your weekend. We will meet again soon, I am sure. Oh, we will try to be quiet over your stalking areas," she said jokingly.

"Please do, madam," Neil responded. "I see you are a little bit more armed than standard issue, Inspector." He nodded towards her holstered revolver that she was clipping on.

"A .357 magnum and the boys here have .38s."

Her two officers were laughing.

"Yes, well, I believe that a woman who finds herself in a gunfight has more of an advantage with a louder bang, and my option of ammunition extends to my officer's supply should I run empty, but of course, you already know that. Good day, gentlemen."

As the chopper ascended into the sky, Adimo could see the hunters at their table and a small girl with a dog waving at the chopper from the rear of the main lodge. Flocks of scared noisy birds were forced into flight from the riverside area. She watched the lodge area becoming smaller and smaller until it became a tiny part of a vast wilderness. She was beginning to envy the life of a pilot. Could this become her next pursuit, she thought.

"Well," Jim said, "I doubt if anyone will get much change out of her. She certainly seems to have her eye on the ball, yeh?"

"Too true, buddy. She could have her eyes on my balls anytime. She is fucking tasty and I reckon that the assumption regarding these folks might be accurate. Are they enjoying themselves far away from this area or has their fate been sealed at the bottom of that river or the likes of? Who knows, mate, who knows," Neil replied.

"You can join the queue for a date with her, Neil buddy," Brad replied.

"No problem mate, *apres vous monsieur, apres vous.*"

"We have a couple of options tomorrow. We can go to try to find your leopard or we can head across the river," Neil said.

"I think better to stick to plan, Neil. Try for the leopard for a couple of days, then think about the river crossing," Jim said.

"Yeh, sure, mate, we will go with that. Are you going to try your buffalo tonight?"

Neil explained that the locals would have it prepared and perfectly cooked in gravy until tender and served simply on a bed of rice. The skinner had dropped off some backstrap and tenderloin that had been marinating for a couple of days.

"Right, Neil, that's beer o'clock time. I will shout them up, buddy!" Brad shouted.

It was 6 p.m. and the breeze had dropped away as if on cue for the chorus of insects to begin their endless chatter. As they were talking, a pair of vehicle headlights appeared snaking their way along the track to the lodge.

"Oh, hey," Jim said. "This will probably be your buddy, Neil."

"No worries, mate, maybe you guys can get her started on the American Civil War or something."

The other Toyota pulled up 40 metres away and the professor and his wife got out and made their way into their lodge tent. The both of them waved over and the lady shouted, "Kudu."

The guys returned the wave and in a quiet voice Neil said, "Yeh, you too." The professor shouted across that they would join them shortly after a scrub and a shave. As the vehicle U-turned to access the rear of the lodge, they could see the skin and trophy of a male kudu on the rear bed of the pick-up. Jim and Brad were shaking their heads, sniggering and looking at Neil.

Neil's cell phone rang just as the professor and his wife were walking the short distance to join them at the patio bar. Neil excused himself to everyone and walked towards his banda to take the call.

"Hi, Neil, all OK there, yeh?"

"Hi, Ron, what's new? All good here, partner. Things going hunky dory, thanks. Are you planning a trip over?"

Ron went on to explain that the other party arriving were delayed by a week, and no problems from their side. All were good to go with permits and paperwork approved.

"So what's the deal, Ron? If you are thinking to head over, we might be able to split into two teams. Tomorrow, we are maybe gonna set up a blind for leopard, but Brad is not too keen. He has a want about him to go for plains game."

"What I will do is let you know tomorrow for definite, Neil. I am not sure if Vince is gonna make it, but if I decide to come, it will be the day after tomorrow. I will be in touch."

"OK. What's new with Vince?"

"It's just the usual, Neil. These Indian boys he has working there led him to believe that a fair-sized job that he accepted was straightforward and they have the equipment to cover it. It was apparently not entirely true. I will get back to you tomorrow, probably late afternoon or early evening."

Neil joined the company at the table and greeted the professor and his wife, Kevin and Sam. He made them aware of the story of the missing Canadian folk, as he forgot to mention the night before. He was chatting away when Sam interrupted him to ask what he was doing. Neil looked at his hand and realised that he was rocking a .375 live cartridge up and down through the fingers of his right hand and the beer in the left.

"Ah shit, Sam, sorry I never gave it any thought, just a pastime of mine."

He slid the cartridge back into his right pocket.

"No worries at all, Neil, carry on. I was just curious."

Neil was surprised, as he actually believed her laughing was genuine tonight.

"I recon you dropped the kudu, Sam?" Neil said.

"Yes I did, from a prone position on that nice, warm, savanna grass."

Neil had never heard the savanna being described as inviting and comfortable as that before. She gave the details of the kill. She had used her Tikka bolt action 30-06 fitted with a high-powered scope at 200 metres with a Nosler-tip 180-grain bullet. It was a heart shot and the animal was long dead by the time they retrieved it from the river's edge after clambering over a barrage of rocks to get at it.

"You are fortunate a croc did not relieve you of your kill, Sam," Brad said.

"Yes, this was mentioned as we dragged it out of the water's edge, yes, lucky," Sam replied.

Kevin enquired if any leopard or other cats were seen or photographed today. He had been informed that a couple of likely areas looked potentially good and the tracker would assist tomorrow. Kevin agreed with the idea and mentioned that these guys were definitely required, as they could read everything he said. Jim asked Kevin what they had in plan for tomorrow. The two of them had one lion on their ticket and were planning to head in a lion direction tomorrow and see what emerged. Kevin and Sam had ten days in the Selous and they had planned to try to relax as much as stalking in the bush.

Sam had agreed and the mention of buffalo meat being locally prepared had her shouting for two carafes of red wine and a cold beer for herself. Neil smirked to himself, as he had assumed that she did not drink alcohol. All the better for him, he thought, as he would not have to strain his concentration too much on his Ps and Qs. He did think that she seemed to be quite more relaxed and laid back tonight but decided to let her dominate any discussion that may arise involving any type of political flavour.

She certainly was attractive, even more so tonight, wearing very casual walking boots, jeans and a loose khaki shirt tucked in. No sign of any makeup at all, and her mousy brown hair looked a million dollars in a simple ponytail. Sam and Kevin headed to the bar to help Tatu with the trays of drinks. Neil caught the attention of Brad and Jim while he was rolling a cigarette.

"Hey, guys, she's looking tasty tonight, yeh? I never noticed last night."

The Americans nodded in agreement.

"So what you are saying, Neil, is you would like to ruffle up that nice hair a little bit, buddy," Brad said.

"Let's put it this way, guys. Given half a chance, the chances of me refusing would fall somewhere between nil and zero."

"She's the wrong colour for you, buddy," Jim replied, laughing. "Yup, you are more into the dusky maiden numbers, Neil, and some of those I have seen you with definitely came under selection when you were wearing your beer goggles. Hey, Neil, I would pay to see one of your K Bar chicks half-trashed arriving and joining you right now."

Loud laughing continued from Brad and Jim.

"Yeh, Jim, that would go down like a death at a fucking birthday party," Brad replied.

"Fuck off, right. Cut it out, you two, give it a rest; they are coming back."

Jim and Brad were laughing quite uncontrollably and this seemed to have an effect on Sam and Kevin who started laughing as they arrived back with the drinks.

"Hey, what's the deal, guys, did we miss something?" Sam said.

"Na," Neil replied, "Just these two guys bringing up some dumb-assed boys talk."

This reply had Brad and Jim battling with the development of more laughter beginning between them.

They continued talking and exchanging each other's backgrounds and enjoying some red wine and beer prior to the meal arriving.

Kevin was a professor in some form of marine biology and Sam was an ex-RAF avionics instructor. They both lived in London. Kevin asked Neil to share some of his hunting experiences with them. Neil said that he was sure that everyone sitting here just now had a few stories to tell of the forests and bush. He certainly had a few hilarious times as expected in this game and also some unfortunate times.

"My colleague, Ron, may arrive after tomorrow. He has a few stories also. We only ever lost a client once, which was unfortunate," Neil said.

"What do you mean *lost*?" Sam remarked.

Neil explained to her that by lost he meant 'killed'. This statement drew everyone's attention and had Sam in an alert, upright and wide-eyed position.

"What, an elephant, a buffalo or lion incident?" Sam continued.

"Nope," Neil replied and carried on the conversation regarding two clients in Zimbabwe about ten years ago. Neil and a tracker along with a Dutch couple were tracking lion tracks along a track that had the appearance of being a rhino path at around 9 a.m. The area was not far from the Manyame River, about a kilometre or so away. They had made their way through some thicket and low branches and had just entered a sparser and more-welcome area. There was not much activity and no sounds at all really apart from birds and insects. The silence was suddenly broken by a sound of movement that quickly developed into something heavy snorting and crashing its way down the path towards them and from the direction they were heading in. They all ran as directed by the tracker into the trees and thicket either side of the path just as a large bull hippo appeared thumping down the path more or less full flight 20 metres away.

Neil and the tracker realised that this big fellow's intention was to stay on the path leading to the river. To their horror, they saw that the Dutchman had not moved off the path and was standing on the side of the path with his rifle over his shoulder as if to give way to the hippo. Neil, the tracker and his girlfriend all shouted franticly at him to move, but the hippo was just feet away from him with those huge jaws wide open and the head tilted to the side in a display of threat. At this point, the Dutchman tried to, bolt but the animal was just a foot from him. With the beast still on the move, it closed its huge mouth on his thigh and dropped him 20 feet down the path.

Neil could barely believe what he had just witnessed and immediately knew the situation was serious. The guy's girlfriend was hysterical and in shock; she was looking at Neil in disbelief and looked like she maybe thought this was sometimes a normal occurrence. It was all crazy. They all ran to his aid and assistance was immediately called. The man was bleeding profusely and Neil and the tracker were shaking as they tried to strap on a tourniquet crafted from their belts. The hippo was gone, but they moved him from the path to the shade of the trees. The blood was flowing at the rate water would flow from a depressed bleach-bottle nozzle and the injury where one of the two lower tusks penetrated right through the left leg had entered just below the inner thigh low on the groin. The tourniquet proved near impossible to apply under the circumstances. Despite several CPR attempts, the man died in less than 15 minutes. The femoral artery and vein were probably severed.

"You know, there is not a day goes by without that incident invading my thoughts more than once. I will never know what that poor devil was thinking about back then, but that poor couple, crazy, completely crazy," Neil stated.

Everyone seated at the table were emotionally touched by what they had just listened to, disbelief at first but genuine feelings of sadness went out to Neil.

Sam expressed that she could only begin to understand how traumatic this must have been for Neil and his group. She hoped that she would never have to experience anything like that. The other guys nodded and verbally agreed. Neil gestured appreciation and wrapped up the conversation by stating that it was over and done with and advised everyone to always expect the unexpected when an unexpected situation arose. Jim gave Neil a head's up on that advice and mentioned that he would never wish himself or any other to leave this world under those circumstances. The food was now arriving and Sam strutted over to the bar to lend a hand to Tatu. The pair of them arrived with the 'entrée' consisting of very large tiger prawns with a tomato-and-garlic sauce. Neil asked Tatu to bring him another beer and she jokingly told him he had drank enough and she would bring him water. The remark prompted Neil to leap from his chair and chase Tatu through the bar area where he caught up with her. Loud screams of laughter were heard from Tatu and Neil strolled back with a large bottle of beer in his hand. Jim shouted over to Neil that a remark like that to an Australian was surely as well-received as trying to stop a dog eating a bone. Bowls of tiger-prawn carcases, sucked dry and squashed head and leg clusters with the empty tail shells lay on the table and reflected everyone's appreciation for the seafood starter. Brad had waited till everyone had finished the prawns, then gave an account of when he had contracted amoeba in Tanzania after eating undercooked prawns.

It was probably in bad taste, considering the timing, but nobody seemed too much concerned. Kevin gave an interesting account of the lifecycle of the sea-dwelling, single-celled organism that was responsible for the amoeba dysentery illness. Sam had let him finish and suggested they move onto another subject.

Not surprisingly, and before anyone realised, the conversation evolved into the subject of firearms and hunting. Sam declared that from all the weapons she had used after advancing on from air weapons, her favourite rifle calibre for target practice and plinking was the .22 long-rifle rimfire. She shared some of her teenage years' experiences with firearms regarding target shooting as well as shooting rabbits, hares and crows with the .22 LR on her uncle's land. Jim complimented her on her choice and stated that the .22 probably has a place in every shooter's heart. Jim praised the .22 rim-fire cartridge for being the dinkiest little cartridge as well as the cheapest and most versatile with no reloading options with the brass. Kevin expressed his interest and ordered some more beers. Jim continued his account of this cartridge, reminding everyone that it had that one-mile maximum range and the standard 40-grain lead bullet is capable of killing a human being out to 400 yards which was an effective range. This was based on a certain copper-washed high-velocity round penetrating a half-inch pine board at this distance. The fact that this cartridge was responsible for the most deaths each year worldwide outside of warzones was mentioned. Neil even mentioned that Robert Kennedy was slain by a .22 Iver Johnson eight-shot revolver, and JFK was assassinated by the 6.5mm military round where an Italian-manufactured rifle was the equipment used in deploying that projectile to the man. "Or so they tell us," he added.

This comment from Neil was well-received by the Americans who awarded Neil full points for his knowledge of some fine details of USA history. They then confirmed to everyone that the attempt on Ronald Reagan's life also involved a .22 handgun. Sam and Kevin were not aware of the Robert Kennedy details and appreciated the information.

Sam enquired how long before the buffalo meat would be served and was informed in around 30 minutes' time.

She had a story on her mind that she wanted to share. Before she commenced, she asked everyone if they had heard of a lady called Bella Twin; she knew her partner had no clue, and she was not sure of Neil. Her main concentration was on the Americans. She quickly realised that Neil had not heard of her; he did quickly offer the fact of this. The Americans after some short serious thought also declared that they had no recollection of the lady.

Great, Sam thought.

"Let me tell you this true account of the lady with her rifle who was responsible for bringing down the largest grizzly bear which was a record at the time in Alberta, Canada, in 1953."

Brad jokingly mentioned that he could be excused from not knowing of this lady, as he was just born around then and she lived north of the border. He asked Sam which calibre she was moving onto now. Sam informed him that she was not moving to other calibres and was still on the subject of the .22. This puzzled her audience and kept them quiet.

Sam continued, "Bella Twin was a little old native Canadian lady of 63 years and probably about five feet tall.

"Bella and her partner were walking along the banks of one of the large lakes in the Alberta area in the hope of dropping some small game for the pot. She carried with her the .22 single-shot bolt-action rifle known as a Cooey Ace One, and it has to be said that this rifle was in a sorry state to say the least. The receiver and barrel were rust-coated and some adhesive tape substituted the broken main mounting screws that once secured the stalk to the receiver.

"The two of them noticed a large grizzly moving out of the cover of the woods and onto the track. They both moved off the track and got behind a large fallen tree. They waited there, hoping that the bear would veer off in another direction away from them. This was not the case and the bear continued advancing towards them. It seemed like the bear hesitated and stood still for a moment, possibly picking up their scent just 30 feet from them. This was when Bella decided that it was better to take a shot rather than not. She hit the animal somewhere between the left eye and the ear and the bear surprisingly went down. She wasted no time in getting closer to the animal and sent another eight rounds from that old single-shot bolt action into the same area of the head where the first shot struck. She apparently had considerable knowledge from some of her past profession 'which is not clear' of animal anatomy and no doubt knew the softest area of the skull. This clearly saved their lives. This 1700lb. grizzly, to this day, is mounted in a standing position at over ten feet tall, and for the records, process and procedure recorded the skull at 16 and

9/16 inches long and nine and 7/8 inches wide, giving a total of 26 and 7/16 inches." Sam, wearing a confident smile, raised her glass and everyone toasted her story.

A couple of welcome remarks were heard as Tatu and the young girl arrived with the especially prepared buffalo meat and the rice together with heated plates. The girl laid down a plate in front of each person and Tatu followed by serving the rice and meat. The gravy boats were left on the table for use as required. No one had tried Cape buffalo meat before except Neil. They were pleasantly surprized how tender this was, and the gravy complimented the dish perfectly. It would be fair to assume that all pallets present were more than satisfied. Neil mentioned that it was quite exceptional the way it was prepared tonight, and he invited Tatu and the girl to join them. They were a slight reluctant, and after the rest of the team insisted, the two of them joined them all at the table.

Nobody could quite comment on what the gravy or sauce reminded them of; it was definitely a new taste. While on this subject, Neil mentioned the dish he had tasted before that had an absolute taste of its own and he still couldn't match it to anything. This was python and his opinion of the snake was, "After your first mouthful, the taste is so alien that the chewing process is slow and reluctant and your face wears an expression which is neither pleased nor appalled, somewhere in between. The second bite is better and tempts more curiosity, and the third mouthful is delicious." Sam stopped chewing and looked at Neil with a slight irritated look on her face. She drank a mouthful of wine and remarked to Neil that snake was one thing that was not on her list to try.

"Never," she said.

Neil smiled and mentioned to Sam, "Never say never." She looked at Neil, smiling with her hand moving up and down Kevin's thigh, and leaned back in her chair, feeling pleasantly satisfied.

A Rewarding Day

The large herd of impala cautiously grazed on the open savanna south of the Rufiji River during the hot and rising temperature of the afternoon.

The undetected danger downwind of the herd had managed to edge in unnoticed and lay low, close to three of the grazing impala. Just five metres away, hidden in the clusters of the long savanna grass and perfectly motionless, lay the patient leopard.

She had skilfully moved in as close as was now possible and was ready to strike just as soon as circumstances reduced the distance between her and the chosen prey animal a little more. The gradual thumping of a distant helicopter rotor momentarily gained the herd's attention and no doubt developed a possible opportunity, if only for a second in favour of the huntress. Before the impala had a chance to react, the savanna grass only metres away exploded and a blur of black-spotted golden cat was dragging her down to the grass, the shrubs and shoots that she had just been feeding on. The cat's fangs delivered a precise powerful bite, immediately breaking the impala's neck, and the leopard quickly adjusted her grip on the neck to complete the kill by suffocation. The 40-kilogram antelope was rapidly hauled 25 feet up and into one of the trees after being dragged 50 or so metres across the savanna.

The big cat lay aloft in her perch, contentedly licking the fur off her prize. She curiously glanced at the distant noisy shape in the sky thumping along at a low altitude over her territory.

The chopper pilot was carrying out a third fly over above an area of interest one kilometre south of the river. Inspector Adimo had taken a few days, following leads on the missing persons and began her first main plan of action. Adimo, along with the two officers and the pilot, agreed that there appeared to be some form of abnormality below at the edge of the lush forest. A sharp reflection of sunlight, alien to the surroundings, was also noticed once by the pilot from a distance as he performed another turn around following a flyby. The pilot circled the area and located a spot to safely land the chopper. He adjusted his controls and descended to a dry firm area in a clearing 150 metres away from where they intended to investigate, and he touched down within sparsely spaced trees of various expanses. Looking in a northerly direction, the forest was lush with a thick canopy that owed its existence to the proximity of the river.

The four of them climbed out of the chopper into the heat of the Tanzanian bush. It was mid-afternoon and the day was exceptionally still, hot and disturbingly quiet and void from any breeze. Following a brief chat with her officers, they decided that one officer would stay with the pilot at the aircraft while she and the other officer would investigate the location. She checked her camera, phone and side arm and they set off through the thicket to the forest. Her officer, as well as being armed with his issued sidearm, carried one of the AK47 assault rifles that were available to them. They stopped to survey the surroundings through binoculars, then carried on through the sparse thorny thicket. From a distance of maybe 100 metres, it became clear that there was something inside the shade of the forest and, by virtue of its nature, did not blend in with the immediate surroundings.

They paused to further take in and become aware of the surroundings when the stillness and the silence encouraged the two law officials to apply some more caution as they approached. At 50 metres away, they could recognise the shape of a vehicle and Adimo's officer took up a more forward position and both had their weapons drawn. It was now clear that the vehicle had been covered with branches, grass and scrub, and the front registration plate was visible. The officer carried out a full visual sweep of the vehicle externally and internally while Adimo covered him and the immediate surroundings.

When all clear was established, they investigated the ground under the vehicle and slowly expanded a search of the vehicle-perimeter area before an internal check. The surface of the surrounding area was dry, and although the officer had extensive tracking knowledge, he explained that it was too dry to determine much. He did point out that there was enough disturbances to reveal a person or persons travelling by foot in the general direction of the river. Adimo was calling in the plate number when the officer called over to inform her that the keys were inside the vehicle. He opened the bonnet and confirmed a cold engine, then had a good look at the underside of the vehicle before attempting to start the engine. The engine spun into life and the dash gauges informed them that the fuel tank was showing empty with the low-fuel lamp illuminated. The engine was stopped and a thorough search of the interior was carried out only to reveal some food and snack wrappers littering the front and rear-seating areas together with a cool box and some empty fuel containers in the rear, covered, flatbed area.

After taking some snapshots, they concluded that so far the area was far short of being a crime scene apart from the possibility of ditching a rental vehicle unlocked and with the keys inside. The vehicle had no signs of being damaged or abused, but this did not suggest that the whole thing was unsuspicious. *Why try to hide it?* Adimo thought. She would surely get some feedback through the rental company regarding rental-agreement information. She made a mental reminder to suggest to the rental company to have tracking devices fitted to all rental vehicles. She radioed the other officer and made their way back across to the chopper. The lieutenant instructed her officers to follow the tracks as best they could and try to come to any conclusion of it.

Adimo waited with the pilot and shared a coffee with him from one of the flasks. They discussed briefly what had been found and she thanked him for his help in locating the vehicle.

"Brian, assume that you were stranded or, intentionally, here, whatever, I do realise that if your intention was to be here, you would clearly have a plan and a route to travel out of the area. Let's go with that one, Brian, and assuming this is the case and you also had the help of two travel companions to assist, how would you proceed?"

"Inspector, we are both aware that the nearest road, or should I say track, is a short distance away, maybe four kilometres I guess. You have exhausted your enquiries along all these villages and small commercial premises connected by these routes and no leads have been forthcoming to you. I do not doubt that the people have been truthful with you either, most know and respect you. Throw in the fact that you have informed them of incentives that you intend to honour in exchange for any useful information leading to ensure their exposure.

"There is a police station not too far from this area that I would have to consider as well. Under these circumstances and the factors in place and assuming that I am involved in something illegal, another vehicle and road trip would be out of the question; we would still be three white folks travelling in the African bush, and travelling on foot would be insanity, especially at night, which would be suicide in this area. I recon a fair assumption of travel from here and I would put my money on it which would be the river, and I don't mean swimming! Maybe a rendezvous with some other help from another party is a possibility, but the river is looking good."

"Hmm," Adimo answered. "My thoughts entirely. I agree with you completely and the vehicle will be collected and taken to the nearest police compound for inspection."

The two officers returned two hours later; she could tell by the confident expressions on their faces that some positive results had been achieved by them. They had followed the tracks as best they could and tracking had become simple when the ground became moister the nearer they got to the river. They reported that three people were definitely travelling and suggested that one was either a woman or a child; a water craft had been launched there.

"Excuse me, ma'am," one of the officers addressed the inspector.

"We noticed clear evidence suggesting that there had been quite a few periods of rest taken between the vehicle and the river along with the markings of something large being transported and being laid down. The distance between the footprints is over three metres with two sets at the rear; we were thinking, ma'am—"

Just then, the inspector politely interrupted, "Gents, please excuse me. Yes, you are thinking correctly and I appreciate your observations, thank you; come on, and let's go check this vehicle again."

The pilot agreed and urged them not to spend too long to ensure daylight return travel. Adimo and one of the officers quickly returned to the vehicle. A quick check of the vehicle roof, sides and rear, hard, canopy sections were checked and photographed. Brackets for securing straps revealed abrasive marks consistent with a load being resting on the brackets, and during this second check, they agreed that there was a smell of gasoline as well as diesel on the rear bed. Both fuels had been transported.

They strapped themselves into the chopper. Adimo requested Brian to follow a course along the river as much as he could before following his main route to Dar S just as a longshot to try to spot anything of interest. The inspector and her officers continued the discussion regarding the boat. They all agreed that the craft and the outboard motor must have been picked up somewhere in the area where the vehicle was located. This craft would be approximately three metres long, probably constructed from lightweight fibreglass or aluminium rather than wood or a rubber inflatable. The lieutenant pointed out that three adults travelling in that river in a small inflatable would be as safe as travelling in a beer barrel, considering the outcome and the fate of the crew, following a serious tear on the small craft. She zoomed in on the photographs she had snapped and confirmed what would suggest an aluminium craft was used. The officers had a look and were able to see that fresh particles of aluminium were present in the concave of the roof contour at the edge of the hard-plastic, fixed-strapping mounts probably due to chaffing.

The pilot followed the river downstream. They were all hoping to get a glimpse at three mzungu on-board some small aluminium dingy but knew the chances of this would be narrow. The amount of small and medium-sized boats sailing up and down the river looked incredible to them, just so many they agreed. No results had been gained and they were in a smooth port manoeuvre en route north to Dar es Salaam.

A feeling of success seemed to be shared by everyone; the day had been productive; it was now fair to assume that these people are not entirely lost. This illusive vehicle was more than irritating, but today's results were now accepted by them as a completion of phase one.

"In the morning, gents, procedures should be underway to have this vehicle uplifted. We will follow up leads beginning with the rental company as well," Adimo announced.

"We have a direction to follow and we can only move forward on this now. I am sure some light will soon be seen in the tunnel and not a freight train, I hope. One of our main advantages is the fact that we are in the dry season in the Selous. The wet season would probably have restricted any travel for those three and we would probably not be searching for them anyway. Or would we?"

Once at the Dar S office, Inspector Adimo thanked her officers and dismissed them early; she was determined to get off early tonight also and she would, she thought.

A quick meeting with her captain to bring him up to speed and inform him of her intent for tomorrow, get home, relax and gather her thoughts over a quiet drink out was this evening's plan.

The meeting went smoothly with her boss expressing his satisfaction regarding today's results; he reminded her of the importance and the pressure attached to the three missing mzungu, which she fully expected.

Diamonds and Gin

She left the station, smiling and contented, and quickly made her way to her vehicle. On her way home, she took a hands-free call from her daughter who was staying with her at present. They both shared the same circumstances in life being separated, and she was very happily separated in her own situation. In her position as inspector, she enjoyed more privileges than in her past positions as sergeant in the anti-drugs support and traffic divisions; the main privilege being in charge of a marked unit entirely at her disposal. The vehicle was a short-wheel base Toyota Land Cruiser which guaranteed commuting through Dar es Salaam City pleasurable. The traffic around her in all directions seemed courteous at all times and was clearly the result of the roof-mounted rotating beacons and the conspicuous battenburg livery that furnished the vehicle body panels.

The plan she had in mind for the evening to go out for a while was in place; her daughter, Jo, would drop her off. It was of some coincidence at this moment in time the ages of the family. She found it amusing to think that she was 44, Jo was 22 and baby Suzan was just two years old. The two of them bonded together more like sisters than mother and daughter, and the fact that she was a grandmother rarely crossed her mind. When it did, she was elevated by the thought. On arrival at home, she parked beside her own vehicle. She had a chat with her daughter and relaxed in a hot shower before changing into her much-adored civilian dress; tonight the choice was blue jeans and a black T-shirt, and she thought, *To hell with it*. Black sued heels also. After another brief chat with Jo, she was ready to go.

The little one was already sleeping and the maid was settling the little girl down for the evening. Jo dropped her mother off at Divas Bar and Restaurant.

The name Divas was actually the former name but still well-used; the new name was now formally The Oyster Bar. Saturday evening in the bar was becoming quite busy as expected and she moved to the quieter bar within the main restaurant. An arrangement to meet up between herself and an ex-colleague was in place to discuss some issues of her case to help her clear up some of her suspicions and concerns in some areas. She had the feeling that some facts were not as they seemed and her usual thoughts of direction and perception were challenged. Adimo needed something apparent to focus on, something more than mere theories developing in her thoughts; it was well-known to her in her line of work during the unclear part of things that the theories had to be ironed in or out to arrive at the proper starting point in the investigation. A little help from a guaranteed source of extensive knowledge and experience would do no harm. She was now three years decorated as inspector. No other promotion was forthcoming, and for her to retire on this rank raised no concerns with her at all.

She was glancing through the menu when her double gin and tonic arrived; she had a few sips of the cocktail through the lemon and ice, and she quickly found herself collecting her thoughts of the events and results of the day in a more clear and relaxed focus.

Some of the more-privileged Tanzanians were arriving in the car park, piloting their Hummers and Range Rovers and announcing their in-car sound systems to the night.

Couples and families would generally frequent the restaurant while the bar area next door took care of the single and group customers. The weekends guaranteed the display of powerful and expensive automobiles, many of these vehicles definitely in the wrong hands and some of the pilots over the limit of alcohol consumption to drive in anyone's book of standards. Unless they were involved in a serious accident, which was not uncommon, 20-thousand shillings would normally put a smile on most of the faces of the police patrol. Adimo knew all this; she had been there before.

Her thoughts went back to some of the more serious RTAs that she had to respond to inside the minority-group areas of the city that were under economic pressure. The scenes encountered there were usually quite gruesome, and the scene in general could best be described as a tragedy. The vehicles, the dead and injured were frequently robbed of valuables before the police and emergency services arrived, especially any unfortunate vehicle carrying people and luggage on route to the international airport. Some of the robbers helped make up the massive number of onlookers and were basically immune from any suspicion. The police could only offer their services and treat the scene as an RTA; the resources available could not be considered to investigate the scene as anything more than an unfortunate accident.

Adimo answered a call from her former colleague informing her that he would be a little late, maybe 20 minutes or so due to traffic.

"Is that 20 Tanzanian minutes, Columbo, because if so, I can eat before you arrive," she joked.

She removed a pen and a small notebook from her bag and began noting down some of the subjects and blanks that she wished to discuss following today's developments and her case in general.

Adimo valued Peter's opinion and any direct knowledge he had in people and certain facts that she was not entirely familiar with. Her mobile phone rang again and was jerking around on the table in vibe mode; her captain's number was displayed on the screen. She accepted the call, and following a brief conversation, she placed the phone back on the table.

Suddenly, Adimo let out a loud scream. Something made her move quickly backwards into her chair, nearly causing her and the chair to topple over. Her pen raced along the restaurant floor and her arm movement sent the glass of gin and tonic smashing on the floor a few metres away. She quickly got off the chair, grabbed her phone and made her way to the bar, her right arm over her chest while catching her breath, with a wide-eyed but relieved look on her face. The barman made himself immediately available to her needs and was keen to know what was going on; he was franticly looking up, down and around with some confusion. Adimo raised her hand and, still slightly breathless, explained to the barman what had happened.

While she sat concentrating and putting her pen to paper, something distinctly touched and moved on her left foot. She immediately pulled her foot back while observing the area under the table, and to her horror, a large, dark, grey rat was present.

The people behind the bar apologised and were relieved to see that she intended to stay, as they knew her very well and promptly replaced her glass of gin and tonic. After collecting her pen and bag, she sat down again, this time closer to the bar in a more-illuminated area. *Oh my God*, she thought and shivered, "Ahhhhh," and without realising, she drank half the contents of the gin and tonic.

Peter arrived and accessed the restaurant through the main bar door; he noticed Adimo and waved before stopping at the restaurant bar and gestured to her offering a drink which she accepted.

Peter sat the drinks down on the table and sat down after they greeted each other with a hug and a kiss.

"Well now, young lady, how is life in our law-enforcement sector treating you?" he asked in a slow, enquiring voice. "I imagine a bit more favourable for you nowadays, Adi, sorry, Inspector Adimo," he smiled.

He drank some of his scotch and laid down his cigarettes and lighter on the table.

"It's marvellous to see you, Peter, and you are looking well as always. Those damned cigarettes contribute nothing towards your healthy appearance either."

He exhaled his cigarette smoke and responded with a relaxed laugh. Adimo smiled and repeated with openness and sincerity on how well he really did look.

The two of them discussed things that two old friends and colleagues typically discuss, mainly family, quality time and Peter's retirement. He never enjoyed his retirement as a subject of discussion and she knew this. He missed the police work terribly, and on this occasion, he asked Adimo if she thought that he looked like someone who was happy to be where he was at in life. He explained with a smile that in his 66th year, retirement 'as they call it' would put him towards the edge of the cliff much faster than if he was still working. Two years into his retirement seemed like an eternity in some kind of a vacuum.

"Retirement should be abolished, my dear, unless of course it is voluntary or dictated by ill health."

The smile never left his face.

Food was ordered and Adimo mentioned the story of the rat; she could now joke about the experience, but she was still scanning the floor area now and again.

"This rat seems to be real lost, Adi; in some African restaurants, they are normally busying themselves either running in or out of the kitchens."

She stopped eating and glanced at the bowl of peanuts that she was picking from.

"Well, come on, Adi, true, yes?"

She agreed and they laughed some more about the incident.

"Since we are on the subject of creepy crawly things, Peter, I cannot think which one was my worst experience, this bloody rat business or that big cockroach that flew right into me and got tangled in my hair a while back."

Peter laughed and elected that the rat experience would be the choice of the day if he was obliged to choose.

Peter leaned closer.

"Anyway, Adi, what do you have on your mind, girl?"

Adimo shared some of her thoughts with Peter and her speculation of circumstances and recent events regarding the case she was working on. Before she could go into any details, Peter interrupted to ask who was in charge of the case, the logistics and the manpower.

"I am, Peter, logistics' pending approval from the chief of course, and the chief, he is definitely in charge of manpower allocation."

"Well, madam, you make sure it stays this way. Now tell me please."

She continued to inform him of the progress she and her officers had made regarding developing events from the beginning. The beginning, she explained, being just a matter of days ago, her task was to look into three missing people in the Selous area who appeared to have possibly lost their way.

At this point early in time, she mentioned that the assumption from the office, including her, was that the people would probably turn up sooner rather than later. When no news was forthcoming over a few days, assumptions began to move towards the possibility of the people in question having met with an unfortunate accident or misadventure. After all she explained, they were adventuring in the Selous with clearly no guide present with them, which was highly unusual to begin with, she reminded Peter. She moved on to refer to him the progress that she made earlier in the day in reference to the Toyota pick-up being located. "This was a game changer for us, Peter," she explained. "I already had a meeting with the chief this afternoon and he obviously agrees.

"The main game changer came to me tonight, Peter, in the form of information during a phone call from the superintendent just before you arrived and the arrival of the rat incidentally.

"We now have another issue to discuss tomorrow as well as developments and conclusions gained from the pick-up searching and checks and the rental-company feedback. Have you heard of the CSIS, Peter?"

Peter's eyebrows raised, and without moving his head, he raised his eyes and focused on Adimo for a few seconds and smiled.

"Adi, if you had mentioned the CIA, I would give you the same answer as I am about to; of course I have and so have you."

"Yes, I know, Peter, sorry; it is just my way of letting you know the subject of the chief's call to me tonight. The latest development, and I mean international development, is the interest and possible involvement of the Canadian Secret Intelligence Service."

"Hmm, it's not very secretive anymore," Peter said with a mischievous grin.

Adimo raised her eyebrows, tilted her head with a smile and carried on talking, "There will be a full briefing tomorrow; I am not sure how I should be reacting to this news. Should I be elevated, euphoric, disappointed, nervous, not sure, but it seems to be coming more interesting."

"And more dangerous I would imagine, young lady," Peter answered. "It would be less than diplomatic to assume otherwise, madam. One fact you can be sure of is if these guys are interested, there is some serious shit involved. Another thing to bear in mind, Adi, is by tomorrow you will be made aware if you are staying on the case or being removed from it."

She was about to interrupt him and he halted her by raising his palm towards her.

"I am only raising the point, Adi, that depending on jurisdictions and the level of investigation, protocol will be dictating the level of involvement of the investigators who will be involved in this 'swoiree'. At present, Adi, think positively and I know you always do. The fact is that you have been chosen to locate three missing individuals and run with that close to your chest. You do not know of their involvement in anything at present, but that will change tomorrow also, my dear."

"Are you in any way comparing this to the USA Embassy bombings in '98, Peter, when you were obliged to step out of the investigation just at the mention of the CIA becoming involved?"

"No, not at all. No comparison would exist between these two cases, and circumstances set them wide apart; to begin with, everyone knew immediately that the CIA would be taking this one as soon as those bombs went off here and in Nairobi. Being a detective, I knew my entitlement of being a direct investigator at the top level would not be required. This was their bad guys to find.

"Four words dictated who would be running that show, American Embassy, bombs, big bombs, I will add, and terrorism. *Excusez-moi, madam*, six words," he said with a smile.

"I have a strong feeling that you will continue on this case in your rightful capacity, Adi. I don't feel that terrorism is in the mix here. Terrorism usually, but not entirely, always has a build-up of information flying around that kind of informs many government agencies that some dumb mindless act of violence is going to take place but nobody has a clue what, when or where. Apart from that, those three are in the Selous area. I can't think of a more appropriate area to be terrorised, and then maybe eaten for good measure if you don't know where the hell you are going."

They both laughed. Peter carried on with some more confidence-boosting conversation with Adimo and reminded her that if any illegal activity was apparent, breaking the law in Tanzania, her jurisdiction, would seem certain. Adimo smiled and leaned over to give Peter a hug.

"Thanks, Peter, that's another drink I owe you. I am more than curious to know what this is all about."

"Me too, Sista, me too."

Adimo and Peter ordered some snacks and drinks and carried on with their evening, reminiscing in times gone by and the memories that never leave one's awareness. They spoke of Adimo's father and his involvement in hunting over the years.

"Do you guys still hunt, Adi?"

Adimo leaned forward, shaking her head, laughing.

"*My father*, well, Peter, if it was suggested for him to refrain from this, the result would have the same reaction as asking a cat not to chase a mouse. I do not hunt anymore. I could never find the time, although I am a regular visitor to the police-training ranges to satisfy my addiction for target shooting.

"You know, I am thankful that certain people were not present here tonight during my tango with that bloody rat," she said.

Peter looked at her inquisitively.

"Some of the people who I have recently become acquainted with during this investigation who are helpful and potentially useful are hunting in the Selous as we speak.

"There are three mzungu guys, two Americans and one Australian. They are aware of the search for these missing three and are cooperating with me favourably in assisting to locate these people. As a parting conversation with them, we were on the subject of firearms, calibres etc. The minimum calibre for large game came under discussion, the Holland & Holland .375 magnum as we know, yes?"

She smiled, shaking her head slightly and showing her pure white teeth.

"I teased them dearly and informed them that the rifle is quite unnecessary, and killing a lion with a spear was as simple as breaking a bar of chocolate."

She drank some of her gin and tonic and cheekily smiled; she watched Peter grinning who was still all ears.

"Can you imagine, Peter, if they had seen me jumping and screaming in reaction to a rat walking over my foot; oh my God, you know what I mean?"

Peter laughed loudly, and following some coughing, he lit another cigarette and had a drink of his whisky.

"You know something, girl. I think even our Masai would have a problem dealing with a rat running over their feet."

The two of them began laughing loud enough to inspire the customers in the neighbouring table to laugh along with them.

The music and the general atmosphere in The Oyster bar were ramping up some, just as it should on a weekend evening. The two of them decided to settle the bill and head home.

Peter offered to drive her home, and they walked past the taxi rank to where he was parked. Adimo's thoughts went back to the inconvenience of trying to find a road-worthy cab in Dar S, and she was thankful that she usually had other options available these days. They entered Peter's vehicle and buckled up.

"We don't want to get into any trouble with the law on our way home, Peter," Adimo said in a frivolous tone.

"On the contrary, madam, we don't want the law getting into any trouble with you on our way home," Peter answered in between laughing and coughing simultaneously.

"Really, Peter, think about what I suggested regarding those dammed cigarettes. You will be doing yourself a favour, and me; you know I am concerned for your wellbeing."

They both chatted for a little while outside Adimo's home.

"Tell me, Peter, tell me your initial thoughts on this developing situation? I am more than curious of your opinion."

"Who says that I have an opinion, Adi? Presently, I am not quite sure what I should be having an opinion about, but I can give you some thoughts and assumptions though, might be something, might be absolute shit." Peter smiled as he stared into the night.

"OK, Adi, this is just coming from a retired detective who knows his way around and still keeps his ears to the ground. A fair amount of information comes my way now and again, never from bad guys, just from guys who know bad guys a little."

Now it was Adimo's turn to smile.

"These folks would rarely go to the law to pass on anything. I get it sometimes because some folk see me as a good guy."

"Do you recall a few years back, not so long before I retired, there were a spate of incidents regarding violence involving foreigners and Tanzanians?"

Adimo nodded.

"Four people were killed, four mzungu to be precise. Nobody really knows how many Tanzanians and other East African deaths were directly related to this fiasco.

"Something came to surface just months ago involving some conflict between some mzungu in Dar es Salaam, yes? You were forced to shoot someone who was just about to shoot some female mzungu who was getting into the passenger's side of a vehicle that managed to speed off."

"Sure, Peter, I remember, but nothing really developed on that and I do not recall an investigation being launched either."

"Yeh, true, Adi, it was all undermined and I heard that the only investigation and resolve was carried out by the mzungu themselves."

"You heard, Peter?"

81

"Adi, I just told you I get fed some information sometimes. Sometimes the information is drip fed, but that is fine. I am not requesting it nor am I working a case as a law-enforcement representative.

"Four murders and God only knows how many more. No investigation and no arrests, and if I remember correctly, the ones who carried out those killing were apparently killed themselves."

"Yes, you remembered correctly, but I know all this, Peter."

"OK, you are aware at this time the word on the street and across the force was that all this was related to ivory smuggling, drugs and maybe the albino body-parts market, yes?"

"Yes, Peter, I was *aware* and that was all. I was never involved to investigate any of that. Who was?" She laughed.

"That to me was all bullshit, Adi. The drug trade in Tanzania is nowhere near large enough to prompt that amount of violence. The albino thing is localised and random and the ivory thing has become too commercial; once it reaches the cities and ports, it is on its way. Any violence or differences relating to the illegal ivory trade is settled out in the bush at the sharp end.

"Anyway, girl, best be thinking about making tracks. My thoughts on this are fairly straightforward and things look to be surfacing again, this time serious enough for the Canadian government to have an interest.

"At least you have a handle on things now. You found the vehicle and you know by now those folks out there in lion country are no tourists," Peter continued and was still looking upwards towards the night sky. "I recon tanzanite and diamonds are involved in all this." Adimo looked surprised.

"Diamonds!?" she repeated.

"Diamonds and tanzanite, with diamonds taking precedence," Peter said.

"What brings this on, Peter? That's a first for me. Nobody in the force has ever mentioned this, at least not in my presence."

"Who knows, Adi, maybe nobody knows or maybe some know and never discuss it. Try to find out the circumstances of how those four were killed, type of weapons, maybe calibres." He smiled. "Just curious."

Peter put his hand into his jacket inside pocket and took out a small leather-type pouch and switched on the interior light. He untied the small cord sealing the pouch and emptied the contents onto the palm of his hand.

"Look, Adi, do you see these?"

She looked intensely at the four small cut glass stones, each no bigger than a small pill, and she touched them and rolled them with her finger and gazed at Peter.

"Are these what I think they are?"

"Yes, they are about 0.4-carat oval-cut diamonds and never been mounted."

Adimo did not know what to say. She told Peter how beautiful they were.

"I had no idea you invested in gemstones, Peter. Where did you get those? Are you going to mount them onto something? Are you getting engaged or married again?" she said sceptically.

Peter laughed and returned the stones to the pouch and returned the pouch to his inside pocket. He looked at Adimo with a stern but inoffensive gaze.

"Adi, remember we were discussing the mzungu killings that took place a while ago just before my retirement?"

Adimo looked and nodded.

"I was not on that case. In fact, I had a feeling that there was a clear effort to keep me off that case—"

"You mean the case that was never a case?" Adimo interrupted.

"Yes. Tell me, Adi, do you remember who drove my patrol vehicle before I took possession of it just two months before I retired?"

"No," she said. "No idea."

"Neither do I. But it is irrelevant. The vehicle that was given to me, following the violence, had been used to transport two of the deceased mzungu to the morgue."

Adimo listened intensely.

"When I took charge of this vehicle, it was handed over to me after a brief clean; it was such a brief clean, I had to clean the remaining blood from the rear myself. Do you know where I got these diamonds from, young lady?"

Adimo tilted her head with a wry-looking smile and rested her cheek on her fist. "That bloody vehicle."

"I have kept these for over two years, Adi, and there was no way I was handing them over to anyone, especially following the way circumstances and events unfolded to accommodate or not accommodate me. These may come in handy to help someone's case in the future, someone deserving." He smiled. "Someone who is right on the button. If not, well, I may just get engaged."

"Well, Peter, with that beautiful little bag in your pocket, I'm available. Peter, your secret is very safe with me and I understand how much-needed vigilance you have just passed onto me regarding the diamond information. Any gemstone talk or information that develops on this case will be brand new to me. Incidentally, Peter, how much are they worth?" she said with a curious smile.

Peter let out some loud laughter along with his coughing; when he recovered, he reminded her that he had already mentioned the weight and the cut and she should consult the internet with her curiosity.

Peter started to buckle in. Adimo thanked him and gave him a kiss on the cheek.

"Wish me luck for tomorrow."

As she was leaving the car, Peter asked her where her police-issue revolver was and she said it was indoors inside the safe.

"I never take it out socially with me, Peter, same as you before."

Peter grinned and opened the left side of his jacket to reveal a holstered handgun.

"I still have my concealment licence, and before is not the same as now. Those dammed poor bastards going around nowadays now have guns, and they have no other reason to live other than to feed their addiction for cocaine or heroin; they don't care who they shoot at. Take my advice, young lady, always carry it. Times have changed, and bear in mind, your briefing tomorrow may tempt you to change that policy."

"Sure, Peter, let's catch up later, yes?"

"Goodnight, madam."

Peter U-turned his vehicle and stopped as Adimo was approaching her front door.

"Hey, Adi."

She turned around.

"Do you have any idea where my vehicle ended up after I retired?"

"Not at all, Peter, but I can try to find out."

Peter started to move away with a smile on his face, pointing his finger at her patrol unit in the driveway.

"Back then, it was dark blue and unmarked; sweet dreams, young lady!" he shouted.

Adi took a couple of steps towards the road with gritted teeth but smiling.

"Peter, you bastard." Two quick blasts from Peter's horn were heard as he drove off. She walked towards the house, shaking her head and smiling. She gave the patrol vehicle a good long look before entering the house and locking up.

The Meeting

The Sunday traffic was quiet and welcomed by Inspector Adimo as she made her way to the station. Eight in the morning was an acceptable time to arrive and there would be no demanding-toolbox meetings this morning. She decided to arrive an hour earlier to arrange some small files and reports.

Driving along, she could not help observing the poor, unfortunate souls sleeping on the sidewalks and in and around the concrete central islands of the traffic circles. They always seemed to be sound asleep even as the heavy juggernauts and buses constantly roared past them just a few feet away. She pitied those people and could not even begin to imagine how it must feel to be in that situation that they were forced to survive in. Nothing on your possession but the clothes you are wearing, persevering with malaria and the likes of and not a soul to help you apart from the Creator. Things normally did not get any better from here. She thought it better to die but then rebuked herself for thinking this on another human being's behalf. She certainly thought it for herself though.

After parking at the station, she observed the superintendent's parking space was still vacant. *Good,* she thought, *at least 30 minutes to relax.* She could not help looking at her unit and trying to imagine it in dark blue. She also had visions of giving the vehicle a complete internal going over. *Peter, you bastard,* she thought again with a smile and entered the building. The distinct smell of insect-repellent spray was apparent as she approached the stairs. The building was hot and humid and the walk upstairs to access the second floor aroused her disapproval.

The elevators were never operational at weekends due to load shedding by the national power provider, and the suggestion of adding an emergency generator to the station's assets always fell on deaf ears. She never saw the point in having suggestion boxes apart from being ornamental.

A few upturned cockroaches lay on the stairs, displaying their uncontrolled death throes, and she dispatched them off the stairs with the side of her foot, sending them to ground level. The cleaners greeted her with smiles and Adimo switched on the air condition in her office and the other units that she could access. She asked the young girl in charge of the kitchen to prepare some coffee for her while she started her paperwork. She noticed there was no printout on her desk, containing the information from the vehicle-rental company; she did realise that the time was quite late when she phoned in the vehicle's plate number the day before. Prime 4x4 Rentals would be open for business around ten on a Sunday. The girl from the kitchen, who was well-known for her perfect preparation of Turkish coffee, arrived. She spoke to Inspector Adimo and handed her a sheet of A4 office paper that she had found on the floor. Adimo immediately recognised the paper was from the station clerk and thanked the girl. The message informed her of the clerk's inability to contact the rental company the previous afternoon. She could relax now while waiting for the boss. There was not much to prepare and he was more or less brought up to speed with the chat yesterday.

The second floor now began to feel comfortable as the air conditioners did their job and began to cool and dehumidify the air in the building. The strong and addictive aroma of the coffee replaced the smell of insecticide and dampness. The office was now operational, she thought.

Inspector Adimo was enjoying a second cup of Turkish coffee at her desk. She heard the sound of footsteps and voices coming closer from the stairs area. Her boss' voice could be heard over the others and the voices faded as they entered the superintendent's office. After a few moments, whilst leaning on the doorframe of her office door which was left ajar, Superintendent Hamisi Hassani gave a light knock on the door and greeted her with a smile. After exchanging greetings, he sat down at her desk; he leaned back on the chair to look through the glass of the main partition on the corridor, glanced in the direction of his office and then leaned forward again.

"I have asked the kitchen staff to accommodate them with coffee and biscuits, and I would like to give you a brief 'heads up' from the relatively small insight that I have at present, just to satisfy your curiosity. You guys will be working together without actually being together a lot of the time. What I mean by that is you all will not be in such close proximity unless circumstances demand."

Adimo thought to herself that this is a good start as she leaned over to him and mentioned that this sounded very acceptable for the time being and they will see how things develop.

"How about rank, chain of command and jurisdictions, Superintendent, and what brings them here?"

"Don't be concerned regarding rank, Inspector. We are not welcoming any territorial issues either. Rank will not crossover between us and them, and I am your direct line manager as always." He smiled. "Jurisdictions are of course ours in Tanzania, clearly theirs too under our rules and theirs will also extend outside our country as well, I would imagine. You guys are two teams working together with the same goal in whatever way you all see fit. What exactly this is all about, I am not quite sure yet, but I have a bit of an idea from our brief conversation during the drive from the hotel and I have a feeling we are about to find out shortly, Adimo."

Superintendent Hamisi stood up.

"Come on, Inspector, and let me introduce you to our guests," he said in a louder and more relaxed voice than they had just conversed in.

"Come, let's go find out what's going on."

He winked at her while smiling and tilting his head towards his office. She found herself smirking and followed him. Adimo could hear voices chatting in the superintendent's office, and when she entered, her assumptions proved correct. A man and a woman casually dressed were seated, holding small cups of Turkish coffee. They placed the coffees on the table and stood up to introduce themselves to Adimo while Hamisi arranged another chair, then sat down behind his desk. The girl from the kitchen then appeared with coffees for Hamisi and Adimo. They both introduced themselves as Victor (Vic) and Zoe. Vic then complimented the coffee and thanked the girl as she was leaving.

"Hey, how do I say 'thank you' in Swahili, guys?" Vic asked.

Adimo quickly said, "*Asante sana.*"

"Hey, my first words in Swahili, *asanti sana,* Inspector," Vic said, smiling.

"I told you she was fast," Hamisi said while laughing.

"Ah, I see I have been the subject of conversation, Superintendent."

"Compliments, Inspector, I can assure you," Zoe said with a confident smile.

Adimo detected a slight questioning look on Zoe's face within her smile and Adimo could swear that as much as she had tried, she did not conceal her surprise as she thought she had when she entered the office.

"Excuse me, Inspector Zoe," Adimo said, laughing. "I may have appeared a little surprised earlier, but I am going to be straight up. I was not expecting one of you to be a lady and definitely not a *black* Canadian lady." They all laughed and the superintendent clapped his hands loudly together once.

"You did not tell her, Superintendent?" Zoe said in between her laughing.

"Hey, nobody told me," he said, laughing with his arms outstretched.

Hamisi, Adimo and the two Canadians exchanged business cards; with today being Sunday and the Canadians still suffering some jetlag, they agreed on today having basically served its purpose for introductions and an overview of things.

Vic formally introduced himself as a field agent with the CSIS (Canadian Secret Intelligence Service) and Zoe an officer (Inspector) with the RMCP (Royal Mounted Canadian Police). This surprised Adimo and she was already thinking how productive the approach to this task could become with three different methods and mindsets working in the same direction. The expression on the superintendent's face was now in earnest and she realised now why his demeanour was so spirited when he led her to his office earlier. *Another black lady inspector indeed.* She chuckled to herself.

"So, Victor," Hamisi said.

"Vic please, Superintendent. Vic is just fine."

"OK, Vic, you mentioned earlier that these persons are known to you guys and operated within a smuggling organization, extending through a number of countries and leads back to Canada. Well, I mean Canada-based?"

"Yes, they only became known to us about five months ago. We were monitoring them and their activities inside Canada and a few other counties which they were travelling to. Tanzania is the first country that we have officially requested to legally operate in and pursue these individuals."

"Does this mean that Tanzania is the hub or is fairly close to the action, Vic?"

Exactly, thought Adimo.

"Yes, it does, Superintendent, bear with me please. Our policy rapidly changed six weeks ago when we gathered sufficient evidence against at least one of these individuals to arrest and most probably convict for double murder, among other offenses."

"Vic, may I enquire into which line of smuggling they are involved in and at what level?" Adimo asked.

"Diamonds, and they would seem to be in there in a high-level capacity, ma'am."

The superintendent and Adimo looked at each other.

"Diamonds!" Hamisi repeated. "Surely they are not robbing the few precious amounts of diamonds that we have in Tanzania. Tanzanite I could maybe be convinced of, but diamonds!"

"We believe they are involved in tanzanite also, the source and origin of the diamonds is South Africa," Vic stated.

Adimo shook her head, laughing a little with a serious tone.

"Well, if all this is fact, it sounds like a serious call. Agent Vic, how are the diamonds getting in and out?"

"At present, we think Mozambique, Inspector. Getting out, no idea. Primarily it is for this reason we are assembled here today. I am confident that your own authorities will be just as interested in exposing this organisation as much as we are."

"Absolutely, Vic," Hamisi said after looking at Adimo and then at Vic and Zoe.

"But to keep things in perspective, we are all clear that we will uphold the law, 'our law', within the borders of Tanzania and Zanzibar together with you. You guys and ladies," he smiled, "will be extending your reach and following enquiries upstream and downstream outside of Tanzania if required, yes? And, everyone, please let us avoid any territorial conflict."

"Yes, exactly so, Superintendent," Zoe assured. "I believe Vic has information packs and photographs in relation to the suspects for you and Inspector Adimo on USB."

"Inspector Zoe, you use the words 'suspects' who seem to be involved in serious crime and murder. Clearly there are warrants on these people and they should be considered armed and dangerous. We can consider them fugitives, yes?" Adimo asked.

"Definitely, Inspector, you will get a good insight into them within the information packs. Yes, fugitives." Zoe smiled.

"Inspector Adimo," Zoe continued, "do you know anything about diamonds?"

"Just a couple of things, Inspector. All women love them and they are far from cheap, two facts for now," Adimo said with a smile.

Peter, Peter, Peter, she thought to herself, *keep those stones well away for a rainy day.*

"OK, people, we hinted on this desire earlier on today. Could we all agree from now on inside and outside of this office, when we are among ourselves, we address each other on first-name terms?" Hamisi suggested. "Oh yes, and Inspector, sorry, Adimo. Please refrain from wearing your uniform from now on, casual is now in."

Adimo smiled and thanked him. They blissfully agreed and Vic went into his bag to retrieve the USBs.

Marc and Odette's Rest and Relaxation

"Sante!" a man in his late 30s said as he raised his glass together with the woman seated beside him and emptied the contents before placing the glass heavily back on the table. He poured another large measure of cognac from the open bottle in the centre of the table. The woman raised her glass a second time and emptied the contents. She also poured herself another, then opened the Marlboro cigarette pack and lit a fresh cigarette. While she was laughing, Marc managed to catch the pack that she awkwardly threw at him and discarded the almost-spent cigarette in his hand and lit another. The food on the table was keeping hot from the burning charcoal trays supporting the dishes, and as well as flame grilled meat and chicken, a wooden bowl of the East African delicacy 'fried termites' sat at Marc's side of the table. The two of them were no doubt planning to sample them after they had consumed enough brandy to alter their gastronomical standards. Odette gulped down another mouthful of brandy and gingerly made her way to the toilets, giggling as she went.

Marc leaned his head back on the chair. He drank more from his glass and quietly said to himself, *Crazy fucking bitch,* while smiling with his eyes closed.

They were checked into a lodge on the bank of the Rufiji River, east of the Selous in the Mtanza and Utete area. They had a rough-looking appearance even though they had showered in the afternoon. Marc's dark facial hair was at a stage in between stubble and the beginning of beard growth, and the both of them could benefit from unpacking the hairbrush and a change of clothing. Odette toddled back from the toilet and dropped herself heavily into the large soft chair that seemed to swallow up her petite frame. She took the mosquito repellent from the table and gave her arms and legs another coat. She wore only flip-flops, denim shorts and a dark T-shirt without a bra.

"Go easy on that spray, Odette, or you are gonna need another rinse before getting into bed with me later."

"Go fuck yourself, Marc," came the reply.

Marc just giggled and smiled at her with his menacing dark eyes.

"Hey come on, babe, our team leader, Dennis, is away for a couple of days. Who's gonna know?" he said, smirking.

She looked at Marc casually and unconcerned, and another drink from her glass emptied its contents, leaving it ready for another top up.

"*Vous etes un salopard, Marc,*" Odette remarked.

Marc let out some loud laughter, then leaned closer to top up her glass. He lit a fresh cigarette and handed it to her and she thanked him. She was a couple of years past 30 and attractive.

"Marc, I ain't your babe, darling or whatever? We are presently and pleasantly together, that's all," Odette stated.

Marc smiled as he leaned back in his chair with his left ankle resting on his right knee.

"Whatever, Odette, but you *are* gonna be my darling tonight."

He blew her a kiss, smiled and raised his glass to her. She let the remark and gesture fly right over her head. They discussed how long Dennis might be gone. Dennis, Odette and Marc checked in the night before after arriving by boat, and Dennis carried on downriver with a local boy who boarded the aluminium dingy in the morning; they were heading to almost the mouth of the river, and then Dennis would make his way to Mafia Island on another craft. From there, Dar es Salaam was his final destination, also travelling by sea.

"I would not be worrying about things; we have all did the Dar run. We are fortunate this time to have two or three days R&R awaiting further instructions," Marc said.

"I suppose that's the way to go," Odette said as she strolled to the bar to fetch another pack of cigarettes.

Dennis was due to arrive in Dar es Salaam the following day with the delivery and meet with his contact there. He was transporting around 1200 cut diamonds ranging in weight between one and four carats. From Dar, arrangements would be made and the process of transporting the stones to Europe would be carefully set in motion. Plans would regularly alter as routine and over the next two or three days. Marc, Odette and Dennis would be made aware of their next task. There were usually quite elaborate methods practiced to move diamonds from A to B. For the three Canadians operating in Tanzania, Marc Dupuis, Odette Gordon and Dennis Vatel, life was adventurous and fast. Death could come even faster if they fell afoul of the rules. Over the next couple of days, the Sea Jay aluminium dingy would be completely coated in fibreglass and resin, painted and put to work on the river in its new role as a local fishing boat.

The haphazard ditching of the rental vehicle had two purposes. These were primarily to transport the occupants and dingy to the preferred spot and to help with a little smoke screening over any investigation. Some traces of contraband had been left around some areas of the vehicle. The firearms and ammunition had now settled somewhere in the murky muddy depths of the Rufiji River.

Odette threw the pack of cigarettes and lighter across the table to Marc from her huge soft chair. They had moved away from the subject of Dennis and transportable items and continued to torment each other with loose insults. Protocol had taught them never to use the 'D' word; they had their own abbreviations for this.

Marc emptied the cognac bottle into the two glasses. He ate some more of the fried Mchwa 'termites' as if picking peanuts from a bowl.

"Try some, Odette. They are very good for you, protein rich."

"*Non merci, monsieur*, be my guest and you finish them."

"This is an East African aphrodisiac, darling, Odette," he jovially said.

"Well, Marc, like I said earlier, you can now have even more fun later fucking yourself. You never give up, do you?" she said as she ran her both hands through her shoulder-length auburn hair, pushing it behind her ears. Her dark eyes expressed a tiring of his advances.

Marc laughed and gulped down his brandy.

"Speaking of aphrodisiacs," she said, "I wish we had taken some of that weed that we scattered around in that rental truck."

Marc grinned as he pulled something from his shirt pocket and lightly threw it over to Odette. Landing perfectly on her crotch, she looked down to see a perfectly rolled long joint.

"Babe, you do know that's forbidden, but we are not exactly on the job at the moment," Marc said casually while smiling.

Odette's facial expression went from bored and discontented to 'the little girl on x-mas morning' look.

"*Tres bien, monsieur, tu es mon sauveur,*" Odette said as she looked around to check if they had been noticed by anyone.

"*De rien, mademoiselle.*"

"No problem with that here, Odette. We could spark it up right here and nobody would give a shit. All the same though, better to head over there," he said as he nodded in the direction of the river.

The two of them strolled towards the river just 50 metres away, following a friendly piece of advice from the barman regarding keeping a safe and sensible distance away from the river's edge. The path was dimly lit by ground-level lamps and nobody was around apart from a caucasian man and a local girl heading back in the direction of the bar and restaurant.

The flow of the river was quiet yet reflected an awareness of such power. The opposite bank could not be seen; the changing movement and shapes on the surface constantly played tricks with the eyes, and only darkness came into focus beyond the vision of Marc and Odette. Sightseeing was not prioritising their intensions.

She placed the joint in her mouth and Marc offered her the flame from his lighter. She took a long draw from the joint, inhaled and paused for few seconds before exhaling. An almost-instant uncontrollable smile developed across her face, and she repeated this another three times. She leaned her hand on Marc's shoulder to steady herself a little and control her giggling.

"Here, take it, Marc, take it!" she said as she put her hand forward, offering Marc the joint. Marc obliged, and after a few lung-fills of cannabis and nicotine, he handed it back to her. He commented on how strong he thought the grass was and found himself quickly giggling along with her. Time did not take too long before the two of them were engrossed in some form of exaggerated, magical, mystical conversation regarding the view and the evening sounds of the river. Marc flicked the finished joint end into the river after his second fill.

"Marc, I am so thirsty I could drink that river," Odette said, laughing.

Marc was quite quiet for a change and was just looking at her, smiling and listening to what she was saying.

"Odette, do you know what would be a slight more than an inconvenience right now?" He decided to drop the 'babe and darling' approach for now.

"Hmmm, no, what?"

"I was thinking maybe a five-metre-long crocodile lunging out the riverside at us," he said.

"Right, that's it, let's go," she said and cracked up laughing again.

"Hey, just kidding," he said as he followed her along the path.

"Yeh, I know, but I'm still fucking thirsty."

They were heading towards their table, fully engrossed and intent within themselves to appear absolutely normal.

"Marc," Odette said suddenly, "let's have a seat and a drink at the bar."

Marc was feeling quite stoned from the grass, as he found himself leaving the dimly lit area of his comfort zone at their table and heading for the brightly lit square cocktail bar. He was wondering if this stone was peaking or increasing. *What the hell?* he thought, soon to find out. They sat down and ordered cold beers; immediately, two frosted bottles of Tusker lager appeared in front of them and the barman uncapped them. The bar was quiet, just the couple who had passed them, the barman and two local working girls who were seated opposite them. Beyond this, there were enough people to almost fill the restaurant area who were seated, enjoying their meals. The two of them quickly quenched their thirst with the cold inviting beer, letting it transform the dryness that had settled in their mouths. Marc looked at her and she at him, and they again started laughing at each other.

"Odette, don't you think the bar here is really bright?"

"No, not overly, why?" she said, looking around. She was thinking that Marc was looking a little serious, troubled maybe.

"I am gonna go to the room and get my shades. This bar is as bright as The Starship fucking Enterprise," he said with a stern look on his face.

At once, Odette quickly twisted herself away from the bar and sprayed a mouthful of beer over the ground and burst out in loud laughter.

"Are you fucking serious, give me a break, Marc."

She laughed and wiped her mouth with the back of her hand. Her laughing was quite uncontrollable.

On this note, Marc requested to the barman to raise the music a little and play the track 'Get It On' by T Rex from his playlist when he had a chance. The track soon began and the barman clearly liked the track, as he raised the volume even more. Odette had managed to control her laughing to a level that allowed her to communicate again. She appeared astonished when she looked at Marc as he had transformed himself from a paranoid-looking moron to a supercool guy leaning on the bar, moving with the music.

"How do you go from 'Starship Enterprise' desole, *excusez-moi, monsieur*, 'Starship fucking Enterprise' and evening sunglasses to 'Get It On'? You are nuts, *monsieur*," Odette said.

The two of them laughed and settled down to enjoying the track. They drank another two cold ones and decided to think about calling it a night.

"Hey, Odette, you know something?"

"Here we go again," she said. "What?"

"I have got a huge hard-on and it won't go away; I have no idea why I just said that, must be that crazy grass."

Odette looked at him saucer-eyed, moved closer and gently squeezed his crotch.

"*Oui, monsieur*, so you have. You can have fun on the sofa bed with yourself tonight, Marc, don't mind me. Do you feel like another joint?" asked Odette.

"If you feel you are up for it, mademoiselle, why not? Our diaries are far from full tomorrow, I have another here." He patted his shirt pocket.

"Cool, but let's go to the balcony. Stuff that river," she said.

They ordered four bottles of beer and a bucket of ice to go and settled the bill. Just as they were preparing to leave, two middle-aged mzungu arrived at the bar and ordered drinks with an American accent. The men had a look around but mainly towards the two local girls. The girls, both smiling, walked across towards the men.

They seated themselves on the balcony of the room. They finished the other joint and managed one cold beer each. The cloud had cleared some to reveal a spectacular star-studded sky with an abundance of light beaming from the three-quarter moon that appeared as if it had just been placed there. The opposite bank of the river now came into view.

"I am absolutely stoned," Odette said.

"Snap completely whackydood."

"Whacky bloody what?" she said.

They moved inside and closed over the mosquito-net doors. No lights were needed. Half the room was basking in moonlight. Marc removed his shirt and jeans and extended out the sofa bed. She walked back into the main room from the bathroom; she looked so tired but widened her eyes to look at Marc. She looked lower towards his slips.

"Well, do you still have that huge ere—!"

Before she could finish speaking, Marc placed both his hands behind her head with his lips covering hers. She did not resist while his tongue was exploring all around her tongue and mouth. She found herself slowly placing her hands around him and sliding them inside his slips and onto his buttocks and pulling herself in against him. They kissed each other slowly and deliberately for what seemed an eternity, then his lips and tongue moved down her neck and he gently but firmly nibbled her earlobes. Her left hand stayed inside the back of his slips and her right hand was now fondling his genitals from the outside of the slips. He drew his head back briefly to look at her and held his palms against her cheeks and started to kiss her passionately again, and she moved her hands to pull his head closer into her. Marc's hands moved down and griped the bottom of her T-shirt. Odette's both arms raised above her to help him remove it.

Odette's T-shirt came straight off and Marc threw it in the direction of the bed. He looked at her, the intense moonlight displayed her breasts, her hair and face so beautifully, he thought. Her nipples were so erect; Marc moved his hands over her breasts, then turned her around to kiss the side of her neck while firmly massaging her breasts and nipples. She was beginning to moan a little and he encouraged her to stand on the bed. Marc now kissed and tongued her irresistible erect nipples, playing harder as she groaned. After a while of this enjoyment, she came back onto the floor and her hands went back to where they had been before. They were now intent on exploring each other's bodies and sexual desires. Their breathing was now heavier and faster. Marc's head was leaning back with his eyes closed, running his hands through her hair and caressing her neck and shoulders. She was softly kissing and licking all over his nipples and he could feel her large erect nipples dragging now and again on his stomach. His slips were being pulled and slid down his legs as she lowered her body to rest her knees on the floor. The slips were tossed aside and the feeling of her cool palm holding his penis was overwhelming. Her hands moved to hold his hips and Marc could feel her mouth slowly wrapping over his entire erect penis as she moved to and fro. He was now experiencing himself taking controlled deep breaths; he could hear his heart thumping, his legs were shaking and he wanted all this to stay this way. She was relentless in pleasuring him and had no intention of stopping anytime soon; she was enjoying this as much as he was.

After a while of this extreme pleasure, Marc raised Odette up onto her feet and they vigorously began kissing each other again. He came down on his knees and unbuttoned her denim shorts. He quickly pulled the shorts and tiny red panties off together and tossed them aside.

She was perfectly shaven and Marc forced his tongue up and down her vagina. Her wetness quickly released and he knew how clean she was. He stood back up and found that kissing her was somehow very addictive to him. Her hand gripped his penis hard as they lowered themselves onto the bed. She attempted to pull Marc against her and tried to encourage him to enter her. Marc resisted and lowered himself down on her and opened her legs wide apart. He found that her vagina was irresistible and nothing would stop him pleasuring her as she did to him. He found himself pleasuring her with every part of his mouth that he could. The more she moaned, the more he applied on her. Odette touched the climate of sexual excitement twice with loud moans of pleasure. Finally, he entered her firmly and directly. He could feel her so perfect, and her wetness was soothing. They kissed each other intensely. She let him know in a loud whisper that she could not become pregnant; her voice was shaking uncontrollably and he found this addictively attractive. He was very erect, almost numb with the effect of the cannabis. The both of them were experiencing magnified sexual excitement from the effect of this. Odette's body shook and tenseness took over all her muscles as she erupted into an orgasmic state a third time.

Despite the air conditioner maintaining the room at a reasonable temperature, both their bodies were saturated with sweat and Marc was beginning to feel exhausted. Odette moved him onto his back and easily manoeuvred her petite, slim body on top of him; he needed the hardness and pressure in his penis relieved. She again took him in her mouth and pleasured him slowly before guiding him inside her again. Marc was groaning and his body was pushing up and down in time with her. She had her hands on the headboard, fucking him harder and harder, faster, faster, faster. Marc now felt the beginning of his orgasm deep in his loins; the moment was coming for him. He handled her beautiful breasts roughly and it soon came. He moaned loudly in bursts while gripping her buttocks so tightly and pulling her down so hard as if trying to move his body inside her.

Death of a King

During the night, some of the savanna received a short downpour of heavy rainfall, enough to send some new green shoots upwards and transform the general vista of the plains. Although welcomed by most species, the nature of the dry season would soon return the scene of the grasslands back to the straw and dusty colours. The flat top greenery of the larger trees would probably benefit with more blooming for a while.

Brad, Jim and Neil were following Juma across a large rocky area leading down to a dry riverbed. The sun was a demon and no signs of the previous evening's rainfall existed in this area. They were around 25 kilometres from the lodge; Thomas was a couple of kilometres away with the vehicle.

They had been on an unsuccessful leopard hunt last week. The male leopard they were pursuing had reportedly been noticed 10 kilometres away from where they had set up their bait and blind. The animal had taken down a young wildebeest, and after feasting on its prey, he managed to safely store its remains at a secure height in an acacia tree. Neil informed the guys that they would try a 'walk and stalk' method next time. Ron and Vince had not managed to make the time to visit the previous week and would rearrange when circumstances permitted.

Kevin and Sam decided to travel out on a photographic safari today. They dismissed the idea of lion-hunting for now. Last week, the same male leopard had lured them out to track and hunt the animal. Their efforts were not rewarded with even a glimpse of the big cat. They had settled for two warthogs that they had skilfully dispatched at a range of over 200 metres. Brad thought he had noticed some leopard tracks earlier in the day, only to be told by Juma that the tracks were made by a lion.

"Are we heading for that kopje way over there, Neil, on the opposite side of the riverbed?" Jim asked.

After confirming with Juma, Neil replied an affirmative to Jim.

Brad was studying every rock, shadow, tree and savanna grass areas as he moved along. The burrows on the side of the dried riverbank made by bee eaters particularly took his attention. "Hey, Jim, I feel I am getting pretty used to stalking these areas now, but I get a distinct feeling that we are being watched."

"Got you, buddy, we probably are."

Juma was following some large fresh lion tracks in a direction downwind of the kopje that had led them all onto level ground on the dry riverbed. They were on the opposite side from where the kopje was up ahead in the distance.

They moved over to the left bank which also offered more shade from where they were. After 30 minutes of quietly moving forward, Juma stopped and stretched out his arm backwards, showing his palm in a gesture to halt the guys. He turned around with his index finger crossing his lips and gestured to Neil to give him the binoculars. After Juma raised the glasses twice to his eyes, he studied a fixed point and gave Neil the glasses. With his arm over Neil's shoulder, his other arm pointed in the direction for Neil to focus on; Neil found the attraction, then handed the glasses to Jim.

"Hey, mate, we ain't gonna find any leopards around here today," he whispered in Jim's ear with a grin.

Jim had a look and, in turn, handed the glasses to Brad. Halfway up the kopje, lying down and stretched out in the shade, facing away from the bank were two large male lions. The movement of one of the beasts' tails had given away their presence to Juma's keen, developed eyesight. Juma gestured everyone to crouch down while they quickly put together a plan of approach. It was clear that no opportunity was possible from their present position. There was probably 300 metres between them and the cats. Managing to pass the kopje would offer a better opportunity for a shot but would put them in a position upwind of the beasts, as well as the lion's acute sense of hearing probably detecting them as they passed by, hidden by the dry riverbank.

This idea was quickly discarded and they decided to carry on as they were until a suitable point of fire was available. They all double-checked to make sure their mobile phones and the two-ways radio were turned off. "It's your call, partner," Brad said as he tapped Jim on his side. Juma reminded everyone to watch every step and to be aware of their surroundings at all times. The latter part of this advice intended for thought towards the possibility of lionesses showing up. They kept as close as possible to the riverbank and narrowed the distance down to 150 metres where they stopped to survey the cats. Both were still there, lying down, making any shot impossible. This suited them, as they were too far out of range and they needed the cats to be focused on napping rather than being fully alert at this distance. Neil had already stressed that the distance they wanted should be around 50 metres; he had mentioned to Jim earlier that a lion in a position of lying down on all fours with the head up, a shot to the neck where the neck joins the chest would be best. Up on all fours, the obvious point to target would be well behind the shoulder just below the lateral midline of the animal. Neil advised that no headshots should be considered. They had moved closer to approximately 80 metres between them now when Juma signalled to halt and this was it, no more closer. They could clearly see why. Although it could not be noticed from a distance, the bank in front of them now was fast becoming longer at a much slower angle that would no longer keep their presence out of sight. Jim indicated that 80 metres was good for him. Jim placed the rifle down carefully in a suitable position on top of the bank, supported by its bi-pod and butt. They decided to stay put and wait a while; one of the lions was sure to change position. Juma had made it clear when they first had a look at the cats and judging the size of the prints that both the animals fell into trophy territory.

The wind had increased a little but had not changed direction. 15 minutes had passed and Neil was looking in all directions through the binoculars. He spotted two male cheetahs out on the savanna, way out beyond the opposite bank about 600 metres away. He tapped Juma's shoulder and handed the glasses to him. Juma had a quick look and gave Neil a 'thumbs up' gesture and focused back on the lions. Neil handed the glasses to Brad. The cheetahs began to make some high-pitched barking sounds. The lions began to stir. The one nearest tried to raise his head and look towards the sound. He rolled over directly onto his back before twisting onto all fours and turning around to face the activity on the plain. The lion was staring deliberately in the direction of these invaders of his territory and flicking his tail in agitation. The other was lying down, watching. None of the beasts had noticed the other four invaders. Jim needed no encouragement to quietly move to the rifle and mould himself around it. He had left the bolt closed, securing a cartridge in the chamber and the trigger pushed forward, engaging the 'set trigger' facility. This facility allowed the shooter to apply a much-lighter pressure on the trigger to release the firing pin. Everyone was behind Jim as he zeroed in on his target. An explosion of dust, spray and hair particles appeared behind the big cat's right shoulder just as the boom from the big CZ rifle rang out with a potential to damage any unprotected ears in the immediate vicinity. The big cat roared as he threw out his front legs, clawing the air before slamming down to the ground on his side, in motion only in death throes. The other cat roared in anger, ready to charge, then quickly leaped down the kopje, paused and roared again before quickly running off in the opposite direction. The cheetahs froze, then began strutting up and down, trying to figure out the disturbance. They too decided to take off quickly away into the grasslands.

Juma arranged with Thomas to have the other vehicle mobilised from the lodge to accommodate the uplift of the kill. The other vehicle did not take too long to arrive and they made their way back to the Toyota to meet up. Neil and the two Americans travelled back to the lodge. Neil was driving when his cell phone began ringing in his shirt pocket and prompted him to pull over to accept the call.

"Ah, good afternoon, Inspector…marvellous, thanks, and you, ma'am?"

Neil could be heard saying. Brad nudged Jim on the shoulder and they carried on looking ahead with small smirks on their faces. Neil could be heard finishing off by thanking the inspector, then motioned to end the call. He quickly changed his mind.

"Inspector, sorry, I wanted to tell you that we managed to spear one *Simba* today."

Neil laughed at her reply, then ended the call.

"She asked me what fucking calibre the spear was."

"Yeh, as we said before, guys, not much change out of her," Jim said cheerily.

Neil passed onto the guys what Inspector Adimo had mentioned and the information she had given was advice regarding the three missing Canadians. She had strongly advised that these people should not be approached, as there was reason to believe that they could be dangerous. Brad protested that none of them had a clue of the appearance of these folk anyway.

"She said she had some more business in this area and would stop by with some flyers with ID photos. Guys, she could just as easy email those; she's already acquainted with us."

"Yeh, but remember, Neil, you ain't gonna get that kind of service because you ain't no cop," Jim said.

"Yeh, true, mate. Anyway, let's get on out of dodge. We can only pass any info onto our acquaintances."

The three of them found themselves discussing what these folk might be involved in until Brad got bored with it and put an abrupt end to the conversation.

The Package

Dennis stood in the shower of his hotel-room bathroom, appreciating the powerful hot water being showered onto his face and body for 30 minutes. He came out clean-shaven and felt the benefit of being dressed in fresh, clean clothes.

He powered on the television using the remote control just for some background activity and poured himself a brandy from the glass-fronted minibar refrigerator. He looked at the price list and laughed to himself. Dennis opened the balcony doors and leaned on the balcony railings, enjoying the brandy and the view; evening was approaching. From his 12th floor view, he could see that a few folk, mainly parents with children and young embracing couples, still occupied the two swimming pools.

Dennis would meet with his contact down at ground level in an hour's time. He decided to call Marc and Odette.

Odette's cell phone rang first. She was relaxing on the balcony of the lodge, enjoying sundowners with Marc.

"Hi, Dennis, yeh cool, everything is fine," she said as she gave Marc a smile.

Marc acted on the hint and quietly left the room for a walk in the direction of the river.

"Yeh, he's cool, Dennis. I think he's having a drink down at the restaurant or the bar."

They had a ten-minute conversation.

"OK cool, see you soon."

Odette sat her phone back on the table and picked up her cocktail.

In perfect timing, she thought as she watched Marc taking his phone from his jeans pocket and engaging in conversation with Dennis. From beyond the bar on the way to the river, Marc turned around and raised his glass to Odette and she returned the gesture. She drank from her glass and made herself more comfortable in her chair and lit a cigarette. While smiling to herself, she thought what the chances were of last night's activities being repeated again tonight. *Absolutely every chance,* she told herself.

Dusk was creeping in as Dennis returned to his room to fix himself another drink. He arranged his small travel backpack that he would take downstairs with him when his contact arrived. Dennis inspected the package. The package was a tough, vacuum-packed, tamper-proof affair that apparently had some integrated circuitry that maintained a nominal millivoltage. The design of this protection had the ability to generate more than enough heat within milliseconds to compromise diamond. Either of these two protections that were in place being breached would signal the detonator within the high explosive inside to explode and, as well as inflicting massive devastation to people or property close by, would also vaporise the diamonds. The protection could only be disarmed through a process involving a controlled environment and/or decoded wirelessly. The concept was simple. In the highly unlikely event of rules being breached during transportation to the planned destination, the catastrophic event would ensure a no-win result as well as the destruction of any trace evidence.

Dennis's contact phoned to confirm his arrival. The contact had arrived and was seated outside in a dimly lit area of one of the large patio areas. Dennis made his way down in the elevator and collected a tray with two shot glasses containing vodka from the bar that he had previously ordered. The contact was seated close to one of the swimming pools that were now void from bathers. It was the time in the evening when families took the children inside to wind them down towards bedtime and adults made their way to their rooms to prepare for dinner and plans for the evening.

As Dennis approached his contact, the man was smiling and stood up to greet him. An embrace and a double-clasped handshake sealed the introduction and the identical backpacks were exchanged. They sat down to chat and sip the vodka.

"Dennis, how are you, my friend?"

The French pronunciation was used for the name 'Dennis'.

Dennis gave his contact an update of events over the past couple of weeks; the contact already had some prior knowledge of what he was being informed of and refrained from making Dennis aware of this. Regards were given to Dennis to pass onto Marc and Odette from him.

They stood up and gave each other a parting embrace just before the contact made his way out of the grounds through the hotel car-park area. He had slipped his empty shot glass into his pocket as he left the table. Dennis made his way into the hotel with the backpack and planned to get quietly drunk later at one of the hotel bars. He would call Marc and Odette later in the evening.

The elevator doors opened and Dennis walked along the corridor to room 1230.

He reached his room and placed the key card over the card reader on the door and entered.

At once, his whole situation changed, his whole world changed. What was happening to him, he thought. He was forced into the room from behind and heard the door slamming shut. He was struggling for his life; an arm was around his neck from the rear and his head was being horribly forced forward and down by a hand. He was locked in and could not find the required effort to defend himself; any attempts were futile, and if he could speak, he could only have begged for this to stop. The pressure increased quickly and firmly just before he passed out.

The attacker, who gained access through the fire-escape stairs opposite Dennis's room, held him a little longer before letting Dennis's limp body rest on the bed. Dennis was checked for a pulse and was quickly intravenously administered a lethal dose of heroin. The necessary arrangements were made to stage the scene as a drug overdose, the backpack, cell phone and fake passport IDs were taken; Dennis's legitimate travel document was left.

The assailant left the lights and television on and the 'do not disturb' card hanging on the door before quickly making his getaway down the fire-escape stairwell. At ground level, he quietly nudged the crash bar on the fire-escape door and surveyed the night outside; it was clear. Coveralls, ski mask and gloves were removed and packed into the backpack. He quickly disappeared and melted into the city streets.

The Game Change

The phone in room 1230 of the Neptune Superior Hotel was ringing out just as it did during numerous attempts by the reception desk to connect incoming external calls the previous evening.

The room-service maid was waiting at the reception desk while the duty receptionist was calling the room. This was now Tuesday afternoon and the guest was due to check out the following morning. Nobody was aware that the guest had already been taken out on Sunday evening, nobody except the intruder.

The manager and the chambermaid ascended in the elevator to the 12th floor. The 'do not disturb' display card was still in place over the door handle. The maid had answered, "No, sir," when she was asked by her boss if she had tried to enter the room. No response was met, following a number of loud chaps on the door. A young lady wearing only a hotel bathrobe leaned out of the doorway of the neighbouring room, curious to assess the noise. She was quickly encouraged back inside by her roommate and could be heard giggling as the door closed.

The key card unlocked the door and the manager pushed the door full open. The maid responded with a gasp in reaction to the sight and smell that greeted them. She was instructed to make her way downstairs and wait in the reception office behind the main desk; he called security and made a call to the police.

He took some steps towards the body that was in a position half on the bed and half off; the upper part of the body was on the bed. It was clear by the smell and appearance of the man that he was lifeless. The manager made his way back out to the corridor and closed the door. He would wait until the security and police arrived. When the security arrived, the three of them entered the room to form an opinion that the man certainly appeared deceased. They again left the room to wait for the arrival of the police. One security guard remained in the corridor outside the room.

Inspector Adimo had just returned to her office, following a second visit to Prime 4x4 Rentals. The rental vehicle was still impounded and was undergoing a thorough search and inspection by the police crime-scene techs. Significant traces of heroin, cocaine and marijuana were discovered throughout the interior. Adimo had the full details of the rental agreement which had been paid in cash. The name on the agreement came as no surprise to her due to the fact that the name meant absolutely nothing to her. The customer on the agreement was a 38-year-old British citizen named Charles Rogers; Adimo passed these details over to Zoe to further investigate. Vic, Zoe and Adimo had discussed some issues the day before and an agreement was reached to establish how many hotels, lodges and camps or any other existing establishments provided accommodation between the points where the rental vehicle was found and a reasonable distance downriver. Vic had put forward the idea that he was intent in quickly going forward with this investigation to pick up a lead. They all recognised this as a constructive idea that was not too much resource intensive. The occupants of the dingy had appeared to have travelled downriver during darkness; upriver would only have led them into a much more remote area. On the Rufiji, darkness was not the ideal time to travel; it was highly likely that the French Canadians stopped somewhere for an overnight not too far downriver. Vic made it clear that he would not devote too much time on this, and he was informed that he would travel together with one of Adimo's officers.

Zoe was following up on the British passport holder through the British Embassy with assistance from the Canadian Embassy. Adimo had insisted to the crime-scene techs to also keep a keen eye for absolutely anything other than drugs inside that vehicle. Deep within herself, she did not imagine that they would come across anything that Peter had previously stumbled on. Peter's circumstances were different, she thought. This Toyota was staged.

The two Canadians and Adimo were preparing to drive out for a late lunch at one of the food courts when the captain entered Adimo's office in a state of urgency. A call had just come through from the duty policemen attending an incident at the Neptune Superior Hotel. Hamisi did not explain too much to them but insisted on them to respond immediately to the scene, as it sounded like a possible connection to their case. They were received at the hotel by the two duty officers and the hotel manager; guests on the 12th floor had been temporary relocated and all existing and temporary room numbers of the occupants were on list should the need to speak to them arise. The three of them entered room 1230 and were confronted by the smell of human remains in the early stages of decomposition and the motionless ridged-looking figure by the bed. The central air-conditioning system was operating but was rendered useless owing to the curtains being closed and the balcony doors open. Adimo enquired if anything had been moved or removed within the room; the duty officers and the hotel manager assured her that nothing had been interfered with. Adimo called HQ to request some crime-scene investigators to attend the scene quickly. Vic offered and opened the curtains. He had a look outside and over the balcony railings. He closed the patio doors after coming back in. The scene became much clearer with the daylight entering the room. The body was in a position at the side of the bed, knees on the floor and the upper body on the bed face down. The right arm was straight out as if reaching and the left hanging towards the floor with the shirtsleeve rolled up. The deceased man was dressed quite well and there was no damage or any signs of disruption inside the room. Some body fluids had secreted from the mouth and nose and the colour of the skin was almost black. If not for the light sandy colour of the hair, it may not have been immediately apparent that this deceased male was white.

Zoe took the opportunity to snap some photographs of the scene before the room became too crowded. She paid particular attention to the contraband, spoon and syringe that were in plain sight on the writing desk; there was also a used candle and cigarette lighter. The three of them had seen the passport in the bedside-table drawer and the passport matched the check in details at the reception. Considering the deterioration of the deceased's features, it would still be a fair assumption that the deceased man was the holder of this passport. A post-mortem, dental records and samples for DNA testing would be carried out as protocol. The three investigators did a full visual sweep of the room and collected some photographs. Adimo noticed something on the floor close to the entrance door. She kneeled down to inspect this and nudged it with her pen into a small, plastic, zipper bag. She studied this and what she had recovered looked like part of a zipper puller, the aluminium type; the way it had broken would have left the other part of it still attached to the slider. She pocketed this after showing the item to Zoe and Vic.

Two crime-scene investigators arrived and both parties exchanged questions and other information. For the record, Adimo mentioned the small item she had found on the floor and requested the investigators to place some emphasis on the deceased man's clothing zippers, if any. The three inspectors left and let the CSI carry out their job. On passing the reception, they enquired into whether or not Mr Vatel had requested any laundry service during his stay. The receptionist checked and pointed to a plastic bag on the floor behind the desk with Mr Vatel's name on it. They were in luck; the laundry was due to be collected by the services company today, but they had not yet arrived. The receptionist informed them that the laundry had been placed at the reception on Sunday by Mr Vatel personally, not long after he had checked in; there was no laundry-contents list with the clothing and, in turn, had delayed the collection. Adimo took possession of the bag and its contents.

They met with Captain Hamisi to discuss the progress of this latest event. Vic and Zoe offered information that would help to discard any suspicion of the deceased being a drug user.

"Things will become clearer over the next few days," Vic said. "We have been fortunate in a way for something like this to arise, unfortunate for Mr Vatel of course."

"Indeed, indeed. OK, Vic, I hear you are planning to do some sailing on the river. I think this is a good starter that could probably reel in some results, excuse the pun. I have approved the resources for you," Hamisi said.

"Excellent, Captain, appreciated. If tomorrow is good to go, even better."

"You are most welcome. Touch base with Adimo here, she will keep you right, and remember to drop the 'Captain' part, Vic."

"Oh shit, eh, I mean sorry, Hamisi, forgot; OK, will do."

"Right, guys, let you all be getting on with it. I have a pile of 'shit' to catch up with here and tight lines, Vic," Hamisi said, laughing.

They proceeded out of Hamisi's office with one intention on their minds, 'lunch'.

Adimo drove to a food court within a well-known shopping mall by the sea. They ordered cold drinks and food from the international menu.

"It's so quiet and peaceful here, Adimo. You can even hear the waves, nice," Zoe said.

"Yes, it is a good choice for breakfast or lunch; there are a few places like this and this one is the closest to HQ. The evening is a different story though. Don't get me wrong, all is good, but trying to get a table for dinner can be just too much hassle sometimes. There is also a live traditional band on usually four nights per week, and loud. I do enjoy live music but absolutely not during a meal."

"I know exactly what you mean," Zoe said. "I am of the same opinion. What do you recon, Vic?"

Vic was relaxed and enjoying the surroundings.

"Hmm, I have to agree with you ladies; loud music and nice dinners don't work for me. I like a conversation over lunch or dinner, breakfast also for that matter."

"You can always try it for the experience sometime if you like," Adimo said jovially. "Don't forget, you will see African people having loud conversations, shouting and singing and dancing before, during and after their dinner, it's just the culture."

The food was not long in coming and was well-received by three hungry people.

"I will talk to you later regarding resources for the river trip, Adimo, if that's cool," Vic said.

"Sure, that's more or less arranged; I will explain to you."

"You know, Dennis Vatel and his tragic demise at the hotel was no drug overdose. What do you guys recon happened there?" Vic asked.

Zoe agreed fully with Vic and gave an opinion of someone wanting to be rid of Vatel; who and why was yet to be established of course.

"Adimo?" Vic looked at her.

Adimo's mouth was half-full and she timely swallowed her food and drank from her coke.

"I won't go into it too deeply just now, but I fully agree with you guys, and we still need to examine the completed report from the medical examiner."

"Absolutely," Zoe and Vic replied.

"I don't know the man," Adimo continued. "The little information I have gained from you guys made my decision for me without even entering any hotel room. Why on earth would a diamond smuggler or mule check into a nice hotel and, on the same evening, proceed to indulge in injecting heroin? My assumption, of course, going by the state of the body providing of course that is the cause of death," Adimo said while rolling her eyes, smiling.

"He met with someone there, we all agree on that, yes?" Adimo asked.

The other two nodded and seemed content being on the same page.

"On another note, had you guys not raised any awareness of these people? Yes, this no doubt would have gone through as some crazy mzungu playing with drugs."

There was doubt in Adimo's mind that this killing could possibly be connected to rivals within the criminal fraternity in which these people existed. Her thoughts were leaning towards Mr Vatel's own organisation. If this was the case, the other two would be in grave danger, but why, she thought. Had they learned from someone of the CSIS involvement and the organisation's interest towards the three missing French Canadians? She thought of Peter, no, no way. Besides, Peter informed her of the diamonds and issues in the first place. No, she convinced herself, definitely not her friend Peter.

In HQ, arrangements were being put together for Vic's departure the following morning. The chopper and pilot would be clear to leave at 08:00. Vic would be travelling with one of Adimo's men as planned and would simply be on assignment as an American magazine photographer together with an armed escort.

"Vic, you seem happy regarding this trip. I would think it maybe patronising of me to ask you if you were familiar with small water craft and helicopter awareness," Adimo said.

"No, not at all. Your concern is appreciated, and if I am in doubt of anything, I will certainly ask your assistance. I am familiar in these areas and confident that your man is familiar with that river."

"Good. He knows the river and the area quite well. You guys will have the use of a four-metre aluminium dingy with a 35 HP outboard motor, more than adequate I believe, and will be appreciated travelling upstream. I would also expect that you choose a good place that is mosquito-free for your overnight stay."

"You think that will be necessary?"

"Trust me, Vic, absolutely. Remember, darkness is on you at seven evening."

The chopper touched down at 09:20 in the morning at the same spot during the previous excursion. They had an interesting conversation during the flight and Brian, the pilot, and John 'Adimo's officer' brought Vic up to speed on recent events in the area and where the rental vehicle was located. As Vic and John exited the aircraft, following correct procedures regarding awareness of exhaust and main and tail rotors, they met briefly with two other men who passed on one bag to John. After a quick exchange of shouting, the two men quickly made their way through the downdraft of the rotor and into the chopper. Brian immediately lifted off and ascended on route back to Dakar. After a couple of minutes, the welcome silence returned to the savanna. John invited Vic to come and see the spot where the rental Toyota was hidden, or partly hidden, as he put it. The two of them were opposites in appearance. Vic being around 5'8", light, brown, thick hair and of medium build in his late 30s. He was very clean-shaven with an almost school-boy look about him.

John stood 6'4" tall, very slim and muscular in his late 20s. His appearance would put him around 23 years old. The contents in the bag that Vic was carrying were camera and lens equipment. He also had a telescopic tripod strapped to the bag. He carried with him a 9mm Glock semi-auto pistol. John was in uniform with his .38 revolver and AK47 strapped over his back. After all, the AK47 is part of the Tanzanian police officer's uniform; just the appearance of this assault weapon demanded respect. Vic was convinced that John probably had the agility of a cheetah and the power of a leopard. *Nice place to be,* Vic thought.

Fresh tyre tracks were visible, highlighting the path that the rental Toyota took when it was driven out to meet the car transporter not so long before. On the way to the river's edge, John explained the dos and don'ts while travelling on this river. He enlightened Vic of the dangers of complacency in regards to creatures in or on the riverbanks.

The dingy looked fit and had certainly been prepared properly. Oars, rowlocks, life jackets, anchor, ropes, harnesses and first-aid kits were all there. Even the drinking water.

"Looks like we have 75 litres of fuel, John. Probably that will be rapidly consumed motoring against the current. The cans are gauged, that's cool. We can get an idea of consumption heading downstream."

John agreed as they sat in the morning heat, consulting a map and getting an idea of distances.

"I will plot roughly where the lodges and chalets are, Vic. I know most of them; they are all quite presentable places, no rubbish, you know."

Vic was searching downstream through a pair of small binoculars.

"I think I can make out some place way down there over on the other bank, maybe a house, John."

"No, no, Mr Vic, no houses around here. Too much maintenance and security costs; the access roads are very rubbish also. That will be the Eagle Lodge, the first one we will be checking over on the right bank."

With their life vests buckled up, they pushed the craft out and away from the riverbank using the oars and lowered the outboard motor and prop into the water. After a couple of attempts with the electric starter, the engine spun into life. John steered the dingy upriver to get a feel of it and asked Vic to sit at the bow. John then applied a generous input of throttle through the twist grip on the tiller. The stern of the aluminium hull dug in and the dingy raced up against the current levelling off as John backed off the throttle some. They both appeared surprised at the power on tap at the motor. The dingy got run upstream for a few minutes, then turned around to head downstream on an idle.

"We seem sorted now, John," Vic said. "No complications, buddy. I have never been on a dingy on a river. Lake and sea only; first time for me. This river looks inviting, it really does and it's not too fast-flowing here. What is it like during the rains?" Vic asked.

John explained that during the dry season, the level and currents were not so demanding, but more respect was required during the rainy season. He advised Vic that the river was never without the presence of danger in many forms. As far as the presence of dangerous land mammals being a concern, the dry season would attract much more.

"We will get ashore on the right bank at the Eagle Lodge first, and it's not too far, about five kilometres. The other thing to be aware of when boating on the river is to keep an eye for any rising sand or rock banks reducing the depth; be ready to lift that motor out of the water. Same rule as any expanse of water I suppose," John said.

Vic was taking in the ever-changing appearance of the riverbanks and edges; both banks were generally separated by 300 metres or so of river. Through the binoculars, he could focus onto water birds and monkeys moving around within the banks and trees. He had his mind on hippos and crocs.

"Are there many crocs or hippos to see in this area?" Vic asked.

"Don't worry, you will see some of these," John said with a smile.

As they approached the Eagle Lodge, a different shape and nature of the river came into view downstream. To Vic's surprise, there was a well-constructed jetty connecting the river to the bank. John explained that these establishments were all equipped with such amenities. As well as tourists arriving via the river, there were plentiful supplies of fresh fish being sold directly to the hotels and guesthouses.

A young boy who had been waiting at the jetty offered his help and assisted in securing the dingy onto the pontoon. Vic kept his handgun hidden inside his camera case as they disembarked.

John tipped the boy who then thanked John, displaying a huge grin as he received his tip. He then ran off barefooted towards the lodge, grasping the coins tight in his hand.

Impressions of this lodge were immediately appealing, Vic thought, and a perfect stopover for a couple of runaways or anyone for that matter. He turned around to take in the breath-taking view of the opposite bank and the distant greenery downstream. The pathway to the lodge was of non-slip wooden decking. As they got closer to the main entrance, laughter could be heard coming from behind a temporary sunscreen on one of the outside patio areas. Vic could recognise the German language being used. There were two men and two women who were obviously guests enjoying breakfast.

Agent Vic and Officer John greeted them in English as they walked past; the Germans returned the greeting in English. One of the men raised his cup to them. On entering the lodge, the reception desk was unattended and a girl was mopping the floor between them and the desk. John addressed her in Swahili, and to save walking through her wet floor, the two of them made their way to the large open-style bistro bar. The cleaning girl appeared behind the bar, and after washing her hands, she served them fresh coffee and small cakes. It was still fairly early, around midday. Some children came noisily running down the stairs, followed by another woman, and joined the guests who were sitting outside. John picked up his AK47 and walked to the toilet.

"Hi," a woman's voice came from the bar area.

A casually dressed young woman appeared from the staff doorway behind the bar. Vic turned around and was greeted by an attractive lady in her mid-20s. She started to wipe down the surface of the bar and replace the beer mats.

"Really nice place you have here, ma'am. How many rooms do you have?"

"We have 14, sir, eight double and six single. You like one room?"

"No, thank you, maybe later. We are passing through downriver just now; how are your rooms? Do you have much mosquitos around here?"

The girl laughed. "We have too much mosquito here; we are on the river, but not inside the rooms, no."

She seemed adamant and confident in her reply. John arrived back from the toilet and became engaged in a short conversation with her. During the conversation, she would sometimes look at Vic with a smile, then her attention would go back to John. John had explained to her that Vic worked for a well-known magazine and had been assigned to photograph some wildlife and cultural interests on parts of the Rufiji River. Vic's employers had insisted that he travel with local security, he told her.

She shook John's hand and then turned to Vic and offered her hand.

"I am Tina."

"Hi, Tina. 'Vic', it's nice to meet you."

"You think my English good? No good? Vic."

"It's fine, ma'am. I can understand you OK."

"You American?"

"Yeh, Ohio. I am working here for a few weeks."

Tina prepared some fresh coffee and served them some more. John picked up his coffee and some cake and mentioned that he was going for a look around outside.

"You are Tanzanian, Tina?"

"Yes, Tanzania no good."

"What! Why do you say this? I am sure you don't mean that."

"Just no good," she replied with pouted lips.

"Do you work here days or nights?"

"I am here all day and all night for two weeks now, not new help coming yet, maybe next week. Only me and my manager and his wife and cleaning girl here."

"Do you have vacant rooms here, Tina? I am not sure, but maybe we will need to stay somewhere tonight."

"Yes, we have, maybe five rooms vacant, I check."

She gave Vic one of the hotel business cards and asked him to call when he decided.

Tina led Vic and let him see the available rooms which he was impressed with and equally impressed by the modest price.

"I am just wondering if you can help me before I go, Tina. I am trying to locate a former colleague and his partner and maybe another man. I know they are planning to spend some time on the Rufiji doing much the same as me; maybe they stayed here."

Vic described Marc, Dennis and Odette to her without presenting any photographs, and he mentioned that they would have been here since last week.

Tina offered him a confident reply to let him know there had been no other guests in the recent past or present at the hotel of this description; she knew everyone that came and went, she said.

His thoughts wondered how far these people were prepared to travel down this river in the dark. He did have high hopes of some kind of feedback from this lodge. *Maybe a little too exposed for them,* he thought, *who knows?*

The appearance of John returning needed no reminding to Vic that they had better get a move onto the next possibility downriver. He finished off the dregs of his coffee and motioned to leave.

"Bye, Tina, you have a lovely day, OK," Vic said.

"And you also, my dear," she replied. "You come back later?"

"Maybe, maybe. I got the card." Vic waved as he left.

The two of them made their way to the jetty and the little boatman was already preparing to untie the dingy. Vic gave the boy some shillings as he boarded.

"No need to give twice," John said. "He will think you have too much money."

"No problem, John. I am still a million dollars short of being a millionaire."

John hesitated for a couple of moments, carefully interpreting exactly what Vic had just said and started laughing and shaking his head.

"Right, Mr Vic. *Yallah*, let's go."

The motor started immediately as if to assure them of the reliability of Yamaha engines. The day was becoming considerably warmer. Vic was sure the river had slowed down its flow but realised that he was most probably just becoming used to travelling on it.

"You like this girl, Vic?" John said with a grin.

"She's nice, yes. That's the problem, John. All the Tanzanian girls that I have seen so far are nice. Is it a big problem for a white guy to have a date with a Tanzanian girl?" Vic asked curiously.

"What! No way," John's voice got louder and he laughed a little at Vic. "No, Mr Vic, you can have many girlfriends here if you like, no problem. How many girlfriends do you think I have?"

Vic tilted his head in thought.

"No idea, John. Hmm, two? Maybe three?"

Genuine laughter came from John.

"Five," John replied to Vic, smiling.

Vic smiled and shook his head, looking at John.

"Nice, very lucky for me, yes?"

"I don't know about that, buddy. That might be a punishment, just make sure they don't know each other."

"OK. How far to go, buddy?" Vic asked.

"About four kilometres and landing on the left bank this time. That's about six down from the Eagle and 11 in total from our starting point."

John took over the tiller and Vic moved to the bow. He took out the binoculars from his bag.

"Hey, John, guess what I can see, buddy?"

John could tell by the enthusiasm in his voice exactly what he could see.

"Hippos, buddy, way far down on the other side."

"That's a good side for them to be at," John said to him. "Did you notice the crocs, Vic?"

Vic's head darted around back and forward, scanning the river. John casually pointed to the left bank.

"Over on the bank, not in the water."

Vic suddenly noticed them in among the gaps and roots of the mangroves, lying motionless, some with their mouths open and just 60 or 70 metres away. He used the opportunity to photograph them. After all, he was on assignment as a wildlife photographer to do just that. They passed by on idle without any of the crocodiles showing any hint of concern towards the little dingy.

Vic was about to ask John a question, but before he did, John mentioned to him that if any of them had fallen overboard, those crocs would have transformed from prehistoric statues into an array of missiles sliding down the mud banks on a rapid subsurface direction towards them.

"Yeh, I thought as much," Vic said.

"So which do you recon is more dangerous," Vic asked, "crocs or hippos?"

"If you are talking about in the water, hippos have a known reputation for being unpredictable and extremely territorial. I don't entirely agree with that," John said.

John explained that while hippos were dangerous, they were only unpredictable and dangerous if you invaded their territory. "Always give them a wide berth on a river or lake to avoid attracting any of their attention; prevention!" John mentioned. "Crocodiles, on the other hand, are another issue," he mentioned.

"These guys want to eat you or anything they feel they can overpower, especially in the water which includes most of the wildlife in Africa, and you really don't stand a chance with a croc.

"They are clever. They will quickly recognise any animal or human repetitively returning to the water's edge at a given spot for one reason or another and will eventually wait for you. You would be lucky to notice any part of that animal in murky water even a couple of metres from you. The croc actively hunts humans, and this guy definitely gets my vote for being the most dangerous on that characteristic alone. Hippos don't hunt us."

The approach to the jetty at the Palms Chalets Hotel demanded a different procedure from the Eagle Lodge. The river's edge was much deeper, and the construction of the jetty was of concrete set on the riverbed and rising two metres above the surface of the river. Once the dingy was tied, access to a converted working platform was via a steel stairway. The dingy could then be free to float with three or four metres of rope between the bow and the concrete riser. Once on the platform, access to the riverbank was gained by crossing a

25-foot rope bridge. The two of them made their way along the wobbly rope bridge. The bridge did not present any danger but at the same time did not inspire a feeling of security. The feeling of instability demanded diligent concentration until the user's feet were on terra firmer.

Morning for the guys had moved quickly and well into afternoon. Time would be against them fairly soon and hinder any intensions of further travel. Concerns had the two of them discussing the possibility of extended time being required to satisfy or exhaust their search. The Palm Chalets had a completely different appearance and layout in comparison to the Eagle Lodge. The complex offered the tourist a four-star rating within the design of a hunting-lodge facility.

John and Vic sat down at a table shaded by the trees and the added protection of a large parasol. Vic's shirt was beginning to be saturated in sweat.

They studied the surroundings and counted 22 chalets spread over a lush mature area roughly the size of two football fields. The place was certainly well-maintained with paved and wooden walkways creating a system of integration to all accommodation and amenities. The whole area benefitted from two natural levels. The land beyond the higher chalets ascended further and could easily support any future investment of further expansion. They discussed the strategy of enquiry they would adopt, and respecting the size and layout of the complex, they decided to take a direct and official approach.

John's presence being armed and uniformed would certainly raise the concerns of any individuals who existed beyond law-abiding boundaries. They decided that John would stay out of sight in the reception-staff area after informing the management of their line of enquiry into missing individuals.

Vic beckoned a waiter to bring him a pot of tea and a bottle of cold water. He noticed a fair amount of guests around the complex, and the tennis courts were empty, no doubt due to the afternoon temperature. The time was 16:10, and today was not yet blessed with a comforting breeze. There was no sign of Marc and Odette. His attention was taken by a few girls seated at the bar within the restaurant that were snapping selfies and laughing and joking. They appeared to be Tanzanian, and one of the girls had a more-coloured complexion than her two darker friends. The coloured girl looked a little embarrassed when Vic had caught a glimpse of her snapping a photo in his direction. She placed her cell phone back on the bar and continued the banter with her friends.

Vic again saw the girl looking towards him as he turned to look in their direction. This time, he was embarrassed and smiled at the girl.

The girl came off her seat and headed in the general direction of Vic; as she passed the toilet entrance, he realised she was coming to him. As he watched her strolling towards him, he wondered why many African women seemed to possess a natural effortless rhythm that drew attention more than some models on a catwalk would.

"Hello, I'm Jacqui," the girl said as she sat down and held out her hand.

"Patrick," Vic said and extended his hand in greeting.

Here we go again, he thought, *another distraction, another attractive young lady.*

"You buy me one drink, Patrick?"

"It's maybe a little early for that, Jacqui," Vic said.

"No, not alcohol," she said. "Coka please?" she replied.

Vic had the waiter bring over a bottle of coke and a glass half-filled with ice. She tipped the ice out into a plant pot, poured the coke and placed a drinking straw into the glass.

"You are American I think, Patrick?"

"Nope, Tanzanian, ma'am."

She drew her head back a little and returned the smile.

"No way."

"Just joking. Yep, American born and bred, ma'am, and you?"

"I am Tanzanian, come from Zanzibar. You know, I not eat yesterday and today," she continued.

Vic was fast becoming educated to the bar girls approach to visitors to Tanzania. He did admire their swift directness. *Maybe they think we live and socialise in bars just exactly as they do here, probably,* he thought to himself.

Vic returned to her with the same directness to inform her that he was a photographer who was not intending to spend the evening here. He told her he was hoping to locate and meet up with two friends who he believed were travelling in this area and he was presently waiting for his security escort to arrive.

"Do you stay here, Jacqui? In this area I mean."

She replied quite openly to him that she stayed here with customers in the chalets and sometimes in other hotels. She shared a small apartment with her friends not too far away.

"Jacqui, I see you are a bit of a photographer as well. You took my photo, yes?"

She laughed and was in denial at first but then showed Vic the photo she had taken of him.

Jacqui had cropped down the photo; it was actually a good photo, he thought. Vic asked if he could take her photo. She poured the remainder of the coke into her glass and agreed. He took out the SLR from the bag and took three photos of her through a 55mm lens and showed her the results on the monitor screen.

"Maybe I will meet my friends tomorrow or tonight. We do not have each other's cell phone numbers yet, but I am sure we will come across each other," Vic said.

He went onto describe Marc and Odette to the girl.

He had not spoken for long when Jacqui, with a more serious look on her face, started to scroll through her clearly endless photo album on her phone screen. Vic knew she was in search of something that would maybe be of interest to him; she was an avid photo person.

115

He noticed her smiling and expanding her screen view. She held out the phone to face the screen to Vic; he was quietly ecstatic. In front of him was a photo of Marc and Odette socialising at the very bar where Jacqui's friends were sitting.

"Whaoh, excellent, Jacqui. That's them. I knew they were around here. May I?" Vic asked as he took out his phone and continued to snap a photograph of her phone screen. "When was this, Jacqui?"

"Last Saturday evening; they were funny."

Vic's phone rang; it was John who informed him that he had important information. Vic ended the call.

"Jacqui, my escort needs to meet with me. Excuse me."

He found himself searching through his pockets. He leaned towards the girl and kissed her on the cheek while handing her 30,000 shillings just as John was approaching them. She was delighted and handed Vic her card with her name and number, which he put in his pocket. She smiled at John before walking back to the bar to join her friends.

"Long story, John. I will tell you shortly," Vic said before John could ask anything.

"Reception!" John said.

The complex manager had the guest register displayed on the desktop-computer monitor. Three individuals who had arrived by boat on the previous Friday evening had checked in. One checked out early Saturday morning and travelled downriver by the same boat. A Mr Graeme Brown, Mr Gordon Mackie and a Miss Wendy Simmons, who were all USA citizens, showed as the guests. The account was settled on Sunday evening by two of them who had arranged to check out on Monday morning.

They had clearly changed their plans and left on Sunday evening according to the manager.

He had assumed they left by vehicle.

The hotel manager respected John's request and provided printed-out copies of the invoices and passports of the three individuals. Vic asked John to contact Adimo in Dar to investigate any external calls that may have come to the Neptune Superior, requesting contact with the deceased or connection to room 1230.

They sat outside, well away from the main bar and restaurant, and photographed everything they had accumulated here at the Palms. The images were sent via cell phone to Adimo and Zoe.

"On a positive note, we have learned quite quickly of their recent moves; they have a three-day start on us, but, still, I think we have done extremely well, John, in one day. What do you recon?"

"I agree with that. I do not think we could have asked for better results. Let's face it, there is no way we were going to walk in somewhere and walk out with them in cuffs."

"Right, buddy. It's time we made a move. The time is coming towards five. We are locked in here until tomorrow, so we can take it easy tonight. Head back to the Eagle for an overnight, John?"

John agreed.

"They found out something happened to their man, Dennis, in Dar, yes?" John suggested.

"For sure they did, and I would bet my bottom dollar that they knew well before we did, the Sunday I recon. Tell you what, John, let's go and see if the management has the keys now to let us have a look inside those rooms, then we can piss off."

The search did not take the two of them long. It was not a crime scene, and the chances of anything being left behind to suggest their plans or whereabouts were slim. Vic briefly spoke to Zoe on the phone. Adimo had apparently relayed information to Zoe in regards to a cell-phone number that had made three attempts to connect to room 1230 without success on the Sunday evening. Vic's thoughts assured him that this sim card would no longer be in existence anymore.

The rooms gave up nothing of interest to them, and they thanked the manager and made their way to the dingy.

Dusk was just around the corner as the welcome appearance of the huge red ball in the sky was rapidly sinking, taking the scorching afternoon heat away with it.

Two young German kids were engaged in a stone-throwing competition, conveniently using the river to measure distance. The young boatman again came to offer his assistance in securing the dingy. This time, Vic beat John to tip the boy. The TV channel in the bar restaurant was fixed on an English-language-learning channel hosted by a Ugandan lady and was probably broadcast from Uganda. Tina was engrossed in the presentation with her elbow on the bar and her chin resting on her palm. Vic and John sat over towards one side to avoid disturbing her educational viewing.

"I knew I forgot something," Vic remarked. "I meant to call regarding reserving our rooms."

"No problem," John replied. "We have plenty time."

They discussed their thoughts on the subject of what Marc and Odette's next moves might entail. Their concluded assumptions suggested that those two guys were in trouble and had probably gained the information on Dennis's fate on the Sunday evening. To slim down their chances of detection, they would be wise to travel separately now.

It would be fair to assume that a possibility existed where their organisation had learned of the involvement of the CSIS being in pursuit of them as well as the Tanzanian police at a serious crime level. The only solution that an organised crime establishment would consider to resolve this situation would be to 'rub them out' so to speak. There was no other solution in their rules; zero -tolerance protocol prevailed.

Vic did not like the thought of this kind of situation: the good guys and the bad guys in a competitive challenge to either apprehend or destroy the fugitives. But that was now the rules in the field; they would have to speed up efforts and tactics. Either way, whether or not the good guys succeeded in their mission, the game was still on for netting the bigger fish.

The CSIS had their views and opinions of Marc and Odette. They were not regarded as 'lambs for the slaughter' or a couple of individuals running scared, erratic and unprepared. The outlook was quite the opposite in fact. These two people were more than likely to have access to contacts, resourceful to requirements and intelligence and to be considered dangerous at any cost. Marc had devoted some of his previous time applying his skills as a mercenary in South America and Africa. Odette had served four years in the Israeli military.

The TV series ended with some music and the ascending tributes on the screen. Tina yawned and stretched her arms and noticed John and Vic as she turned around.

"Hey," she greeted them. "You guys gonna stay? Of course you are." She smiled. "It's gonna be dark soon."

She made her way to the opposite end of the bar to serve the lady of one of the German families.

Arrangements were in place for the chopper to arrive to pick them up at 10:30 in the morning. No planned destination had been favoured yet. It was mentioned that some reconnaissance in the area may be beneficial before heading back to Dar. That would be a positive day's work for everyone. This would be discussed formally in the morning with HQ.

John interrupted their conversation by nudging Vic with his elbow. Vic looked in the direction of John's head nod to see Tina bouncing along happily towards them, carrying the hotel register.

She greeted them. "I will get you drinks, yes?" she asked.

"Yes, Tina, please. Two cold beers please."

"Hey, John, go and slip into some casual wear, buddy; we ain't going anywhere tonight."

John thought about the offer and picked up one of the key cards that Tina had left.

"Room ten looks good," he said to Vic as he looked at the card.

"Go for it, buddy. I will get your beer put back in the freezer."

"I see you have been enhancing your English, Tina."

"Enhancing?" Tina replied.

"Eh, sorry, improving."

"Ah yes, 'improve' I understand. Yes, this lesson on TV is good. Every Wednesday it comes. Today, I learned three new words and some little things. Important, recognise and gentleman," she said as she consulted her notepad.

John appeared back from his room, dressed in shorts, sandals, police polo shirt and a police ball cap. Apart from the AK47, his appearance was regular.

"OK," Tina said, "can I have your passports to make copy please, 'gentlemen'?"

Vic applauded her with some light clapping.

The two men looked at each other and could not contain their laughing while Vic was rummaging through an abundance of passport copies in his bag, attempting to find his.

Minutes later, Tina arrived back with Vic's passport and John's ID. They ordered drinks and poured the bottled beer into the frosted glasses.

John complimented Tina on the presentation of the room. She explained that the two rooms were identical and reminded them that there were no mosquitos as she glanced at Vic, smiling.

John finished his second beer.

"Come on, let's take a look outside, Vic."

"You like another beer?" Vic asked.

"No thanks. The customers may term me as an unwelcome distraction armed and holding a beer in my hand," John said, smiling.

"Right enough, buddy. I suppose you can't leave that weapon out of your possession," Vic said and got himself another beer.

With the sun now gone, the moon was rising and transforming everything into an illuminated, colourless landscape. The two German kids were rapidly throwing their last barrage of stones into the river as their parents were instructing them to get prepared for bed. They checked the dingy and John answered a few of Vic's questions relating to the river. Vic sat down his bottle and glass on a table. He selected a stone from the flowerbed and hurled it far out into the river.

He laughed and let John know that he had an urge to do that since he noticed the kids when they first arrived.

"Do you think you can reach the opposite bank?" John said, laughing.

"What! Not even you could manage that, buddy."

John headed indoors. Vic stayed a few moments, admiring the moon and the silence and gave some thought towards the task that lay ahead for them. Things were going to become more demanding for them now with the presence of danger increasing, he knew that. Marc and Odette were the known, what were the unknowns? he thought.

Vic went indoors. The time was approaching 22:30. Tina offered more beer for them, John declined. She was finishing off the cash report and stock count for the day.

"Yeh, why not, ma'am, one more," Vic said.

She came over and sat down two bottles of cold Tusker beer.

"I will come and drink one cup of beer with you guys in five minutes," she said.

John stood up and bid goodnight to Vic. They shook hands and Vic thanked John for his efforts today. John looked in the direction where Tina was discussing work with the duty receptionist. He laughed a little while shaking his head slightly.

"Good luck," he said to Vic as he raised his eyebrows and tilted his head upwards.

Vic turned around to see Tina at the reception area, then quickly turned back to John with a wide-eyed smile.

"Hey, buddy, with one of the hotel staff, no way Jose," Vic said with a defiant look on his face. John smiled as he made his way to his room.

"Remember, you are not in Canada, my friend; enjoy your beer, Mr Vic, goodnight."

"Goodnight, John. 07:30 for breakfast then?"

John was in uniform and already seated for breakfast, enjoying fresh fruit and coffee when Vic arrived just after 07:30. They exchanged greetings and Vic explained some of the content of Adimo's phone call to him at 07:00. Vic excused himself and made his way to the breakfast buffet before the kids invaded. He returned happily with more than enough scrambled eggs and sausage on his plate. John arranged another pot of coffee for them.

"You're looking happy, Mr Vic."

"Oh yeh, let me tell you. We are not heading back to Dar S at the moment. Apparently, Adimo and your colleague, Winston, are arriving soon at an area not too far from here, some hunting lodge. She will send the chopper for us a little later after they are dropped off, around 11:30."

"I know that place; we know some people there. That's true, it is not too far, providing you are fortunate enough to travel by air, about 75 kilometres," John replied.

Adimo suggested to them to spend some time getting some inspiration from the air and giving some thought into which exit roads from the Palms area could be desirable for a couple of runaways to travel. Some aerial photos of the area were also suggested.

Vic and Zoe had already brought Adimo up to speed with the scale of resources that the two fugitives could, or more than likely 'would', be able to access.

They would touch base with Adimo and Winston in the Selous camp in the afternoon before they all headed back to Dar S.

"Are we just about ready to head upriver then, John buddy?"

John visited the men's room, then thanked the receptionist. As John arrived back, Vic finished off his coffee and also paid a visit to the men's room.

From the mooring point, John could see Vic thanking the staff and giving Tina a hug and a kiss. Vic then made his way to the mooring.

John smiled and thought to himself that the hug and kiss was probably just a friendly end to a short acquaintance. He also reminded himself that in Tanzania, they had a few sayings to compliment this parting gesture.

John handed their harbour master his final tip, bringing another smile to the boy's face.

"OK, Captain, I've checked the fuel," John said. "Let's sail."

The hour-plus journey upstream was hitch free. Vic sadly had no more croc or hippo appearances to enjoy and photograph.

They sat down in the shade of a large mature Kigelia tree close to the trunk. The chopper would be due to arrive in 20 minutes, if on schedule.

Vic commented on how quiet and peaceful this area seemed to be. So very peaceful, he said. John agreed and added that the ambience would always be changing and the time of day that accommodated their visits was maybe why.

"What are these things hanging from this tree, buddy?"

"Sausages," John jovially replied.

"Yeh right, bullshit, like what I had for breakfast, only mine did not come from this baby here."

John laughed.

"No really, Vic. This is the Kigelia tree. The nickname is 'sausage tree', on account of those big sausage-looking seedpods hanging from it, those are the fruit. There are plenty in our country, and the tree should be due to flower around now or maybe next month."

"OK cool. I am assuming you can eat those?" Vic asked.

"Not if you value your life, my friend. They are highly poisonous to humans. I have heard that some tribal people have some special knowledge on how to cook them, but I would never go there; just avoid them. Most birds and animals that can reach them feast on them. Hippos usually scoop up the ones that have already fallen to the ground. That is how the seeds are dispersed, through the animals' dung droppings wherever they shit," John continued. "They do have a traditional medicinal value though."

"Absolutely. I understand that part, John."

"You know something, Vic, those sausages can easily weigh up to 10 kilos and more. It would be unwise to pitch your tent under the Kigelia tree, especially a big one. This tree has to be carefully managed also if hanging over roads and footpaths in towns. Here in the savanna, they are free, but be aware, my friend."

Vic was now aware of himself, scanning the branches above him for any potential hazard that could become detached from its fixture and transform him into an undignified heap on the ground.

John laughed loudly at Vic's awareness and concern above him.

"Don't worry, my friend, I already checked before we sat down."

Vic shook his head, laughing.

"You are some piece of work, buddy, some piece of work you are, John. I'd be screwed here without you."

Suddenly, the familiar thumping sound of the chopper blades startled them, and immediately the aircraft appeared in the sky, banking to the right, on approach to the landing spot.

Brian brought the chopper down quickly and smoothly and shut down the engine. Brian, along with the two casually dressed policemen who were responsible for the dingy, came out of the chopper.

"Hey, guys, ya'awl help yourselves to some drinks," Brian said as he sat a cool box down on the ground.

They moved over to the shade of the Kigelia tree where John and Vic had their bags. Vic chatted with Brian and informed him of the recent education he had gained on the subject of the Kigelia tree and its reproductive cycle.

"No shit," Brian said. "I heard about that tree before. Rings a bell, buddy."

John handed the other two police the boat bag and they set off for the river.

They had a quick discussion on the subject of some aerial exploration over the area mainly focusing on the road networks. The river was now of no interest to them.

Following this, they would rendezvous with Adimo at the hunting lodge.

"Yup, we can do that," Brian said.

"Is there any developments on information at the lodge, Brian?" Vic asked.

"No idea, buddy. They got out and I lifted off. You will find out soon enough."

They finished their drinks and climbed aboard the aircraft. Brian went through the start-up procedure and spun the machine's turbine into life.

They followed the river downstream, and within minutes, they were over the Palms Chalets area at an altitude of just 1500 feet. It soon became clear from the view that any vehicle leaving the Palms and heading northeast in the general direction of Dar es Salaam would quickly gain advantage by being able to change to different road networks easily. They could gain no information at this time, but Dar S could easily be quickly navigated, providing they had a vehicle. Vic told himself that they did.

The manager at the Palms provided some information that was probably significant rather than nothing. The manager who was in bed at the time had been absolutely certain of hearing some kind of confrontation involving a male and female voice around midnight on the Sunday evening. He then heard a vehicle driving off in the opposite direction of Dar S. He had said it meant nothing to him, as he had heard this kind of thing on many an occasion. As he put it, maybe boyfriend and girlfriend, husband and wife, prostitute and customer, husband and someone else's wife, who knows, he said. The most significant information had come from one of the reception girls who mentioned a man requesting the room location for Marc and Odette on Sunday evening, a non-resident.

"How long until we touch base at the hunting lodge, Brian?" Vic asked.

"As long as you need, Vic. It's still early. We can make it in 30 minutes without breaking records."

"OK, we can go for that one. We can observe and photograph as we go." He looked at John.

"OK with you, John?"

"Yeh, go with that."

The vastness below fascinated Vic, but at the same time it placed a feeling of 'the needle in the haystack' to deal with in his mind. *Never mind,* he thought, *never mind.*

During the flight to the Mambo Hunting Lodge, they got a much better idea of the road and track network below them, heading into the Selous game reserve. They discussed their thoughts and gut feelings of what these two fugitives may be planning and where they may be heading.

To head back to Dar would seem the obvious, but there were many eyes in Dar that would be looking out for them, especially now when the Tanzanian law enforcement was aware of their physical appearance, let alone their own organisation.

Dar requirements were covered in regards to boots on the ground and organised intelligence methods in place by the Tanzanian police and the CSIS.

The not-so-obvious routes to disappear would be through the Selous; they agreed that this should not be overlooked and some serious efforts should be concentrated in this area at least until efforts proved absolutely fruitless.

John did explain that the Selous was the largest game reserve in Africa and probably the size of some states in other countries.

If they could, and it was a big 'if'; John mentioned if they could make it to Zambia or DRC, then they would be well on their way to freedom. The DRC would not be an easy place for any outside authority to operate in.

Brian offered his opinion as a bush pilot to inform them that using the Selous as a platform to escape would not be a bad idea at all. He reminded the guys of the amount of airstrips in this vast area that accommodated small fixed-wing aircraft. He also reminded them of unofficial airstrips that could pop up fairly quickly at any time as a convenience if a situation demanded, especially during the dry season.

They decided that a meeting among them was required. It all made sense and brought a feeling of excitement to Vic. They were now at 2,000 feet and Vic carried on photographing the vista below him, what was left of the green areas supported huge herds of blue wildebeest and zebra; elephants came into view also. He looked forward to zooming into the images he had taken later when he had some peace and quiet.

"There we are," John said.

John pointed to the large curve in the river and the lodge not so far from the bank.

"I've never seen a hunting lodge before," Vic remarked. "In Canada, we have more like small cabins for hunting that are sometimes very remote purpose-built things."

They descended down to the landing spot, creating a small typhoon and displacing debris and dust in all directions. Brian shut down; the dogs could still be heard and their barking subsided as the chopper engine fell silent.

Adimo and her officer, Winston, were seated in the shade of the open restaurant, enjoying tea and coffee. The restaurant was exceptionally busy.

"Hi, Inspector. Officer, how goes it, guys?" Vic asked.

"Marvellous, Agent Vic, marvellous. Please have a seat, guys," Adimo said.

John and Adimo officially greeted each other and had some verbal exchange in Swahili; they ordered some drinks. Adimo leaned towards Vic's ear and quietly mentioned not to discuss anything outside the fact that they were engaged in locating some missing visitors to Tanzania.

"Of course, ma'am," Vic assured her.

123

"How was your stay over there, Vic?" Adimo asked. "The Eagle Lodge I believe? Did you have a pleasant stay?"

Vic could see John's eyes casually looking over at him and then moved away back in conversation with his colleague, Winston.

"Absolutely, Adimo, faultless. It's a really nice place to spend time."

"Good, that's nice."

"Hey, Adimo." Vic was gazing over her at the parking area. "What the hell is a sports bike doing out here? It's a bit out of place, yeh?"

"Hmm, that belongs to one of Neil's friends or colleague or whatever, an American."

"Neil? American?" Vic replied. "Excuse me two minutes, ma'am."

Vic walked over to look at the motorcycle and take a couple of photos with his cell phone. He seemed to admire the machine before walking back.

"Do you like motorcycles, Vic?" Adimo asked.

"Hell yes. I have had a few in my time and I have owned one of those as well. Nice bike, Honda Fireblade. I was not sure of the colour until I went over there. It's black, but it is so covered in mud and dust, it is hard to tell. It just looks like something out of that old Mel Gibson movie 'Mad Max'. How about you, Adimo, do you like bikes?" Vic continued.

"I do, some, but only to look at."

"Who is Neil? Is he American?"

Adimo laughed and had to take the coffee cup away from her mouth.

"No," she said. "Two different people. Don't be asking Neil if he is American," she whispered. "He is Australian, a PH here in Tanzania 'Professional Hunter'. He is around, and you will meet him. He and some other Americans around here have been quite helpful to us during our early stage in this investigation."

"Tell you what though, ma'am, that bike rider must be keen and have a big heart to ride that type of machine on some of these roads. Is there somewhere we can talk?" Vic asked Adimo.

"Yes, of course. Let's walk towards the chopper."

As they started to make a move, Neil appeared from the bar area, holding a sandwich and a bottle of beer.

"Hi, Neil, I thought you had left us and went off on another hunt," Adimo said jokingly.

"No ways, ma'am, day off today," Neil said as he took a bite from his sandwich and raised his bottle of beer.

"Neil, this I my colleague, Vic," she said as she introduced them to each other.

"Nice to meet you, buddy. You're Australian, I see," Vic said.

"Yep, too true, mate, Australian/African more like. You sound kinda North American, Canada maybe?" Neil said.

Neil's statement hung for a few seconds before Vic replied.

"Yeh, I am actually," Vic said with a smile.

He seemed impressed, as most people's first choice if they were having a stab would usually indicate an assumption of him being American.

Adimo had a curious admiring smile on her face towards Neil's confident innuendo.

"Would you like a drink, guys?" Neil asked.

"Later, thank you, Neil. We are going to the helicopter to check some material," Adimo replied.

"No worries, guys. I got them waiting for you."

With Adimo in civilian dress, the appearance of the three of them could have been three casual friends or even people having a safari holiday.

"Nice bike!" Vic shouted to Neil as they walked off.

Neil gave Vic a thumb's up gesture as he mingled his way in towards the bar.

"Seems like a nice guy," Vic said.

"Yes, I like him actually. He is very helpful when he can be. He has lived here a long time, you know, and he carries a wealth of knowledge and experience of this area and the wildlife."

"That photo I sent you, at best I can put that down to last Saturday evening at the Palms. At that point, they look pretty carefree and enjoying themselves, but something went down on Sunday though. They either got wind of something or something got wind of them. Which direction they headed in is anyone's guess at present, but the possibility of heading into the Selous should be seriously considered," Vic said.

"Ah, I meant to mention to you yesterday, your man, John, is a star, clever guy, Adimo."

"Thank you; they both are."

"I would normally say to you 'how so' regarding your theory of the Selous Vic, but I did put some thought into that along the same lines as you just mentioned. It is a possibility worth investigating."

Adimo mentioned that Zoe was involved in the mammoth task of searching for clues in Dar S with a 'boots on the ground approach'.

They were trying to locate any witnesses in Dar that may know someone or something relating to the death of Dennis Vatel. Adimo had managed to get the captain's approval for another three officers, but only two to help out on the case during the day and one on evenings.

Adimo knew the perfect one to assist on this case, but that could never be. He was already retired; only she had 24/7 access to him, only her. Adimo had put some thought into the possibility of Peter coming out of retirement to help with this case. It was something she dismissed the thought of as she always regarded this as impossible. She had decided to start by putting this idea to Peter when they next met. *Never say never,* she thought to herself.

"So, ma'am, what do you have in mind? Zoe is in Dar, no doubt, doing as much as she can, and what she is involved in is of paramount importance. You and I are in the open park which may or may not be productive, but in a way, we have just got started and quickly picked up a good lead on things now. How much are we going to concentrate our efforts in the Selous, the bush, the savanna?"

"A lot," she answered. "The fact that one of them has been accounted for and two are still missing, this is what we know. I cannot suggest that they are on the run, dead or otherwise just now, this we will have to find out ourselves.

"If they turn up dead, Vic, then that is the end of our involvement and you guys will be destined to whatever path is open from then on, unless of course there is any proposal to apply a change to protocol.

"At present, in this region, we are eagles stalking from the air. We are in need of change now, and when we identify exactly the process we wish to apply, I think we can get the approval."

"OK, I will buy that."

"On the subject of eagles, Adimo, why is the Eagle Lodge named so? I only seemed to see crocs, hippos and monkeys there."

Adimo paused a little and tilted her head back to look at the sky.

"You should ask my father that question," she said. "He taught me how to see them."

"See what?" Vic asked.

"Eagles of course. If you have time on a clear day, early morning or afternoon, lie flat on your back and scan the sky above you for a while; once your eyes are adjusted, look carefully and slowly sweep all over. At some point, you will get lucky and see one or two. They are very high up. Vultures are up there too, but they tend to be bigger and have much more squared wings, and they group. Concentrate on finding lone birds hunting in their territories; you will know when you see them."

Vic found himself looking at the sky for a few seconds.

"Thanks for that, ma'am. I think you have something there. That answers my question I suppose."

The Crocodile, Hippo or Monkey Lodge just would not cut it anyway, he thought.

Adimo noticed the time was 14:00 and suggested heading to the restaurant for lunch before travelling back to Dar.

"You should need a change of clothes," she said jokingly to Vic.

"Do I smell that bad?"

"Come on, let's go to the restaurant. Brian is already there," she said.

The plan they had discussed and set out would be run past Zoe, then a meeting with Captain Hamisi would be required to present their proposal for approval.

Travelling back to Dar today was essential. Zoe would continue her endeavours in her role in Dar. Adimo and Winston would cover Dar and the Selous region. Vic and John would be based in the Selous to cover areas, as they became of interest. With their main tool being the chopper, they could operate as a kind of rapid intervention team when circumstances demanded. Adimo sat having lunch with her two officers. They shared information and entered some input into present requirements. She was thinking to alternate

Winston and John in their duties but decided to leave things as they were at present.

She was due another meeting with Peter, she thought, then she corrected her priorities in thought. She was not 'due'; she wanted another meeting with him. This was voluntary, off the record, conversing that could maybe lead to constructive development for her and her team.

Brian, Vic and Neil seemed to be engrossed in conversation while having a stand-up lunch at the bar. No doubt Vic's curiosity over the motorcycle would be fulfilled following a chat with Neil.

Bloody motorcycles, she thought to herself with a smile. Her opinion of motorcycles that she had given to Vic was not entirely true. She disliked them and had no interest towards them at all.

Winston received a call on his cell phone. He covered one ear and left the restaurant to avoid the surrounding noise. Adimo returned from talking to Brian at the bar and informed John that they would be making a move shortly. She had her cell phone in hand with an intention to call Captain Hamisi.

As she manoeuvred her way through the chairs and tables of the diners to make her call, Winston was making his way back inside. He stopped and beckoned Adimo to come towards him as he again turned around to move outside the restaurant. Adimo could see a clear expression of concern on his face.

John watched them engaging in conversation as he was finishing off his coffee and snack. He could tell by their expressions, arm movements and body language that something was about to demand attention. She beckoned John to come outside and instructed Winston to go inside and inform Brian and Vic to make their way out. She then made a quick call on her cell phone as John made his way towards the chopper.

She completed her call to her captain after informing him of the news she had just received.

When they were all together outside, she shared the news with them that she had just received from Winston.

"Gents, a situation has arisen within the past hour or so, not so far from here. The local police are in attendance at present. At this point in time, we know that there is a body; a deceased white male has been discovered in the direction of the Palm Chalets area on the riverbank side of the main road."

Vic looked confused as he looked at John who shrugged his shoulders and shook his head.

"I have informed Captain Hamisi," she continued. "He has requested us to investigate and deal with it accordingly, and he was brief in his instruction. Brian, we need to forget Dar at this moment and prioritise this. This may be something or nothing relating to our investigation, we will know soon enough."

"OK, what do you have in mind? How many people travelling, all of us?" Brian asked.

"Yes, unless anyone has a constructive reason to stay here?"

"No, ma'am, let's get to it," Vic replied.

Adimo requested five minutes and walked back towards the restaurant. Brian had left the chopper cocked so a quick start-up was in progress. Adimo made her way to Neil and thanked him for his help. She explained that something had come up and they had to leave.

"You have my number, Neil. Could you find out the availability of accommodation in the lodge here and let me know?" she said as she made her way out.

"Crikey, are you guys coming back?" Neil shouted.

"Not sure; later, Neil."

Adimo ran bent over as she approached the chopper under the constant speed of the main rotor. A hand came out of the access door to assist her in boarding.

After lifting off, Brian kept a low altitude and followed the river downstream as advised by Adimo's officers. Adimo caught Vic's attention seated opposite her and pointed down from one of the starboard windows. Vic soon focused on the Eagle Lodge down below and nodded to Adimo in recognition.

"Maybe number two?" Vic said.

Adimo drew air through her teeth.

"It's looking that way, isn't it."

Winston signalled to Brian and pointed down. They could see the activity down ahead of them. There were people and objects just outside the cover of the forest a few hundred metres from the river. At the other side of the forest, at the road, the police vehicle came into view. Brian nodded and banked the chopper over to negotiate an approach from the river. The chopper descended in an approach towards the scene. Adimo and Vic could see the Palms Chalets maybe just a kilometre or so away through the starboard window.

"Well, here we go," Adimo said with a smile to Vic.

Brian brought the chopper down 200 metres away from the scene towards the river. The savanna grasslands here were quite short due to an abundance of base rock that assisted in quick drainage into the river. Brian and Winston stayed with the chopper, while the others made their way towards the scene.

Two policemen with two villagers and their dog were standing quite a few metres away from a yellow tarp spread across the grass. When the investigators were within a distance of around 100 metres from the scene, they were periodically breathing in the unmistakeable stench of decomposing human remains. The four guardians of the remains seemed to have positioned themselves upwind of the tarp.

They first walked around the tarp to greet the police and the villagers. The local villagers were fishermen that had been netting the river close by and had noticed vultures above and descending on the area. The presence of the vultures so close had prompted the men to tie up their boat and investigate. Adimo and John had a conversation with them in Swahili.

Vic tried to change his position now and again; the smell was unbearable, but he could not find any sanctuary.

The policemen walked towards the tarp and the investigators followed.

"This is apparently not a pretty sight," Adimo said.

"I can imagine; let's get on with it."

The stench of decomposing flesh was intense as they got closer; Adimo could feel it clinging to her throat. The policemen moved two of the rocks being used to weigh down the corners and pulled back the tarp.

A huge swarm of large flies broke the silence as they came off the remains and swarmed around the immediate area. Adimo gasped and briefly turned away before returning her focus on what lay before them.

Vic handed her a handkerchief which she accepted and covered her nose and mouth.

Apart from the head, shoulders, one leg and the remains of the upper arms, there was not much else there. The entire abdominal content was missing, allowing the vertebrae to be visible.

"God Almighty," Vic said. "What the hell happened here?"

He moved away a few metres and sat down his bag and returned with the camera.

"Please, John, could you go inside the forest with the two police and have a look around? We still have a female missing also. Ask the fishermen if they could work their dog around in there?" Adimo said.

Vic took shots of the remains. Adimo explained to Vic that while the fishermen had been fishing the area close by for the past three days, it was only this morning they had seen vultures. She had agreed with the fishermen in their assumption of the body being dragged out of the cover of the forest by a predator or predators during the night. Probably hyenas, she mentioned.

"Adimo, please," Vic said as he handed her the camera.

Vic slipped on a pair of latex gloves and squatted down, tolerating the flies. He fondled with the head of the corpse. As he moved the head around, it was clear that the eyes and lips were gone; it was more or less unidentifiable by facial features. His hands ran through the hair with fingers searching. Adimo observed him and she could tell he was no stranger to this. The only clothing remaining were partial blue jeans, a black T-shirt and a high-quality walking boot on the remaining left leg. Vic turned the back of the head around to face Adimo; his index finger was depressing the small holes in the back of the skull. She knew what he had found. Vic smiled and asked her to photograph the head; there were three small entry holes within a two-inch group.

Vic peeled off the gloves and placed them on the tarp next to the remains. He stood up and put his arm around Adimo and walked her to where his bag was.

"Small calibre?" Adimo asked.

"Yeh, and no exit wounds. Probably subsonic 22."

"Can we assume this is, 'sorry', was Marc Dupuis? Vic, to me there is something that does not match the hair colour to the photos."

"Bravo, madam, one minute please."

129

Vic took out his mobile and made a call. He put the phone back in his pocket and slipped on another pair of latex gloves. He squatted down with the remains again and poured his bottle of drinking water over the hair to reveal a reddish-blonde colour and checked the upper arms and shoulders.

"Bingo 'not'," he said. "Well, ma'am, as we suspected, it's not Marc. Marc also has a tattoo of an eagle on his upper right arm."

He took a small sample of flesh and placed it in a tamper-proof specimen bottle. He gazed up at the vultures that were not so far away, patiently gliding the thermals.

"Well, in a way, I am glad that this pair would appear to be still at large. I have a feeling that their fellow colleagues may have underestimated them," he said.

Adimo widened her eyes and slowly nodded as if to partly agree with what Vic said.

He ditched the gloves and stood up.

The police and fishermen strolled out of the forest in discussion of their findings. Adimo instructed the police that they had completed their inspection of the remains. They again covered the body and informed Adimo of the procedure they would follow to have the body sent to Dar S. The dog had easily located the original location of the body, and Adimo and Vic followed John to this location about 60 metres away. John handed Vic a single 22 casing that he had found nearby. It was quite clear to them that an assassination-style killing had taken place here. Adimo maintained her public-relations credibility by gifting some money to the fishermen. Time was on their side for a change; it looked like they would make it back to Dar S this evening.

Guests of the Selous

Marc and Odette had underestimated the task before them after deciding to choose west into the Selous as their route. They accepted this as the incident at the Palms left them narrow on choice. Heading to Dar would have probably proved disastrous for them. The assassin whose task was to silence them was now en route to Dar es Salaam in pieces. The two of them were now in a vehicle that did not belong to them, and they had taken charge of the few firearms and ammunition stored within the vehicle. They were thankful for the firearms cache, and the fact that the vehicle could not be traced back to them had to be two plus points in this scenario. Marc, Odette and Dennis had a code between them; the code was simple. If any of them did not get an answer from the person dialled after three attempts in close intervals, it was then assumed that the person had been either compromised or incapacitated. The situation they had encountered last Sunday evening had dealt them those very cards.

Be it luck or vigilance, they had another piece of good fortune on the Sunday evening as they were hastily packing their belongings in preparation to leave the Palms by taxi. Marc had left the accommodation just to make sure their taxi was there waiting. He had noticed a vehicle approach and park outside the security barrier with its lights on. As he approached, he observed a man in the reception, leaning on the counter, waiting for one of the staff who was crouched down on the floor, retrieving some folders from a low-level shelf. He recognised this visitor whose appearance raised an immediate red flag with Marc. He quickly moved towards the Toyota 4x4; the engine was running with the dipped headlamps on; the taxi behind was his. He paid the driver and sent him on his way and then got into the Toyota rear-seating area. He moved his body down as far as he could to the floor after adjusting the interior courtesy lamp switch to the central neutral position, disarming the lamp circuit.

Less than a minute later, he could hear the footsteps approaching the vehicle and the driver's door opening; as the driver stepped in, Marc acted fast. Before the door was closed, he raised himself and the driver found just enough time to turn around to catch a glimpse of Marc but was too late to lean enough forward or sideways to avert his assailant restraining him. Marc's left arm had gone around from the back and across the man's neck with his right hand securing a tight grip on his left wrist.

He tightened his hold, forcing the driver's neck hard against the headrest assembly. The man in the front struggled and choked; his flaying arms and hands fell short of making any contact with Marc in the rear. Disaster almost changed the circumstances when the man's left arm struck the gear lever and engaged a gear, but the efficient hold on the well-maintained vehicle's parking brake ensured the engine to stall with a quick shudder of the vehicle. Time seemed to pass slowly before the man started to show signs of being completely incapacitated. Marc finally let go and took some time to regain himself by taking deep breaths. There was still a pulse present when Marc managed to pull the victim between the two front seats and over into the rear of the vehicle. He found some heavy cable ties in the rear and zip-tied the victim's hands behind his back and bound his ankles. He put his other cell phone to use for the first time to call Odette. He noticed this guy was unarmed and quickly searched the interior; inside the glove compartment revealed a semi-automatic 22-calibre pistol with a fitted moderator. Odette appeared running towards the vehicle, carrying her bag and Marc's backpack. Marc took some verbal abuse from her as she opened the rear door of the Toyota to throw in the luggage. She gasped when she saw the man in front of her crumpled on the floor.

"Shit! What happened?" she yelled. "You killed him. Do you know who that is…?"

"Of course I fucking know. Get in!" Marc demanded.

She got into the vehicle and Marc quickly drove off. Odette looked around the vehicle and its contents; she opened the glove compartment to reveal the handgun, and she then looked at the guy on the floor again.

"Marc, I'm sorry. Really, I just got surprised back there."

"Well, that makes three of us."

She read the situation and realised what must have unfolded and what had to be done.

"Where are we going?" Odette asked.

"No idea; we have to deal with him first."

They travelled for a while along the main track to an area void of any lights or dwellings, where Marc stopped the vehicle. He concentrated and felt for a pulse at the man's neck; he looked at Odette anxiously.

"Alive?" Odette asked.

Without answering, Marc got out and dragged him out of the vehicle. The two of them dragged him into the forest, well away from the road. The man began to become conscious and kicked his legs violently and easily broke free of Marc and Odette's hold. He had managed to break the cable tie binding his ankles; he was shouting and cursing them and kicked the legs away from Odette who crashed to the forest floor painfully. Before Marc had even realised that this man had managed to get up and onto his feet, Marc was shoulder-charged and knocked to the ground. Now running with his hands tied behind his back, he was making his way towards the vehicle. Marc, still on the ground, flipped over onto his stomach and squeezed the trigger of the pistol when a muffled sound could be heard. Their captive lost his stride and impacted the forest floor heavily. The 22-calibre bullet's point of impact found the man's lower back; he was powerless and seemed unable to control his legs when Marc and Odette stood over him. His cursing had not been affected, and after directing some profanities at the two of them, he was able to spit on Odette's legs. Marc instructed Odette to go to the vehicle. Halfway to the vehicle, Odette heard a sound like three, rapid, muffled handclaps coming from the darkness she had just left. Marc returned, holding both cable ties and three 22 shell casings; the two of them got inside the vehicle.

"That is what was intended for us. Are you OK?" Marc said.

They drove west and into the Selous region; there were clusters of lights visible far in the distance. They decided that until they got their bearings, it would be best to carry on towards those lights.

It was early morning when Marc was filling up the fuel tanks with diesel fuel being delivered by a small boy via a hand pump. The village was small and the access road to this sparse little place branched off the main track. Odette lay motionless on the rear floor covered with some blankets. Four 20-litre jerry cans full of diesel fuel were strapped in the rear pick-up bed of the vehicle. The boy spoke in Swahili, commenting something to Marc. Marc displayed some actions and gestures using his face, voice and hands in an attempt to declare his lack of knowledge and understanding of the Swahili language. The boy laughed and pointed at Marc's boots with a 'thumbs up' gesture.

"Good, very very," the boy said in English.

Marc laughed and lifted his right boot off the ground to look at it, then thanked the boy and tipped him along with the fuel payment. After a check on the oil and fluid levels, he turned around and drove through the village to the main road. He picked up some water, cigarettes, sodas, chips and camping odds and ends. Odette sat up in the backseat when Marc gave her the all clear.

"That's both tanks full and reserve; we have range now, but I wish I knew where the fuck we are heading," he said. "How is the cell phone signal, babe?"

He smiled at her in the rear-view mirror. The signal was non-existent. The two of them decided to contact some people they knew in Tanzania as soon as any signal was strong enough. Marc pulled in under some trees close to a kopje to benefit from the shade. He leaned his chin on his hands over the steering wheel and stared at the vast wilderness in front of them. He shook himself out of the semi-trance.

"OK, babe, stock take," Marc said.

He moved over to the front passenger's seat and the two of them checked over the firearms. The 22 semi-auto pistol had already proved useful; another two spare clip magazines for it were found. The other two firearms were an AK47 and a 30-06 Springfield-calibre hunting rifle fitted with a high-powered scope. All had liberal supplies of ammunition and in perfect condition.

"This guy was sure prepared, eh?" Marc said.

Odette was arranging the ammunition.

"Yep. When was the last time you seen him?"

"Last night." Marc grinned. "About two years back in Dar S."

"Last month for me, Dar S also. He was with Dennis."

Marc looked at her in a 'matter-of-fact' way as he cleaned and loaded the Browning 22 pistol.

"One thing is for sure; it could not have been that monkey who caught up with Dennis last night. His name was Kyle yeh? South African?" Marc said.

"Yes, Kyle. I never knew any other name for him."

"Anyway, to hell with him, Odette. Better him than us over there."

Marc thought of how easily the outcome in the forest could have ended differently if the cable tie binding this man's hands had failed.

Their plan was to travel into the Selous and arrange to be flown out of Tanzania. First, they had to establish where they were and where they would have to head to. They would try to get some information at the next village in the morning. Receiving a mobile-phone signal of significant strength was crucial for them to get out of Tanzania. Tonight, they would concentrate on getting some proper rest and some much-needed sleep.

Odette completed the ammunition count and loaded the assault and hunting rifles. She expressed how hungry she was.

"Sorry, Odette, this will have to do for now." He handed her a can of coke and a couple of packs of chips.

"Sit tight, babe. I will have something for the pot tonight, promise."

He looked around briefly and noticed a few groups of large pigeons coming and going on the branches above them. Odette looked up at the birds, then back at Marc, smiling. *No, we won't starve tonight,* she thought.

"Whaoh, ooh, Marc," she said excitedly. "We have a signal."

Odette's vivid dream made no sense nor had any meaning and was interrupted by the process of awakening with a sound that had taken her from her sleep. She lay still for a few seconds, collecting her thoughts on where she was and how she got there. She quickly sat up in the rear of the vehicle to watch a massive herd of buffalos strolling slowly past in the direction of the river. Marc was gone and there was no pistol or hunting rifle and the AK47 lay beside her. She felt a little apprehension taking over her. *What time is it, what day is it?* she thought. It was then the realisation flooded back in her mind, beginning with the incident in the forest close to the Palms Lodge. Her cell phone informed her it was 07:40 on Tuesday morning. A message was highlighted on her phone and she immediately knew the sender would either be Marc or the network provider. 'gone for a stroll, c u soon' was displayed on the screen; relief took over the anxiety. She watched the stragglers of the herd strolling past the vehicle as if the vehicle did not exist. She drank from a can of soda that lay opened from the evening. She felt the need to urinate and cursed the buffalo herd.

The previous evening, they had dined on pigeon cooked over an open fire. Marc had dispatched four birds using the 22-calibre pistol. To save time, he had removed the breast meat and legs for roasting and burned the rest in the fire.

Odette was well-aware of lions following buffalo herd, but the desire to urinate was the focus of her attention just now. As she was entering the vehicle again, she noticed the pigeon's congregating on the same branches where their flock members had met their end on the previous evening.

She answered the incoming call on her cell phone.

"Hey, Odette, good morning, just making sure you are up. I got a call this morning. We can be picked up at an airstrip around 180 kilometres from here, that's our closest option."

Odette was about to speak.

"Save the sim credit, I will be there in 15 minutes."

He lay for another few minutes, observing everything out in front of him through the high magnification of the riflescope.

No sign of any vehicles was apparent, but there were signs of pastoral land that would indicate some form of settlements would have developed in those areas. Could his organisation have people in these remote areas looking out for them, of course they could, he thought. An all-out-guns-blazing Bonnie-and-Clyde-style confrontation was not an event he would like to take part in. Marc observed Odette inside the matt green vehicle through the aid of the scope; his thoughts went back to the Palms Lodge and the previous Saturday evening. How he would like to turn around and check in as a couple of casual guests. He smiled at the thought and thought of this being the least expected move they could play. He saw that the last of the herd had moved on past the vehicle. There was no sign of predators following the herd, but they may well be flanked from the sides. He strolled the 500 metres to meet Odette.

"Hey, Odette, ain't you fixing breakfast yet?"

She smiled and threw him a bag of chips.

"I think we should get this vehicle deeper into the thicket and make some preparations for travelling at night; what do you recon, Odette?"

She savoured the smoke from the cigarette she had just lit and exhaled the smoke towards the blue sky.

"Well, I do appreciate you asking, and if my opinion is of any value to you, I would agree with you entirely."

She kissed him, then sat on the hood of the vehicle and gazed around at her new surroundings.

"Hey, Vince, where are you from in Texas then?" Brad asked.

"Nassau Bay in Harris County, buddy. I grew up there at least. I moved around a lot before I joined the military. Do you guys spend much time in Africa?"

"Yep, certainly try to. Tanzania is kind of new for us. Jim and I have spent more time in Namibia and South Africa, once tried Burkina Faso before also. We should be heading back home next week. KLM via Amsterdam and Minneapolis, not too bad that flight. You got any plans to head to the US anytime soon, Vince?"

"Hell no. I'm here just over a year now, trying to make a go of things; a lot tougher than I thought though. Just ain't got the infrastructure here for any type of support services. Standards defy what we are used to, and any sense of urgency is non-existent half the time. Apart from that, you do manage to become used to it. It seems that pretty organised and acceptable standards are applied out here in these environments."

Brad smiled and nodded in agreement.

"Yep, buddy. Out on these excursions, you have all the dumb-assed and rich mzungu shooting fucking game and trophy hunting. Lots of money generated in this game, I mean lots! It's a massive industry. They got to maintain the standards or people will walk. Tanzania has got to be one of the most expensive, if not the most expensive, gig in Africa. They all differ. Take Namibia for example. Very reasonably priced and you are treated like a king from pick-up at the airport to being dropped off again. Then there is Kenya. They banned hunting years ago altogether, obviously concentrating on safari tourism. Whether or not their conservation approach to wildlife is more attractive for bringing in a high level of tourism, I have no idea.

"When I first came to Africa, I was under the impression that it was a very cheap continent to live, 'man' it's the exact opposite. I ain't seen anywhere in this God-dammed continent that's cheap for anything, it's way OTT, especially for the mzungu.

"Maybe if you are African, it is different, but if you ain't, you're screwed, man."

"Hey, Tiger, cool your jets," Jim said as he approached the table. "Is he busting your balls, Vince?"

"Na, we're just discussing how we can join this African club and live like kings as all the folks back home see our existence here."

"Hey, bullshit yeh? I'm gonna get myself a cold beer. Could you guys use one?"

Jim headed to the bar and returned with three cold bottles. Vince and Brad were still on the African subject and had moved onto the woman part.

"What do you recon, Jim?" Vince asked.

"About what?"

"The African women."

Jim gulped down a large mouthful of cold beer, then laughed.

"Oh boy, I've seen some fit babes and I've been with a good few of them, but hey, you got to set yourself some boundaries when you participate in that pastime in Africa, buddy. If you don't, a three-week game-trophy safari is gonna seem like a smart way to economise. I mean, check out Neil. When he has his fucking beer goggles on, he thinks he has a season's ticket with these girls, you know what I mean?"

Brad and Vince could not agree more and shared some laughter on this thought.

"Shit! Here he comes now. Change the subject. We don't want to get him started on this," Jim said.

Neil had spent the day meeting with some business colleagues who were taking care of Brad and Jim's game trophies. The trophies were being prepared for export and import into the US by the dip-and-pack process and the completion and mounting would be carried out in the States. The dip-and-pack process would normally involve the boiling and drying of skulls. Skins would be prepared and all dipped in a solution to kill off any bacteria before being wrapped and ready for export. It would make sense for them to have the final preparation done in the US in case of any abnormalities that needed rectifying.

Ron had stayed back later at the taxidermist's place to catch up with some chat with some friends there.

The two Americans were pleased with their homebound trophies of the lion and buffalo; the leopard opportunity had not arisen for them, not yet anyway. They again tried today but were unsuccessful in luring one of the big cats to their bait location. Ron had offered an educated suggestion agreed by everyone. He mentioned that the presence of the two male lions over the past week or so had probably encouraged the smaller cats to lie low for the time being. This would not last long, he mentioned.

Ron was first to be up and about on the Saturday morning. The time was 06:30 and he had sat down with Kevin and Sam for 20 minutes as they were finishing their breakfast. They were heading out to the savanna early, hoping for some plains game opportunities. They agreed to catch up later and left to get on-board the prepared and waiting vehicle. They too had plans to complete their time in Tanzania shortly.

Ron had made his decision to leave for Dar in the morning; Neil was happy to stay with the Americans for the short duration they had left. He studied Vince's motorcycle parked in the parking area. A glimmer of filtered sunlight was beginning to reach out through the trees onto the bike and enhance its aggressive appearance. It began to take on the shape and presence of some wild-looking creature ready to pounce on its prey. With Vince in mind and a smile on his face, he thought to himself, *Crazy bastard.*

Ron greeted Tatu as she approached with his pot of coffee, eggs, sausage and toast.

"How was your night, Tatu, late?"

"2 a.m. Mr Ron, Mr Neil, Vince and the Americans were enjoying their time."

"Well, I would expect them to arrive late for breakfast, in theory at least," he said.

Tatu laughed and turned and started to walk towards two guests who were making themselves comfortable at a table close to the bar.

"Tatu, one minute please."

Tatu returned and Ron handed her a 50 American-dollar bill. She had a puzzled look on her face as she looked at the money, then back at Ron.

"Take it, Tatu; it's for helping me yesterday with the phone calls and easy directions to my contact's place. Appreciated."

Tatu was a slight reluctant and looked a little embarrassed, but she accepted.

"Thank you, Mr Ron. God bless you."

She hurried off to attend to the arriving guests.

The stillness of the morning with the rising sun casting its rays and bringing everything in sight to life again was worth being there to watch. The peak of the vista lasting only minutes, seconds sometimes, encouraged Ron to stay longer at the lodge. On this occasion, he could not extend. Business requirements demanded his presence in Dar. He would be back soon though, as always. Vince's decision to stay longer at the lodge and not return to Dar the next day had surprised Ron. Maybe the workshop activities were covered by his mainly Indian workforce, he thought.

He found himself scraping the remainder of the egg yolk from the plate with the edge of the fork, then ordered some more sausage, toast and coffee. Time was approaching 07:15 and the restaurant was as quiet as one would expect on a Saturday morning. The two ladies seated at a table close to the bar having breakfast were not overly loud in their conversation but clear enough for Ron to recognise their American accents.

"Good morning, Mr Ron," the voice came from behind him.

Ron turned his head to see Simon approaching.

"Hi, Simon, nice to see you so early. I heard you were arriving today; sit down, man," Ron said as he offered a chair at the table.

More coffee was ordered as well as some mango and watermelon.

"What's new, Bro?" Simon asked.

"Things are looking better than last season. Two weeks ago we got some new customers bookings and due to arrive over the next few months. Good for us and good for you, partner."

"Excellent, keep them coming; hey, how about the two ladies over there?" Simon asked quietly.

"Na, mate, no idea, not through us; Americans but not ours. I'm not sure when they arrived. I got here on Wednesday."

Simon walked to the bar and kitchen area to talk to Tatu and the kitchen staff. He returned to the table, carrying the tray holding the coffee pot and fruit.

"I've did all this before," he said, laughing.

He poured coffee for Ron and himself.

"Ron, have you heard any talk or information of any adverse incidents since you arrived?"

"Nothing of interest, mate, no. The only thing that I heard out of the normal was some visit from the law on Thursday; I was not around. Uniformed and plain-clothed police visit, helicopter and all that carryon. As far as I know, there was a visit here from the law before regarding missing persons."

"Yes, yes, they have been here before conducting enquiries. Inspector Adimo and her team, nice lady."

"Yeh, well, I heard all about that."

"Well, Ron, apparently there was a man found dead on Thursday."

This statement got Ron's attention.

"I stayed at a relative's home yesterday evening, 30 kilometres from here, and my relatives passed this story onto me," Simon continued. "They said torn to pieces by hyenas or some other predators. The body was found by some local fishermen; white man, they say."

"Wait a minute, Simon, where was this?"

"About 150 kilometres east of here, not too far from the Palm Chalets Lodges and visitors centre in the Utete area."

"Torn to pieces eh!" Ron said as he carefully sipped the hot coffee. "Looks like these Frenchies are maybe starting to pop up now. Excuse me, Simon, 'French Canadians' allegedly."

They continued their conversation on the latest event for a while. It was clear to them that this was probably the reason for the hasty departure of the law last Thursday.

They had chatted much longer than intended, then Simon excused himself at 09:00 to resume his duties running the lodge. Ron checked the time on his watch at 09:20 and had Tatu bring him some more coffee. He thought about phoning one or two of the guys but decided against this after considering the late-night socialising they had enjoyed the previous evening. A few more guests arrived for breakfast before the 10:00 last orders.

Vince appeared walking towards his motorcycle and waved at Ron. He was checking his drive-chain tension, then came over to greet Ron.

"Need to remember to give that some lube later; give me a minute, Ron, just going to wash up in the men's room."

The other three appeared, Neil and the Americans. Ron was surprised that none of them had any appearance of that 'morning after' look about them. He knew that Neil's appearance was difficult to evaluate. Neil generally maintained a kind of a baseline rugged look. A man for all seasons would be an appropriate description.

The three of them sat down at the table.

"Man, I ain't half peckish. I could eat a scabby dingo, mate," this was Neil's entry to the conversation.

Everyone just smiled and reached eagerly for the coffee. Vince joined them and returned Neil's knife back to him that he had borrowed in the morning.

Ron shared the news with them that he had received from Simon. Everyone appeared surprised but unconcerned.

"Could be anyone, Ron. Sounds like he was close to the river if fishermen found him, maybe too close. Don't sound like crocs though. That ain't such a remote area over there, surely happened in darkness. Yeh, well, maybe it's one of the missing or some unfortunate pisshead walked too far from his vehicle to take a leak," Neil said.

"Mind you, buddy, they will have no problem identifying anyone through a vehicle registration. If it was one of the missing, he was surely not together with his buddies," Jim said.

"Maybe you will hear through your cop friend, Neil," Vince said.

"Yeh maybe, but I don't really give a fuck, mate, police business."

They discussed the program for the next few days. Ron would be chilling out and packing in preparation to leave in the morning. This left the other four to travel out with Neil in charge. They had decided to take one vehicle and the tracker. The skinner could have some time off, as their plans to hunt some

139

small plains game would not require much effort to transport any kills back to the lodge.

"Right, guys, that's 10:40. Are we good to leave at around midday?" Neil asked.

Midday was agreed.

"Vince, I will leave you my 270, mate; Neil can sort you out with ammo," Ron said.

"Too kind, buddy; I will keep her in good shape. Cheers, Ron."

They ordered late breakfasts from Tatu.

"Neil, Neil McPherson!" the voice came from across the restaurant, towards the bar.

"Neil…!"

Neil was startled and glanced over very reluctantly and petrified of who had recognised him in the middle of nowhere. About eight tables away, smiling and waving at Neil, sat Nancy Bell accompanied by another woman.

"Hi!" she shouted, also waving at Brad and Jim.

Neil quickly raised himself from his chair, determined to greet Nancy at her table rather than the other way around.

"Jesus," he said quietly. "I won't be two minutes, guys."

Neil shook hands with Nancy, and she could not have been more pleasant. He was introduced to her friend, quite an attractive lady in her early 50s.

"This is Brenda, Neil."

They exchanged greetings and Neil sat down.

"I have so much to tell you," Nancy said, "but later. I realise you are just about to break bread with your friends; you are here later, yes?"

"Yeh, sure thing. We will be out for the day, but later, sure."

He noticed that both the ladies were drinking coffees and white wine from a bottle chilling in an ice bucket. Nancy's friend was enjoying a cigarette that looked like the same brand as Jim's. A waitress arrived with fruit for the ladies.

"Look, Neil, we won't keep you, darling; we will have a rendezvous tonight for a drink, OK?"

"Absolutely. I will look forward to that, Nancy," he found himself saying.

They shook hands again and Neil left to join the guys for breakfast.

Crikey, fucking hell, Neil thought to himself.

Neil sat down, almost dumbfounded by his brief encounter with Nancy Bell.

"What's up, Neil? You look a hell of a quiet, mate," Ron said.

The Americans were enjoying their breakfast and were detached from Neil's disposition on his return to the table.

"I recon I may have misjudged that lady, Ron. That's the lady I met on the aircraft a while back when I arrived here."

"Hey, ain't that the dame you were with when we picked you up at the airstrip, Neil?" Brad said at the same time as masticating half his sausage.

"Hey, mate, don't speak with your mouth half-full. Fill it…!" Neil replied. "Yeh, Brad, that's her all right."

"Well, mate, looks like you may have a new friend. Right, guys; I'm off for a rinse and some chill out time. Catch up later," Ron said.

Ron got up and strode through the restaurant to his room.

"So much for first impressions," Neil said and continued eating his breakfast.

Neil followed Ron's advice and instructed Juma to drive them to the Gomma Plains area. This was one of the areas that attracted an abundance of browsers and grazers. They reached a point where Neil asked Juma to pull over to let Vince try out Ron's 270-calibre rifle. Ron had informed them that the rifle was zeroed at 100 metres. It was perfect conditions for some shooting practice, as there was not even a hint of a breeze.

Neil and the others were happy to stretch their legs and have some refreshments. Vince stood with his hands on his hips, searching for a target to concentrate on. Eventually, he turned around, smiling, and approached the cool box. He picked out two cans of soda and proceeded to walk out on the savanna.

"Hey, that's a bit ambitious, Vince!" Neil shouted.

He turned around, smiling, and kept walking. He stopped after a short time and raised his arm.

"That's 200," Neil shouted.

Vince sat down one can of soda. He carried on walking out away from them and repeated the action.

"300!" Neil shouted.

Vince shook the remaining can of soda and placed it down on top of a small rock. Neil reminded Juma to use the electronic ear defenders from the vehicle.

Vince opted for a Hyde bench rest placed on top of the vehicle hood in favour of a tripod. The first shot rang out and a distinct explosion of dry earth and gravel appeared in front of the target.

"Way short," Jim said.

An adjustment was made to the scope elevation. A second shot soon rang out.

"Short but not much at all, buddy," Jim confirmed.

The target could not be seen without using the spotter scope that Jim was monitoring through. Vince dialled in another adjustment, took aim and squeezed the trigger. This time the point of impact was a foot or so left of the target.

"Get it on, buddy, you're about there. That was a foot to the left," Jim said.

Another adjustment was made to the windage on the scope. Vince had a quick look at Neil and was wearing a confident grin on his face.

"Second last round in the mag," Neil said.

The big gun boomed out again, and 300 metres away a burst of earth, soda, gas and tatters of aluminium filled the air around where the can had been placed.

"Last round," Vince said as he felt the temperature of the barrel.

He carefully took aim at the soda can 200 metres away, and as soon as the trigger was squeezed, this can was also vaporized over the savanna.

It was quite late in the afternoon by the time they reached the Gomma Plains area. The time they had to spend here would only amount to a couple of hours to avoid travelling in the dark. Jim and Brad were of the same opinion this day, both being content to relax and enjoy the day's activity without firing a shot. If any opportunities arose, Vince would be welcome to have a go. He certainly left everyone no challenges to improve his marksmanship. They took the time to have a coffee and sandwich; they had left things too late today as a result of the previous evening in the lodge. Neil had brought along the remainder of his unfinished breakfast in between two large slices of bread.

Juma, who was walking around the area habitually, looking for any type of animal spoor, was crouched down, observing something in among some rocks.

"Hey, guys, come and have a look here," Juma called over.

"Sure, buddy," Brad said as he and Neil walked over.

Juma was moving around some burned remains of a fire and the charred area with a piece of dry tree branch.

"What's the deal, Juma, recent campsite?" Neil commented.

"Yes, this is maybe as recent as last night."

"Poachers, you recon?"

"No, too tidy for poachers, and the bones look like remains of some small game, savanna hare maybe; poachers eat more chic than this. It is not tribesmen either, no animal spoor around, just some tyre tracks over there."

Juma pointed to an area 40 feet or so away.

"The footprints are from two people wearing quality outdoor footwear," Juma said.

"Well, the only folk we know are Kev and Sam and they would be nowhere near this area this morning," Neil said.

Vince was having an intense look around the ground and he scanned the grasslands and hills in front of him in the general direction of the tyre tracks through binoculars.

Some distance away, as the plain became a gradient forming the landscape into more hillocks, he could make out tree and scrub-covered areas. The distance was maybe four kilometres and some vehicle track formation was visible on one side of the hillside. He scanned the area thoroughly, but no sign of anything or anyone was visible.

"Hey, Vince buddy, we are heading back in the direction of the base camp. Are you good to go?" Brad asked.

"Yeh sure. I don't see any bush meat out there anyway, just a whole bunch of nothing; maybe somebody before us spooked everything."

Vince lowered the glasses and walked to the vehicle. He secured the Browning rifle onto the rear rack and sat up back with Jim. Neil stamped out the end of his cigarette on the reddish savanna dust and poured some soda over it. He headed back to the vehicle with Brad and Juma.

"You still keen to have a shot at something today, mate?" Neil asked Vince.

"Na, not really. I've enjoyed today, buddy; next time around, too late to bed and up too early."

"Yeh, I'm bushed too, man. Leisurely ride back I recon," Jim said.

Juma did a walk-around check of the vehicle, then began the drive back. Unknown to them, out in the huge Gomma Plain of emptiness, they were the ones being watched.

They were fortunate to get some snapshots of two black rhinos on the plain prior to heading onto one of the main tracks. Vince was giving some thought to the fact that most of the largest mammals on earth were in fact herbivores. Things seemed to appear the opposite in the human race, he was thinking.

"What you got to smile about, Vince?" Jim asked.

"Ah nothing, Jim. I was off on one there."

"Hey, if you like, we could do some fishing; I recon I am gonna have another bash before heading back home," Jim said.

"Sounds cool. Yeh, might take you up on that, let me know, buddy, sound."

"OK, Vince, sure, I can do that. To be honest, I get fed up squeezing fucking triggers after a while."

Vince looked at Jim with a surprised look on his face.

"God dammed. Believe me, Jim, I know the feeling well."

"Where did you learn to shoot like that?" Jim asked.

"The military."

"Ah, say no more, buddy, got you. You would have been paid for squeezing triggers, and we are out here paying to do that, crazy eh. What do you recon of those Canadians folks, Vince? Some white boy turns up very dead down by in that Mohoro area a couple of days ago, animals apparently. Do you recon that campfire and the vehicle tracks today are connected to these guys?"

"Who knows, may well be."

"Well, if those dudes are trying to be illusive, they sure have a reason for it, I dare say. I'll tell you what, partner, they ain't half doing a good fucking job of it if you ask me," Jim said.

"That cop lady, maybe she will fill Neil in with an update next time. He seems to know her pretty well," Vince said.

"Yeh, I've met her on more than one occasion, buddy. Nice lady, pretty sharp too. That other dame that Neil was chatting to at breakfast goes by the name of Nancy; when Neil arrived here, she was sat in the seat next to him on the flight." Jim went into laughter.

"Fuck me, when he got his feet on the tarmac, he couldn't get away from her quick enough. He reckons she is some kind of tree-hugger nut. She sure didn't look like that to me this morning. I mean those two dames were throwing back the vino big time for breakfast, 'man'."

The two of them shared a laugh over the thought of it.

"Yeh, you will meet her tonight, buddy. Tree-hugger my ass," Jim said.

On arrival at the lodge, they were looking forward to a quick sundowner before getting cleaned up. Ron was doing just that in the company of Sam and Kevin.

Juma drove the vehicle to the rear of the lodge for cleaning and lending some help to Ron, returning the guns and ammunition to the gun safe. Vince's

Honda motorcycle had attracted some admirers. They were local kids from one of the nearby villages who were there with their guardians.

The villagers would make occasional visits to the lodge to trade freshly caught river fish.

Through courtesy, Vince walked over to join the kids at the bike and he was immediately confronted with a barrage of questions. The majority of the enquiries focusing mainly on how fast the machine could travel and how would one go about securing an opportunity to ride pillion. Vince humoured them for a while before giving them a handful of small currency, then walking over to the bistro area. The discovery of the vehicle tracks and the campfire on Gomma Plain was brought up. Neither Ron, Sam nor Kevin seemed remotely interested in expanding on the subject.

"We could spend all night exchanging ideas and theories on that one," Ron said.

Neil made a mental note to mention it to Inspector Adimo. He thought she may be interested. He would give her a call after he freshened up.

An old diesel-fuelled pick-up close to Vince's bike cranked over and quickly polluted the area with a thick black cloud of exhaust smoke. The kids, who were admiring the bike, raced towards the vehicle and they clambered onto the rear bed of the small truck.

As the pick-up sped away, the kids, sharing the rear bed with the empty fish crates and a dog, yelled, smiling and waving to the guests seated outside the lodge.

"Right, folks, what time are we touching base back here tonight? I may just snack it tonight. I feel kinda full," Neil said.

"You might feel different after a couple of drinks," Sam said. "See what happens, how about nine-ish?"

"Nine-ish it is," Neil said. "Right, I'm off for a shower, shit and shave."

Ron wondered if Neil would honour his declaration of assurance regarding the shaving part.

With the sundowner drinks finished off, the hunters and huntress departed to their rooms. Ron stayed behind for a while on his own to take in the complete change of vista until the shadowy demeanour of dusk settled in. He engulfed himself in the sounds of the night that was beginning to be announced. A different world was being born again on the African savanna. He was a man who was well-accomplished to the African evening world in far more remote areas than here, sometimes with only canvas between him and the mesmerising and sometimes merciless darkness. The lioness, he would never forget her, the big she-cat, the huntress, the mother. The memory to this day occasionally had him turning in his bed and into an almost-foetal position.

Nancy and Brenda arrived following a short walk around the grounds, and they seated themselves down at the same table where they enjoyed breakfast. Their bottle of chilled white wine arrived, surrounded by fresh cubed ice in the bucket. They agreed that their appetites would increase later, and for now, they ordered a bowl of the house catfish pepper soup to share. They were assured by the waiter that this river fish was feeding on the riverbed this very morning. Brenda Monroe did the necessaries by filling up the glasses. A verbal exchange of 'cheers' was heard, followed by the clinking sound of glasses in contact.

"The boys are back from their excursion out on the savanna; both jeeps are parked up," Nancy said.

"I did notice, boys and girls," Brenda corrected Nancy. "There's a lady among them also, uh huh."

"Oh yeh, you're correct, honey; I saw her in the morning, fit-looking, jeans and a khaki top."

"Eh, excuse me, sir." Brenda waved over one of the waiters and requested an ashtray. She lit one of her Marlboro cigarettes and sat it down on the ashtray.

"Top up, darling," Nancy said as she topped up the two glasses with the chilled South African dry white wine.

"So when do you think you will be heading back home, darling?" Nancy asked.

Brenda took a draw at her cigarette and exhaled the smoke directly above her and into the night.

"I ain't going nowhere soon, honey," she replied to Nancy with raised eyebrows and a mischievous smile on her face.

Nancy laughed and leaned over and placed her hand on top of Brenda's hand.

"OK, darling, I won't bug you with that anymore. I wish I could say the same for myself."

"How about you and Norman?" Brenda asked.

"You know, the more I think about it, I may just join you and extend my stay in Tanzania. He is in Dar with his buddies at meetings. Do you think he is gonna visit here even for a day or two? No, like hell he is. He is due to leave, sorry, we are due to leave in a few days, next coming Thursday. He may just be boarding that flight on his own. That's me and Norman these days, honey."

"Bring it on, girl, go for it," Brenda said encouragingly.

The steaming hot bowl of catfish pepper soup arrived, mounted on a charcoal base and enough cutlery, bowls, condiments and napkins to occupy the remaining space left on the table.

"Just make sure there's enough room for the ice bucket and the ashtray," Brenda instructed the waiter.

"Your friend, Neil, is over there by that motorcycle, Nance."

Brenda was looking beyond Nancy towards the car park. Nancy turned around to see Neil and Vince chatting.

"Seems they are all appearing now. The big guy and the others just arrived at the top end of the bar," Nancy said.

The hot spicy soup was quite addictive and was getting more attention from the two of them. They found themselves sipping it frequently off the spoons, only taking a rest from it to consume the cold white wine.

She was looking in the direction of Neil and Vince with a content smile on her face.

"I really like his accent, you know," Brenda informed Nancy.

"Who's accent?"

"Your friend, Neil, dear."

"Oh I see. Yes, the Australians certainly get noticed, I suppose, outside of Australia at least. Do I detect a glimmer of admiration for the man, Madam Monroe?"

"Hmmm, there is an attraction, presence maybe, definitely something about him, Nance."

"Yes, I must agree with you, dear; a bit of rough I think it's known as."

The two of them shared some laughter and other whispered comments to each other.

"Well, it's true, Brenda, I don't know him well; I only sat next to him on a short flight. To be honest, he is quite direct without being offensive, and what you see is what you get. Yes, definitely, that on its own can be an attraction. We will join him and his friends later on, honey."

Neil and Vince were discussing how many more days rather than weeks they would spend in the Selous. Brad and Jim were already fixing plans for departure, and Ron was bound for Dar the following day. The trophies belonging to Brad and Jim, in their incomplete form, would be going through the dispatch process as they were speaking.

"That was good shooting today, mate, from a rifle you ain't used to. I know the military was your learning platform, but I have seen lots of ex-military folk that had no interest in firearms and couldn't even set up a fucking scope. You seem pretty methodical, mate," Neil said.

Vince smiled and stared towards the ground, looking at nothing in particular.

"Well, Neil, first off, that rifle is set up well and feels well-looked after, and I have no doubts that your reloads are finely tuned. I was involved in a small, special, elite-operations team in Iraq. We taught ourselves a lot of the time. It wasn't so elite or special either. There was fucking loads of those teams, you know what I mean? I'm glad to be away from it, buddy."

Vince cranked over the motor on his motorcycle to let it run for ten minutes.

Neil was walking towards where Nancy and Brenda were seated when he remembered of his intention to call Adimo. After checking the time, he dialled her cell-phone number.

After a few rings, Adimo picked up.

"Good evening, Neil. How are you? Not out on the savanna at this time I hope?"

"Na, back in base, Inspector, not so long back though. How is your enquiry going?"

"Oh fine. I can let you know some details next time we meet. We are moving on with the enquiry in a couple of different directions now as we speak. It's a pity I did not get to meet your colleague, Ron, on Thursday. He was out on business, and as you know, we had to leave urgently to attend an incident. I am sure you have heard some rumours and truths regarding that by now, Neil."

"Yeh, we have all heard the word on the street, no big secret. In fact, the reason I was calling you was to inform you of something we came across this afternoon in the Gomma sector—"

"Gomma, you guys never really head there, do you?" Adimo interrupted.

"Na, that's correct. It was a suggestion from Ron to check out plains game. The leopards are lying low just now. Anyway, it may be of interest to you, Inspector, or maybe 'f'...sorry, nothing at all."

Neil almost became loose in his term of 'nothing at all'.

"No, please, Neil." Adimo laughed. "Carry on, and please, no need for the 'inspector' title either. Adimo is fine."

Neil went on to let her know the detail of what they had come across in relation to the campfire and tyre tracks and assured her that none of them or Sam and Kev was involved.

"You say Gomma, Neil. I know that this area is not your regular beat, but whether or not this is of interest to me. I do appreciate anything you pass on to me, thanks."

"OK, no worries. I already had a word with Juma and best you have a chat with him. He will explain the location and things better to you."

"Brilliant, I will call him this evening; John, my officer has his contact number. So, any plans tonight, Neil? It is Saturday in Tanzania," she suggested.

"Gonna play by ear, Adimo; Brad and Jim will be heading to the States soon and Ron is Dar-bound tomorrow. My other friend is here; you missed him also on Thursday. Vince, the guy with the bike. I will be heading out bush with him on Monday, couple of fly-camping nights, something I promised him. So how about you tonight, anything interesting?"

"Actually, I do have plans tonight. Meeting up for some drinks and a chat with an old friend and ex-colleague; he retired a while back."

"OK, Inspector, oops, sorry, Adimo, enjoy your evening. I'm off to see a man about a dog!"

"Thanks again, Neil," she said, laughing. "That's a couple I owe you."

On his way back to the bar-restaurant area, Neil paid his respects to the two American ladies.

"G'day, girls, *bon appetite*. How is the soup?"

"Delicious, just a snack. We plan to eat later, please try some!" Brenda offered Neil.

Neil took a spoon from a nearby table and sampled the soup.

"Bloody delicious right enough, nice one. So what are you guys up to tonight? We are here for the night, organising some drinks and some food later, no doubt. You are welcome to join us, the more the merrier," he said, looking at Brenda and Nancy.

"Very kind," Nancy said. "We would love to, darling, yes, Brenda?"

"How long are you girls here for?"

"Hmm," Nancy sounded and smiled at Brenda. "Brenda is undecided at the moment. I am supposed to leave on Wednesday, but it's not written in stone."

"How is your old man, Nancy, still in Dar on business?"

Although Nancy did not reflect any signs of feeling regarding Neil's enquiry, she was a slight irritated by Norman being a subject of conversation outside of herself and Brenda.

But then again, she thought Neil was only being polite in regards to the little he knew about her.

"Yes, Neil, he's doing fine, and we are enjoying a welcome break from each other for a bit."

"Yeh, I know the deal, a healthy practice I always say. Anyway, girls, I better spend some time over there. Ron is off in the morning. Catch up later, eh?"

"He doesn't give a shit." Brenda smiled at Nancy with raised eyebrows.

Neil arrived back at the bar with the guys.

"Hey, Ron, fuck me. That's us well-outnumbered now, mate. Looks like we have five Americans for dinner. Not to worry, our Commonwealth reinforcements should be along later, Kev and Sam," Neil said.

Neil managed to get his usual order in at the bar before anyone could return any remarks to him.

"Change of opinion towards the Nancy dame, buddy?" Brad asked.

"Yep, definitely, Brad, ain't nothing formal about her now. The two of them seem good company; we can have some crack with them later," Neil replied.

"Hey, Neil, did you get a chat with your cop-lady friend?" Vince asked.

"Yeh, I had a bit of a chin wag with her. She appreciated the info about the campfire and shit. I got time for her; she's a sound banana."

"Crazy business, missing folk in this area of all places. If that is one of them that turned up half eaten, maybe the other two are fully fucking eaten. Would not be anything unusual out there," Neil continued.

"Hey, Ron." Neil turned around and noticed Ron had moved outside to talk on his cell phone.

"Vince and I may be going fishing, ain't that right, Vince?" Jim announced to Neil.

"Well, if you fish as well as you shoot, mate, we ain't gonna starve," Neil said.

They continued discussions over the day's events as well as Jim and Brad's departure plans. Neil reminded everyone that Sam and Kev were due to leave fairly soon also. Ron appeared back at the bar area, smiling and shaking his head.

"That was Debs on the blower there. Apparently, there was a dead body; a male of British, American or Canadian nationality turned up in the Neptune Superior Hotel in Dar S."

"Was he attacked by wild animals as well, Ron?" Jim said.

"Not in that place. He may have got himself involved with a poor choice of local wildlife for company though. Is that right, Neil?"

They all shared some loud laughter at these comments. Neil nearly choked on his Jack Daniels as he was throwing it back.

Brad lit one of his special brands of Cuban cigars and filled the air around them with the pleasant aromatic scent of the burning prime tobacco. This was a sure sign of Brad settling down for the evening. Neil's cell phone vibrated in his pocket. He viewed the screen to see Adimo's number displayed on the screen, and he took the call outside in the car park.

"Hey, Neil, apologies for disturbing you, just a quickie."

"No worries. How can I help, madam?"

"Listen, I had a chat with Juma and I need to ask you a favour, a big one. Could you spare him for a couple of hours either tomorrow or Monday? It's no problem if you can't; I understand you have people leaving soon."

"Hey, you are in luck, Adimo. I already gave him the weekend off, so he's all yours if he's up for it."

"Fantastic, Neil, thanks a lot and I really appreciate. I don't have much of an idea how to get to this exact spot. John or Winston can take over once we know where to start. That's great, we can pick him up in the chopper either tomorrow or Monday, not quite sure yet. Byeeee, Neil, have a good one!" she shouted.

"You too. That's a case of beer you are heading towards now."

He could hear her laughing as they disconnected.

"Well, that is that sorted, Peter. He is a decent guy as I mentioned to you. Drinks and nibbles?" she asked.

Peter beckoned a waitress over to their table.

"Please, young lady, could we have a large scotch and a large G-and-T with ice and lemon for the lady. Oh, and please, one ashtray."

He reached into his inside jacket pocket that was hung over the back of his chair and took out his Marlboro cigarettes, lighter and a cigar tube-container. Adimo came back from the buffet area, holding a small tray containing bowls of olives, sushi and fresh oysters on ice. She cut and detached one of the oysters from its shell and removed the top shell. "Mmmm," she expressed as she immediately let one slide into her mouth without adding the lemon juice. She chewed twice before swallowing.

"Marvellous. Try, Peter."

"Shortly, Adi. I am a little bit stand offish on fresh oysters. Let me have a sip of my honey first."

"Honey?" she commented.

Just then, the waitress arrived with Peter's order. He smiled and raised his glass of scotch.

Adimo ignored the whisky and focused on her double gin. Peter shrugged his shoulders.

"Save you ordering another soon," he said.

"Peter, I am sure you heard of the incident in the Neptune here. Another deceased male was discovered in the Mohoro area last Thursday. I will explain," she said.

Peter gave a nonchalant shrug. "Two bodies already, Adi. There will be more, I'm sure."

The two of them planned an evening of discussion on events and exchanging information relating to the Dar and Selous incidents in the hope of forming a direction that might prove fruitful in this investigation.

Vic and Zoe were working on the identity of the remains found in the Selous. There were no obvious items of evidence found on the body or the surrounding area apart from the 22 shell casing and the projectiles themselves that had not exited the skull. The bullet type used were subsonic, hollow, point lead. This would make identifying and matching a bullet to a barrel through rifling markings almost impossible due to serious distortion and fragmentation. A barrel was also a necessary item required to conduct these comparisons.

Samples of DNA and dental X-rays had been sent to Canada and North America for analysis. Adimo was aware of all the information that was fact and other reports from Vic, Zoe and Peter that flagged up South African involvement.

South Africans were a main source of suspicion to probe into. She had already discussed a proposal with Vic and Zoe to quietly monitor any South African residents or visitors to Dar. This was one of the recommendations inspired by Peter. It was another branch of the investigation created that required more resources or multitasking officers who were already more than busy in their allocated assignments. It was also an area that Peter had mentioned he would be happy to assist in, following some of Adimo's manipulation and applying her powers of persuasion of course.

Brad, Jim, Vince and Ron were introduced to Nancy and Brenda soon after the ladies arrived to chat to Neil. Ron thought to himself that Neil had been 100% correct on the announcement regarding being outnumbered by the Americans. He quickly became aware of the infestation of American accents dominating the conversation. The Americans were spending a fair amount of time discussing their routes and areas of birth in the US.

Neil and Ron took advantage of the moment to have a beer and a non-alcoholic beer together and a catch-up chat. Although Ron could appear to most folk quite composed and almost uninterested during discussions in regards to the recent unfortunate events in the Selous and Dar, he was all ears and perceptive enough to end up with the correct figure if he decided to put two and two together in his chosen areas.

"Whatever is going on, Neil? Just take care around here, because nothing seems to be making much sense so far. I get the feeling that there are issues on a fairly high level of investigation going on by the law here. Those two out-of-town suits that you described last Thursday stick out like a couple of spare pricks at a hookers wedding, and I've never even seen them."

"Absolutely, mate, I am well-aware. You know me, but I tend not to give a fuck, you know that too."

Ron laughed and slid the freshly washed ashtray that the girl laid on the bar towards Neil.

"All kidding aside, Ron, I appreciate your concern; really, mate, I will focus more in what you mentioned. These boys here I am sure have their deep feelings about it also."

Nancy appeared with a fresh glass of wine in her hand and introduced herself to Ron a second time. They were soon engaged in conversation, and at this moment, there was a polite interrogation from Nancy in search of Ron's recent background. Neil took the time to have one of these moments when himself and himself happily got together to enjoy a couple of drinks and some shared thought. He leaned on the bar facing the gantry relaxed with his drinks and cigarette. He could just about hear every word in every conversation going on around him. He could not help hearing Ron bring up the subject of trophy hunting in the Selous with Nancy and the revenue that the industry creates in Tanzania. *You bastard, Ron,* Neil thought to himself as he smiled, *you fire her up on this and piss off tomorrow.*

Nancy's demeanour and her answer to Ron surprised Neil even more. "Not at all, Ron. You guys and your professional activities out there make ya'awl part of the conservation process of the Selous as well as other permitted regions. No, there are complexed issues here. It's not just a matter of creating a 'for and against culture'," was her answer. She actually chinked glasses with him. "But I will tell you what, Ron, to hell with those poacher bastards!" Nancy said.

Neil took a drink from his Jack Daniels, then a drag from his hand-rolled cigarette, inhaling through his teeth and smiled. *Crikey,* he thought, *that woman is beginning to appeal to me.*

The Chase

Sam and Kevin arrived and first announced their departure plans to Neil; the coming Tuesday was the date they had decided on. Jim and Brad had their departure set on the following Saturday.

"Who are the ladies, Neil?" Sam asked.

"Oh yeh, that's Nancy and Brenda, Sam; Nancy arrived here on the same flight as me, American Conservation Society."

"Oh, I've heard about her," Sam said while smiling at Neil.

"Ah, I may have misjudged her, Sam. No worries, and Brenda, I don't know at all apart from a quick chat. She seems pretty cool though."

"Some more Americans eh?" Kevin said.

"Yep," Neil said. "That's five of them now. It's gonna be a lark at dinner, especially at the rate those two girls put the plonk away. Anyway, what plans do you two guys have for tomorrow and Monday?"

"To be honest, mate, no frigging idea. We plan to kind of plan that this evening," Kevin replied.

"That sounds like a kind of plan," Neil said.

"I would imagine everyone here has the same thoughts in regards to tomorrow at least. I ain't got a thing in mind for tonight, just gonna go with the flow, guys. Saturday night ain't it?" Neil continued.

Sam grabbed her large glass of red wine when it arrived at the bar.

"*Excusez-moi*, guys, I'm off for a mingle."

"Did you hear anything about that hullabaloo, Kev? You guys left early this morning. Did your driver mention anything?"

Kevin lowered his glass after a long drink of cold beer and let out an uncontrollable burp.

"Excuse me, mate; no, the driver never mentioned anything. Always a bit of hullabaloo around here I suppose. So what's new, mate?"

"I suppose he would not mention to you, Kev. The guys tend to let the big white hunter pass info onto the other big white hunters, with their upmost respect in mind of course, just their way."

An update from the news of the corpse that was discovered and the campfire at Gomma was passed onto Kevin.

"Bloody hell, Sam will find all this stuff interesting; she loves all that mystery and investigation shit. Maybe better not to tell her or she may get ideas to extend our stay here."

Kevin had no idea where Gomma Plains was located, and as everyone had thought, he and Sam were nowhere near that area today and they never noticed any other parties of people during their travels.

Neil took a call on his cell phone from Adimo, confirming that she would pick up Juma tomorrow, and she let Neil know that she would now contact Juma to arrange a convenient time.

The dogs began to bark, and some of the children of the lodge staff ran out to the parking area, excited and clapping their hands. Neil looked up while he was loading supplies onto the vehicle. The chopper came into view and the loud thumping and downdraught of the blades invaded the relative serenity of the area as it descended. Adimo had a change of plan and decided to mobilise on Monday; it was 07:00 hours. Brian kept the chopper in flight idle while Adimo got out to meet with Juma and bring him aboard; she met also with Neil and expressed her thanks to him again. Vince strolled across and received an admiring glance from Adimo.

"You must be Vince? Ex-military, Neil tells me," she said as she offered her hand.

Vince placed the cool box on the truck hood and shook hands with her.

"Yes, ma'am. Vince Kelly, nice to meet you; I missed you guys last time around."

"Likewise, Vince." Adimo smiled and hinted that they needed to get a move on.

"OK, thanks again, gents. Catch up soon, yes?" Adimo and Juma walked quickly to the chopper and boarded.

"You will know all about those things, partner, eh?" Neil said as he watched the chopper ascend and tilt to quickly fly off.

"Me!" Vince protested. "Never been known, buddy," he said, grinning.

30 minutes in the air had them approaching to make a landing in Gomma in the area of interest. They had circled the spot and surrounding area before landing, but nothing of interest was in the vicinity for them to focus on. Vic and Juma searched around the fire area. Vic picked up the discarded cigarette butt.

"Mr Neil's," Juma said to Vic.

Winston and John followed the direction of the vehicle tracks but did not pursue this, as the tracks simply appeared to merge with one of the main, permanent, well-worn tracks. Adimo, along with Vic, stringently searched the area in an outward direction from the fire pit. Juma decided to take a more closer look at what seemed the only place left to search, the fire site and ashes itself. He gathered up all the charred material and laid it down on an open piece of cloth. Much of the material that seemed to survive the fire's heat were bones consistent with small game animals and birds. He was left with bare earth at the base of the fire and he started to inspect everything he had laid out on the cloth. It soon became apparent to him that the charred remainder of the skull was more than likely from a savanna hare. Some of the skull separated away as easy as completely burned pieces of wood. Something in the tougher part of the skull took his attention and prompted him to break it open with the help of two rocks. He walked to the chopper and poured some drinking water over his cupped palm to clean whatever he was holding.

"Inspector, please."

Adimo and Vic approached and Juma held out his open palm to reveal a small, dull, tarnished and distorted piece of metal.

"This is a 22," he said.

Vic moved the object around in Juma's palm.

"This was in among the remains, in the ashes and bones," Juma said.

"Hey, my man, you are so correct, buddy." Vic pointed out to Adimo the distinctive heeled formation part of the lead projectile bullet common to a 22.

"I agree, gentlemen. Well-spotted, Juma, that's a find, that is."

They bagged the bullet, and thanks to this, their thoughts were taken in a more positive direction within the investigation.

Adimo, with her hands on her hips, looked around the area in all directions with a calculating, determined look on her face.

"We need a couple of vehicles and some boots on the ground. We need to be able to communicate more with locals at their level and be able to move day or night if required."

"I couldn't agree more, ma'am, knowing what I know now," Vic said. "Let's discuss this as a team, yeh?"

Everyone was made aware of Juma's find, and including Juma and Brian, they had decided to have a discussion together before boarding the chopper. Everyone's ideas and conclusions all seemed agreeable to each other. The chopper, as well as an eye in the sky, was regarded as an excellent fast responder, but the operational restriction to daylight hours and vulnerability to catastrophic results from a firearms conflict were agreed as the main negative points. An understanding of the fugitives digging in during the day and exercising movement during darkness was now obvious to them. Adimo placed a call to her captain with the latest suggestion to complement the existing procedures. This time, she was taken by surprise; Captain Hamisi agreed.

"I hope you all enjoy spending some time sleeping in tents," he joked with her.

"OK, that seems pretty much kosher, gentlemen," Adimo announced. "And without any negotiations to render the procedures already in place, I may add."

"Excellent. I had a little scent of something the other day, that the Canadian contribution to the investigation and operational cost was under consideration to be increased," Vic said.

"Let's make a move on this now before someone changes their mind. We could head back to the lodge with a fly over those hillocks on the way," Adimo said.

Juma was asked to help in locating two vehicles in Kiba, suitable for the purpose they required.

"We need vehicles with sleeping capability, yes? To hell with tents, and thanks again, Juma."

"Of course, ma'am, no problem," Juma replied.

On touchdown at the Mambo Lodge, Juma, along with Vic, John and Winston, got out. They had finalised their plan on route and planned to mobilise this evening. Adimo accompanied the pilot back to Dar es Salaam. The four men arranged transport into Kiba Town after Juma had contacted Adimo and a rental company where they could enquire and maybe negotiate a rental deal on a couple of specialist vehicles.

On arrival at Prime 4x4 rentals, at a glance, there looked like more than enough choice of stock to meet their requirements.

They were met by a large overweight Syrian gentleman named Nasir, the rental fleet manager for the Kiba branch.

"Good afternoon, gentlemen, *salaam ali ayekum*," came the greeting from Nasir in a loud, cheerful voice. The three Tanzanians and Vic returned the greeting in Arabic.

"Inspector Adimo just called me. I've been expecting you; come inside and talk and have coffee," Nasir said.

Nasir made sure they were all lavished with strong Turkish coffee and knafeh, the sweet Lebanese dessert combining syrup, nuts, gooey cheese and pastry. Shear decadence for anyone with less than a moderate palate for sugar.

They chatted a little on the subject of the Prime 4x4 vehicle that the police still had in their custody in Dar es Salaam. John hinted that he was sure it would be returned to their fleet soon. Nasir was aware that the company was being compensated for the vehicle being taken out of service. The Africans clearly enjoyed the sweet dessert. Vic observed, when John finished his helping, he was immediately given more.

Vic decided to take his time with the dessert and hopefully politely 'almost finish it'.

Nasir led them around the fleet which was mainly Toyotas, Land Rovers and some much older larger vehicles. His attempts to swing the police towards the Land Rover models failed; the preference of the officers was focused on the Toyotas. A 15-minute negotiation of shouting and arm movements developed, which Vic refrained to enter, ended in pleasantries, smiles and handshakes. A deal was complete with a two-week rental of two 2008 model Toyota J7 2.5 diesel Land Cruisers finished in matt khaki paintwork. These particular vehicles were South African-converted troop carriers fitted with complete fibreglass rear-covered coachwork.

Fuel-tank capacity had been increased to 190 litres between three integrated tanks with an option of three separate supply and return lines using isolation valves between the tanks if required. The rear section could easily accommodate and sleep two adults.

They left the rental premises after politely declining a second offer of coffee and refreshments from Nasir.

The start of the plan was to secure some supplies. Vic and John drove to some of the stores and small mini markets. John would cover the first of the driving. Winston and the local policeman, Omar, travelled to the police headquarters to secure some additional firearms with ammunition, bedding, clothing and one of the tracker dogs. They would all rendezvous at the HQ prior to mobilising. There was no option of an overnight stay at the lodge or any other establishment; they would make haste during the evening in the direction of the Gomma Plains.

Vic caught up with the latest developments in Dar during a phone conversation with Zoe. There were no leads as yet regarding any information on the perpetrator responsible for ending the life of Mr Vatel in room 1230. Zoe was fast becoming a welcome part of the African team in Dar es Salaam particularly through her ideas and approach to aid everyone involved in her team and the drive in the investigation. Vic could sense a yearning from Zoe to become involved in the Selous part of the investigation. He had the same sense of understanding that Adimo's preference would probably lean towards the outback challenges.

Adimo had begun to apply a new strategy in Dar with an emphasis in keeping her more involved there. Although the savanna side of things had not yet yielded anything significant to date, she was sure that some valuable exposure was just around the corner.

The time was the other side of 8 p.m. when the team, in their two vehicles, left the police HQ in Kiba to begin their journey southwest. They kept to the higher road, keeping the Mambo Lodge vicinity approximately eight kilometres south of them. Winston and Omar were the lead vehicle. John explained to Vic that travelling in daylight hours would permit a journey of around two-and-a-half hours to reach the campfire area they had seen earlier. Evening travel of course being dependent on a hitch-free journey would dictate a journey time of four or maybe five hours. They were confident of maintaining a steady pace and reaching their destination late this evening or at latest within the first wee morning hours. The one main advantage that they welcomed was the steady mid-20s temperature of the evening.

Vic made himself more comfortable by adjusting the seat back and reclined and resting his left foot high above the glove compartment on his side of the instrument panel. They were still travelling on more or less solid and fairly even ground at 40 miles per hour. John and Vic's visibility was disadvantaged by the amount of airborne dust generated by the lead vehicle and increased the distance between each other.

Vic's attention was focusing on the darkness outside the open window on his side in an attempt to have his eyes become more accustomed, but the headlight beams dominated what his eyes took in as images. This area did not offer much to see, just stubble, sparse trees and open plains.

"It makes a real difference to travel in something that feels proper and you know that it is fit enough to take you anywhere, Vic; look at the panel gauges, all nicely lit and all working," John said gleefully. "Thank you, Mr Nasir."

"Yeh, thank you, Mr Nasir, for the cake also. What was the name of that thing, John?"

"Knafeh. You liked that?"

"Na, no way, buddy. Way too sweet for me. You boys seemed to enjoy it though."

"In Africa, we like sugar probably too much, Vic."

"Yep, sugar and Nido, I've noticed and I don't think you will get much change out of Mr Nasir."

Vic had his eyes peeled in search of any wildlife as they cruised on through the darkness. There was not much to see, but an abundance of bats were constantly appearing in the glow of the headlamps clearly attracted by the mass of flying insects that were being drawn in towards the source of the light. A small mammal darted across the track in front of them, much too fast to even guess what it was.

Vic leaned over the seat to the rear and picked up a bar of chocolate, which he broke in half and handed half to John.

"Hey, bro, what additional rifles did you pick up from the HQ? We got two in the rear here, yeh?" Vic asked.

"Yes, sure. There are four. The guys in front have the other two. They are all 22 calibre."

"No way. You're shitting me, right?" Vic said while seriously smiling at John.

"No, really, Mr Vic. You don't believe?"

Vic leaned further across into the rear and dragged an ammo box towards him and lifted it over the seats. He knew immediately exactly what he was looking at, but still he shone his small torch at the base of the shell casing around the centrefire area; 223 Remington was stamped clearly into the brass.

"Ah, thank heavens for that, buddy. 223, handy tool."

"Yes, 22 calibre," John said, looking puzzled.

Vic realised that the African guys among other nations loosely used the base calibre size to describe any rounds within that family of ammo despite the casing type or projectile.

Vic reminded himself that most of the time, or all of the time, where he came from, the mention of a 22 and the British and maybe European term two-two represented a particular round. This referral would be describing a .22 rimfire using a 40-grain lead-heeled projectile which is a tiny round but certainly lethal. The .223 is of the same calibre but a high velocity full-bore centrefire cartridge with a copper-jacketed projectile that has the capability of shooting out through 600 metres. The difference of the two is like night and day.

A bit like comparing a Ford Mustang 2.3 inline four-cylinder motor and one with a 5.0 V8 configuration motor, he thought.

Vic discarded the confusion and quickly moved away from the calibre subject.

To carry on the conversation gently, he asked John the manufacturers of the rifles.

"Howa," John said proudly. "They are Japanese."

"Yup, I've heard of them, buddy. Never seen one, but I believe they are pretty capable rifles."

"We don't use them often; they are quite new. They get used at the range on Sundays but just sometimes. If we don't clean and polish them after use, woh! Big problem is coming from the captain," John said, laughing.

"We have two bolt-action and two semi-automatics with us. This is only because of the request of Captain Hamisi in Dar, Vic."

"Well, God bless Captain Hamisi," Vic said.

John does seem to know his firearms outside of his standard-issue AK47 and .38 special sidearm, Vic thought to himself.

As they progressed on their journey, the track narrowed by giving up its width to some large rocks on either side. Potholes were in no short supply, and progress lent some time to slower, careful manoeuvring to avoid any underside damage. Like lasers targeting the vehicles and occupants, occasional white, red or yellow light reflecting from some night creature's eyes could be seen. Something ahead of the lead vehicle prompted Winston to abruptly bring the vehicle to a halt. John reacted in the same manner to halt the Toyota.

"What the hell!?" Vic said in surprise.

Not far ahead of them, something large was moving quickly through the forest from the right side of the track. It was appearing in and out of their vision, depending on the spread of the thicket separating the vehicles and this large, moving entity. Things became more clear as metallic reflections could be seen coming from this bulk. To everyone's surprise, another vehicle came into focus. A dilapidated pick-up truck crossed the track in front of them at a pace that left no room for mistakes and carried on through the forest on the other side of the track. No operational lights were working on the front, rear or sides of this truck. At best, Vic could make out a type of frame or cage fitted around the side capes of the bed with a light-coloured horse, possibly two, standing upright in the bed. Above the cage, there was a trailer secured upside down, with its axles and wheels being the highest point of this rig. The pick-up melted into the darkness just as quick as it had invaded their path from the darkness, leaving nothing but excessive exhaust smoke behind it.

"Shit! What was that all about?" Vic said.

John engaged first gear as the lead vehicle moved on in front of him. John looked at Vic, grinning and unconcerned.

"Crazy, yes?" John replied.

"Crazy…! Absolutely. Different, that's for sure. No lights, no nothing and the speed he crossed the path, whaoh! Maybe no brakes."

"Actually, this guy should sound his horn for safety," John continued.

Vic let out some genuine loud laughter.

"Horn…!" Vic shouted. "That's a hoot, John. Excuse the pun, buddy. I reckon that vehicle couldn't see a horn with a telescope."

Both of them laughed and giggled for a while over the incident.

Vic's realisation of the diversity of both their cultures was becoming much more apparent to him. The track began to level out again from the hard-rippling surface, and they were thankful for a break from the constant jarring of their bodies over the past 45 minutes.

Their first view of any sign of civilisation appeared in the distance in front of them. A few soft glows of light at different levels were visible at both sides of the track. The track had been widened considerably now, giving the impression of it being used more commercially at this area. As they approached closer, Vic could make out the outline of small dwellings and the unmistakable eyesore of a view of tired 20-foot shipping containers. The strained sound of a small generator could be heard with its frequency raising and lowering. The light bulbs dangling randomly by their supply wires from tree branches and facia wood were constantly dimming and brightening in tandem with the generator power supply. *No doubt a result of poor maintenance or system overload, probably both,* Vic thought to himself. Both vehicles pulled up to a halt and Omar approached John's open window and discussed something in Swahili. This triggered a sleeping dog outside a dimly lit container to begin barking in defence of protecting its territory.

"Hi, Mr Vic, are you tired?" Omar said, smiling.

Vic stretched and indicated that he was fine and then began to rearrange and secure some of the things in the rear that had become scattered. Omar walked towards the container entry door, and to Vic's surprise, the dog's barking had ceased with Omar down on one knee, patting and clapping the animal. When the dog finished a quick thorough sniffing of Omar's clothing, it strutted away and lay back down in its dusty bed outside the container. The dog in the lead vehicle had sat up and watched the events without making a sound.

John explained to Vic that they were stopping just to make some enquiries regarding any strangers who might have passed through the town. A few minutes passed and Omar returned to inform them in English that a man, a white man driving a jeep, had bought some fuel last week. He had come from and left in the same direction that they were heading. Both the vehicles cranked up and got on the move again. The container dog got up from its bed again and resumed its barking until the vehicles were a reasonable distance away.

An hour or so would pass until they reached their planned destination being the campfire site in Gomma. They reached an area of flat terrain, and even in the dark, Vic thought he recognised this area. John confirmed to him of his correct judgement and mentioned that they were just ten minutes away from the campfire spot.

John took some time to follow up on Vic's inquisitive requests for wildlife information. He explained that the creature's eyes reflecting the light on the plains were most probably wildebeests, buffalos and antelopes along with hyenas, leopards and lions.

"Whaoh, amazing, buddy. Some look so close, I would imagine that hunters would be at an advantage at night. Where I come from, although I don't hunt, some of my hunting buddies spend a fortune on certain riflescopes that intensify the light before dawn when they are after elk and moose. I recon they are paying for light."

"No way, Mr Vic. Hunting is not permitted after dark in Tanzania, and no matter what you think, it would actually be more dangerous for the hunter. Remember, you're not the top of the food chain here, and the carnivores out there are expert hunters in the dark. The only people that do this in the evening are these poaching gangs. They are dangerous and can be shot on sight. There are many who have been killed mainly by lions at night."

"Yep, got you, buddy. You would not catch me out there at night, rifle or no rifle, no way, Jose, sack that."

Both vehicles came to a halt.

"We arrive," John said.

The vehicles were switched off along with the lights. Immediately, they were enveloped in complete darkness with the stars above ever present like a million down lighters.

"Just sit for a minute, Mr Vic. Your eyes will accustom quickly," John said.

Next moon would be in a couple of weeks, but had there been a full or large moon, they would have travelled without lights, John had explained to Vic.

"It didn't deter that boy in the forest with the pick-up truck, buddy," Vic replied, laughing.

"Hey, John, tell me something. How does that work anyway? Ben-Hur flying along with no lights in total darkness. I mean, the fucking horse wasn't driving," Vic said.

John and the other Tanzanians laughed at this.

"This is bush people, Vic. They are born in this; I don't really know. Maybe you should ask the witch doctor, my friend," John said as he fed the laughter even more.

"Yeh, yeh, yeh, and how much is that gonna cost me?"

The guys enjoyed some more laughter at the unimpressed look on Vic's face during his reply.

They were all eager to stretch their legs and have a snack before getting some sleep.

"How about snakes?" Vic asked. "Any around here?"

"Plenty," came the reply from Omar. "You will be fine, sir. They will be well away from us and won't come near. Just remember not to leave any remains of food around though, very important."

The time was approaching 01:00 hours and they shared some coffee and cake. John unwrapped some leftover knafeh from Nasir's place and offered some to Vic who politely declined while giving attention to the display of stars above.

Suddenly, everyone jerked quickly as Vic yelled and seemed to move two metres in a single leap.

"Shit," Vic said in relief and to the relief of the others.

While Vic had been engrossed in the stars above and recognising the same ones and systems as he could view from Canada, the cold, wet nose and warm tongue of the dog had pushed into Vic's hand that was by his side, holding a piece of chocolate.

"Sorry, guys," Vic said as he poured himself a fresh coffee from the flask.

Vic climbed up onto the hood of the jeep and sat on the edge of the roof to finish his coffee and stargazing before settling down for the evening.

While they were clearing up outside and preparing their sleeping areas, Vic asked if the dog stayed outside.

"No, Vic, he will stay inside the front of the other vehicle, unless you would like him in here?" John smirked.

"No, but I thank you kindly for the offer, sir."

"He would probably attract unwanted attention if he was kept outside, Vic."

"Oh, yeh, what type of attention?"

"Any other canine or cat, especially leopards."

"Really? I would have thought that big fella would see off a leopard, no?"

"No, no way. Leopards love dogs. I mean they love to kill and eat dogs. A leopard would most likely kill him."

Vic made a mental note to upgrade the leopard within his newfound recent thoughts and interest in African wildlife.

To his surprise, Vic found himself last up in the morning; a little startled and quickly taking in his new surroundings, he grabbed his cell phone to check the time, then lay back down for a minute; it was just before 07:00. Vic gave his eyes a rub and slipped on his T-shirt, shorts and boots. Winston and John were tending a pan over a fire that was clearly the source of the smell of food Vic had noticed as he awakened.

The dog was bounding across and around the savanna grass with some encouragement from Omar. Vic walked across to greet them at the fire.

"Morning, guys, or *habari*," Vic said with a tired smile on his face.

"Ah, who teach you?" Winston asked.

John spoke in Swahili to Winston, and Vic could make out Adimo's name being mentioned; Vic looked at them and nodded.

"*Habari* is OK, Mr Vic. It can mean 'hi' or 'hello'. *'Habari za asubuhi'* is complete 'good morning' if you like."

"*Asante*, Winston, I will try to remember."

"Sit down please. Eggs, coffee, bread," John said.

Coffee was just what Vic needed. It was the beginning of a beautiful day. A blue, hazy sky developing with the sun beginning to turn on the heat.

Vic jokingly commented on the convenient readymade fire surround that they were using.

"Look, Vic, your friend," Winston said and nodded towards the dog.

Vic smiled and shook his head a little.

"Well, he ain't having any of my eggs this morning, guys."

Vic then commented on how well a sleep he had. He had almost expected some kind of wildlife to be heard or coming close to the vehicles. John assured him that nothing had come around and there was no sign of any spoor apart from some snake tracks not far from where they were sitting and tracks from the dog. John explained to Vic the difference of dog and cat tracks and mentioned that the snake was more than likely a puff adder. Vic's inquisitive mind asked if that type of snake was dangerous. Winston told him that it was and that it was best to maintain a policy to consider all snakes as dangerous.

Vic went to the rear of the vehicle and splashed his face with some water from a container. The plan was to be on the move in an hour's time. The vehicles were kitted out with simple shower systems which were gravity fed from the bag. He planned a shower later this evening.

Omar jogged past and greeted Vic, with the dog following. The dog stopped to look at Vic with his tail wagging and head tilted in curiosity. Vic somehow felt encouraged to pat the dog on the neck and rub him hard on his back.

"Hey, buddy, howz you?"

This dog was a strong animal, Vic thought. He was sure this dog could bear his weight if he sat on his back, not an experiment he was about to carry out.

Omar called the big animal as he poured water into a plastic basin and the dog quickly left Vic and raced towards the basin. Vic's thoughts went back to the leopard. John had told him that even the smaller of the species, the female cat had the capability to carry that dog high into a tree.

The only probable chance of a dog surviving a confrontation with a leopard would be awareness before the cat attacked and to always keep facing and threatening the cat in defence.

"Which breed is he?" Vic asked.

"Simba? He's a ridgeback," Omar replied.

"Simba, that means lion in Swahili," Vic commented.

A brief rundown of the Rhodesian ridgeback breed and its popular title 'The Lion Dog' followed. Omar explained the history of the breed and the activities that the dog was generally involved in regarding hunting lions. Vic had learned that they also make excellent tracking dogs. When Vic was told that this particular dog weighed around 40 kilos, his thoughts touched again on the leopard and the strength that this cat must possess.

"Mr Vic," John said, "you see that grass over there, the short and medium-length savanna grass?"

The grass in question was 25 metres away.

"There could be a leopard in there watching and you would not even know; it could be on you in two seconds," John said. "Simba would scent it of course, but only if the leopard was at a disadvantage by wind direction."

"You know, John, I believe you. Let's get our shit together and get out of dodge."

John laughed and gave Vic a hearty pat on the back.

The tracks left by the vehicle that was probably associated with the original campfire seemed the obvious direction to follow. The drive uphill on the only track available was easy to follow. A good steady pace could be maintained even though the camber was fast changing and the uneven surface was consistent but shallow rather than sharp bumps. The dry season had its effect on the trees and parts of the forest that did not benefit from being close to the river where the roots were rarely parched. The trees on the high level were much sparser in comparison. The Tanzanian officers had a good, sound knowledge of the immediate surroundings. When the track offered a choice of three directions at the top of the hillock, they followed left in a westerly direction.

They were full on now and sharing a feeling of being properly involved in the game. This was a completely different feeling from being in the sky in the chopper where no surprises could confront them. Anything could be just around the corner here and they were now in the arena.

"Do you have any kind of plan in mind, John? Maybe we can get together and have a chat after you guys ask some questions to the locals in the next village?" Vic asked.

John agreed and pointed out that they should be at the next village after another 20 kilometres. Between their present location and the village, the surroundings would be carefully examined for any signs of interest or suspicion that could assist their task.

Both vehicles arrived at the village and parked up. Not far before they reached the edge of the village, they were halted by a police checkpoint that had been briefly set up to target suspects in a recent wave of poaching. The local police manning the checkpoint had more questions for the officers than the officers had for them in regards to unusual activities and movement of strangers.

John and Winston left the vehicles and made their way towards an area of small huts within a large fenced-off sheep pen.

While Vic was sitting, waiting in the vehicle, looking down the road through the village with his attention on nothing in particular, he was suddenly startled by sudden movement and a voice next to him at the open window. He quickly arched back and turned to the side to see an old man dressed in a white kaftan-type shawl in a hunched-over position; he seemed to have appeared from nowhere. The man was holding a long stick, more of a pole to assist in walking, and his other hand was held by a small boy no more than eight years. The old man's gaze was directed above Vic and more towards the sky.

His eyes were no longer eyes but just a pair of opaque, pale, white inserts unable to receive images and void of the ability to transmit any sign of emotion, feeling or recognition.

Vic found himself very uncomfortable in the situation that he could not leave, but he would not have left if he was able to. He struggled to find some money in his pockets and handed some Tanzanian notes to the boy who smiled and nodded a gesture of thanks together with his old relative. *Despite having this unfortunate disability, this old man wearing a pure white cloth over his head and his silver well-groomed beard in contrast with his almost-black leathery skin shined handsome, majestic,* Vic thought to himself.

Vic's surprise and embarrassment with himself blended into respect and a feeling of humbleness against this man's power of survival in life.

The both of them then toddled away on the sidewalk towards the town centre.

163

Vic transferred a number of small denomination bank notes into an easy-to-access pocket after the experience.

Winston and John arrived back sooner than Vic expected.

"Hey, bud, how did you get on?"

John sat down and closed the vehicle door, unfolded a piece of paper and studied it for a minute.

"Well, OK and not OK," John replied. "I suppose OK actually."

Vic could tell that he was disappointed.

"This guy in here recons that he was aware of four vehicles coming through here over the past couple of weeks, vehicles carrying white people. He can't remember the manufacturer or the colours of the vehicles, and he sure did not see any women. The only clear thing he recalls is a vehicle with three white guys inside. He remembers this because the vehicle parked on the opposite side of the street while they eat ice cream bought from his friend's store. Then they were gone, travelling in the same direction as us. He says this was just a few days ago. The positive thing with this is that he was sure they did not return back through the town. Anyway, Vic, no problem. We are the investigators, not them."

"Too true, John, absolutely, and we both know that anyone in a rush does not usually park up for a while, eating ice cream, and they don't seem to be trying to be illusive. It may all be nothing related to our interests, but you never know. Are we off then?"

The two vehicles got gassed up in the village, then set off at a quick and comfortable pace again, taking advantage of the acceptably level surface of the road.

Vic's cell phone pinged, indicating a received message.

"Hey, that's the first my phone has connected to a network in a while, John. I had forgotten about the thing."

He ruffled through the contents of the bag to retrieve the phone. John's phone let off a notification sound also. He studied the message and saw that it was from Adimo.

"Some news from your boss, John. She says they got an ID on the John Doe who was found at the Palms area. A South African national by the name of Kyle Kotze… Well, there's a start, buddy. Apparently, 42 years old; well, at least he 'was'. You will have the same message on your phone."

Vic sent a return text to Adimo while the network had a signal.

"You know of this guy?" John asked.

"Nope, but you can bet your ass we will all be sharing the story of his life soon enough."

Night Travel

Odette moved closer to Marc and squeezed him from behind as she woke up to another hot and humid morning. Marc raised his hand behind him and pulled her head to the side of his face. He stretched his neck upwards, and after kissing her, he let his head fall heavily back down on the makeshift pillows. She sat up and got onto her knees to look out of the windows, a privilege she enjoyed each morning.

"Hey, it's just like being on holiday in a motorhome."

Some unintelligible mumbling came from Marc.

"What?" Odette asked.

"I don't know, never been in a motorhome."

He appreciated her enthusiasm and knew now that he could rely on her. She was strong and certainly not unequal to him; she could handle pressure and demanding situations.

"You got fish," she said happily.

Marc had purchased some monofilament fishing line and some hooks from the boy at the fuel stop. They were parked close to the river edge on the north bank, hidden under some dense canopy, completely out of sight of any aerial search. Over the last couple of nights, they had thrown out some baited setlines into the river, which was proving productive. Mainly eels and catfish got hooked.

Odette could see one of the branches supporting a line thrashing now and again as the fish tensioned and jerked the line in its efforts to free itself.

"I am going to get it, Captain."

She began getting dressed into her t-shirt, shorts and boots.

"Hey, madam, remember what I mentioned. Make sure there ain't nothing or nobody out there, and don't go near the river edge. And remember to check on top and under the vehicle," he shouted as Odette opened the rear door.

Through concern, Marc got up and watched her pulling the fish from the depth. Another catfish of a few kilos got dragged up and well onto the riverbank. She pinned it down and hit it hard twice over the head with a piece of tree wood.

She turned towards the vehicle as she knew Marc would be watching her and held up the fish, encouraging him to snap a photo. He looked at the photo on his phone screen. A smiling girl with a big fish was displayed.

"You see, just like a camping holiday," she said.

She pulled in the other two lines to find no bait or hooks with the line cleanly cut.

"Nothing, all gone."

"No problem, babe, something with sharp teeth; we don't have any wire. Hey, Odette, move further away from that river's edge. Don't hang around there."

He looked around in all directions, paying particular attention to the more-shaded forest interior. Odette sat the lifeless fish down on top of the vehicle hood.

As they were eating the fish, which was roasted over a small fire, they tried to recollect some thoughts and put their ever-changing plans into perspective. They were still in the Selous game reserve and, for now, had decided to lie low for a bit at their present location while waiting for instructions from their contacts. After all, a phone signal, even though it came and went, was fairly reliable and bed and breakfast was guaranteed.

No definite arrangement of where and when they would be picked up was in place yet, but plans were going through a process. To date, they had travelled only 160 kilometres from the Utete area in ten days; it was suggested to them that they may be picked up in an area called Iringa. Marc was convinced that lying low in their present position was an advantage, as it would probably be expected by any pursuers that they had travelled much further. They had not heard any helicopters in a while, but it was impossible for them to constantly monitor any movement on the tracks or roads.

Their cell phones let them know their position in the planet after they realised and familiarised themselves with the integrated GPS facility that was becoming commonplace with cell-phone manufacturers this year.

The vehicle had a basic, integrated, satellite-navigation system, but they had decided not to make use of it. It was clear that there was no tracking system fitted in this vehicle, otherwise trouble would have knocked on their door long before now.

"Hey, babe, according to the map and phones, we should be around 300 kilometres from Iringa. We have the fuel to reach there and then some if needed," Odette said as she prepared coffee. "I wish we had a refrigerator though," she said, smiling.

Marc was carrying out a modification to the gravity-fed shower system by hauling the reservoir bag 12 feet up and suspended by a tree branch rather than relying on the head pressure created from the height of the vehicle roof. Water supply was not an issue at this location.

"I don't think we are going to get out of here, Marc."

"What...! Bullshit," Marc protested. "What has brought this on, babe? Just sit tight. We dealt with one problem that was gonna see us dead, surely that's a positive. Things might look like we are fucked up, but we ain't, trust me. Hey, this morning you were on a wild camping holiday," Marc said, smiling.

Marc knew she wasn't scared, not with her background. He just put it down the women's prerogative in thought when changes were not coming quick enough.

"I know that, babe," she replied, "but sitting around, waiting for an airlift don't seem as easy as it sounds. I am as confused as hell. Why was Dennis taken out? He delivered the fucking package, and it's us who are holding shit now."

"Odette, Odette. Yeh, and we are gonna hold it, fuck them. They just proved whether we had the gear or not; they were gonna whack us, yeh? They bust the deal, not us. C'mon, babe, we are out of here and out of here with the shit. It won't be a picnic, but you cover me and I will cover you, deal?"

Odette smiled and brought over the coffee. She lit two cigarettes and handed one to Marc.

"OK, deal, hotshot."

Marc put the idea across that they would benefit by spending some time making a plan, and they agreed to take the drive to the vantage point that they knew and take into account what they could see. They would put a careful observation on every road and track that they could see. They would try to get some sight of any vehicular movement without compromising their own location of course. Just as Odette was pouring coffee, they were taken by surprise by the sound and vibration of Marc's cell phone ringing. Marc answered and was immediately engaged in conversation. Odette was confident that the news was welcome by the expression on Marc's face; he was concentrating more on listening than talking; this was a good sign, she thought. Marc beckoned her to provide him with a pen and paper.

Odette started to move everything back into the vehicle in preparation for the short drive to the vantage point. When they moved, everything moved. Their packages were taken back in also, as those were generally carefully buried outside with one of the vehicle wheels parked on top of the site.

She heard Marc happily shouting, "Yes," and he then began to inform her of the news. He took some items from her hands and laid them on the vehicle hood. He put his right arm around her waist with his left hand clasped on her right and proceeded to perform a waltz dance. This had the desired affect and cheered her up some.

He unfolded the map and had a keen look outwardly at their surroundings and laid the map down on the vehicle hood.

"OK, we can be lifted in a few days, all going well. At present, there is a two-day window and this is planned to happen on one of those days, probably Thursday or Friday.

"It's important that we stay north of the Ruaha River, although we can be picked up at either of two locations north or south of the river; it's not yet clear."

He could see the excitement in her eyes.

"Now Iringa is out of the question I was informed. Too far away, and, apparently, the chances of us making a 300-kilometre trouble-free trip at this stage may be considered impossible, according to our guys at least. They know our location and they want us to travel to a point within Morogoro by Friday. There is a suitable landing strip there that is fairly concealed in a forest clearing. It has some history attached going back to the Idi Amin days and the Ugandan war. Here, let me show you."

He ran his finger across an area of the map, starting from the Utete area where they stayed at the Palms to where they were now. He then had to focus a bit more closely to identify and point out the pick-up destination to her.

"It's about 110 kilometres from here."

"So close, Marc, so close."

"OK, here's the 'not so good news'. It was mentioned that there is some people in the Selous right now, some people who are to compromise us at any cost, at least two were mentioned."

"Surprise, surprise," Odette said dryly.

Marc raised his hand gently in a gesture to request that she let him finish his briefing.

"We can expect the Tanzanian law enforcement to be covering aerial searches and they are not sure, but there may be some involvement from a higher authority."

"What higher authority!" Odette demanded.

"Hey, Odette, how the fuck should I know, hey? If they are unsure on that and not even sure they exist, what the hell would I know? We can only assume, and hey, you ain't stupid. Anyway, toots, I don't see it as positive or negative news anyway; we knew there would be goons on our tails. We know Mr Kyle was the first and certainly won't be the last. I don't need to spell it out for you, babe. A man with a wooded head can work that out."

She could not contain her laughter and removed his hat, and she clasped both her hands around the back of his neck and tiptoed up and kissed him.

"What about a woman with a wooden head?" she said in his ear.

"Get out of here," Marc said, laughing at her comment.

"I am just blowing off a little and I know our pickup is sound; I just want us to get there, Marc."

"Exactly, babe, *moi aussi*."

"Hey, hotshot, I ain't your babe or your girl."

The both of them laughed and Marc put his arms around her and pulled her towards him.

It was a fact that their airlift was 100-percent guaranteed, ensuring a safe departure out of Tanzania, providing the aircraft stayed in the air. Both Marc and Odette were in possession of four packages, two each with four separate deactivation codes. Marc knew two codes as well as Odette. Their rescuers would be well-compensated for their services. The other executors of the deactivation codes would be the hierarchy of the people pursuing them. The knowledge of the codes was definitely not a 'get out of jail' card if they were captured by these people unless they themselves were intent on jumping ship.

The both of them cleared up their area and Marc took some time to bait the three lines and set them in the river. They got ready to take the short drive to their vantage point to carry out some observation. They had decisions to think about regarding their departure from this location. Apprehension niggled at the two of them, as the only time they had travelled in daylight was at first when they had no choice in the matter. Around this time, they were also at an advantage during the night with some moonlight to illuminate their path with cut headlamps.

After four kilometres of uphill travel, they reached their intended point. The vehicle stayed parked in the darkest shaded area of this sparse hilltop forest to prevent any reflections being sent out from the glass.

The main vantage point was a dead tree that looked as if it had been around for hundreds of years. Marc could reach the area 20 feet up on the trunk quite easily. Odette was on varmint watch and she preferred to do this from inside the vehicle, with her upper body outside of the rear section turret armed with the AK47.

"Hey, Odette, there is no restriction on visibility today, crystal clear, quite beautiful actually. I can see the track, road or whatever the hell you want to call it that we will be using. Well, there ain't any sign of anyone or anything outside of wildlife out on the savanna. I'm coming down, babe."

Marc got himself down and walked over to the Toyota inside the edge of the forest.

"I recon we should move tonight, tiger. Fuck daylight travel. Are you good for that?"

Odette was more than relieved to hear this.

Three South African nationals were enjoying the remainder of their breakfast in the early morning next to their campfire, not far from the north bank of the Ruaha River. They too were feasting on rod-caught river fish. They were in discussion, comparing the Kruger National Park and the large reserves in Tanzania and Kenya.

All had an appearance of experienced safari men clothed in khaki shirts and trousers, and on their heads was Australian-looking bush hats. The tall one named Marquis in his early 50s touched on the subject of a curious crocodile close to them while they were fishing close to the time of dusk on the previous evening. These men were familiar with river carnivores and dangerous game. The crocodile would have been shot for the pot had it been a little smaller, as this reptile had been two-and-a-half metres in length. Not your four or five-metre giant that is commonly found in Tanzania but still too large for their requirements. All of these men had dispatched crocs before with a well-placed headshot from a small-bore rifle such as a 22 long rifle round. This time their real prey was Marc and Odette and the contents of their carry luggage.

Marquis sat on one of the large rocks that surrounded their campsite which was secluded behind a huge kopje north of the river. He studied his text messages with a cigarette hanging from his mouth; the other two sitting at the fireside were involved in much the same practice.

Marquis cleared his throat and spat towards the fire at the same time as flicking his cigarette end in the same direction. The cigarette fell short, but one of the other two men picked it up and discarded it into the fire. The plan was to get moving around 07:00 in the general direction of Marc and Odette's route.

These people knew the details of the vehicle that they were pursuing as well as its contents. They also had knowledge of airstrip locations north and south of the river. Two main river crossings were known to them, although they thought it doubtful for them to be following their quarry across the river; this was still a consideration.

"Right, let's boogie," Marquis said as he got up and made his way to the vehicle. He stopped at the fire and urinated over the smouldering charred wood.

Marc and Odette had made a complete clear out and tidy up of the site and set off the previous evening around 10 p.m. At this point, the distance between the two camps was around 50 or 60 kilometres. Taking into consideration the condition of the road, the two of them should have managed to increase the distance between themselves and the South Africans to 120 kilometres by sunrise. As the dawn was arriving, Marc and Odette discussed a plan to select a stopping point and rest during the day. They explored a route off the main track to observe the river-crossing point in case they had to alter their plans. They were greeted by one man and two teenage boys, all local Tanzanians. This was a point where the river took a wide curve and the current's flow was slowed down by back eddies created from the opposite bank. There was almost a calmness of a small lake here.

The ferry itself was crude but probably expensive to manufacture. It was a fairly buoyant-looking affair that could carry two large vehicles and the amount of passengers, pedal bikes and mopeds was anybody's guess. Port and starboard drive units were in place with single propeller drives submerged below the power plant. The drive units seemed to have what looked like a facility to rotate through 180 degrees allowing bow, stern and beam propulsion. Power was transmitted from canopied diesel engines probably through mechanical and hydraulic drives through to the final drive. The cargo was already full with two vehicles and an amount of people and their two-wheeled transport to fill a small stadium as it powered its way out on the river. There was another car in front of Marc and Odette. One of the boys approached Marc and informed him of the crossing cost and mentioned that the ferry would return in 40 minutes.

"Is that your father over there, 'your papa'?" Marc asked the boy in English.

The boy nodded and beckoned his father to come over.

Marc explained to the man that they had no intention to make the crossing today. Marc spoke very clearly to the man who fully understood the request and accepted the offer with a handshake.

Marc had given the ferryman two 50 American-dollar bills to inform anyone who enquired about them to confirm they had made this very crossing today. He then made the awkward manoeuvres required to turn the Toyota around, and they both continued back up the hill to the main track. Their plan was to cross the Ruaha River at the second point and avoid more than 100 kilometres' travel and another crossing to get to their destination.

"You realise that we are definitely the first people to pay for not boarding and probably the first people to travel back up that one-way decent," Odette said.

"I never thought of that," Marc said, laughing.

They discussed the possibility of travelling during the day due to the fact they had noticed much more traffic obviously on route to the ferry crossing points. They considered this but declined the temptation and stuck to plan.

Marquise and his comrades were on their way, staying on the main track road westward and taking the time to slow down to investigate and side roads of interest. Any fresh tyre tracks made from well-shod tyres would raise their suspicions.

They were disadvantaged in their role as the hunter but could not afford to have their quarry behind them. They had not taken into account that Marc and Odette were following a strict policy of travelling in darkness.

Occasionally, they would stop and scan the area around them with binoculars. They had come to a change in the road surface that transformed from the long, smooth, uneven stretches of different gradients and cambers. They now had a flat, hard-packed, rippled surface in front of them with only a few inches between the peaks, causing the whole vehicle to vibrate violently at their speed. Marquis had no hesitation in shouting to the driver to slow down for fear of the cooling-system radiator or delicate electrical components becoming fractured. The driver slowed down to reduce the vibration and shouted something back at Marquis that could not be heard over the noise. This demanding part of the journey looked like it would have to be endured for a while

They had tolerated an hour of this and eventually reached higher ground where they stopped to make some observation of what lay ahead. The shortest of the crew opened the rear door to retrieve a coffee flask. An amount of the vehicle's contents spilled out onto the ground as the door was opened. They chatted over coffee outside the vehicle and wiped sweat from their faces and necks with wetted cloths. They were grateful to be taking the time to recover from the constant noise and vibration that their bodies suffered along this track.

The smallest of the three returned to the rear of the vehicle with the intent to again secure the rifles and carry out a bit of housekeeping in the vehicle.

Marquis reached into the vehicle and retrieved one of the packs of cigarettes. He addressed his companion who was also drinking coffee and smoking at the front of the vehicle.

"Do you recon they are still in front?" Marquis said as he looked intensely around him and into the distance ahead.

"I would put money on that, yeh. From what we gathered from that village, it looked like they planned a bit of distance bashing," his colleague replied.

"OK, goed, goed. I will go with that. Let's get those ferry crossings checked out just in case. I recon they may have just considered that. It's not too far from here."

As they descended the incline down the track towards the ferry-docking point, the craft was already on its way across the Ruaha River; at the riverside point, the ferryman approached them with a smile.

"Hey, my friend, could you help me please?" Marquis said. "We are trying to locate some friends who should be on the other side by now, a man and a lady, white folks. I recon they made a crossing recently."

"Yes, Chief, a white couple did this morning."

"OK, boss, thank you," Marquis replied.

Marquis instructed his colleague to manoeuvre the vehicle into a position to be first to board the next crossing.

As Marquis was guiding the reversing vehicle, he noticed fresh tyre tracks already cut into the earth where their vehicle was backing into. Marquis halted his colleague and studied the tracks, noticing that they had been freshly made by a vehicle that was well-shod and had a perfectly distanced wheelbase as their own vehicle. Marquis glanced suspiciously with a disgruntled look at the ferryman and the man purposely turned to look away. He marched towards the troubled-looking man and grasped him by the front of his shirt. He pulled out the contents of the man's top pocket and threw the money on the ground along with the American-dollar bills. Within a second, the man was looking at the muzzle of a .45-calibre revolver pressed against the side of his nose.

"When and where?" Marquis demanded.

The shaken man had trouble replying. "Four hours ago, they go west, boss, for sure, no crossing here, please sorry, sir."

Marquis let him go and angrily got into the vehicle. They raced up the track, narrowly missing a descending pick-up truck laden with goats.

Odette awakened to the familiar sound of insects claiming the peace of the encroaching evening. She sat up and noticed Marc outside, preparing and checking firearms and ammunition. She knew the rules of the game were stepping up a few notches now.

"Are you good, Odette?" Marc asked.

She yawned and stretched her arms upward, then made her way out of the Toyota.

"Yeh, I'm good. Have you been up long?"

"Not long. About an hour, just getting some stuff ship shape, but if I was completely honest with you, I'm fucking bored waiting."

"OK, cowboy, let me have a pee and a coffee and I will help you saddle up the horses," she chuckled.

"Keep an eye out for those snakes, Odette."

"Yeh, yeh, yeh, thank you, Marc."

This location was sparse in comparison to what they had been used to. The river location in particular was a welcome and precious commodity. This location was in higher ground within a formation of huge rocks that bore an appearance for probably thousands of years, that some of the couple of hundred-ton specimens were about to topple off each other and crash to the ground below. They were effectively and completely concealed by barriers and overhangs of this ancient formation. 50 kilometres of progress had been made since leaving the Ruaha River, which was more than they had expected. The distance covered by them was usually dependent on the discovery of a suitable place of concealment and preferably able to support cell-phone-signal coverage. Their rocky stopover had pockets supporting a good signal. At this stage in the game, the phone signal was of paramount importance. A call was expected this evening to shed some more clarity on evacuation plans.

Darkness was already upon them as they enjoyed some cooked fish and biscuits with coffee; their scheduled departure from this spot was around 22:00 hours.

"Marc, where do you recon our destination will be, assuming we get on this airlift and things work out?"

"Kwazulu-Natal, hey, just kidding, babe. Put your money on Zambia or DRC. Personally, I recon Zambia. DRC is inaccessible to most and dangerous to many. Depends on just how far our contact's friends and associate's loyalties extend, I suppose. Remember, in reality, loyalties between them, us and their friends, don't really exist; it's the packages that are cementing it all together. These packs are absolutely no use without us and us without them. They all know the term 'impossible' applies to any thought of safely releasing the goods without our codes."

"Yeh I know, even one deactivation attempt with the wrong code demands our other codes entered to abort the countdown to destruction and vaporising process."

"Do you still remember your codes, Odette?" Marc said jokingly.

"Fuck off, Marc."

"Our main problem is these fucking goons on our tails or ahead of us. These people are in a win or maybe win situation, providing they get their hands on the diamonds. What do you recon you would do if you were them, Odette?"

"What!? Providing they find the packages, I recon protocol would take precedence and ask us nicely for the codes, and when that fails, we would be asked or persuaded not so nicely, failing that we would be dispatched and they would run back to their masters with their tongues hanging out and tails wagging. If they were clever, they would simply take possession of the goods, pop us a couple of times in the head and take the goods home to their superiors."

"Hmmm, why so?" Marc said, smiling.

"You know 'why so', smart ass. Anyone hauling me into a vehicle beat up, handcuffed and gagged to surrender codes would need their heads testing. They would get the codes all right, the codes to guarantee vaporisation of everything around a 20-metre radius. What would you do, cowboy? Anyway, Marc, that ain't gonna happen."

"Damned right it ain't." Marc flicked the remains of his coffee across the ground.

A message notification chimed on Marc's cell phone. He opened the message to see it was blank. The phone began to ring, then stopped and Marc moved quickly towards another area of more clearance. The call came through again and he answered. The conversation had been brief and Marc walked back to Odette to inform her of the pick-up time of 18:00 hours on Thursday evening had been agreed, just a couple of hours short of 48 hours' time. This ensured another overnight for them and some imminent daytime travel.

Marc gave the vehicle a check over. All was sound and the fuel on-board was probably enough to power a Challenger Tank to the airstrip area. The both of them tidied up and removed as much trace of them ever being there.

The track was firm and the main track road lay three kilometres ahead. Marc was using only the small side lamps which proved successful this evening, providing they travelled slowly.

The AK47 was now making use of one of the various strapping points above them on the cab interior roof. Once they were 300 metres away from the junction where the main road crossed, he stopped the vehicle, switched off the lights and they made an observation of either direction of the main road.

Things looked clear as he switched on main headlamps and accelerated quickly to join the main road. Being on a small track made them more vulnerable to being trapped in. They were just about to join the main road when Marc was forced to brake and quickly bring the Toyota to a halt. "Bastard," he shouted as a large overladen truck appeared out of the left in the darkness using no lamps whatsoever; he was forced to turn right and join the main road behind this metal behemoth swaying dangerously from side to side.

"Shit, we need to get past this thing," Marc said.

He steered to the right and came close to the rear of the truck but soon found that the road was too narrow at this point to allow any overtaking. Marc was far from impressed, as they needed to pass this slow-moving obstruction sooner than later. He again steered to the right of the rear of the truck and sounded the horn in an attempt to encourage the driver to pull over more to allow him to pass. Another pair of headlamps approached from the opposite direction; the truck came to a halt and forced Marc and the oncoming vehicle to do likewise.

"Fuck," Marc shouted.

Odette looked behind and was able to make out vehicle headlamps quite far away in the distance. She spoke to Marc calmly, suggesting to him to relax, as they could not afford to bring any attention on themselves. The truck now proceeded to slowly move to the left.

The passenger in the truck had now pointed a torch out of the window to illuminate the roadside hazards as the truck driver slowly edged the vehicle over rocks and bushes. A reasonable gap developed now on the right-hand side and the oncoming vehicle wasted no time in passing through. Marc pulled out and quickly took advantage of the opportunity and raced past, pressing his horn. The truck driver returned with loud sharp blasts on his air horns.

"Fucking typical, perfect horns and no lights," Marc said.

Again, he must have tickled Odette's sense of humour with his remark. She laughed hysterically for quite a few seconds.

"What do you mean, Marc? They had a torch!"

The South Africans drove off the main track on the left-hand side towards an area that looked suitable for a stopover. They discussed the vehicle lights that they had noticed in the distance in front of them. It was difficult to determine the distance in the darkness, but they thought maybe as much as five kilometres. The vehicle lights descended from high ground on the north side and probably joined the main road. It was decided that they would get back on the main road and drive some more distance to catch up with this vehicle. As they approached the crossing of the main track, one vehicle passed heading west. The driver turned west on the main track and carried on along this route; they soon found themselves not far behind this vehicle. They kept pace with this vehicle, keeping a distance of 30 metres, with the intension to overtake given an opportunity. Marquis noticed, as did the driver, of approaching headlamps behind them. The front vehicle displayed a plate number that was of no interest to them, but Marquis's thoughts were on the vehicle behind and the possibility of this vehicle being of interest. Marquis instructed the driver to reduce speed and let the vehicle behind get closer to them. The driver obeyed, and as he was paying as much attention to the rear vehicle on his mirror, he was startled by realising the front vehicle had come to a halt.

The driver brought the vehicle to an abrupt halt, causing the front wheels to loose traction for a couple of feet. The three South Africans watched as a uniformed police officer stepped out of the passenger side of the vehicle and approached them, carrying a torch and an AK47 assault rifle. Winston greeted them at the driver's open window and asked the driver to switch off the vehicle lights and cut the engine. Without being too intrusive, Winston shone his flashlight in and around the vehicle. Another armed officer approached them from the rear vehicle and walked past them on the passenger's side to the vehicle in front. He finished a brief chat with Omar, took details of the South African vehicle plate number, then joined Winston, and he also greeted the South Africans. Marquis stepped out the vehicle and lit a cigarette and he did his best in his attempts to offer himself as the main spokesman. Although the officers conversed with Marquis constructively, they did have questions for all of them. All the paperwork in regards to their firearms, hunting licences and visas were in order, and after a brief search of the vehicle interior, underside and under the hood, the officers were satisfied enough to let them carry on.

"What are your intentions for the week ahead, gentlemen?" Winston asked.

"Actually, Officer, we travelled west a bit further than intended, so now that evening has settled, we are going to kip up overnight. Tomorrow, we may keep going to have a look at the floodplain area, then head back east to find a good hunting lodge to use as a base. Can you recommend any?" Marquis asked.

"Depends on your intended game. I know you South Africans favour blue wildebeest," Winston replied. "It's still dry season, remember, and quite open.

You have the calibres there to cover plains and dangerous game, and let's say the .45 is the .45. The Mambo Lodge may suit you."

Winston wrote down the lodge phone number and handed it to Marquis.

"Did you come across any white folks on your travels, gents?" Winston asked.

The reply was, "No," along with three heads casually shaking.

"OK, guys, I am sure you all know what you are doing and where you are going, so sleep well and good hunting."

Omar drove the vehicle over to the side to let them pass.

"Do you trust them, John?" Vic asked as they moved off.

"Nope, I do not. I will pass all the details to Dar HQ tonight and see what comes back tomorrow."

"Sounds like a plan, buddy."

The two vehicles were parked up not far off the main track. First light would creep in in 30 minutes. They had been wakened by a freak rain shower that lasted just a few minutes but boomed like marbles on a tin roof. The dog was anxious to get out probably due to the rainfall and the abundance of short-lived rainwater around outside. Omar opened the rear door and let him out earlier than schedule. Simba bolted out like a cork from a champagne bottle and raced through the wet grass and puddles, flushing startled guinea fowl into the air and into the safety of the trees. Winston and Omar organised the fire and began the preparation for breakfast. Vic, now a seasoned outdoor survivor, applied his skills to preparing the coffee as soon as the fire was prepared.

"I have a feeling that we will be chasing some folks pretty soon, guys," Vic said. "I will sure be surprised if those guys last night are not tied up in this party."

"I agree. HQ should advise today, I would think," John replied. "It would seem easy, yes? Two vehicles, four of us and Simba, then air coverage probably tomorrow. What about those other two? What are they up to, are they even alive? They are elusive for sure."

They began to eat some ugali with some carrots prepared by Winston and Omar. Vic commented on his preference to the ugali over Mr Nasir's knafeh. John passed Vic the salt and encouraged him to season his.

Return to the Savanna

The Dar es Salaam HQ received some feedback from their investigative resources regarding the request from John on the previous evening. Adimo asked Zoe to pass on the critical information to the guys in the field and walked off to the captain's office.

Vic's phone rang at 11:15, displaying Zoe's name.

"Hey, Vic, howz ya'awl doing? Say hi to the guys for me. Listen, we are passing this info to you guys in the first instance. More information is probable according to Adimo, but there is enough to act on suspicion at the moment. One of the names, specifically Mr Marquis, would be a person of interest and to be termed as dangerous. Please consider the others accordingly, Vic."

"Sure, Zoe, will do. We kind of figured this but needed confirmation and grounds for suspicion from you guys. No doubt they will be well-aware of our findings on them by now."

"Any sign of Mr Dupuis or Ms Gordon at all, Vic?"

"Nope, a 10-60 on that one. I would put money on those boys last night in pursuit of them, but as you know, things don't always pan out as they seem. The one sure thing is we have an interest in them all now."

"OK, Vic, Adimo will be in touch. She's trying to get the bird arranged. Signal becoming grainy now, take care, over and out."

"10-4, partner."

Zoe took a couple of sips from her coffee and leaned back in her chair. She closed her eyes and sleep took over her easily. The past couple of days, Zoe, Adimo and two assignees had been working excessive hours without being rewarded with much sleep. She was giving a lot of thought to her partner, Vic, now that party time could be very close, at least in the Selous area. Her brief sleep was interrupted by Adimo and the captain walking down the corridor, engaged in conversation in another language, a language that she was beginning to pick up in small instalments.

The captain carried on down the corridor and Adimo entered the office.

"Hey, girl, you look just the way I feel. I could use one of those," Adimo said.

She ordered herself a coffee from the girl in charge of the kitchen.

"How are things going, Adi, any development with the chopper today?"

"Yes, very well but not till tomorrow. It's apparently having a component change out as a mandatory upgrade today. Tomorrow is probably good considering this."

Coffee and biscuits arrived for the both of them.

"No doubt intelligence will get back to us this afternoon with a wider report on the other two South African fellows. We're ahead now anyway, yeh?" Zoe said.

"Yes, that's a point, but it does not really matter if they write up as Frank and Jessie James or Batman and Robin; they are on the wrong side of the ball park, Zoe."

The both women joked a little over the situation and finished up with their excess charges of caffeine.

Adimo let Zoe know that she had to go to collect her daughter and granddaughter from a local clinic nearby and would return shortly. She advised Zoe to take it easy and informed her that she was in the process of arranging an early finish for the two of them.

"I will drive you home today, Zoe," Adimo said as she picked up her bag and walked towards the open office door. She turned around while rummaging through her bag for her car keys.

"Oh yes, are you good to fly tomorrow?"

"Well, yeh, absolutely. You want me there?"

Adimo gave her a genuine smile. "I need you there, Sister, thanks. We can be aboard the test flight," she shouted as she made her way down the stairs.

Zoe picked up her cell phone and began to text Vic. She stopped herself and decided it was better to call him in the evening.

She went through the office drawers and cabinet, assessing what she would need to take home with her today.

Neil had not done any river crossings in a long time, and now he found himself along with Vince about to board the second vessel within a few days, crossing the Rufiji River.

South was their direction of intent, and they had reached the ferry barge crossing point not far from Kikola, about 25 kilometres north of Shuguin Falls.

Vince traded his offer of a fishing trip with Jim in favour of Neil agreeing to travel south on a hunting trip. Neil raised the fact that with most folk preparing to leave left an opportunity to do such things.

Neil already had the go-ahead from Ron who was now back in Dar; the other drivers would assist in the departures to the airstrip with Kevin and Sam.

They planned to return to the lodge on Thursday to catch up with Brad and Jim prior to their departure.

The ferry began its crossing, and in comparison to their first crossing, the distance from bank to bank was considerably shorter. This particular craft had a large notice in Swahili and English, stating the maximum capacity being one vehicle at a time was the SWL. This gave Neil a much better sense of security, as he calculated that the chances of being confused with the amount of 'one' was highly unlikely and overloading was practically impossible.

On arrival at the opposite bank, they would meet with one of Juma's relatives who would offer some advice to them regarding areas of opportunity that could prove productive for hunting smaller game.

This area was as far south as they planned to travel. The wetlands that began more towards the west had been discussed between them, but time would not accommodate further travel.

As they waited in the ferry-docking area, sweating and resting on the hood of the vehicle, the heat was rapidly increasing. The crowds noisily moved quickly towards the ferry, pushing and nudging each other, intending to secure their place aboard the vessel.

Vince handed a bottle of water to Neil.

"Hey, buddy, I wonder what the maximum amount of bodies is allowed on there," Vince said, tilting his head in the direction of the ferry.

"What's your plans when you get back to Dar, Neil?"

"Depends when we get back, mate; next Monday we planned, yeh? I will give Ron a bell probably on Saturday. I can't see mobilisation of clients for ten days or two weeks, permit process and the usual red tape. I'm sure we can handle a few cold ones when we get back for sure."

"Absolutely, partner. Well, this will be the last weekend at the lodge. I've really enjoyed it all so far. Oh yeh, those two dames of yours will still be around," Vince said, laughing.

"Yeh, fine, but I don't fancy yours much."

"Which one would that be?"

"Who do you recon, mate? The Nancy one," Neil shouted.

Vince grabbed Neil by the shoulders from behind and laughed while shaking him.

A local man approached them, wearing a white kaftan, carrying a stick and leading a large goat secured by a rope collar around its neck. This man being the only person to be walking in the opposite direction of the ferry could be assumed to be Juma's relative. They greeted each other and the man introduced himself as Juma's brother named Ziad. Neil immediately noticed the facial resemblance. Following some interesting advice from Ziad, Neil handed him two cold sodas and the money from Juma. Neil had insisted to Juma that he would gift his brother the money from his own pocket.

"Can we offer you a lift anywhere?" Neil asked.

"No, no, thank you. I am entering this boat here, it's leaving very soon."

Ziad and his goat melted into the packed crowd of noisy pedestrians on-board the ferry that was already beginning the crossing.

A silence prevailed replacing the hustle, movement and shouting that dominated the past hour.

The Australian and the American smiled and exchanged glances at each other while dabbing the sweat from their foreheads and faces with handkerchiefs in the intense heat.

"OK, mate, let's get moving and some air moving around us. I'm sweating like Stevie Wonder in a darts final."

Vince lay back on the vehicle hood, laughing for a minute before settling into the passenger's seat of the vehicle.

179

Neil navigated through some savanna after crossing a main road; some sparse thicket was developing but was not yet becoming an obstacle. The concern on Neil's mind was some of the River Rufiji's contributories that may have developed into mud baths in this dry season. He had a fairly competent knowledge of this area, but a few years had passed since his last visit. Neil stopped to have a look around. He explained to Vince that it would be advantageous to get onto the higher ground around the area at the moment.

"Hold on a minute," Neil said as he steered towards the edge of one of the contributory banks.

"What do you recon, Vince?"

The both of them were looking at a steep decent towards the completely dried up riverbed about 20 metres wide.

"Let's go for it," Vince said loudly.

Neil released the parking brake and let the vehicle roll down the embankment with the transmission in the lower ratio option. He kept the vehicle steadily pushing its way through the soft sandy surfaces and without hesitating, negotiating up the hard rocky assent to level ground on the opposite bank. He stopped the vehicle and applied the parking brake.

"Fuck me, Vince, I know it is dry season, but I did not expect to see some tribs as dried up as this. Mind you, I did hear that there were some new irrigation support projects in this area, maybe rice or something. Anyway, we got one more to get across and things should be a little bit more hassle free. It's good to know we can come back the same route as long as there ain't any big flash floods. Just kidding, mate."

The other contributory that demanded crossing was wider and dried up apart from a trickle flow running down the centre that was surrendering to the sun and rapidly evaporating.

They crossed the next riverbed easier than the last one, which was hardly a difficult task for the vehicle they were using. As they drove along the more or less flat plains of grassland, Neil's cell phone began to vibrate. He took the call from Adimo.

They were late in arranging some sleep due to their evening travel. It was now Wednesday and Marc and Odette planned to rest late afternoon. There would be no evening travel tonight, providing there was no change to evacuation plans which would be highly unlikely. They had taken the second Ruaha River barge-crossing and headed directly south towards the rendezvous point in the Kilombero area. They had chosen a fallen tree within the thicket of the savanna that also offered a wall of cover in the form of its uprooted layer of grassland surface. The mass of dry white-and-black branches proved a perfect platform to lay some natural material and grasses to adapt the tree into a shade and blind for the vehicle. Most importantly, they were fortunate again to be in an area that allowed their cell-phone networks to transmit and receive. Marc began his daily checks on the vehicle and asked Odette to try to calculate the distance between them and Kilombero.

The South Africans had covered more than average distance, following their Ruaha crossing at the second point. Obtaining information from the ferry-barge operator regarding Marc and Odette crossing earlier in the day had come to them easily. Both police vehicles had also used this crossing point following the information received from the ferry operator. The police had checked the second point first simply due to the queue of vehicles causing an obstruction at the first point, making progress to the ferry almost impossible. By not investigating the first crossing point, the police had deprived themselves from obtaining information of an incident involving a South African and a .45-calibre revolver.

With the idea in mind that the two vehicles of interest to the police were west-bound, they decided to ascend to some higher ground through the forested areas.

They reached the summit of this hillock that was not very high by any standards. Omar and Winston left the vehicle with the dog to have a look around the immediate area for any potential threats. Simba was entered back into the vehicle and the two officers sat down on one of the large rocks that was creating an overhang and provided a view over the trees below and the adjoining savanna.

Omar settled down to scan everything in his vision through the binoculars. The afternoon heat haze forming in the distance like an impenetrable abyss blurred out everything beyond to a barrier of colourless movement.

Omar began quickly shifting his body backwards, away from the rock edge in an attempt to conceal his presence from the view in front of him. Winston naturally adopted the same movement.

"What's wrong, Omar?" Winston enquired in a loud whisper.

"It's them. They are moving above the first dried riverbed down to the left and moving towards this area below us, maybe one-and-a-half kilometres away."

Omar handed the binoculars to Winston and urged him to be careful, then headed to the other vehicle to inform John and Vic. The three of them returned to the rocks. John viewed the scene, then handed the glasses to Vic. They were pleased at this development, but apprehension reminded them that they should adopt some caution in planning their next move. The vehicle had now entered the riverbed and was out of sight; their view was blocked by trees and the general contrast of the surrounding features between them and the changes of direction of the riverbed.

They waited, but the vehicle had not emerged at the next visible part of riverbed to their right. The South Africans must have parked up within the area out of their view. They could only guess for how long.

They needed the element of surprise to reduce the risk of armed conflict, and they agreed to make their move around early evening. Omar moved the vehicle downhill, away from the rocks. Simba was kept inside the vehicle to avoid any noise being created by the dog. They took it in turns to keep an eye on the situation below. John was in position on the rocks, carrying out his lookout duties, enduring the 38-degree heat from the afternoon sun. The time was between 2:30 and three, and something caught his peripheral vision to the left, a general southwest direction. He focused the binoculars and just caught sight of a vehicle disappearing out of sight due to the contours of the riverbed it was travelling on. This was not a welcome situation, as the vehicle was moving on the same riverbed as the South Africans were camped at.

Locals maybe, he thought to himself. Now a situation had developed that would require some decisive action, and soon. This vehicle was just around a kilometre away. As John waited for the vehicle to come into view again, he signalled Vic and the others to come over.

He replaced the binoculars with the rifle and bipod they had used earlier to have a closer view on things. The others were briefed of this latest development. He focused the riflescope on the maximum x24 magnification and had a crystal-clear view of this vehicle as it emerged into view once again. Things were becoming more of a problem than some locals on the move.

"Shit," John muttered. "Shit, this is not good."

Without any further comments, John left the rifle for the others to observe.

After Vic had a look, he displayed a kind of concerned laugh, looking at the ground and shaking his head.

"Man, this is all we need 'not' but is probably easier to deal with than we think, John," Vic said as he reached for his cell phone.

"I was thinking the same. Hold on, I will give you his number," John said.

"On second thoughts, buddy, let's bring Adimo in on this one. I think a call from her will receive more attention."

The vehicle that was gradually moving on the same riverbank and towards the South African camp was none other than Neil McPherson's Land Cruiser from the lodge. Vic had explained their dilemma to Adimo. She responded in surprise but then quickly realised that Neil and his friend, Vince, had a plan to explore other game areas further out from their usual sectors.

"Leave it to me, Vic, I will get back to you," she said.

Their conversation was brief and Vic strolled back to the rocks.

As he approached, he heard the guys laughing. He had a check through the binoculars to the right of the riverbed where they expected the South Africans to emerge. There were no changes there. In this short period, to the amusement of the guys, the lodge vehicle had come to a halt. This was clearly a result of Adimo's communication with Neil. Prior to Neil turning the vehicle around, Vince and Neil had got out the vehicle and were hopelessly looking around in different directions in an attempt to locate the task force who had monitored and identified them. Adimo had been quite straight with Neil and was not economical with the truth when she explained the present situation to him. She asked just one thing of Neil to refrain from creating any gunshots for the next couple of hours, which he readily agreed to. They turned around and left the riverbed at the first convenient exit path that they found.

The location of the lodge vehicle was more or less southwest, and with the blind spots being more numerous due to the bends and curves of the dry riverbed, they altered their plans to approach from this direction.

At 17:30, both the police vehicles headed back down the hillock on the same route as they ascended. They followed the bank southwest in search of a convenient point of entry down onto the riverbed. They entered about a mile from the South African camp. Dusk was beginning to take over quickly, transforming their surroundings into a colourless arena and distances now being more unfathomable to judge. They set off in the direction of the three suspects.

As they steadily moved north with all vehicle lights off, their plans became disrupted once again. Coming towards them out of the darkness were powerful beams of light rapidly becoming more intense and carving through the darkness with sporadic changes of direction; there was no refuge from this. The beams suddenly beamed directly at them and lit up their two vehicles like a forecourt security lamp. Both police vehicles halted with the gap between them and the oncoming vehicle being 300 metres at best.

"Fuck," Vic commented as they watched this vehicle quickly manoeuvring to proceed in the opposite direction, and in seconds, they were now looking at the red tail lamps moving away from them. This time John and Vic were in the lead vehicle. John switched on the lamps and raced towards the escaping vehicle. They were in a proper 4x4-purpose vehicle, but the surface conditions dictated the speed and approach in order to avoid serious underside damage. The conditions were far from ideal for a high-speed pursuit. Far ahead, the vehicle they were pursuing veered off to the left, most likely exiting the riverbed. As they arrived at the point where the vehicle drove out the bed, the reason became clear. The obstruction was not possible to pass. This part of the riverbed appeared to have a wide deep basin that had managed to sustain water and an abundance of hippos occupied this. Some of them visible by their eyes, nostrils and ears aligned on the surface of the watery, muddy sludge and some roaming the banks on either side.

John accelerated hard to bring the Toyota up the bank's gradient and out of the riverbed. Both vehicles came to a halt nose to tail within some sparse thicket that they found themselves in on the savanna. John climbed out and stood on one of the spare wheels mounted on the hood.

"Can you see anything, buddy?"

"No, nothing, Vic, not a thing."

The other two in the vehicle behind were of the same opinion.

It seemed only moments away when the vehicle headlamps had exposed them in the fast-approaching dusk, but they were now enveloped in total darkness. They made the decision to abandon any pursuit during darkness and continue at first light. Both vehicles turned around and descended back down into the riverbed to make camp for the night.

"It definitely looks like these guys' intentions is to travel south," Omar said. "And they are sure not going to pass through this route again tonight."

Odette was trying to adjust from her nocturnal activity to settling down for the evening. The two of them appreciated the dark, dark surroundings and the beautiful night sky. For a while, during the night, they had only roads and tracks illuminated by vehicle headlamp beams to enjoy. Now the sounds of the night made them acutely aware of the variety of life forms that they were sharing the evening with.

The menacing roars and grunts of a territorial lion reverberating across hillocks and valleys invaded the relative silence. Odette shivered in agitation and began vigorously rubbing the goose bumps on her forearms that already had a thin coating of sweat in the 28-degree heat and humidity. Marc was sitting at the rear of the vehicle on top of a plastic bucket, cleaning and lubricating the semi-auto pistol.

"Yep, we are certainly catapulted a few notches down from the top of the food chain out here, Odette," Marc said as he watched her displaying a short quiver of fear.

"Yeh, well, it certainly gets my full attention and respect, Marc."

"Mine too, Odette. I find them pretty fascinating and I am afraid of them. Let's get some coffee together, babe."

Odette had calculated the distance between them and the arranged pickup point to be closer than they had assumed, six kilometres.

Marc would happily accept her judgement and calculations in these matters due to her past background with the IDF and the Combat Intelligence Collection Corps.

"Where do you recon the posse is just now, Marc?"

Marc admired her sharp facial features which were made even bolder by the glow and shadows created by the embers in the fire. He thought how much more attractive it gave her appearance. Her alert, intelligent eyes were on him.

"Well?" Odette continued as she ran her fingers through her hair, resting it behind her ears.

"Hey, tiger, two posses, don't let them get you down. I recon they are not too far away; the farther the better. To hell with them, I think we both know that we are likely to cross paths tomorrow. Tomorrow is our day and don't forget that and we are going there."

Marc raised his voice a little and pointed in the direction of west. She leaned towards him and squeezed him tight, with her face pushed into the base of his neck. The two of them embraced as if to recharge each other's body and soul.

"It's not the fear of them, Marc, it's the fear of not making it."

The night level of silence and insect sounds that they had become accustomed to was suddenly breached again by the lion. This time, he was louder and closer and prompted Odette to tighten her grip on Marc.

"Hey, shhh." Marc put his hands on her shoulders and kissed her.

He assured her that this territorial beast was still a few miles away.

Marc retrieved the thermal-imaging goggles from the vehicle that they previously used at the river area and gave the area a 360-sweep.

"No nasties, Lieutenant. You know, the sound of a lion's roar apparently can be carried something like seven or eight kilometres I think, and the lioness can make a fair sound also. The first time I ever heard a lioness roar was in a zoo enclosure when I was a kid. I nearly shit myself. It was so loud and so close."

Odette laughed, then stood up to take in the view of the night sky.

"Na, babe, that big fella is still more than a few blocks away."

Being the last evening before the planned evacuation day, some apprehension had settled into them. The both of them had taken some time to encircle their stopover area at a 40-metre radius with some fishing line and a few empty soda cans from the bulk spool that Marc had previously purchased. Marc handed Odette a plastic cup and produced a bottle from under the driver's seat. She looked curiously at the bottle when Marc turned the label side towards her to display an unknown brand of French brandy.

"You bastard, Marc, where did you get that?"

Marc was about to open it.

"No, Marc, let me."

Odette took the bottle from him and slowly turned the tamper-proof lid to produce the crisp raspy sound of the seal breaking.

"Just one or two each, babe," Marc said as she poured two small measures into the cups.

Marc squirted some brandy from his mouth into the glowing embers of the fire, producing a bright blue flame that quickly dissipated. He laughed and swallowed his next sip.

"*Tu es un connard,* Marc."

The effect of the brandy flexed the spine of agitation that influenced their normally heuristic attitude to challenge. They smoked cigarettes and enjoyed some of the smoked fish prepared at the resourceful riverside location. Marc stood up again and scanned the area through the thermal-imaging apparatus.

"Are you expecting anyone, Marc? Maybe these yarpies just want their jeep back, hun bun," Odette said, laughing in her facetious temperament.

Marc could only join her in laughing.

"Hey, Odette, you don't come out with them too often, but when you do, 'class'! Tell you what though, they can have it and all the contents when we are done with it less the goodies buried under that rear wheel. I may consider investing in one of these when we are out of this shit. That vehicle will take you around the planet and back again. Apart from our transport, it is our bed, haven, shower cubicle, you name it."

Marc kissed the hood of the vehicle as he walked back to Odette by the fire. He took the brandy bottle and poured another two measures of the distilled grape juice into the cups. They sat together, thankful to be safe in this African paradise this evening from all the hidden dangers that possibly surrounded them. The bottle of liquid courage that Marc had surprisingly supplied and the calming effect it gave them was appreciated on this evening. Tomorrow would prove to be their most demanding day, but they were glad to have reached this point in the game. After all, it was a game. It had always been a game to Marc, Dennis and Odette, a dangerous and profitable game but still a game. Circumstances had forced Marc and Odette to take this game to another level, another level of uncertainty. They had changed the rules just as their mafia board of directors had changed the rules and decided to have some unfortunate individuals compromised after being termed surplus to requirements. They both now hated the organisation for this.

The grunts and roars of their lion king could be heard again. This time, his announcements were fading more to into the distance. Odette did not tremble, and they stood up after a mutual decision to tidy up and settle indoors for the rest of the evening. Marc held her snuggly and said the one word into her ear that was on both their minds, "Tomorrow."

She began to unbutton Marc's denim shirt and slid her arms around his waist. She pushed her crotch hard against him.

"Tomorrow is tomorrow, and tonight is tonight, cowboy."

He kissed her passionately and let her enter the Land Cruiser. He poured two more small measures, then capped the bottle. Before Marc entered the vehicle, his cell phone chimed a message. The rendezvous time for the next day was now 16:30.

Adimo, Zoe and the two additional officers packed themselves into the chopper at the heliport in Dar es Salaam. The earlier briefing in the morning covered the intention to secure arrests today. They were now aware of four vehicles identified in the area of interest with the fifth vehicle until now unaccounted for. Vic, along with her police colleagues, would be met at a pre-arranged point as soon as they arrived there.

"Is Vic expecting you, Zoe?" Adimo shouted over the noise of the turbine during lift off.

"Yes, I let him know last night. I decided surprises would be a bit unprofessional. I hope all goes well today. I was going to say 'smoothly', but these South African guys seem to be shrouding their intentions in uncertainty."

"We will get a better idea when we touch base with the guys, Zoe, and they will be glad to see us, trust me."

The meeting was planned in an area 25 miles northwest of Kikola on the north side of the Rufiji River, and they only had a couple of hundred miles' journey to reach this location.

Zoe was using her time to take in the vastness of the savanna below. That brown river snaking through savanna, valleys and forests was never out of sight for long.

"Ten minutes to go, guys. I'm gonna take her down and do a sweep to port. I would appreciate your eyes on the ground, folks," Brian remarked.

The officers on the ground were located during the port sweep. Brian then swept to starboard to make his approach for landing. They touched down 50 metres from the two vehicles and Brian shut down the chopper.

As they all became reacquainted, it soon became clear that Zoe and Adimo's intentions were to travel with the vehicles and the two other officers would continue to occupy the chopper with Brian. This arrangement was met with no surprise to Vic while Winston, John and Omar had not assumed that the ladies would be part of the ground crew.

Adimo jovially asked regarding the details of when Neil McPherson and Vince Kelly appeared into their area of surveillance. Vic, who had taken up a position of lying down on the grass, just shook his head while running his fingers through his hair, offering a sign of disinterest to her. Zoe looked at him while making a gesture over her cheek, suggesting that he needed a shave. Vic motioned a salute to her and smiled. John conversed with Adimo briefly, informing her of the incident with Neil's vehicle before they all joined in a discussion in regards to the South Africans. Although they had an idea which area the three South Africans would be at, they had no idea of the whereabouts of Ms Gordon and Mr Dupuis. They did agree that all of them would be in fairly close proximity of each other and the chopper should confirm this. It was 10:30 and was now time to make a move. Brian and the other two officers lifted off to begin some searching from the air. Adimo and Zoe climbed into the vehicle with Vic and John while Omar and Winston along with Simba took up as lead vehicle. They set off in a south-westerly direction.

"Those hunter boys, Adimo, were the last folks I expected to see around here."

"They do get around, Vic. You never quite know what game they are hunting or how far they are prepared to travel to locate it. Last time I spoke with him, he was actually at a loose end on where to go and was considering some different location."

"Well, they have arrived in or around this area, so I suppose we will just have to deal with that if and when we have to, Adimo."

Vic leaned back over his front seat position.

"Do us a favour please, Adimo? Don't let him know that we were focused on him through a high-power riflescope attached to a high-powered rifle."

Zoe could not keep from laughing, and John and Adimo smiled. Adi turned her head to look upwards out of the window in an attempt to restrain the laughter that seemed to be developing within her. Her attempts failed to produce the intended result and she had no choice but to release some loud laughter.

"Vic, you have no idea how crazy that sounded. You guys were actually monitoring a magnified Neil McPherson with crosshairs over him?"

"Yep, and his buddy."

The laughing eventually faded away; the bumps and the violent jarring of the vehicle aided with this. The pace they were travelling was as fast as the road surface and conditions would allow. Adimo explained that she had requested to Neil to cover the rear section of his vehicle with a bright white form of cover. He had complied and used one of the large, white, heavy sheets that they carried for lifting small game. The aim was to benefit them being recognised by the chopper. She was confident this would prove effective since the lodge vehicle had surprisingly appeared in the area. An hour had passed since setting off when Brian had radioed through, trying to make contact. Adimo requested John to halt the vehicle. They all listened intensely as Brian's message came through to them from above. They identified a safari-type vehicle 15 kilometres southwest from the police vehicles' position. The vehicle did not furnish any form of white marker over the rear section and had moved into the forested area probably due to the presence of the chopper.

Brian informed them of his essential requirement to gain altitude and warned them of a large dust storm advancing. Visibility had changed to zero for Brian and his passengers for the time being.

"Shit, what's the deal with these dust storms?" Vic asked.

"No telling," John replied. "They are a fairly frequent occurrence in the dry season in some areas, sometimes minutes sometimes hours."

The two vehicles carried on regardless of the oncoming dust storm.

Since entering into the forest, Marquis and his colleagues had stuck to a rough track that was bearing signs of little use in the past. In a way, they were thankful for the sudden arrival of the dust storm if only to benefit them temporarily from the eyes in the sky. Choppers were bad news in their book. They joked and discussed how easy it was to take one down with a large bore rifle, but who in their right mind would execute such an action? Unthinkable, they agreed, unless of course they were in a position where they would be returning fire. It was not difficult for them to calculate the intensions of Marc and Odette after they had received information regarding a disused airstrip in the area. They would interrupt the plans of the two ex-operatives at any cost. The one important piece of information that was not available to them was the time of arrival. This would also be dependent on the absence of dust storms.

One of the colleagues had returned, following some reconnaissance at Marquis's request; he was having trouble catching his breath after his sprint back to the vehicle. To the surprise of them all, the man had reported to them of his sighting of the two targets. They sounded to be just a couple of kilometres away. Marquis instructed one man to stay with the vehicle while he followed the other through the scrub and boulders. They arrived at a spot where Marquis's partner instructed him to crouch down. He checked the sun's position, then viewed through the binoculars. The glasses were handed to Marquis to view for himself. Marquis appeared happy and satisfied, an appearance not normally displayed by the man. They were less than a kilometre away. The dust and wind was intermittently coming and going. After the dust that had enveloped them for a minute or two, Marquis raised the glasses to have another look and assess the situation.

"Fuck!" he whispered, then checked again and around the area where Marc had been.

"Gone, fucking gone!"

Marquis handed the binoculars back to his colleague and instructed him to stay where he was before racing back in the direction of their own vehicle. Ten minutes passed when the vehicle appeared a short distance away, signalling the man to return to the vehicle. The man hurriedly approached the vehicle, again forced to run awkwardly, carrying the binoculars and a rifle. He saw the urgent demeanour of Marquis. Marquis was in the driver's seat. A sight never witnessed with the exception of leisurely entertaining some female company during an evening in a location that supported this activity.

The shorter man had just entered the rear seating of the Toyota, and before he could close the door, Marquis raced off. The track they were on was riddled with small potholes and the surface was as even as ploughed field. The jarring, rolling and zigzag motion that Marquis was maintaining under his control forced the man in the rear seat to lie across the seat and refrain from even thinking to secure his safety belt.

The vehicle was ascending on the track that had now narrowed down to a metre with one side of the vehicle negotiating grassy virgin ground and undergrowth that was inaccessible. Heavy branches crashed off the front of the vehicle, and the noise on contact with the windshield was so alarming that the glass appeared unbreakable. It was at this point that Marquis followed advice from his colleagues to slow down in fear of any failure occurring and rendering the vehicle out of service.

They were approaching a large kopje, and the forest was beginning to thin out, exposing some dry, grassy savanna. Marquis halted the vehicle and got out to make his way up the rocky formation as high as he could. He cursed again as he made his way back to the vehicle and mentioned something in regards to having to go down before going up.

He armed himself with a rifle and instructed his colleagues to follow him as he made his way down and around the right side of the kopje, through the thick, dry grass and uneven ground.

He used hand and arm signals to guide the driver and indicate halting or commencing. He was not happy with the delay and the thought of being in an exposed area should the chopper return. They would have to make their way up the hillock again in the general direction towards where Marc had been seen after they completed their slow progress through the rough ground. Marquis was also convinced that they had not been noticed, although this assumption was not entirely accurate. Marc Dupuis had caught a glimpse of them and was grateful for the sudden onrush of the dust and wind activity as they moved out of their concealment.

During the South Africans' gradual accent on the hillock, the progress of Marc and Odette was more predictable as they descended towards a more level part of the savanna, graced with some forest, scrub with dry and wet tributaries of the Rufiji River. There were breath-taking contrasts in this area and the landing strip was in close proximity. Marc brought the vehicle to a halt in between some massive rock formations still quite a distance from where the savanna clashed with the deep-forested area. They got out and trained their binoculars on the hillock that they had descended. To attempt to move down on the other side and come around unnoticed would result in their path being blocked by large rocks and cut off by the river's path of direction. There was still no sign of their pursuers.

The roar in the air above them caught them suddenly and completely off guard. Marc almost dropped the binoculars and Odette instinctively dropped to the ground to make herself as small as possible. The chopper had approached from the huge rocks behind them, heading towards the hillock that they were observing, at an altitude of 600 feet.

"Shit, what the fuck? Do you think we got spotted there, Odette?"

Marc was already making his way to the vehicle with Odette quickly doing likewise. They got inside and started the engine.

"They must have, Marc, but hey, look, they are carrying on without as much as a tack. I recon we just got lucky there, that's cops. Let's get out of here."

They drove quickly towards the forested area and higher vegetation growth that would offer them cover. They drove behind the cover of some more large rocks surrounded by ten-foot-high elephant grass, not far from the edge of the forest. The panic had subsided and they felt more concealed in their present location.

"It looks like that chopper has taken an interest in something on the hillock, Marc."

"Yeh, give me a minute."

Odette was already looking through the binoculars and handed them to Marc.

"OK, got you, hovering but just disappeared out of sight now on the other side. What do you recon, those goons?"

"Yep, for sure."

"Where the fuck are you?" Marc said as he had another intense look at the hillock area.

Just as they had expected, a vehicle appeared descending the hillock as they had done earlier. They watched at their distance of three kilometres away and Odette was now putting herself closer by using the riflescope.

"I count two, Marc, no, three, three in that jeep."

Odette tried to locate the chopper without success.

"Marc, what time is it?"

"13:20, just over three hours before evac. These bastards know our plans, babe, I'm sure."

Odette agreed. The landing strip was visible from where they were; it was a patchy view through the trees. They had to establish an obstruction-free route to that location and it looked like a kilometre away at best. Odette informed Marc that they were at the correct end to be at as instructed. He never advised her to recheck. This jeep was heading their way but seemed to be staying on a track on higher ground. This unexpected development encouraged the two of them to reconsider their judgement and wonder if they had missed something. Maybe during the panic following the chopper's appearance that forced them to rush away, impaired their judgement.

"No way, Odette, fuck knows what the hell they are up to, but we took the route that we took and that route is correct; it got us here, yeh?"

Brian had not taken long in locating the two police vehicles and landed a short distance in front of them on the hillock. They got out and waited for the team to arrive. He then explained to them the risk involved for the chopper to remain in the area of a possible conflict. He described how he witnessed one of the occupants of the jeep being outside of the vehicle, carrying a rifle.

"You know, guys, the search and location is complete from my side; it's just not worth the risk of the chopper taking a hit in the air or the ground."

The officers could not agree more, and it was decided that the aircrew standby further over in the valley until required. Brian and the two officers gave an update of the situation on the opposite side of the hill and advised of the quickest way around to connect with negotiable tracks.

"Well, looks like we are all in close proximity now. Do we have a plan?" Zoe asked.

"I wish we had, Zoe," Adimo replied, "but I think we will have to assess what develops on the other side first. No telling how these people will react now. You will see what I mean over there; in a way, they are boxed in because of the river, its tributaries and the general rocky terrain, not to mention the wetlands beyond."

Brian assisted in them adjusting their thoughts when he mentioned the disused airstrip presenting itself as a forest clearing that looked as wide as a football pitch and 500 metres long.

"That we assumed to be well overgrown," John commented.

"Nope, I can assure you it is only clear from the air and it looks to me like nothing but dried soil and savanna grass; nothing green at all."

The other two officers agreed with Brian and offered some more comments in Swahili to their Tanzanian colleagues.

"My guess is you are going to find your Canadian friends over there somewhere unless they have not arrived yet. We can take a short period to check in the opposite direction and return to here," Brian continued.

The two vehicles began the ascent and tested communications with Brian. Brian and his crew lifted off and set a north-easterly course to spend some time on the chance of locating the other vehicle of interest. There was nothing of interest to be seen; following communications with Adimo, they set a course back and landed on the pre-arranged area. Brian carried out his usual visual checks, strapped down the main rotor blades and the officers made their way to the welcome shade of a wide acacia tree. The heat and humidity was becoming unbearable for Brian. He soon understood the sense in exploiting the shade of the tree and made his way over there to join the officers.

"Piss pot hot, guys, eh?" he said as he stood for a minute, dabbing the sweat dry on his face and head with a cloth.

Without any warning, the hot and humid conditions sustained by the high pressure that cocooned Marc and Odette was transformed into a violent swirling gale moving in all directions at the same time. Odette managed to grasp her hat before it was taken by the wind. Her hair was directed upwards as if a huge vacuum was above her. The both of them moved to enter the vehicle just as the vegetation and thorny thicket became a noisy arena of potential flaying weapons. The sand and dust blasted their faces as they entered.

The blue sky had vanished and was replaced by a gun-smoke-coloured fog, allowing just enough light through to remind them which direction the sky was in. The vehicle rocked sometimes violently in this sudden tantrum of Mother Nature. They were thankful that the goods were still inside the vehicle on this occasion. The storm subsided after 20 minutes but soon began to demonstrate its fury again. The short break in white, brown and grey dust opened a view of the sky to them. The sky had become a dark slate grey as if primed to release an arc of electrical energy. The cocoon of dust and debris was now darker and cooled the area. 15 minutes became 30, and 30 became over the hour before the day was transformed back to the hot African savanna paradise.

The only movement of air that seemed to be left in the stillness of the savanna were the small precipitous random dust devils that disintegrated not long after they appeared.

Marc got out of the dust-covered Toyota and kneeled on top of the hood. He raised himself slowly to view over the top of the tall elephant grass to find there was nothing to see in all directions. This made them uncomfortable, at least until they were aware of the other vehicle's location. To make a move now from their concealment would not be wise; they decided to avoid the risk and wait.

"These dust storms are concerning, Marc."

He agreed and advised Odette to banish the thought of this from her mind. If a dust storm interfered with any aircraft approach or, even worse, 'take off', disaster would be inevitable.

The thing they had to concentrate on was to be in control of that airstrip for the period of time during this planned operation.

They wondered what had happened to the chopper, maybe exceeded its operating range and returned to refuel somewhere. It would be bound to have backup or an intervention alliance on the ground.

"I see something, Marc. It's them." She handed him the binoculars and pointed to guide him in a direction.

"I see that, yeh. That is the roof of a vehicle, looks about a mile away, stationary. Odette, we got to put these fuckers out of action."

"Marc, the only way is an ambush, surprise or a booby trap, land mine or something, you know, but unfortunately we don't have the latter." Odette's past military experience was apparent in her suggestion of options.

"Babe, we could sacrifice one of the packages that would toast them," Marc suggested.

She managed a smile and admired his power of unpredictably moving in and out of reality in difficult times. Marc agreed with her again and accepted that the advantage was still theirs at this point in time.

The Airlift

A loud distant rifle shot followed quickly by another broke the silence. Odette focused the binoculars back in the direction of the vehicle. At first, she thought that the vehicle had managed to make its way back up the hillock, until she realised that this was another vehicle making its way down.

"Shit, another vehicle, Marc, bound to be connected to the chopper."

This vehicle had stopped and appeared to be attempting to take some cover behind some raised ground between them and the lower vehicle. These two vehicles were involved in an exchange of gunfire. Circumstances had now encouraged the two of them to make a decision. They decided to move out, and the only direction open to them was into the forest in the direction of the airstrip. They got into the vehicle and Marc engaged reverse.

"Wait, Marc, wait, stop."

The vehicle nearest to them was now moving quickly in their direction. The amount of dust created suggested that this vehicle was travelling at speed. Marc pulled back into their cover and watched as a second and third vehicle were now in pursuit of the first one. These three vehicles, although they were heading in a general direction towards Marc and Odette, were on a different level. They were heading away to the left of their cover position, which would take them to higher ground, overlooking the forest and possibly part of the airstrip.

"Our options are slim just now, Odette. We have to sit tight and see what develops here. All that's missing is that God-dammed chopper."

The two of them got out the vehicle, armed with the hunting rifle and the assault rifle, and took up precautionary positions within the large rocks that safely cradled them out of sight. It was clear why the vehicle had chosen this other track. It appeared the choice had been done in haste or panic, as this track offered a smoother surface to facilitate speed. These vehicles were approaching fast, possibly 80kph and visibly stable-looking. They were not experiencing much bouncing or rolling.

The pursuing vehicles were not wasting time in trying to catch up as they watched the first vehicle speed past their view 500 metres away before moving out of view behind the forest tree line. It was not long at all before the other two vehicles repeated the action; all three vehicles looked pretty much identical in their passing.

"I wish that airstrip was on the opposite side of the river, Marc, and we had a powerboat."

"Wait right here, Odette, be back shortly."

Marc picked up the assault rifle and made his way towards the riverbank at the south side of the airstrip. Odette was on alert again, following some exchange of gunfire on the higher ground where the three vehicles had driven towards. Marc was catching his breath on return from the river.

"No way, babe. I was checking the riverside for any access with the jeep, not a chance. I never noticed any powerboats either."

He gave her one of his confident mischievous grins while checking the time on his cell phone, 15:00 hours and no messages.

A powerful-sounding impact on the rock formation close to them sent the two of them to the ground for cover. A blast of sand, dust and shattered rock rained down on them. A loud deep sound of a ricochet travelling upwards quickly faded away.

They were almost under the vehicle.

"It would be a long shot to think of that as a stray bullet, Marc."

Just seconds later, another projectile struck the vehicle on the edge of the roof and exited through the opposite side rear window before burying itself in the undergrowth. Glass particles scattered over the area around them.

"We need to do something about this, Odette."

"Marc, when you hear me firing my second shot and only then, get into the vehicle and drive as fast as you fucking can into the cover of the forest."

Before Marc could react, Odette was gone, racing towards the kopje with the hunting rifle.

"Shit," Marc cursed as he watched this girl in blue Levis, black T-shirt and hiking boots moving as calculating as a leopard.

She was 30 metres away from the vehicle and scaling the rocks of the kopje with the rifle strapped over her shoulder. After positioning herself confidently in a concealed position, she checked the sun's position before slowly raising the binoculars to view the area that could be concealing this shooter. These hills had a sparse coverage of trees, and she managed to locate one of the vehicles. Another round impacted the rocks close to her vehicle, this time without any ricochet sound. Like most shooters, she hated ricochets, especially incoming ones. She once just about lost a friend when she was in her teens in Canada. Her friend took a shot at a rabbit from 25 metres with his .22 LR rifle. The 40-grain lead went clean through the small animal, then ricocheted off an exposed snaking tree root before embedding into the boy's neck. He had bled a lot by the time he reached the hospital accident and emergency and was lucky to survive. Had a main artery or spinal column been struck, circumstances would have probably been catastrophic.

She detected movement behind rocks and vegetation approximately 500 or 600 metres away, not far from where the vehicle was. She knelt down and chambered a round into the 30-06 rifle, then positioned the rifle stalk resting on her hand using the rock as a bench rest. The crack of an incoming high-velocity projectile was loud above her, this time not contacting anything. Again, she focused on the rocks through the scope at 18 times magnification and confirmed that a figure wearing a hat was moving around. She knew Marc had zeroed this rifle at 300 metres the day he was playing with it, so she would act quick and set her crosshairs around two feet above her target. Without wasting time, she quickly exposed herself for the shot and the boom sent one round up that hill. The big spent brass ejected out of the rifle's receiver as she quickly re-chambered another round. When the rifle recovered, she observed the rocks through the scope; the dust emerging from the rocks told her where her bullet had impacted. It struck low.

"Excellent," she told herself. This was all she needed.

Aiming a little higher, she sent another round up into the same rocks.

"Marc, go, go!" She sent another towards the rocks, determined to keep this shooter down and hidden. During this, the Toyota cranked up and raced into the cover of the forest. Odette boomed a fourth round into the sniper's den, then immediately took off as fast as she could into the forest. She ran heavily into Marc and he relieved her of the rifle.

"Careful, Marc, still one round in there," she said, panting.

Marc kissed her. "Catch your breath, babe."

He began to reload the rifle, this time chambering a cartridge and closing the bolt before locking the steel magazine into the receiver loaded with five rounds of ammo. He then engaged the safety system on.

"You made an amazing decision there, babe, and gave me no time at all to think about it. Bravo, *mademoiselle*. Did you see much up there?"

"I found the shooter's hide and a parked vehicle; no time to take the time to recce though. They were trying to put the vehicle out of action, Marc, not us."

"Really, that was nice of them. I will remember that when they are at the receiving end of my muzzle."

He grinned and gave her a hug. More gunfire began again on the hill beyond the trees.

Neil nudged Vince awake from his nap in the passenger seat of the Toyota.

"Hey, check this out, mate."

Ahead of them, off the main track, was the chopper that they knew so well. As they approached, Brian and the two officers made their way from the shade of the tree to meet them. Brian studied the rear of the vehicle as Neil was parking and commented on the white material that he had been made aware of firmly fixed down.

"Hey, what's up, man?" Vince said as they welcomed each other.

They walked to the acacia tree to have a chat in the shade. They updated each other in regards to the recent events developing beyond the hillock and the previous events that Neil and Vince had stumbled into on the dried riverbed.

Brian advised Vince and Neil that certain areas beyond the hillock would be best considered out of bounds; he was referring to the valley areas that Adimo and her crew had planned to pursue. They understood Brian's duties being in standby.

"Yeh, no worries, mate, maybe we should travel with a white flag fixed to a pole on the back. What do you recon, Vince?"

"You're a crazy bastard, Neil, you know that, yeh?" Brian commented in laughter.

"Well, Brian, I'm glad I don't have a South African accent today, mate."

"Is there much difference between an Australian and South African accent?" Vince asked.

Vince just managed to move his backside quickly enough to avoid contact from Neil's boot.

"Right, Vince, we need to boogie, mate. Thanks for the heads up, Brian."

They parted company and headed for the hillocks areas in front of them.

"What a fuck up, Vince. That's twice we have been in among this shit."

"Yeh, what the hell, buddy? We may as well enjoy this fucking road trip that has been laid on for us and head on back early doors tomorrow."

During the vehicle chase, an absence of coordination resulted in both police teams becoming separated. Adimo, Vic and Zoe had driven to the peak of the hillock. John had made his way down on foot to check on Winston and Omar and had not returned; he had called Adimo to notify her that he was with the other two. The existing hurdle now was the fact that the South Africans were dug in and spread out in between both police and agent teams.

"This ain't gonna be easy, ladies, but I guess none of us really expected these guys to walk up and let us cuff them."

"We will work it out, Vic, and we will have to concentrate on a solution to try to avoid this going into nightfall," Adimo mentioned while smiling at Zoe. "These guys appear to be in a position of being unable to move up or down."

Some more shots rang out below, causing Vic to display signs of being overprotective to the female officers. They began to calculate the best positions for each of them to be in on this high ground. An assessment was made between them, and it was fairly accurate for them to assume that the South Africans were 150 to 200 metres below and spread out. They based this acknowledgement on the sound of the gunfire. Their colleagues' positions further below were more difficult to calculate. One thing they could correctly assume regarding their colleagues was that they were not over the other side of the track where this part of the forest engulfed the airstrip.

Vic and his female colleagues did have a view of part of the savanna-coloured airstrip that lay 500 metres away from them. Anyone below them would find it impossible to have the same view as them.

"Shit!" Vic said aloud. He realised that the airstrip was not void of any activity. He had detected at least one individual moving within part of the forest through the limited daylight that the dense forest offered in its infrequent sparse sections. He scanned further in all directions, trying to locate a vehicle without results. He relayed the news to Zoe and Adimo.

"That's got to be our Canadian or Canadians. I think we can assume at least one of them is alive and kicking."

Adimo and Zoe agreed.

Vic picked up one of the rifles that they had loaded earlier. He choose the bolt action. He lay down and took aim towards the airstrip and randomly fired a

196

round from the Howa rifle into the dry, grassy, savanna surface of the strip. The eruption of dust and debris was instantly visible after he squeezed the trigger.

"Just experimenting, girls. These are supposed to shoot out through 600 metres I believe, .223 or 5.56 or whatever."

Between the three of them, they had the two rifles and four handguns. John had set off downhill with his issued AK47 and sidearm.

John, along with Omar and Winston on the lower level of the forested hillside, were well-spaced in distance between each other and knew roughly where each other was. They had also noticed some form of activity taking place towards the airstrip area. Omar signalled to John to make him aware of his intention to move from his present position to a small rocky formation a short distance away on a higher level. He was trying to get to a point where he could pinpoint any of their adversaries. As Omar got up and ran in a crouched posture, John squeezed the trigger of his assault rifle in burst mode to release two rounds at a time in random directions where the South Africans' positions were thought to be.

Omar reached his rocky haven without incident, and he positioned himself to carefully survey the area of interest. He had to wait for incoming fire that would surrender the shooters' position, but he strongly suspected an area of various mounds of earth and some large termite mounds. Marquis had tasked his subordinates to concentrate on reaching the proximity of the airstrip. As well as this being his main priority, they needed to be between the law-enforcement officers and Marc and Odette. Marquis set his own task of getting to the higher ground and compromise the officers who held this area. While these officers occupied this area, they were pretty much in command of disrupting any events developing on the airstrip. Heavy-calibre bullets began impacting around the rocks and trees where Omar had dug in as well as beyond and lower down the hillside. He could tell there were both a bolt-action and a semi-automatic weapon in use. The general direction from where the shots were coming from appeared to be from the termite-mound area that he suspected.

During these gunshots, Marquis was beginning his ascent to the higher ground. It was crucial for him not to be detected from those above.

Winston was hidden at a location closest to the track, separating the forested area on the hillside that they occupied and the part of the forest that surrounded the airstrip. He attracted John's attention and indicated his intention to cross the track to enter the forest to access the airstrip side. John directed some fire in the general direction of where the last incoming fire came from. Winston raced towards the track and threw himself down into the heavy foliage at the edge of the forest to assess his options of crossing over. The dense grass he was waiting in concealed him from the view of anyone within the trees that he had just left. When the next occurrence of gunfire began, he quickly made his move and entered into the dark forest floor of his new surroundings. He kneeled down for a while and carefully took the time to observe these surroundings, hoping to detect some sound or movement to react to. There was nothing; he was welcomed by a silence and stillness that had him imagining that he could be the only living thing in there. The same tranquillity also appeared high up in the canopy. This came as no surprise to him and required no explanation, considering the amount of recent gunfire that took place. He decided to move in the general direction of the airstrip. He stood up and moved carefully using pre-selected trees as a stopover point to help conceal movement. The end of the airstrip was now 100 metres away, distinctly noticeable from the daylight invading the edge of the forest. Exchanges of gunfire began again, interrupting the silence that it had helped to create in the first place. He decided to move to the airstrip to have a view of the tree-lined areas meeting the airstrip savanna. He was also keeping a careful eye on the area behind him when he realised that he was just a good stone's throw away from the savanna grass that surfaced this disused airstrip.

Winston was taking the surroundings here into account before he moved towards the contrast of the forest and the savanna.

The menacing silence was suddenly broken by two unnerved pigeons taking flight above him and fluttering out of the forest. Startled and shaken, Winston pressed himself backwards against the tree, then turned side on to walk around it, observing all around him. The only visible movement was a contour feather given up by the bird that was slowly swaying on its way to the forest floor.

An explosion of sort preceded the stinging on his face, eyes and neck. He found himself on the canopy floor on his hands and knees, blinking repeatedly in an attempt to clear his eyes of the contaminant that was in there. He induced enough tears to flush out this source that was causing him so much pain and irritation, and he was relieved to discover that his eyesight was still with him. His temple area and earlobe were bleeding slightly, and dust and particles of tree bark were deposited on his cheek and neck. Winston began to recover his senses and looked at a large gape in the tree bark that was surrounded by wood splinters facing outwards in every direction. The sound of the bullet's impact and energy when it struck the tree trunk so close to him reached him before the report of the rifle; he had heard no gunshot.

His options were slim and he lay down where he was trying to plan the best way to move away from this area; moving on his stomach was the obvious course of action. The scar on the tree offered a general direction from where the shot was fired from. Nobody could be seen or heard moving towards him; this surprised him. His cell phone began to vibrate. Although the timing was less than convenient, he found himself welcoming the contact from John. He quietly informed John of his wellbeing while John informed him of one of the South Africans' entry to the forest that Winston was exploring.

He began to belly crawl in a direction where the trees and plants were offering more cover and less exposure than the area he was presently in.

Marc and Odette positioned themselves at prime locations, surrounded by heavy growths of greenery with rocks and thicket in abundance along the edge of the forest. They were 50 metres apart, and a deep, natural trench integrated the two points that they occupied. The trench allowed them to quickly access each other discretely as well as offering alternative firing points if desired. They were far from the vehicle, too far to consider moving back. Circumstances now presented new challenges, and the use of the vehicle was neither a requirement nor an issue.

Odette was in high alert within herself. She was well-hidden and the 30-06 hunting rifle had become part of her. She was glad of the light weight of this rifle.

Had Officer Winston been one of the South African mercenaries, she would not have taken aim at the tree trunk and the tree would be required to have fragmented skull bone and brain matter removed from its bark. She noticed Marc crawling along the ditch towards her.

"Odette, news! Not sure if it is good and bad, good and good or bad and fucking bad. Pickup time is unchanged, but pickup plans have changed."

Odette almost sighed in disappointment.

"They made contact just a couple of minutes ago; after giving them an update, they made the decision for us to board at the opposite end of the airstrip."

"What the fuck, Marc!?"

After considering the facts and circumstances, they quickly realised that this was not such a bad idea and probably the best procedure for the aircraft to follow. It meant that they had to adjust their plans to comply. It could produce advantageous results if all went well.

"We can do this, Marc, yeh?" She looked for reassurance from him.

"You bet, babe. What's the latest on the cop front? This yarpy bastard is a couple of hundred metres away, moving slowly."

"I would imagine the cop is moving in a commando crawl away in the opposite direction from that tree to reassess the situation," Odette replied.

They recognised it was now paramount importance to get back to the vehicle. The time was 16:05 hours.

They made their way in the direction of the vehicle. Odette was straddling the edge of the forest and Marc moving 30 metres in and avoiding the heavier undergrowth. He detected some movement to his left and reacted quickly to what he found. Winston made the choice to lie low when he heard them approaching, but his final movement to conceal himself caught Marc's attention. Marc was quickly in control and commanding the situation with an assault weapon. He signalled to Odette to halt and wait, then handcuffed Winston's hands behind his back with the handcuffs taken from his uniform pocket. Winston was quickly helped to his feet. Marc took possession of the AK47 and the police issued .38 and ordered Winston to move quickly in front of him. Winston could barely believe how quickly his circumstances changed. It was outlandish for him to see the presence of an armed athletic-looking girl moving stealthily in tandem with them just a short distance away. This strangely gave him some comfort over the thought of the dangerous situation that he was now in, but he would not confuse this with a false sense of security.

They arrived at the vehicle without incident. Marc helped Winston into the front passenger seat and got into the driver side. Odette, armed with the assault weapon, stayed 25 metres away outside at the forest edge in a prone position, scanning the area where they had come from. Winston's cell phone vibrated in his pocket, suggesting a message notification. Marc removed the phone and checked the message, '*ok to enter*'.

"Who is John? Your partner?"

"Yes."

Marc returned the text, '*No, delay some, let you know.*'

"Why no Swahili?" Marc asked.

No answer came from Winston, and Marc checked the time which was now 16:17 hours. 13 minutes, he thought. He watched Odette updating herself with the time.

Only Marc and Odette knew what event was about to happen. It was the first big advantage they had so far, and they prayed for a healthy outcome. Others were also risking their lives to make this happen.

Odette was still uncomfortable, wondering why there was no sign of this South African tailing them. She noticed some activity to her right beyond their last location inside the forest. She made her way back to the vehicle and replaced the assault rifle with the 30-06 from the rear floor.

Winston glanced at her and she returned him a quick nonchalant glance before her eyes moved downwards to concentrate with loading the magazine. Marc held his cell phone towards her, displaying the time at 16:20 hours. In seconds, she was back in her prone position, concentrating on the images displayed through the scope. She was in full view of Marc and their hostage. The instantaneous roar of the twin turbo props just 120 feet above came from behind as the shadow of the aircraft quickly passed over them. The sudden event caused Winston to panic and lower his position in his seat.

Marc started the vehicle engine as the aircraft smoothly touched down on the savanna, generating a mass of dust into the air.

The arrival of the aircraft clearly prompted the figure at their previous location to expose himself by moving out of the forest edge onto the savanna. He appeared confused and seemed to move in the direction of the aircraft. The dust was now spreading fast in the hot, still afternoon and her view was about to become impaired.

She squeezed the trigger and the boom of the rifle sent the heavy-calibre bullet towards him; she immediately ran to the vehicle. She had seen the man go down just before her view became no more than a curtain of dense red dust. She entered the rear of the vehicle and placed the rifle on the floor.

Marc drove fast and smooth along this savanna airstrip towards the aircraft that was now manoeuvring 180 degrees in preparation for take-off. The dust stirred up by the landing was a bonus in respect of the circumstances. He drove to the tail end of the airstrip where the trees and foliage convulsed heavily in the draught of the turbines and turned the vehicle around to rest 20 metres from the aircraft, facing the same direction on the port side.

The door was already open on the fuselage, and Marc and Odette were already out of the vehicle, wearing their backpacks. A man at the aircraft door watched as they started to take the rifle and assault rifle from the Toyota.

"No weapons; c'mon, move," the voice shouted from the aircraft door.

The pilot began to raise the rpm of the engines and the two of them raced to the entrance door; they were helped by being pulled up the access stairs.

The De Havilland DHC-6 was already in full throttle and disturbing enough dust behind it to completely screen the Toyota and the immediate area.

In seconds, the aircraft was high in the air and banking sharply to starboard high above the river.

With the exception of Marc and Odette, the arrival of the aircraft caught everyone by surprise and the quick departure even more. John had made his way into the forest surrounding the airstrip and was met with the lingering eerie silence. He quietly and carefully made his way to the strip, and on arrival at the edge of the savanna, he could hear or see nothing. He crouched down and dialled Winston's cell-phone number; he made three attempts without an answer. To the left and right of him, there was no sign of movement or sound, not even the sign of insect activity. The dust was still lingering over the area but was now beginning to thin out. John cleared the forest edge and began to walk in a direction to the right, staying close to the treeline of the forest. It was not long before he noticed something ahead of him at the edge of the forest, among an abundance of foliage; he approached with caution. An arm and a leg became visible, confirming the body of a man wearing khaki shorts and a matching heavy shirt lay in front of him; a large-calibre bolt-action rifle lay beside him. John checked for a pulse but found none. On a closer inspection, he could see one entrance wound on the left-side ribcage and a large exit wound at the base of the throat.

He visioned this man's life ending before his body met with the ground. This was a single shot and he knew Winston carried his AK47 to the airstrip, but he had not heard the distinct sound of that type of assault rifle from there. The police-issued .38 he carried could not have delivered such a fatal wound. He had remembered one loud rifle shot as the aircraft landed but had earlier thought this had come from the hillside; he was happy to conclude that shot had come from here. His concern grew for Winston; where was he?

As John stood up, he saw that the air above the savanna had now cleared of the reddish-brown dust and the jeep at the end of the airstrip stood out like a tree in the desert. There was no activity, but his hopes grew and he began cautiously making his way in that direction. John approached without taking his eyes off the jeep and the edge of the forest, and he was convinced that he was not being tailed by anyone. The jeep was still a couple of hundred metres away from him when he froze, then got down flat on the ground in the undergrowth that blended with the forest's edge as the passenger door opened on the jeep.

As clear as daylight, this was Winston who got out and he was alone.

Vic and Adimo were using some rocks and surface contours to take cover from some incoming fire on the upper ground.

"Zoe, are you OK?"

Vic was calling for her every now and again and he was hoping she was close enough to the shooter and staying silent to maintain her concealment. It was difficult to pinpoint the exact position of this shooter from the nature of their cover which gave the gunman the advantage of being aware of their position. Another heavy round impacted the rock that Adimo lay behind, allowing her to feel the energy of this bullet from her side. Now and again, Vic would elevate the .223 semi-automatic rifle above the rocks to blindly fire off a few rounds in the general direction of where he thought this gunman's location might be.

Marquis was in a rage. He did not give any thought to an aircraft to attempt a landing and recovery during broad daylight; he felt he had been outsmarted. He was dressing a wound on his upper left arm. During the noise of the aircraft landing, he had been making his way up towards the crest of the hill through thicket and rocks when he and Zoe were equally surprised to encounter each other. She had opened fire with a handgun, but he had moved so fast and came down on top of her, pinning her to the ground. Her shot had unfortunately missed the vitals and struck Marquis on the shoulder area.

Seconds later, Zoe was facedown with her hands tightly bound behind her back. She was now insurance for this gunman and could make a move towards the others less-challenging if needed. Marquis had Vic and Adimo pinned down to the spot where they took cover, but he had to plan to relocate; he could not shoot through rocks.

More shots began being directed at Vic and Adimo from another firing point, forcing their concealment to be compromised some. There were now two shooters with knowledge of their location.

Adimo's anger was increasing. She positioned herself to allow her to fire off a full cylinder of ammunition from her revolver towards the threat.

Omar signalled to her from lower down the hillside and quickly made his way up and belly-crawled over beside them. While Adimo and Vic returned more fire towards their assailants, Omar ran beyond the vehicle to a deep shallow in the ground and took cover. Firing continued between them when Marquis was struck by a round from Vic's rifle. He had been struck on the right side of his face, along the cheek, where the bullet gouged flesh from him right to below his earlobe and carried on its high-velocity path.

He fell backwards, dazed for a moment when Zoe used the moment to try to escape downhill. Her attempt was short-lived and Marquis's strong grip dragged her back to where he wanted her. Marquis had taken two hits and preserved any vitals from being damaged.

Adimo nervously reloaded her revolver. She glanced at Omar's cover location and was taken by surprise to see that he was no longer in the safety of the deep hollow in the ground.

She searched frantically for him and she caught sight of him. He had succeeded in securing a new position behind the second South African gunman. This gunman had heard Omar approaching him from behind but was too late to respond to the situation. The rifle's butt came down on him firmly and squarely on the centre of his face like a blow from a huge hammer. He completed his capture by cuffing the unconscious man's hands behind his back and securing his weapon.

Two shots impacted the ground close to Omar. He did not realise he had been seen by the other assailant and made plans to get back to his original cover. He first made it back to Vic and Adimo when two rounds tore up the ground close to him just as he plunged in beside them.

Vic responded by quickly raising himself and began rapidly firing in the area of the gunman in the hope of putting an end to this struggle.

Simultaneously, the rifle fell from Vic's grasp and he fell backwards, hitting his head heavily on the earth. Adimo gasped in disbelief and pulled him in deeper behind the cover of the rocks. They both got to work, laying Vic on his back, and tore open his shirt to assess his injury. Blood was coming from his front and his back, and he had an exit wound at the rear of his shoulder area; the bullet had entered under his collarbone on his right side. Omar removed his jacket and placed it under Vic's head.

The incoming bullets impacted the rocks, their energy causing loud unbearable thuds and frequent howling ricochets. Omar tapped Adimo on the shoulder, and during a break in gunfire, he ran quickly to the depression on the ground that he had previously occupied.

"Vic, Vic!" Adimo shouted. Vic was losing consciousness.

She tore up some of her jacket and clothing to compress the wound areas to slow down the bleeding. She got herself more under control and shook Vic's head while squeezing his hand.

"C'mon, Vic, c'mon!"

Vic's eyes opened again; he was as pale as a ghost, his breathing appeared regular with occasional, deep, fast, short breaths with no signs of bleeding from his nose or mouth.

Exchanges of gunfire sporadically continued between Omar and the shooter, and her ears were now ringing from the persistent sound of it.

Again, Vic's head slowly tilted sideways. She checked the bleeding again and shook Vic. She had no other ideas what to do in this situation; it worked in the movies and it should work for her. She slapped his cheek lightly and continuously while talking him back to this present moment on the savanna. She was frightened and distressed and tears were beginning to form in her eyes. Vic came around again and looked at Adimo, then direct to the clear blue sky and said something. She came down close to him. The heat of the day was extreme and the absence of a breeze presented more of a challenge for them.

"Yes, Vic, tell me."

He gave a faint smile and told her that he could see the eagle. She looked up, and in seconds, a huge eagle soaring above them came into her view. It instantly reminded her of her father and it was as if the bird was there for them.

She turned to smile at him, but his head was already resting sideways with his eyes closed; she checked his pulse: pulse OK, breathing OK.

"Vic! Vic!" she shouted and shook him. "Vic! Don't you fucking leave me here, don't you fucking dare, Vic!"

He came around again, looking more alert, and she sat him more upright against the soft grass barrier between him and the rock. Adimo's use of the 'F' word jolted him and he was back with her. She checked the bleeding again and held a bottle of water to his mouth after pouring some over his head and face. She looked at him with relief overcoming the anxiety that had begun to settle within her.

Vic's bleeding had subsided considerably and he managed to thank her as she changed the improvised dressings. She knew that he had not lost so much blood, but her thoughts were still on the first-aid supplies in the vehicle. Present circumstances presented too much danger to attempt any retrieval. She knew whatever injuries he had sustained were not as bad as it looked, and the exiting bullet probably fell short of damaging any vitals. Things would have proved more complicated had he been shot with a low-velocity bullet not exiting and leaving fragments inside him.

"Can you lift your arm?"

"I think I could, but the pain is preventing me."

Adimo had to stop him attempting to lift his arm; the pain and the stress showed in his face.

She saw the change in his facial expression as Vic glanced to her side with a look of concern in his eyes. She had just realised that the gunfire had gone quiet for a while.

She looked, and to her dismay, she watched Omar standing upright, moving out of his cover with his hands on his head. She clasped her revolver in her hands, then saw what nobody wants to see. 15 metres away, a large man was walking towards them, restraining Zoe and holding a large revolver in his right hand, with the muzzle pressed under her chin. He nodded at Omar to move and join Vic and Adimo, then bellowed at Adimo to ditch her weapon.

"Shoot him!" Zoe shouted.

Adimo did not hesitate and threw her weapon towards him; she felt like she was deflating and close to becoming empty. This man was also bleeding and had an assault rifle strapped over his right shoulder. Zoe was bound by some kind of restraint around her neck, fabricated by her shirt; she was being held by the man's left hand. He glanced around and paid some attention to the inside of the vehicle where he noticed the keys present in the ignition switch.

"Where's the other two? Where's the other fucking two?"

He pushed Zoe violently, sending her stumbling 15 feet before crashing down heavily in among her colleagues. He placed the assault rifle in his right hand and levelled the muzzle at Omar.

"They are in the forest somewhere. How can we know?" Omar said.

Marquis could not contain his anger.

"You set of stupid bastards!" he shouted. "Fucking stupid bastards. I got no time to waste on you."

As he began to step towards them, his colleague ran to join him, dazed, bleeding and handcuffed.

Marquis looked at him in disgust, then back at the officers. "Keys!" he demanded.

Omar slowly put his fingers into his shirt pocket and retrieved the keys. He threw them to Marquis who immediately kicked them back to him.

"Un-cuff him and get back there. Tinus, collect these weapons, we're leaving," Marquis instructed his colleague.

He returned the .45 back into its holster and cocked the AK47.

He was starting to say something, maybe adios, maybe some more profanities, but his speech abruptly ended and was replaced by an indescribable sound as his head and face exploded, scattering bone, blood and brain matter. His large frame seemed to jerk and his body sagged to the ground on its back in what seemed like a millisecond. His colleague dived for cover, and he once again fell victim to Omar who, with the assistance of Adimo's revolver, quickly restrained him and returned the cuffs to his wrists. Adimo looked at this man lying in front of her who no longer looked human, no face and half his head gone and reduced to a third of the size it was just seconds before. What was left was so red, grey and so fresh-looking, she dismissed the thought of this being human. They were all in confusion as the rifle shot that followed the deadly impact was quite distant but clear. The two ladies hugged each other tightly with tears of relief filling their eyes. Zoe gave Adimo a break and quickly retrieved some first-aid supplies from the vehicle and attended to Vic.

Omar pulled Tinus to his feet from the back of the shirt. The South African cursed, voicing profanities and insults. Omar kicked him hard from behind, sending him crashing into the rear of the vehicle and falling to the ground.

"Be quiet and get in there, Mr, before I change my mind and put you in beside the dog."

Armed with the assault rifle, Omar searched around the areas and the cover points that the two South Africans had used. Adimo, shocked and dazed, looked around, taking into account what had happened over the past 40 or so minutes. She thought that she must now get in touch with Brian, but she realised the area was not secure; there were still three people unaccounted for. Why were John and Winston not breaking cover after their shot? She thought it must have something to do with the other South African; there were no other shots. Maybe he had fled and her officers were in pursuit of him. They were still on alert and well-armed for the time being. John's phone was returning an engaged tone and Winston's was unreachable. She walked a little and looked in the north direction, then she saw the vehicle about 300 metres away in among the thicketed woodland on higher ground; two figures appeared to enter the vehicle. She made her way back to her colleagues. "I see them."

Adimo pointed in the direction of the vehicle that was slowly approaching them. She wondered why John and Winston were located north of them. Of course the third South African, she thought. Omar arrived back from searching lower ground, looking cheerful.

"Ma'am, look down at the southwest end of the airstrip and you will see them. John just called me and is coming with Winston."

He was beginning to explain to Adimo of the body of the other South African being with them when she cut him off.

"Wait, we may have a situation, people. Best take up cover and defensive positions. Who the hell is this?" she shouted.

The vehicle approaching from north had stopped 250 metres away, looking more sinister in among heavier thicket.

She was about to retrieve the binoculars from the vehicle when her cell phone rang. Neil McPherson's number displayed on the screen.

"Hey, Adimo, are you guys OK? It's me and Vince in the vehicle north of you guys. Is everything OK there?"

Upset and holding back tears, she walked away from her colleagues with her phone held by her side. Neil's voice could still be heard voicing her name. She levelled her breathing and put the phone to her ear.

"Neil... Neil, what on earth..." She paused. "Yes, Neil, we are OK, but help is needed. Vic took a hit and Zoe needs attention. Yes, come, we are secure now."

As they approached, John and Winston had already arrived and joined their colleagues. They were standing over Marquis's body in discussion with the team. All eyes concentrated on Vince and Neil as they stepped out of the jeep. The two hunters could see the trauma among the law officers and agents, anger, fear, injury and relief, the prisoner in the vehicle and the body on the savanna. There were photographs being collected of the body.

Nobody was quite sure what to say to each other following their solemn greetings during this unfortunate time when Neil McPherson broke the silence as he looked at the body.

"What the hell happened to him?" Neil said in profound earnest.

Adimo came back over talking on her phone.

"Listen, please, everyone. I realise we are all pretty shaken. Brian will be here in a few minutes; me, Vic and Zoe will board the chopper and get to Dar and the other two officers will join you here. There are four vehicles, a prisoner, two bodies and two missing, presumably out of Tanzania by now. In your own time, everyone. Is everybody OK with that? Neil and Vince can make their own choice what they are doing."

She received a positive response from everybody.

"I think we all did well today with a good end result. I would like to thank everyone for that. We all have a lot to discuss in Dar before we even think about processing an official report."

She looked at Neil and took him aside to talk quietly. She held his hand, thanking him. After Neil spoke, she looked at Vince, then back at Neil. He let go of her hand and they walked towards Vince. Vince was staring at the ground in an attempt to disengage himself from everything that was going on around him. Adimo clasped her hands around Vince's hand and sincerely thanked him.

"Listen, guys, we will discuss all this back in Dar. I thank God for this outcome today. Thank you two again."

"I'm sure you guys did a hell of a job here today, Adimo. We can keep this a secret if you like; one of your guys took the shot," Neil remarked.

Adimo smiled a little. "I think there's a slight too many folk here to keep a secret, Neil."

"What about a stray shot!?" Vince suggested.

Adimo looked at Vince and could not contain her laughter. She needed a laugh; everyone here did.

"You are just as crazy as him," she said, pointing at Neil. "This will be sorted out; you guys deserve a medal."

Adimo got her officers together for a quick chat before the arrival of the chopper.

The chopper could be heard approaching, and Brian tonight would have to bend his rules on evening aviation. Zoe helped Vic to his feet and checked the binding that she had fabricated to hold his arm firmly against his body.

"Everything OK there, guys?" Vince asked.

"Good, buddy, it's good," Vic replied.

As the chopper touched down close by, Zoe approached Vince and Neil to thank them. She turned and thanked the rest of the officers and left with Vic to the chopper. Vic halted to thank the officers and Vince and Neil; he patted Vince on the shoulder.

"What calibre did you use, buddy?"

"270," Vince replied.

Vic gave a long whistle and smiled. "Must be a hell of a round you used. Talk later back at base. Not sure what calibre this was, but I will sure as hell find out." Vic gestured at his shoulder wound. They laughed and parted.

Happy New Year

In Dar es Salaam, on Monday morning, Zoe and Adimo arrived at one of the city's mortuaries where the bodies of Marquis and his colleague rested. They planned to visit Vic in hospital once they had concluded their business here. The task in hand at the morgue was to have a visual of the colleague of Marquis and to snap some photographs.

"Are you OK with this, Adimo?"

"Yes, I will be fine. We have had the weekend to get over all that. Don't worry, I will be OK."

They were led through to the cold chamber by a large overweight lady with an unemotional attitude. The woman approached a four-body refrigerator and slid out two body trays, then left. The bodies were loosely covered in very lightweight, white-coloured polythene. Zoe wondered if some morgue attendants developed their attitude or if it was a contributing strength considered desirable in the recruitment-selection process. They concentrated on the smaller man and collected the photos that they needed. They had both already been acquainted with Marquis. Adimo walked to the door to let the woman know that they had finished with the bodies. The woman left her coffee, then entered the cold chamber to slide the bodies back into their resting place. Adimo then asked the woman where they could find the clothing and personal effects of the two men. They were directed to another room where two large cardboard boxes sealed with police tape lay in the corner. The two inspectors slipped on latex gloves and set about cutting open the boxes. The pockets gave up two mobile phones but little else, then something caught Adimo's attention as they were returning back the items of clothing. Instead of lace up boots like his colleague's, Marquis's boots used a zip fastener with a Velcro flap that sealed over the closed zipper band. She inspected the left boot and noticed that the zipper-pull tag was broken. Zoe was focused on her as she pulled her wallet from her pocket and produced a small grip seal bag.

Adimo looked intensely at the small object that she just shook out the bag onto her palm; it was clear that the two halves matched perfectly.

"Yes," she said aloud.

"I know where you got this from, Adimo?"

"No less than room 1230 in the Neptune." She grinned with delight, they both did.

"Well done, Sista. Well, that closes another door, Adi. Unless this guy had a time share in a pair of boots, this puts him in that room."

They bagged the boot, thanked the big lady and left.

Vic had received quite exceptional emergency treatment and his injuries were, thankfully, not life threatening. He was approved to return to Canada in a couple of days for the required surgery and Zoe would be travelling with him.

The meeting at Captain Hamisi's office began the following day with the absence of Vic. Adimo had previously submitted signed reports from her officers. Neil and Vince were invited to attend, but due to the unusual circumstances they had become involved in, they decided to decline the offer. Neil was still to have his own meeting with Ron to explain the involvement of his rifle in the incident.

"Well, Madam Zoe, I hear you are going to be leaving us soon along with Mr Vic? It's a pity this incident occurred, but God willing he will be fine now. I spoke with him yesterday. He looks well and I believe the surgery he will receive in Canada is quite routine. The extraordinary involvement of Mr Vince seems also to have been a Godsend, unbelievable but fact. In the progress of your investigation, where do you stand now, Zoe? I know things must be pretty much concluded."

"It is ongoing, Captain, but I could probably guarantee that the Tanzanian operation side of things is now officially closed. The South African names and leads that we have acquired have already led us to new pastures in South Africa and Mozambique as we speak. Thanks to Adimo here, we have closure on the death of Mr Vatel. We arrived here originally to try to locate three Canadians that included Mr Vatel. The other two are at large.

"We emerged into pursuing other individuals who seemed to be pursuing the three Canadians. The person or persons responsible for the death of the other individual, Mr Kyle Kotze, at the Palms Lodge is still unclear, but as you know, we all have a fair idea of what unfolded there. The two that got away are still a bit of a mystery. We do know that they were field operatives at the sharp end involved in the logistics of moving merchandise from A to B, not big fish by any means. They certainly had serious connections, an illegal non-governmental air evacuation out of a country does not come cheap by any means."

With his elbows on the table, Captain Hamisi listened and rolled his pen between his fingers. He smiled while nodding his head in agreement of what Zoe had just said.

"I do wonder if they arrived safely at their intended destination; it's a dangerous game they are in," Zoe continued.

"Remember, they excel in looking after themselves, Zoe," Adimo added.

"Hmmm, Adimo, I read your officer's report regarding the time he spent as a captive by these two individuals. He was not mistreated, and this young lady routinely dispatched this South African aggressor at long range with a high-powered hunting rifle; extraordinary, don't you think? Don't get me wrong, Adimo, I am aware of your more-than-competent use of hunting rifles," Hamisi said.

Adimo was writing down some notes or maybe a 'to do' list on her notepad.

"Yes, Captain, I find it quite intriguing actually. They are no longer in Tanzania, and, sadly, my, or should I say 'our', involvement in the investigation is at an end. Before we conclude this meeting, Captain, may I put forward a request to you from the hunters who miraculously freed us from a dire situation?"

"Yes, absolutely."

"They wish to remain anonymous in reports and in the investigation as a whole; very bad for business apparently. Vince has decided to return to USA for some R-and-R if he is not required for anything in our departments. Do you have any need for him, Captain?"

Captain Hamisi raised his arms with outstretched palms.

"I would say we owe him. Based on his actions and shooting skills alone, he can have anything he wishes from us if we can provide it. I do realise his situation and that is why I have decided not to invade his privacy by trying to meet with him personally; you guys can be my ambassadors there. We still don't know of any undercurrents or paybacks that may exist out there; it's a good idea for him to take some time out. No, case closed on Mr Vince."

"From our side, the case is closed on him also, Captain. It never happened," Zoe added.

Three weeks passed since Zoe, Vic and Vince's departure. Adimo had settled back into her routine of apprehending the type of individuals that kept her in a job and spending quality time with her family. She had heard some pieces of information that there may be some promotions awarded at the turn of the year. The Savanna House was as busy as ever, keeping those western hunters with disposable income happy. Neil was making up for lost time on his occasional evening activities when he could, and, to Ron's delight, Osaya was well on the mend and would soon be back on-board.

Neil's cell phone rang, displaying a country code that he was not familiar with, but this was nothing unusual.

"Good morning, Neil McPherson, Outback Expeditions speaking."

"Hey, buddy, how goes it?"

"Vince! How are you, mate? A bit of interference here, the line's a fuck up."

"No worries, just gonna be quick to ask a favour. Listen, Neil, I may be away a bit longer. Could you disconnect the ground cable on the bike battery please? The battery is under the seat. Just unlock the seat with the ignition key."

"Sure, buddy, consider it done. You need anything else? Where are you?"

"Doing a bit of travelling, Neil."

"What!?"

"Line's going shit again, Neil, will get back to you soon, buddy."

Neil was preparing to leave The Savanna House in the morning to meet with Osaya when he remembered to disconnect the motorcycle battery. He returned to his room and collected the ignition key and entered the garage area. The seat popped off without any problems, and the first thing Neil noticed were two small envelopes taking up the limited storage space common with super-sport motorcycles. One marked 'Neil/Ron' and the other 'Adimo'. He disconnected the cable and refitted the seat. He sat in the vehicle and opened one of the envelopes and a key slid out onto his palm. The key looked like a quality security-type key. Neil pulled out the small paper note from the envelope and read the scribbled message of a Dar es Salaam bank address and instructions to hand the key back to the bank when finished.

What the fuck? he thought. The number 270 certainly got his attention, but whatever Vince was up to was beyond guesswork. Some kind of a laugh, no doubt.

He kept his meeting with Osaya and they arranged his schedule for him returning to work the following week. His curiosity needed satisfying and he found himself driving to the address of the bank; he did put two and two together to regard this key being attached to a safety-deposit box. He entered the bank and produced the key to a clerk sitting at a large desk. The lady greeted him and unlocked a door with a code and let Neil enter.

"Take as long as you like, sir."

The door closed behind him and Neil could not believe the amount of boxes in there. There must have been a thousand, with access to another door with additional boxes. This was an experience for him. He located 270 and entered the key into the barrel and unlocked the drawer. There was a small jiffy bag inside containing a small non-descript package. He quickly put the package into his backpack, closed the drawer and pressed the alert button for the clerk to let him out. On leaving, Neil handed the key to the clerk and bid her goodbye.

"Excuse me, sir, the other key."

Neil explained to her that his partner had the other and would be along separately.

She seemed happy to hear this and carried on with her duties at her keyboard.

Neil decided to carry out Vince's wishes and phone Adimo to get her envelope to her. She was available at home for a short while and invited Neil to stop by. He arrived and found her in the garden, watering some plants, and he explained Vince's wish for him to deliver the envelope to her. Neil made no mention of receiving any gift from Vince and handed her the envelope; she was holding Suzan who was keeping her occupied and accepted it with her free hand. He noticed her looking oddly at this package as she shrugged her shoulders just before they parted company. Neil's curiosity naturally necessitated him to return home to inspect the envelope from Vince; the package was neither light nor heavy.

Alone in his room, he began unwrapping the jiffy bag tape and opened the envelope to reveal a large matchbox, the type that would occupy the rear of a wall-unit cupboard in the kitchen for years beside some emergency candles. He shook the box, then cut off the scotch tape securing the tray to the casing, then slid out the tray and lifted out a black moleskin-type pouch and untied it. What he found inside the pouch triggered a reaction in him, but he was unsure whether to react to a joke or the shock of his life. Neil tilted the pouch and let the contents flow out and onto his bed. He was looking at diamonds, or what looked like diamonds, and lots of them; a small note was inside the pouch.

Round Brilliant, 3.87 Ct, SA, untraceable, real deal $3.500.000 approx, followed by a scribbled smiley. Neil knew this was no joke. This was not a stunt that Vince would orchestrate, and no, this was not him. This was real. Neil's mind was racing back and forth, trying to recalculate Vince as another individual even though he knew him so well; he could not succeed; they were best of friends.

Neil knew nothing of diamonds; he breathed condensation from his breath onto them and the beautiful cut gemstones would not hold any film of condensation, maybe this was an old wives tale, he did not know.

He counted them three times and counted 170 in total. He could feel a feeling within him as he looked at these glittering gemstones on his bed cover. A feeling he had never experienced in his life; this feeling was ultimate power, freedom.

The thought of Adimo came back to the front of his mind and his mind raced again without making any sense and wasting his thoughts in reaction to all the 'what if' scenarios that his mind was throwing at him. He felt there were now two people inside him; he had to take control here. What was done is done, he thought. What Vince has done is done and what Adimo will do will be done. He was tenacious enough to convince Adimo that he had not received any gift or envelope if circumstances deteriorated. He reminded himself that anyone going official or public with 'diamonds' would only encourage depravity on themselves and open up a monstrous can of worms or even snakes. After all, he had no idea what was in Adimo's envelope anyway. One thing he knew was he was now the curator of 170 cut diamonds in his safe, destined for him and Ron. He would not think about Ron's reaction to this at the moment. Time for that, he thought.

A few days passed and Neil was entering one of the government game departments in Dar es Salaam as part of the process to declare the game and trophies taken by Jim and Brad. His cell phone rang and displayed Adimo's name. His heart was thumping, but he welcomed this call. This was a weight off his shoulders even before he answered; he had no sleep worth considering over the past few days.

"Good morning, Neil, how are you, dear? Just calling you to let you know that Vic is now up and about and well on the mend. Zoe called this morning and he asks for everyone. He asked to pass onto you and Vince that the rifle that caused his injuries was a Winchester 308 calibre."

What the fuck? Neil thought, *Be your normal self!*

"Oh, yeh, no worries. I will pass that on. Yeh, tell Vic I did not realise that he was shot with a girl's gun."

"I will pass that on," Adimo jovially said.

a, all kidding aside, Adimo, it's better to have a big round like that ing cleanly out the other side rather than some gutless little lead thing sting up inside you; that sucks."

"Exactly, Neil. Tell me how is Vince, is he enjoying his R-and-R?"

"Yep, I am doing a few things on his bike for him for when he gets back. I think he is gonna extend some though, Adimo."

"That's lovely; it will be nice to see him back in Tanzania, and anyway, Neil, I need to move. Catch up later."

Neil was happy with that one. She did not mention gifts and neither did he, and she sounded as happy as a pig in shit. Was this for Vic? he thought. Neil had one bolder move to make to help elevate him out of the feeling of anxiety that was smothering him. On impulse, he found himself driving to the bank again. Judging by the police-radio transmissions he could hear during the phone call, he knew that Adimo was at the other side of town in her HQ.

With all caution thrown to the wind, he parked his vehicle and made his way into the bank where he was greeted by the same lady.

"Excuse me, ma'am. I was concerned regarding your other key, my partner—"

Before Neil could finish, the lady informed him that everything was fine. The lady had collected her belongings and returned key 357 two days earlier.

Neil thanked her and made his way out of the bank. A smile developed on his face. *357,* he thought to himself, *you twat. Vince.* He had received the answer he needed.

He walked briskly around to the backstreet, looking in all directions as he moved, paid the unofficial parking warden and blended back into the Dar es Salaam traffic.

The following day, Adimo did receive an actual call from Zoe and she asked after Vic's welfare. Zoe explained that although she was aware of the Tanzanian law enforcement being no longer involved in the case, she was going to pass some 'off the record' information to Adimo's private email in regards to the ones that got away. Just to satisfy any curiosity she may have towards them. They chatted a while, then carried on with their business.

She had too many questions in her mind, wondering why Vince would bless her with a fortune in gemstones. She still had not accepted that this was even true. Vince was not a diamond smuggler; she hesitated. *Was he? Did Peter acquire the stones he had through the means that he informed her?* Nothing was clear now. Her mind was troubled over the past few days, trying to calculate what she should do about this. Report the incident and generate a huge troublesome investigation, probably bigger than the last one that would no doubt see her being the main focal point. *N...O, no,* she thought, *that's a no.* She would accept this for the way it was. This man making her rich beyond her imagination and saving the lives of her and her colleagues. There was no other way to deal with it, and this was one dilemma where she would definitely not require Peter's advice. *But why, Vince? Why? And Neil, did Neil receive a similar gift from Vince? Of course he did.* She would lay a bet on that. *What about Peter, was Peter always in on this?* She was asking herself too questions. She decided to stop thinking and accept her own situation; to with the rest.

That evening, Adimo spent some time with Suzan to free up some time fo Jo to carry out some of her new studies she had taken up. When the child was sound asleep, she shared some wine and exchanged some chat with her daughter.

She was about to make her way to bed when she remembered to check her email for Zoe's mail. She used the desktop and opened her inbox to find the mail simply headed FYI. She noticed two attachments and clicked on the first one. The connection was not so good and she patiently waited for it to open. Her screen eventually displayed the photo of Marc Dupuis much clearer than the hand-outs they had been supplied with at the beginning of the investigation. This time there was some history and personal details to compliment the image. She read through the personal details and found them quite interesting; this guy had been around and been involved in a few African conflicts in the capacity of a mercenary no doubt.

The second attachment opened to reveal an image of a woman, again much clearer than the flyers from before; at first, she thought this was a different woman due to the clarity. She scrolled to the personal details briefly, then back to the image, then returned to the personal details.

USA, Canadian and Israeli passport holder.
Odette Gordon.
Born 6 May, 1979, Harris County, Texas, USA.
Married at the age of 19 to Israeli citizen and spouse Uri Gordon and moved to Israel.
Separated 2002 when she joined the IDF serving four years.
Maiden name: Odette Kelly.

"Oh my God," she found herself saying aloud. She displayed Odette's image back on her screen and gazed deeply at her. She rested her head in her hands and began to cry. The hair was different, but she now recognised the woman. This was the woman she had saved from a bullet months ago on the streets of Dar es Salaam. And the eyes, she thought, the eyes!

This was the sister of Vince.

Adimo wakened in the morning, feeling heavy and tired after being in a deep trance-like sleep, and she would now neither worry nor be afraid of anything more that might come to her attention. She had already done all the thinking last night. *Enough,* she thought.

She was convinced that Zoe and Vic had already excluded Vince from their enquiries.

"It did not happen," that's what Zoe quoted.

And who would want to open an enquiry into someone who was responsible for saving their life; that's a nonstarter, she thought.